The Candidate
Jack Quinn

For Teague:
You were my sunshine.

CHAPTER ONE
Washington, DC
February 1976

Senator Charles Robinson rose from his seat and looked around the chamber. I was standing with one of the Capitol Guards near the tall double doors at the back of the room, and when we established eye contact, the Senator raised his arm and gave a little wave of his hand.

The Secret Service had installed new procedures after two assassination attempts were made on President Ford last September by Lynette 'Squeaky' Fromme and Sara Jane Moore. But security is tight inside the Capitol building, so we tend to relax a bit when we can. Protectees give us endless reasons to stay alert in public.

I'd been observing the Senator for three days but would not be officially responsible for his protection until the full detail came on board the following morning when we would be on the job around the clock. Even so, I wanted to keep him in sight. That ramrod posture, full, close-cropped white beard and black eye patch, Senator Robinson was hard to miss.

No matter how many times I go there, the United States Senate never fails to impress me. High vaulted ceiling with recessed lighting, blue velvet draperies against curved walls of pale gold, one hundred hand-polished mahogany desks almost two centuries old. Despite its often conniving, fallible members, I could sense the dominant spirit of history and dedication throughout the muted tone of the wide room from the brass-railed spectators' gallery, across thick pile carpet to the stars and stripes and senate flags on either side of the dais.

The President Pro-Tem was engaged in private conversation at the edge of the gray marble podium while a junior senator from the mid-west prepared to address his colleagues from the lectern below. Many of the seats on the floor were empty, senators stood in the aisles talking to one another, their aides, lobbyists and other members of legislative process. Most would leave soon because outsiders are not allowed on the floor while the senate is in session.

I started moving toward Senator Robinson before he dropped his arm, snaking around people blocking my way, expressing polite but firm apologies. By the time I reached him, the Senator was listening to a short Hispanic man, moving his head in little nods, his one eye fixed like a beam of light on the person speaking. The pressure of his grip on my arm acknowledged my presence, but his attention remained fixed on the man in front of him.

I could never figure out why the Senator seemed so large when you were farther away. Up close, he wasn't much taller than I am. He's lean and hard with broad shoulders--really good shape for fifty-six. The premature white head of hair adds to it: thick, parted in the middle and combed to the sides. Anyone else would look like a pirate with the beard and eye patch, but not him. The press says it gives him an 'avuncular' image, warm and concerned. He looked important, like a Senator should.

"I wonder if you would do me a favor, Jared." The Hispanic man had left and that clear blue eye was boring into my soul. "I promised to support a bill that wasn't due out of committee until next week." He pulled a leather case out of his pocket and detached a single key. "It will reach the floor this afternoon and my notes are at home."

I guess I must have paused a beat before I said, "Of course, Senator, I'd be glad to." He gave me that thousand-watt smile, assured me he'd be perfectly safe in the Capitol Building while I was gone and would not leave it until I returned. His expression said that I worry too much, but he appreciated it.

"Have John drive you to my condominium complex and wait while you run in. My notes are on my desk in the den." He glanced at his watch. "You'll be back within the hour if

2

you don't get too engrossed in my condo layout again.

Guarding a presidential candidate after the New Hampshire primary, eight months before the election is different than being responsible for the life of the President of the United States. With the former, a Secret Service agent can use a little discretion. With the latter there is none. The Senator had announced his candidacy the previous October but didn't rate Service protection until two days ago when the polls confirmed he'd take more than five percent of the popular vote.

I was scout for the two seventeen-agent details that would provide Senator Robinson twenty-four-hour protection while he campaigned across the country for the most powerful elective office in the world.

My assignment and that of several other humps delegated similar responsibilities began an hour after they announced the results of the polls. I called the Senator's office to get briefed on his schedule, met for the third time with John Goddard and arranged to evaluate the logistical problems we'd have to overcome at his home and during his normal activities while he was in Washington. On the road his schedule would dictate our coverage. I had worked out alternate commuting routes when he was in the District, drawn up a floor plan of the Senator's condo, made copies for humps on both details, verified his workday and leisure habits, learned about his nightly walk and the kinds of political/social functions he attended. Any change in schedule, we'd be more alert for potential trouble.

We'd bring in enough weapons to make a difference to "The Charge of the Light Brigade" and were prepared to counter the usual scenarios we drilled for constantly. We established guard routes and the best way for exterior humps to provide front and rear surveillance of his condo unit, which was located in the middle of a 'U' shaped building, one of thirty in the luxury condominium complex.

To the average taxpayer these precautions seem like overkill, money wasted on a handful of men and women who for one reason or other were under threat of harm or whose stance in Congress made them targets for every deranged sociopath in disagreement with their policies.

The Senator's condo was not a target or direct threat from anyone, but my boss, Ken Burnett, wanted to make a good impression right off the bat for the man who we would probably be guarding for the next four years.

* * * * * *

I buttoned my trench coat as I dashed down the long granite steps and got into the front seat of the black Lincoln Town Car.

"You must feel pretty special, jumpin' up here with me," John said, pulling out into traffic.

John Goddard was a lean black man with salt-and-pepper hair trimmed close to his head. He didn't say much, but when he did, it usually went with a half-smile and sideways look to see if you knew he was pulling your leg. In the short time I'd known him I discovered I enjoyed tugging John's chain as much as he did mine. The Senator liked to ride in front but that would stop when we started guarding him.

"You were holding the front door open for me," I told him, "what do you want me to do now, crawl over the seat into the back?"

"Guess it don't matter anyways, nobody gonna see how special you be up here, all this snow. How come you drag me outta my nice warm office in this lousy weather?"

"You love it, you old fake. You were probably bored stiff shuffling papers or on the phone practicing your political arm-twisting."

John liked driving the Senator. His black suit was always pressed, his chauffeur's cap square on his head, its visor polished like a marine sentry's. The Senator told me he'd been a congressional driver-aide for twenty years and the federal government was his hobby. John turned onto Constitution Avenue and we became stalled in traffic opposite the Ellipse. The wet flakes sticking to the side window made it difficult to see, but I could make out the White House beyond the wide lawn covered in a layer of pristine snow.

I said, "Your boss could be living over there this time next year."

John nodded, keeping his eyes on the cars beyond the wipers clicking rhythmically on the wet windshield.

"Couldn't ask for a better man."

"How long you been driving him?"

"Thirteen years. Almost the whole time he been Senator."

"What happens to you if he wins?"

"That makes no never mind." John pressed his foot on accelerator and the long car moved ahead in traffic.

"What happens to the country if he don't?"

"You really think he'd make that much difference?"

John smiled as we crept along toward the Potomac and the Teddy Roosevelt Bridge. The Senator had a reputation around Washington Mother Teresa could have been happy with. I'd only known him a couple of days, but I had to agree. Senator Robinson seemed to be one of the few politicians in town that tried to make the government work for the people instead of the other way around.

"It's a pretty big job," I said.

"Funny thing about that, ain't it?"

Somehow, I knew he was going to answer his own question, so I just turned my head to look at him.

"Mr. Nixon probably the most qualified man to live in that big old house since Thomas Jefferson," John paused for effect before he continued. "Little man named Truman, least."

I saw what he meant. But it didn't stop me from thinking about it. One minute a man walks up and down the street like a regular person, the next he's the most powerful man on the planet. The ancient question: could one man really make a difference? Could Senator Robinson? Who knew.

We crossed the river and started to pick up speed on Route 66 in Virginia, then turned off at a little town called Falls Church, about twelve miles from the center of D.C. John took the back roads to the exclusive condominium west of town and pulled up at the guardhouse standing next to a high stone wall that enclosed the entire complex. The guard leaned down to speak to John through his lowered window.

"Senator send you out to check on the workmen, John?"

"Checkin' on you," John said. "Brought the Secret Service to make sure you doin' your job."

The guard was a young black man who wore a yellow poncho with a hood and seemed to take his job seriously.

"You just worry 'bout yo' own self, my man. Senator's office called ahead, guys had all the papers. I know what I'm doin'."

John fired his parting shot as he started moving the big car through the gates. "Never can be too sure 'bout somebody stands out gabbin' inna blizzard."

A big white box truck sat blocking the entrance to the Senator's townhouse, one guy smoking in the cab with the fogged window cracked a couple of inches. 'Alford Girard Carpentry' was painted on the door. John couldn't pull up to the walk, so I was going to get pelted with wet snow again.

"I ain't supposed to be your momma, too." John said, reaching over the backrest to the jump seat in the rear of the car, "but I guess I'll do for today." He tossed the Senator's wide-brim slouch hat in my lap.

"Don't let it give you no big ideas."

Sometimes it seems futile to come back on John with a snappy answer and I guess I thought that was one of them. Now, I wish I'd said something. Anything. But I just jammed the floppy hat down on my ears, opened the car door and ran for the entrance.

I expected the house to be unlocked with the workmen inside, so I didn't bother getting the key out of my pocket. I stood there in the foyer for a few seconds thinking I should probably take off my raincoat and hat and hang them on the coat tree instead of dripping snow all the way into the den.

Why was it so quiet? Where were the workmen? Why hadn't the Senator mentioned they'd be here? I slipped out of my coat and unbuttoned my jacket. I took a few steps into the living room and stopped. Nobody was on the first floor, but I heard a noise above me. The stairs were on my left and

I started toward them. My mistake was not getting the hell out of there and calling back-up. A rookie cop would do it. Not the Service. We're taught to intervene, protect the subject at all costs, even at the risk of our lives. If those guys up there weren't workmen, the Senator was being violated.

I drew my .357 snub-nosed Magnum out of its shoulder holster and started up the stairs.

The carpet was thick, and I wasn't making a sound. They were though, and the work they were doing was opening and closing drawers. Burglars, maybe spaced-out druggies, but more likely pros with the truck, the advance phone call and fake papers. Either way, they could be armed. How many were up there? I had to confront them all in the same room or I'd have trouble covering all of them. And I'd better do it quick or the guy in the truck would join us.

Now I remembered why cops call for back-up. 'Dumb, Jared, dumb, dumb, dumb.' A voice called out off to my left as I stopped halfway up the stairs.

"*Scheisse! Die Schlussel noch papier sind nicht hier drin,*" the voice said. "*Hier its auch kein Safe oder Geheimfach. Nichts.*" [Fuck! The key and paper are not also here; is no safe or secret compartment. Nothing.]"

The Service likes us to be fluent in a second language and officially mine was German. They were looking for some key and document and that guy out of sight couldn't find them. A man in brown coveralls wearing latex gloves stepped out of a room into the hallway and I dropped into a one-handed shooter's stance with my left index finger up to my lips. The guy got the message and raised his hands in the air. An instructor at Treasury told us that stress was a great fixative of images on the mind. You're pumped up, adrenaline flowing, scared stiff. If you just thought about absorbing it for a second, you'd carry the image with you for the rest of your life.

The perp was in his early thirties, about five-ten, a hundred and sixty pounds, sloping shoulders, standing like a gymnast on the balls of his feet, ready to pounce with the good sense not to. Straight black hair cut short, low forehead, high cheekbones, deep-set eyes and a square jaw thrust out like a threat. He didn't look scared or surprised and he didn't speak, but his dark eyes never left mine. A real pro, no druggie, whoever he was.

There were noises coming from the room across the hall and I motioned the guy toward it. As we entered the Senator's bedroom another character in a brown jump suit was going through the Senator's closet with his back to us. Before I could open my mouth, the first guy spoke real easy not realizing I understood him.

"Hinter dir. Ein Mann mit einer Pistole. Dreh dich schnell urn und schiess." [Behind you, a man with a pistol, turn quick and shoot.]

If the guy at the closet hadn't moved so fast I would have swung around between the two perps, a second's hesitation as he dug in his coveralls pocket that told me what was coming. I saw the gun in his hand as he turned and that's when my Service training made up for my earlier stupidity. We don't say 'freeze,' we shoot.

His arms flew out and he slammed back against the wall taking the night table and everything on it down with him. I caught him square in the chest, confirmed by the blood and fragments of tissue forensics scraped off the closet door. I understand they had plenty to work with. We load with soft lead designed to spread when it hits bone and stop an assassin through massive shock.

I knew I had to swing back on the first guy before he could drop his hands but saw my problem in the eyes of the guy I'd just shot. The wounded perp, slumped halfway in the closet in front of me, pulled a gun out of his coveralls, still in the game, as I heard the soft spit of the silenced pistol from the man behind me. One second, I was starting to whirl around, arms out, both hands wrapped around the crosshatched grip, knees bent, still feeling the kick of the gun, the sound of my shot filling the room.

Next, I got punched between the shoulder blades with one of those huge iron balls they swing from the end of a crane to demolish buildings and dropped into a deep, black hole.

In my line of work, you try not to think of what 'might happen.' But you can't help it. Jumping in front of a bullet meant for the president. Blown into little pieces because you're standing next to some controversial politician or foreign dignitary.

But not this. Getting wrecked by a punk thief because I was too gung-ho to do it right. I must have faded in and out of consciousness a couple of times before they found me. I hoped John had been smarter than I was and gone for help before the third guy got out in the truck and came into the house. I wasn't betting on it. I remember feeling worse about letting John down than letting myself down. I still do.

Just before I heard the sirens, I started getting cold, everything coming into sharp focus and I thought they'd be too late. My face pressed into the tufted beige rug, its twisted wool fibers standing out as separate strands before my dilating pupils. Petals of red and purple flowers on the shards of broken lamp. Spider webs of cracked glass in the silver picture frame lying inches from my nose, the black and white photograph of my mother and father.

When she was alive it always sat on the mantle above the fireplace in our home, now on the bookcase in my apartment in Georgetown. What was it doing here? A photo taken thirty-four years ago aboard my grandfather's yacht in Narragansett Bay. In my picture, my father was standing on my mother's right, his expression serious, her face bursting with a mischievous look that I had never seen in real life. This photo that lay on the rug less than a foot from my nose did not have my father in it. The blond stranger standing on my mother's left was vaguely familiar, not a childhood recollection or college friend, but someone I might have seen recently.

Seconds before I tumbled down into that black hole again, I recognized the tall, awkward young man in that cut-down version of my family picture. It was a youthful version of Senator Charles Robinson.

CHAPTER TWO
Washington, DC
February 1976

John Goddard was found by the security guard slumped behind the wheel of the big Lincoln, bleeding from the single bullet hole in his left temple. The guard didn't hear my shot, but a neighbor did. After the contractor's truck sped out of the complex, the guard drove back to the house, discovered John and called it in.

The shooter hit me under the left shoulder blade and ruined the Senator's carpet. The EMT's arrived in thirteen minutes and I was inside the trauma unit at George Washington University Medical Center twenty minutes later.

The Senator refused to leave the hospital until I was out of the woods. Thirty-six hours and the man sat in a private waiting room under full Secret Service protection, his secretary or runner showing up periodically with more work. Despite his recently announced candidacy, he refused to meet the press at the hospital. When the surgeon told Senator Robinson they had me stabilized, I understand he slipped into intensive care, stared down at my sedated body with that piercing look of honest-to-God sincerity, whispered a couple of words of encouragement and left.

Several days later, one of the surgeons told me that if the bullet had hit a half inch to the left it would have saved them five hours of hard work. Neither one of us felt sufficiently relieved to say the cliché.

John Goddard might have. I missed his funeral and the Senator told me that half the administrative staff in the senate office building showed up. I felt a lump in my throat, knowing I would feel it whenever I thought of John. That would be often, I realized. If I hadn't been such an idiot, as soon as I sensed something was wrong, I should have walked right back out of the Senator's condo, got in the car an called the police. If the man in the truck had given us trouble I would have been there. John would still be alive.

The doctors were not pleased, but the police questioned me as soon as I woke in intensive care. Two Secret Service agents conducted their own private interview the same afternoon, but I was not alert those first few days after surgery with antibiotics, morphine and other intravenous solutions dripping into my veins. I was able to get the facts straight but did not start making sense of them until later. So they had a B&E that turned into armed robbery and murder. Not an unusual occurrence in the District of Columbia with one of the highest crime rates in the country that spills over into surrounding communities on a regular basis.

Senator Robinson came back later that week when I was feeling better and I asked him about the picture of my mother and him in his bedroom.

"Everyone's supposed to have a near-double some place on this earth," he answered. "Doppelganger. Your mother must be a lovely woman to be mistaken for Caroline."

I explained the circumstances of the photo, my mother and him leaning against the furled sail on the boom of my grandfather's boat, the pose, the clothes she was wearing, her hair, the barrette.

"Are your parents' sailors, too?" he asked.

"My father crossed the Atlantic single-handed. He was killed in World War II. My mother passed away three years ago."

"I'm sorry to hear that," he said with profound sadness, not automatic like most people who seem more embarrassed to have brought it up than truly sorry about your loss. "I've been sailing all my life. That picture was taken in Newport in the summer of '41, six months before Pearl Harbor." His smile was weak and thoughtful. "Not much sailing after that for a while."

He said Caroline Masterson had been his fiancée but

had married someone else while he was overseas. "One of the few regrets of my life," he said, shrugging into his top-coat. "I should have married that girl before I joined the navy." The Senator turned on that smile, only two hundred watts this time at something that happened a long time ago. "Things might have been different." I suddenly experienced the strange feeling that Senator Robinson was talking about my own love life or lack of it. Like his old romance recalled some universal truth we both shared.

"Get well," he said, buttoning his coat, then walked out of my hospital room.

Did I really imagine that was my mother in the picture? No question I was not at my best when I saw it. How could I be sure? A United States Senator, the avowed pinnacle of integrity in a den of political wombats? How could I accuse him of lying about knowing my parents?

* * * * * *

My boss, Ken Burnett, paid me three visits. The first was the debriefing in the ICU, part of the initial investigation. The second was social, buck up, get well. The third was a combination of both.

It was mid-morning and the sun streamed through the windows making the stark white-and-chrome hospital room seem bright, almost pleasant.

"The Bureau ran into a dead end," he said. "Put it on the national wire--nothing."

Since when was murder, breaking and entering a federal offense, I wondered. "Why do they have it?"

"Three reasons," he sounded like he was quoting from the manual. "Assault on a Federal officer," he pointed at the sling on my arm. "Attempted robbery where the United States Government may be an interested party, Senator Robinson, and the interstate transport of stolen property."

"What was stolen?"

"Nothing from the house, according to the Senator. They stole the truck in Charlottesville, left it in Waldorf, Maryland."

A crime artist from the Service had come in the week

12

before. "I didn't get a copy of the perp sketches."

He raised his eyebrows and sat looking at me for a few seconds. Then pulled out two folded sheets of paper from his inside coat pocket and placed them on the bed.

I studied the face of the man I'd confronted in the Senator's upstairs hallway and described to the crime artist. It was fairly accurate. I couldn't describe the driver who shot John because I didn't see him, or describe the perp I shot, but the guard did. The truck driver and the inside perp must have taken the wounded or dead pal with them.

"What'd they get from forensics?" I asked.

"Nothing they can use yet. Serology showed the guy you shot had '0' positive blood and we got a tissue profile, both useless 'til we have something to compare them to."

I slipped the sketches into the drawer of my bedside table like they belonged to me. "No prints, hair, fibers...."

Ken shrugged, lifting the palms of his hands. "You saw the gloves, the coveralls. The whole house was clean."

"Guy I nailed must have croaked if he didn't get treatment."

"Maybe he did if they were smart as they seemed."

Ken was mid-forties, sandy hair, receding hairline. He could stretch up to five-ten, five-eleven when he tried to crane over the heads of a crowd. Just average looking almost by design, same as the rest of us.

I had a private room and the door was closed. Ken was sitting by the window in one of those plastic chairs someone had substituted for the padded seat the Senator had sat in, pretending we were just shooting the breeze.

"Come on," I said, "that guy would never survive with some back-room sawbones." I waved my good right arm at the wall. "He probably wouldn't make it in here."

"So, he didn't make it. Lots of ways to dispose of a body."

"How about the language angle?"

"You thought it was Germanic. Swedish, Dutch...."

"German, Ken. Dutch is my family language, I'm fluent in German." He knew that.

"OK, they're looking for German burglars." He frowned

and cocked his head, a mannerism I had seen Ken use before when he was not sure he understands what he's hearing. "You making it something else?"

"They were tossing the place for some document and key."

"You were mumbling about that earlier."

"I heard them talking."

"In German."

"Yes, in German."

Why was my supervisor resisting the first-hand testimony of a trained eyewitness? One of his own. I knew Ken would have jumped at information like this in any other circumstance, from any other witness.

"You were delirious when they found you." Ken folded his arms as though he had to relate something that would embarrass both of us. "Crying for your father, John Goddard, weird stuff they didn't get."

"There's more to it than B&E."

"Is that where you're going? Some political conspiracy? Espionage?"

"That's impossible?"

Ken nodded. "The Senator doesn't buy it. Says he doesn't have any papers at home burglars or spys would want."

"Maybe he's working on some top-secret project he can't talk about."

My favorite nurse tapped on the door and came through it. She was a heavy black woman with a ready laugh and a soothing touch. Before Burnett could respond, she moved to my bedside held my wrist while she looked at her watch.

"Not talkin' serious business, are you?" she asked, sticking a thermometer in my mouth and wrapping a blood pressure cuff around my bicep. "Felicia, I'm going home in a few days," I mumbled around the glass rod.

"Not back to work I hope." She shot Ken a challenging glance. "He was one sick puppy."

"He'll be on disability leave for at least a month."

"Oh?" That was the first I'd heard about it. As a matter of fact, I'd been worried about being brought up on charges for not calling backup. Or getting booted off the detail for

14

messing up the Senator's rug.

"The Man wants you in top form when he hits the campaign trail in earnest." Burnett winked at Felicia. "He's got a Rabbi in high places."

"Gonna have to pray a lot harder, keep this boy outta trouble. Outta here, anyway." She fluffed my pillow and left the room closing the door behind her.

"A month?" I asked Ken.

"Yup." Burnett was grinning like he had just given me a Christmas present.

"Thirty days' recuperative leave, a week retraining."

"I'll go nuts!"

"Take a vacation. Visit Disney World, Club Med."

They have me doing therapy already. I'll be fine in a couple of weeks."

"Out of my control." He lifted his hands off the arms of the chair palms up. "See you 'round mid-April."

My disgust was evident. I hated people meddling in my life and it looked like the Senator had decided to do just that. A whole month was ridiculous. But my mind kept going back to the robbery.

"The silencer doesn't fit with house burglars, either."

Burnett crossed his arms again glancing at his watch as he did it. "Why not? They're going into a condominium; they don't want twenty people calling 911 if they have to shoot."

"Burglars don't want to shoot. They want to steal, disable if they have to."

"Coughlin," Burnett's tone shifted into its official timbre, "the Service has determined that the incident at Senator Robinson's home was not an attempt on his life. The only reason we were involved was one of our agents happened to be on the scene." He gave me a hard look to emphasize the finality of his message.

"We closed the book on it."

"How about the Bureau?"

"It's being pursued like any other Federal crime."

"But no leads after what, two weeks?"

"That's right."

"Don't you smell something, Ken?"

Burnett shook his head and said no. "I think you're reading more into this than there is, Jared," his voice dropping the sharp edge it had a few minutes ago. "Being on the scene and all, getting hit. The driver, Goddard."

I looked past him, out the window across the narrow air shaft at a blank wall of gray bricks. There would be no point telling him about the picture of my mother and Robinson.

"Take your vacation," Ken continued, "get away somewhere. You'll see it better when you add a little distance to it."

I flashed a smile at him like I'd seen the Senator do--open, friendly, agreeing. "Maybe."

Ken stood up. "Remember, I don't want to see your ugly face for a month." He grabbed my good hand and shook it.

"Send me a postcard."

* * * * * *

I wrestled back and forth with a hundred loose ends for the next few days until the morning I left the hospital. Senator Robinson insisted on sending his car to take me home.

It was a cold, sunny day when I sat in a wheelchair on the hospital steps inhaling the crisp winter air, a nurse's aide shivering behind me. I realized the doctors and nurses had saved my life and had taken good care of me, but getting out of that place was only second to coming home from 'Nam. I had been shot on Valentine's Day. When I was still in the ICU, I remembered thinking I didn't have anybody to send flowers to and it felt kind of good in a way.

I had been living with Melissa Thurston for two years until the previous October when she was made junior partner in her law firm and decided she wasn't ready to make a commitment. So, she left. She had stopped in at the hospital once, but after that awkward visit, I acknowledged the loose reciprocal of Yogi Berra's dictum: 'when it's finally over, it's all over'.

Even when we were living together, Melissa accused me of being a loner. She was probably right, because after she left, I relished a sense of freedom. In retrospect, I felt the years

16

with her had been confining. I was ready for a new relationship in my life, but something less restrictive.

Maybe I should sign up for a singles cruise, look into a group tour after all.

* * * * * *

Jorge was a fat young Hispanic who seemed nice enough, but content to keep his own counsel. He turned west on Pennsylvania on his way to Wisconsin Ave. and my Georgetown address. After coming out of Washington Circle, Jorge extended a large brown envelope over the back seat without taking his eyes off the road.

"Sentor say geeve you."

The doctor advised me to keep my left arm in a sling for another week to immobilize the shoulder as much as possible, but I had full use of my hand. I opened the envelope and slid out two pieces of protective cardboard. In between them was an 8x10 black-and-white photograph of the youthful Charles Robinson with a young woman who looked remarkably like my mother. Same hairdo, same kind of blouse, same pose, standing on a large wooden sailboat with an indistinct shoreline visible in the background. Same everything. Except the young woman in that photograph was definitely not my mother.

CHAPTER THREE
Georgetown, DC
February 1976

Senator Robinson took the New Hampshire primary in a landslide. The polls predicted it, the party was behind him and as long as some dirt-monger didn't drag a skeleton out of his closet, his nomination at the national convention that summer would be a formality. According to *The Washington Post*, if the administration didn't get the lead out quickly, the Senator would be the next President of the United States next January.

I lived in a one-bedroom apartment on 'T' Street in back of the University, a typical town/gown neighborhood with low crime, high rent and zero parking.

Melissa had fixed the place up like a real home during the two years she lived there, but most of the furnishings were hers and she took them with her. When she left, I bought a new mattress and box spring that would probably sit on the bedroom carpet until I got around to shopping for a frame and headboard. Or found another girlfriend.

As an alumnus, I could use the university gym, so I put a couple of layers of sweats on over some old turtlenecks and started walking the three blocks to the Georgetown campus. It must have been twenty degrees, but the sun was shining and I was glad to be out of that hospital room. Glad to be alive, too. I started jogging a little, inhaling cold oxygen down into my lungs, blowing little silver clouds into the dry air. My chest felt tight, my arm awkward in the sling, but other than that, I was doing fine.

Pedestrians were dressed in bulky coats peering out between scarves and ski hats, jiggling up and down at bus stops, walking briskly to the subway. The early commuter traffic sounded loud and grating to my ears as it fed onto

Wisconsin toward the downtown area, the stink of exhaust offensive in the winter morning. After two weeks of virtual isolation, everything seemed more pronounced, three-dimensional.

The gym was usually quiet in the morning, the vinyl tiles freshly buffed by the night cleaning crew, wide corridors lined with trophies in glass cases waiting silently for the noisy exuberance of hyperactive athletes. A group of students was shooting baskets on the big court and I could hear the muffled echoes of their shouts and jibes bouncing off the high walls of the cavernous room.

I came to Georgetown as pretty hot stuff from a Maryland prep school with a two-year record as the 175-pound All-State Wrestling Champion. Whenever I looked back on my early life, I saw a lone, sullen youth I almost refused to acknowledge. I knew I'd been adrift in those days and as a man, wondered how much or if that early isolation had changed.

I entered the deserted wrestling locker room where the pungent odors of liniment, sweat-soaked cotton, adhesive tape and Tuff Skin welcomed me back like old friends. I took off the layers of clothes and sat on the wooden bench using a full-length wall mirror to examine the ugly red scar on my back, manipulating my left arm to see how much I could swing it without pain.

As I pulled on gray shorts over purple tights representing the colors of the Hoyas, my gaze fell on the framed black-and-white photographs on the far wall. Most of them were group shots of young men with hard bodies in dark tights and tank tops, several taken during the years my team fought their way up the division ladder. One was of me during the heavyweight title match I won, giving Georgetown the two points we needed to take the Eastern States Collegiate Championship in my senior year.

The wrestling team of the Jesuit institution wore ear guards and kneepads, grappling with some other sweating slab of gristle, bulging muscles sharply defined against an out-of-focus background of cheering spectators.

19

Was I ever that young and innocent? The blond hair was shorter now, the same long face that my mother claimed I inherited from my father's Viking ancestors and stubborn jaw she attributed to my pure Dutch lineage. I remember hearing the word 'cute' from giggling girls I passed on campus in those days, but all I saw in these pictures was a gawky, self-conscious kid, younger looking than my twenty-four years, outwardly unmarked by my tour in 'Nam. Maybe some of the edges had worn off during the past thirteen years, a few squint lines starting around the baby blues, but essentially the same straight arrow that had bored Melissa half to death.

I put on a pair of paper slippers, grabbed a towel and shuffled into the overheated PT room where I climbed into a whirlpool tub that immersed me to the neck in warm swirling water. I placed the folded towel between the back of my head and the metal rim of the tub and closed my eyes. The room was empty except for a maintenance man working on a maze of pipes and valves in the corner, the occasional clang of his tools on the damp cement floor ringing above the sound of the water sloshing around me.

John Goddard was a widower. I had hoped to speak to his children after the funeral, but they had gone back north right after the service. I should call them.

The heated water moved against my chest and shoulders, relaxing the damaged muscles as it worked to pull the tension from my body. I couldn't beat myself up about John forever. Or the way it happened.

After Burnett's reaction to my misgivings, I would not pursue that with him again until I could prove my basic contention. The silencer, German-speaking burglars, the way they were searching for a document and key. They were not on drugs. The men I saw in the Senator's home were two of the coldest pros I had ever run into. I grabbed the edge of the tub to shift my position in the churning water and my butt on the wooden seat.

First, the Falls Church police brought in the Virginia State Troopers, then handed it over to the Federal Bureau of

Investigation. It should be our case. Why were Burnett and the Secret Service standing mute on the sidelines? It didn't make sense. I needed to know what was going on. What was being done about John's murder. Why my mother had her photo taken with Charles Robinson. Get some answers to everything that had been bothering me since I got clobbered in the Senator's bedroom.

* * * * * *

The Embassy of the Federal Republic of Germany is on Reservoir Road not far from my apartment. A large redbrick mansion three stories high with black shutters, white trim and widow's walk, built in the late nineteenth when Georgian architecture was *de rigueur*, the tall fence of black wrought iron added later. I didn't know where else to look for three killers who spoke German in normal conversation while trying to steal some document from the home of a U.S. Senator.

My '71 Camaro was black with foot-wide red racing stripes running back along the hood, roof and trunk. Not the best stakeout vehicle, but it was in good shape for a five-year-old bomber that didn't look out of place among all the other city bangers parked along the side of the road. Melissa used to say I kept the car cleaner than my suits, but that was from someone who wouldn't wear the same dress twice in a month.

I found a space a half block down on the opposite side of the street with a clear view of the FRG entrance and driveway. It was one of those mild days the capital gets in late winter, with no wind, a pale blue sky and weak sunshine that held the promise of an early spring. I had the two I-dent-a-kit sketches taped to the dashboard but saw no one who looked anything like my perps go in or out of the embassy all day. Sitting in front of the German legation was a long shot and I knew it. I really didn't expect to see the burglars waltzing in and out of the front gate. That wasn't why I was there.

The uniformed police who guard the White House are part of the Secret Service Executive Protective Service. That branch of the Service also has a Foreign Missions Division whose job it is to protect the embassies around Washington if they request it. The German legation did, and the EPSO day shift was scheduled to get pushed at four o'clock per orders, right on the button. They peeled out of the front gate, three heading west, the other toward me on the sidewalk where I'd parked my Camaro. I stuffed the sketches into my pocket, locked the car and crossed the street with my badge in the palm of my hand.

"How you doing?" I asked the EPSO, flipping open the double fold three-by-five leatherette case the guard had seen a thousand times. "Got a minute?"

He was a light-skinned black man, average height, thick waist, wary, with a wrinkled cobalt uniform under his winter coat after a long day on duty. A good job for any kid smart enough to graduate from high school, especially a Black man who had risen from the high rate of unemployment among the 18% Afro-American population in the District.

"Coughlin," he answered as I fell in step beside him. "You the one caught it in the Senator's house."

His name was Ed Dekins and he was curious but asked no questions.

I said I was and asked him, "How long you been on this detail?"

"'Bout a year now, off an' on past month."

"Hear any scuttlebutt about the Feebs snooping around, cornering any of the legation?"

Dekins kept walking with eyes fixed in front of us, shaking his head. "I ain't heard nothin'."

We could have gone on like that for a couple of blocks.

"I need your help if you can keep it quiet."

The guard looked at me and raised his eyebrows. We were at a corner of 38th Street in back of the G-town campus. One of my old student watering holes was half way up the block.

"Can I buy you a beer?"

Georgie Porgy's has a narrow bar that leads to a big room where they served Schlitz in pitchers and thick pizzas at long wooden picnic tables. The dim light comes from ersatz

Tiffany lamps hanging three feet above your head on brass chains coming down from the ceiling. The bar was crowded with college kids, but the back room was almost empty, waiting with confidence for the evening traffic. We sat in a booth along the far wall and ordered two bottles of Pabst from a young waitress who interrupted her reading at a nearby table to serve us.

I filled Dekins in on some of the background and slid the sketches across the table. "Ever see these characters?" He studied the two portraits for several moments while he made up his mind, then stabbed his finger at the full-face rendering of the guy I encountered in the hallway.

"Gunter Knopf's this one. Security, according to the roster." We both knew that could mean Knopf was anything from a tourist aide to an espionage agent.

"Ain't seen him in about a month."

Staking out the German Embassy was not such a long shot after all, considering the man whose home had been broken into. I tried not to let my excitement show as I touched the edge of the second sketch. "How about this guy?"

Dekins picked up the sheet of paper and narrowed his eyes. I had gotten a good look at the first man, so that drawing was fully developed. The second sketch of the driver, the one who killed John was based on the description given by the guard at the condo, who admitted he was not too good at faces, especially white ones.

"Could be Kurt Henzler," Dekins said. "Ain't seen him lately, either."

"Think they went home?"

"Coulda done. They don't tell us nothin'."

"Their names still on the roster?"

"Don't know. I could check."

"There may be another guy missing," I told him.

Dekins tilted his glass, poured the last of his beer into it and looked up. "That's right, you shot one, didn't you?"

That part had happened so fast all I could remember of the perp I shot was a blur of facial skin.

23

"He needed serious medical attention, or they had a body to dispose of."

"We wouldn't get to know nothin' like that."

The FMD guard mashed his lips into a tight line and gave a shake of his head. "These foreigners are very private people."

We finished our beers and tried to figure out if the apparent departure of Knopf and Henzler coincided with the date of the break-in but could not do it. Dekins agreed to call me at home after he checked the embassy employee roster and found out what he could about the two or three missing attachés from the other guards on the FRG detail.

* * * * * *

Headquarters of the Secret Service is three blocks down from the White House in an unpretentious office building at 1800 'G' Street NW. That's where the Director's office is with his assistants, deputies and administrative staff needed to run 2,500 agents in all our field offices across the country. Most of the technical support departments are located there, too. Forensics, the counterfeit lab and mainframe computer system.

Burnett, my own desk and most of the people I worked with were in the Washington Field Office in the Potomac Electric Power Building on 21st and Pennsylvania. With a little luck, I would not run into anybody at headquarters who knew my disability status.

* * * * * *

Alex Shertinsky could find your high school sweetheart's shoe size from the first three letters of her married name. Short and round, with a perpetual smile behind his sandy beard, he sat in a glass-enclosed office looking out on the nucleus of the Secret Services Information Services Section. I crossed the well-lit room that housed the Cray computer in tall gray cabinets with spinning tape drives and the men and women in casual clothes who tended the humming beast, reading flashing lights, changing reels, working at terminals on desks scattered throughout the area.

"Jared, my good fellow," Alex said in his clipped British accent, "I hear you've been playing at coppers and thieves." He did not lift his considerable bulk from the big leather chair surrounded by computer terminals, keyboards and printers, but extended his hand for me to shake.

"How are you healing?" he asked.

Alex motioned to the small sofa against the wall, where I shrugged out of my Bean parka and put it beside me. We exchanged scuttlebutt during which I tried to steer Alex away from the shooting incident and the inquisitive data-fanatic attempted to pry every last detail about it from me.

Alex and I had worked several cases together over the years, one ending in the capture of a gang running a major U.S. savings bond counterfeit operation. I had been able to feed Alex seemingly innocuous information that enabled him to locate the printing plant. Alex had done all the work, so I faded into the background when they passed out the kudos. The role Alex had played in the case had earned him the glass enclosed office we sat in.

When he realized I was evading his questions, he leaned back in his comfortable leather chair and folded his arms across his chest as best he could.

"Exactly what is it that you require?"

"Everything you can dig up on three guys: background checks, affiliations, financials."

"You have their names, I presume...."

"Gunter Knopf and Kurt Henzler."

"Germans." Alex stroked his beard and turned to the terminal on his left.

"Could this be related to...." He waved an arm at the door and I got up and closed it. "I don't suppose this particular inquiry has a case number...."

I didn't reply, and Alex began typing into one of his keyboards. "May we assume D.C. or environs?"

"They're with the FRG Embassy."

Alex continued tapping, scanning the data that flashed on and off the screen. The process began to absorb him, and he hummed an unrecognizable tune to himself as he searched voluminous data banks at his disposal. I couldn't suppress a smile as it occurred to me why data processing mavens seemed to cloak their work in a shroud of technical obfuscation from computer semi-illiterates, which elevates their status, but more important, they often figure out how to gain access to external sources they're not supposed to hack into.

"No priors." He tapped in another series of commands and waited. "As you know, our free society doesn't keep track of foreigners well, but we can hunt down our own citizens quite adequately."

He straightened up and stared at the monitor, then turned to the terminal on his right and hit a couple of keys. I couldn't see that screen from where I sat, but it looked as though Alex was using a password to call up a directory. He shut that down, flipped on a modem that would access some remote computer though a special phone line and began working on the main terminal again. It took about two minutes.

"It appears that your Teutonic duo were operating in unison," he said. "Checking accounts, VISA and ATM cards all opened the same day, same bank." Alex smiled and turned the terminal on its base, so I could read the information on the monitor. "Along with a third man named George Berger."

"Those are my guys," I told him, and began copying the information into my pocket notebook.

The screen listed their diplomatic passport numbers, West German addresses, their employer as the Federal Republic of Germany and residence the embassy on Reservoir Road. All three had made minor financial transactions through February 15th, then Knopf and Berger's accounts were closed. Henzler made a $300 withdrawal with his ATM card on February 17th. No activity since. Alex tapped a finger against the CRT screen.

"The bank accounts were opened on January 16th."

"About two weeks," I said, "after the New Hampshire polls came through and the Senator became a serious contender

26

for the presidency."

"Does that help?"

"Alex, you're a veritable magician!"

His broad smile faded beneath his beard and his eyes became serious. "Their collusion might put a sinister spin on it."

"Can you get the embassy phone bills?"

He shrugged his heavy shoulders as though nothing was impossible. "Give me a couple of hours. Ma Bell's system is more secure than some of our own."

"I need to know who they've been calling since the middle of February."

"Since your altercation and the Germans disappeared."

I rose to my feet and put on my parka. I had a lead on John's killers and a link between Senator Robinson and the German legation.

I couldn't wait to drop the information on the Bureau. Maybe earn a citation, jump a grade or two. Show Melissa.

"This is unofficial," Alex gestured toward the screen, "So I trust you will protect the source of this data and your prestidigitator."

"Hey! They don't call us 'secret' for nothing."

The big man leaned forward in his chair, shoulders hunched, thick forearms braced on the desk between us, his wide hands folded before him and shook me back to reality.

"Be careful, my friend. Be very, very careful with this."

CHAPTER FOUR
Georgetown, DC
March 1976

I went home for dinner, dropped a bag of frozen chicken a la king in boiling water and started heating up a can of lima beans just as the phone rang. It was Ed Dekins. I heard kids playing in the background as the FMD guard read the list of German staff members slowly, so I could copy them down. George Berger's name was on it.

"I checked our humps on duty the week of the break-in," he said, which impressed me. Dekins must have been on the phone since he got home, calling his buddies on the detail. Then he hesitated like he knew what he wanted to say but was not sure what it meant. "Gunter Knopf, the security guy, took a pouch home the day after you got shot."

"What, like a briefcase?"

"Anything with the ambassador's seal on it is a diplomatic pouch, nobody can inspect it. This was metal crate."

"Did he take it out on a commercial flight?" I asked him. "Lufthansa?"

"We don't know. They drove a van in at three in the morning, probably shoved the crate in some government or corporate plane with Knopf and his luggage."

I sensed Dekins anxiety in his low tone of voice. "They don't have to show us nothing. Our guy was lucky to read the seals in the dark."

"What about Henzler?"

"We don't think he's been around four, five weeks."

"Since John Goddard was killed?"

"About then."

Secret service 'uniforms' were assigned to foreign embassies to protect them, not watch them. They had a roster of authorized personnel but did not log them in or out.

"Anybody else go missing around that time?"

"Man by the name of George Berger we think. No one's sure."

"Ed, this is good scoop, I really appreciate it"

A tone of uncertainty crept into his voice again as he said, "Sounds fishy, don't it?"

I agreed that it did.

The phone was silent. "This ain't official, right?"

"Right."

Silence again. Dekins said, "Hey, man, we're just humps, like you."

The brotherhood. And Ken Burnett was not in it.

* * * * * *

There were seventeen German nationals working at the embassy whose alleged functions ranged from ambassador to domestic servant. In between, there was a consul, first secretary, a couple of attachés, clerks and other mid-to-low-level employees. I made a quick trip back to 1800 'G' Street where Alex had left an envelope full of computer printouts with the uniformed guard.

The FRG February phone bill details I brought home on a stack of green-bar sheets absorbed me until midnight. Three calls had been made from the German embassy the day after the shooting to a number with a (301) area code on February 13th in Western Maryland.

Western Maryland. The same number was called from the embassy again on February 17th, then several times thereafter from the home of Gustav Klauber a technician on their employee roster who looked like a go-between. I decided not to brace Klauber yet, but Kurt Henzler could have gone to ground at the address listed for the Maryland phone number. Or people there might know where he is.

Information in (301) told me the number was listed to an Irmgard Bauer at 317 Hockley Street, Germantown, about twenty-five miles northwest of DC. Smart. The hell with hiding a needle in a haystack, hide it in a pile of needles.

He'd blend in with the dominant German population, speak the language, probably pose as an illegal alien with everybody ready to hide him and he'd be close by if someone at the embassy wanted him. I needed to know more about what Shertinsky told me, but his wife aid that Alex had gone to Vermont for a long weekend of fly-fishing.

After I found out who had the case at the FBI it took Special Agent Roger Talbot two days to return my phone call. In spite of urgent hints about what I had learned, he would not agree to meet until three days later. I tracked John Goddard's son and daughter down through the Senator's office and spent an afternoon writing letters. I found it difficult to express my feelings on paper and promised myself I'd call them soon.

There wasn't much to do around Washington in February during the day with everyone else working, so going on vacation was probably a good idea after all. I picked up some brochures at a travel agency, then threw them in a kitchen drawer when I discovered that most of the cruise ships and packaged tours were double occupancy. I decided to check on Club Med. Until my meeting with the FBI changed my mind.

* * * * * *

I laid out most of my story as we sat in Roger Talbot's cubicle in the middle of a vast floor of identical partitions in the WFO in Buzzards Point: identifying Knopf and Henzler through our Protective Service and the two Germans departing. I held back on Irmgard Bauer.

Each agent had a government issue gray metal desk, padded swivel, two side chairs and one file cabinet. Talbot fit in beautifully with his lean build, neatly trimmed brown hair and rep tie. Blue serge suit, of course. He was about my age.

"We can't just let you dig through our files," he said with a twitch of his mouth that was as close as he got to a smile. "You know how it is."

I knew exactly how it was. Inter-agency competition, what have you guys ever done for us, we're the Bureau. The Secret Service Investigative Division had turned the case over to the

FBI as soon as they concluded there had been no attempt on the Senator's life. Talbot implied that the only reason he was talking to me was that I was one of the victims.

I asked about the driver waiting so long to come into the house, then killing an unarmed man. "Why didn't the guy in the truck follow me right away? Why did he wait, then shoot John before he came in?"

"What should he have done?"

"Bring John in at gunpoint, he'd have the drop on us, tie us up. Take what they came for and leave."

I shook my head, still unable to answer the questions that had gnawed at my brain for weeks.

"Why escalate a simple crime like burglary to murder, unless the stakes are a hell of a lot higher than just B&E?"

"You were sitting up front where the Senator rides, right? Wearing his hat? We figure the driver thought you were him and his guys inside could handle it."

"How would the driver know the Senator rode up front?" I asked. "Or whose hat it was?"

"Whatever...." Talbot shifted his weight in his chair and waved a hand in front of his face. "Slouch hat, snowing, you had your head down, running for the door. Point is, he didn't realize you were Service and packing."

I decided not to argue. "Then what?"

"Driver walks over to the car, Goddard rolls the window down, the guy asks what's up." Talbot picked a yellow pencil off the desk and began twirling it in his fingers. "Soon as he realized an armed Secret Service agent just went inside with his buddies tossing the place, he pops Goddard, runs in and drops you."

"What was the weapon?"

"Nine-millimeter automatic."

"What kind?"

"Lugar, 7.65 Parabellum."

Dragging information out of Talbot was like pulling tree stumps.

"German," I said. "Like their language."

"Your boss, Ken Burnett, told me about your theory."

Talbot gave that little twitch to the corner of his mouth that was beginning to annoy me. "You still reading espionage into this?"

"Geeze, Talbot, don't you?"

Alex had learned that FRG ran a cargo flight out of Andrews Air Force Base two or three times a month. "Knopf was on the plane that went out the day after the shooting," I said. "The man I shot must have died, so they pack him in a metal crate with dry ice or something and slap a diplomatic seal on it. Neat"

Talbot squinted. The big room was surprisingly quiet with all the people in it, but the partitions acted as baffles and they piped that white noise down from the ceiling to absorb conversation and the sounds of typewriters. The ring of a telephone in the next cubicle broke through the low-level murmur.

"We hate dealing with ambassadors. We never win."

"You think the German ambassador's in on robbery and murder?" I asked.

"Of course not," Talbot answered. "But they rarely waive diplomatic immunity. If a couple of low-level staff members commit a crime, the diplomats don't want their country's image smeared with the extended press coverage of a felony trial."

"Suppose it wasn't robbery?"

Talbot gave me a patronizing smirk. "German interference in our political process?"

"It makes more sense than robbery."

"Senator Robinson doesn't think so," Talbot said.

"What makes a U.S. Senator an expert on criminal behavior?"

"We agree with him."

The Bureau would shut me right out of this if I didn't smarten up.

"Well, that cuts it." My self-effacing grin tried to acknowledge their superior opinion.

"What about Henzler?"

Talbot stated the obvious. "He's missing."

They must have picked this guy for his endurance, because he was certainly wearing me down.

"Doesn't that look suspicious under the circumstances?"

"It happens all the time."

"What," I asked, "legation staff disappearing into the heartland of America?"

"Mostly non-essential employees, domestics," Talbot replied. "They get in on a diplomatic visa, then take off for one of their tight little ethnic communities a thousand miles from here and burrow in."

I was glad I had withheld Irmgard Bauer. "Can we get Knopf back to answer questions?"

Talbot shook his head. "We need a lot more than your description to extradite a foreign national from his own country that has D.I. here."

"Henzler may still be in this country or as far as we know, he could have gone home. INS doesn't keep track of outgoing diplomatic passports unless they get a Stop Order."

That did not surprise me. The Immigration and Naturalization Service had all they could do to keep illegal's from getting in, never mind getting out. They didn't get a stop order because these ham-and-bone guys were playing patty cake instead of the job they could do when they wanted.

"You're going to look for Henzler," I said, "right?" He's the one who killed John Goddard."

"We put a wanted and Stop Order out on him after you called me," Talbot said. "As soon as we bring him in, we'll ask his ambassador to waiver."

Not if you don't find him, I thought. The FBI wasn't getting tired, but I was. Special Agent Talbot seemed prepared to sit there forever and let me extract meaningless bits of information from his molasses personality.

"So, you're going ahead with the investigation?"

"Full-court press," Talbot assured me.

I bobbed my head up and down like I believed him.

"I'd like to help."

"You're on medical leave from the Service." Talbot put on

his cold little smile that made me feel like a Cub Scout. "What makes you think you're fit enough to work with the Bureau?"

"I'm involved," I told him. "John Goddard was my friend. Henzler shot me. I was assigned to protect the Senator."

Talbot leaned forward, placing the palms of both hands on the arms of his chair. "Maybe you're too involved, Agent Coughlin."

He stood up and tugged at the starched white cuffs under the sleeves of his navy-blue suit coat.

"You just relax. We'll handle it."

I didn't buy it. Three Germans had been searching for some key and document in the home of the man who could be the next president of the United States. They killed a decent human being to insure the secrecy of their mission. And the top law enforcement agency in the country was covering it up.

CHAPTER FIVE
Georgetown, DC
March 1976

If the Germans had diplomatic immunity they could not be detained, arrested or prosecuted. I was not sure how that worked if murder or espionage could be proved. I knew a woman at State well enough to set up an appointment without getting into a long explanation on the phone. She was a friend of Melissa's, a serious GS-12 government employee currently working her way up the ranks in protocol, which was exactly what I needed.

Judith Silverman's office was in the State Department building on 'C' Street. She agreed to meet me for a cup of coffee in the third-floor cafeteria and I waited forty-five minutes for her in the wide marble hallway outside the main bank of elevators, a high-traffic area with people hurrying through the huge doorway carrying file folders or cardboard trays of food and drinks back to their desks. Secretaries, shirt-sleeved clerks, administrators and bureaucrats lifted their voices to talk above the conversation of the moving throng.

"Are you back on the job?" Judith asked in lieu of a conventional greeting.

"Not yet." She didn't break her stride as she headed for the double doors and I followed her into the massive cafeteria. "They gave me two months' disability," almost adding, 'but the bullet wound's coming along nicely, thanks.'

We got in line and Judith held up traffic at the cash register digging around in her pocketbook for thirty-five cents, refusing to let me pay for her coffee. She led the way to a pair of empty plastic chairs at a table in the center of the room as I made a conscious effort to keep my eyes off her compact derrière that bunched and swayed beneath the clinging fabric of her red knit dress.

Judith was a petite woman, about thirty-five, with a cheerleader face made up like a New York fashion model. I once remarked to Melissa that Judith must spend a fortune on brassieres, because her breasts rippled like two sacks of Jell-O jutting proudly from her chest. I was sure my comment had been passed on and interpreted as sexist.

"It's a shame about you and Melissa," she said when we were seated. I knew she never thought I was enough of a politician to make it into the top echelons of the Service or any position in government worthy of her friend's growing stature in the Washington legal profession.

I smiled at her observation. "Probably best for both of us."

"What did you want to see me about?"

"I need to know about diplomatic immunity in a specific situation."

She frowned and cocked her head. "What ever happened to channels?"

"I'm not ready to go through that yet." I sipped my coffee and tried to sound casual. "It may be nothing." I put the cup down and stroked my left arm inside the sling. "Not supposed to go into the office 'til April."

She probably didn't believe that but was curious. "Does this have something to do with the shooting?"

I explained why I thought the burglars might be German nationals attached to their embassy. "But I'm not sure and don't want to go out on a limb until I am."

"What's their rank?"

"I don't know. One's in security, I think."

She frowned again and looked across the room for a couple of seconds. Ask a government employee a question and you get a snotty answer or a slow trip to boredom. Judith could do both.

"Full immunity from criminal acts depends on how sensitive the person's job is to the diplomatic function of the mission." She took a tiny sip of coffee and placed the Styrofoam cup in the center of her folded paper napkin. "It's not a courtesy or privilege like most people think but designed to guarantee foreign service personnel they can conduct official business in another country without reprisals or intimidation."

"Even if they rob and murder?"

"Ever hear of trumped-up charges?"

"We don't do that, do we?"

"You don't think our good old CIA could be tempted if the stakes were high enough?"

We were getting off track, but I didn't answer. I needed information, not an argument.

"D.I. is a concept the Greeks came up with a couple of thousand years ago," she continued, "to keep the bearers of bad news from getting killed.

"If the guys who murdered John Goddard have it, we can't touch them?"

"I didn't say that. We can ask their ambassador to waive immunity and let us arrest and prosecute. Or we can pull their visas. Send them home."

"How do we do that?"

"First, you need a damned good case."

"How about an eyewitness?"

"A Secret Service agent?" she asked. "We'd need more."

"Suppose the ambassador refuses to waive?"

"We can declare them PNG, *Persona Non Grata*. Ship them out and they can't come back. If they do, we can prosecute."

I didn't like the sound of that. If I lucked out and found John's killers, we might be able to confront them, but have to let them walk. Telling somebody to go home was not my idea of appropriate punishment for murder.

We finished our coffee and left the cafeteria that was starting to fill up with the early lunch shift. Judith was a standout in a city full of attractive women, getting appreciative looks as we waited for an elevator.

"Police agencies usually let up on investigations," she told me, "when they learn a suspect has D.I. That's a mistake."

I thought of my meeting with Roger Talbot. "Why so?"

"We can't ask an ambassador to waive if we don't have conclusive evidence." She reached out to jab the UP button that was already lit. "Even if it's granted, a D.A. might not be able to get a conviction. And we can't impose maximum sanctions if the investigation is incomplete."

"You're saying push this to the hilt."

"If there's anything to it."

The doors of the elevator opened and she stepped between them, turning toward me. "And keep me informed. I'm writing a memo on this which makes it official business."

The doors closed.

What a bright, dedicated, attractive lady. Why did she have to be such a pain in the ass?

* * * * * *

That night I went to bed early and exhausted. Either the effects of my healing wound or stress from my ambivalent feelings about what I had learned and done during the past few weeks were catching up with me.

When I awoke, the west wall of the room was bathed in the streetlight shining through my bedroom window. I lay there staring at the ceiling for several minutes, evaluating the "clues" I had stumbled on since getting out of the hospital. Was I just beating around the mulberry bush trying to convince myself I was getting somewhere in a serious or pointless investigation that law enforcement professionals were discouraging me from pursuing, and those who weren't were probably laughing behind their hands.

Maybe I needed a break from the German conundrum. Like Burnet said, get a little distance from it. Finding out if my parents really knew the Senator thirty-four-years ago or I was just whistling Dixie on that, too.

It was almost dawn and I was hungry, lethargic and morose. Murder and espionage were not my areas of expertise. I had spent two years in the Dallas office on bond fraud and credit card scams, then transferred to WFO where I'd been working interstate counterfeiting. I did not feel comfortable with what I was doing but could not stop. I was afraid it would end badly.

It was still dark when I forced myself out of bed, threw on pants, sweater and moccasins, then started the coffee.

When my mother passed away I had sold her condo in Florida with everything in it, gave her clothes to the Salvation Army and packed her papers and memorabilia in a steamer trunk which stood unopened in the back of my bedroom closet.

My mother had induced conflicting emotions deep within me ever since I could remember, and she did so then as I dragged the big trunk into the middle of the living room. I pulled a straight-back chair to it and began sifting through souvenirs, familiar knickknacks, snapshots, costume jewelry and loose personal papers.

After her death, her attorney had urged me to go through all of her personal possessions to make sure they had not missed any insurance policies or other financial records, but I did not look at them closely. Most of the things in the top shelf were items from her desk and table tops that I'd packed in a hurry. Nothing new, unfamiliar or revealing there. I thumbed through a leather-bound address book which contained names, phone numbers with cross-outs and notations indicating birthdays, anniversaries, her Christmas card list and deaths. I recognized some of the names, but nothing indicated who the people were or how long she'd known them. I removed the shallow upper compartment and set it down on the floor.

The bottom section of the trunk was a mass of letters bound with colored yarn, spiral notebooks, manila envelopes, file folders, scrapbooks and photo albums. Three years after her death and a lifetime of discord, I found it almost as difficult to confront my mother's intimate past as I had the woman herself. The smell of brewing coffee tore me away. I sipped it black, calming my mind, watching English muffins turn brown under the toaster broiler.

The chronological sequence in which her most private possessions had been placed in the trunk propelled me back through time in my mother's life, from the recent years I knew best to her middle age and youth that had always seemed vague and remote to me. I did not believe many people thought a great deal about the lives of their mothers and fathers when their parents were young, but most knew a lot more about them than I did mine. Not that I believed my mother had a lot of secrets or anything, that was just the way she was.

She was fifty-six when she died of a stroke. The doctor said they might have been able to save her in a hospital, but she'd been known to stay drunk for days, and her neighbor didn't find her for almost a week. My mother had divorced her third husband in the early sixties and had lived alone ever since.

Before number three, she was married nine years to Maxwell Coughlin, who adopted me and gave me his name. He left when I was fifteen and I started going to boarding schools. My mother came from an old New York Dutch family and some pretty serious money, both of which died out as the result of an investment banking scandal in the nineteen-fifties. My real father was Pieter Kramers, a Dutch boat captain employed by my maternal grandfather. My mother's family was hardly ecstatic about the marriage but provided a Christmas wedding in New York society for their only daughter during the somber winter of 1941. Less than a year before my father had drowned at sea.

Except for a few fleeting details and half-remembered anecdotes, that was all I ever knew about my parents' background. If Senator Charles Robinson had his picture taken with my mother around that time, where did he fit into my parent's history? What was the relationship between those three people thirty-four years ago--and why wouldn't he acknowledge it?

My mother and I lived in Manhattan with her parents when I was a child and in Connecticut with Max Coughlin while I was growing up. No one in her family ever volunteered information about my father, and none of her later friends seemed to go back far enough to have known him.

The oldest photo albums contained snapshots of Pieter Kramers that I had seen before--on the forty-eight-foot wooden hull ketch he sailed across the Atlantic for my grandfather; at the van Oudgaarden estate in Newport,

Rhode Island; their Miami honeymoon; and the single Christmas they spent together three weeks after the United States entered World War II.

There were no photos of the Senator or any reference to him in her letters, the spiral-bound diaries she started some years on the first of January (then aborted before the winter was over) or in the notes and papers I found in the Manila envelopes and file folders.

One envelope contained a yellowed news clipping from the August 27, 1941 *Providence Bulletin* I had never seen before. It was a single column eight-inch item with my father's fading picture under a headline that read:

DUTCH RESISTANCE HERO DROWNS OFF BLOCK ISLAND

Newport—A Dutch resistance fighter who escaped German occupied Holland in a daring single-handed transatlantic crossing last year, drowned early Wednesday morning in tragic boating accident five miles west of Block Island.

Pieter Kramers, a thirty-one-year-old professional yacht captain from the Netherlands was lost overboard during a routine Coast Guard Auxiliary patrol of the yacht, Dutch Master, *owned by George B. van Oudgaarden of Newport and New York City. Also presumed dead in the same incident is U.S. Coast Guard Ensign John Andeweg, twenty-two, from Chicago, Illinois, a recent graduate of Brown University.*

Both men were serving in the newly inaugurated Corsair Fleet. Fellow crew members, including Marijke van Oudgaarden-Kramers, wife of the deceased Dutch yachtsman report that both men disappeared from the yacht during their midnight watch while the rest of the crew were below deck sleeping.

When the motion of the boat became erratic about two am, the off-watch crew came on deck to find Kramers and Andeweg missing along with the yacht's dinghy. The crew began an immediate search of the area summoning assistance from the Block Island Coast Guard station.

Although seas were moderate with ten to fifteen knot southwesterly winds, the search was hampered first by darkness, then by rain and fog, which reduced visibility to under one mile throughout the day.

Kramers' body was found tangled in a rope attached to the yacht's over-turned dinghy at 4:45 PM yesterday by Coast Guard Cutter CG-577. Andeweg has not yet been found.

Authorities speculate that the two men saw something in the water which they tried to inspect or retrieve from the dinghy. It is believed that a problem ensued which caused both men to end up in the water.

"Whatever it was," Coast Guard Lt. Edmund Gilmore commented, "It must have come on them awful sudden to keep them from waking the crew or radioing for help. This should not have happened," Gilmore said. "Both men were good sailors."

In addition to Mrs. Kramers, the crew of Dutch Master *consisted of James A. Barnum, fifty-seven, of Washington, D.C.; Paul L. Graham, forty-one and his wife Ellen, both of Wickford.*

Owner George B. van Oudgaarden was not on board and could not be reached for comment.

Besides his wife, Mr. Kramers leaves an infant son, Jared, and Kramers parents who reside in Roosendal, the Netherlands.

Dutch Master *is on loan to the Corsair Fleet established by Congress in the U.S. Coast Guard Auxiliary Act last March. The 'fleet' is comprised of private yachts manned by competent yachtsmen who are disqualified for military 'service by physical problems or age and can serve for ten-day periods on offshore patrol.*

Often referred to as 'Hooligan's Navy,' the Corsairs perform an invaluable role protecting coastal shipping by alerting the Coast Guard to un-identified vessels, thereby preventing enemy infiltration from the sea.

* * * * * *

A hero in the Dutch resistance? My mother never told me that! Giving me sketchy details about my father drowning in a boating accident was understandable when you think of the trauma she must have experienced waking up to find her new husband had gone missing in 20-fathoms of pitch-black ocean.

But why hide the truth that my Dad was a war hero? I had little enough to look up to as a child, embarrassed at my inability to describe to my peers the ghostly shadow who had sired me; why had she robbed me of this?

I must have reread that article thirty times, conjuring up the feats of bravery suggested by the words, 'resistance fighter, daring single-handed sailor. Hero. 'My father! Suddenly more substantial, no longer an elusive concept in my mother's past. Why had she kept that from me? Who was she trying to punish, my father or me? I was never told that another man died that night, either. Or the circumstances described in the article or the names of the other crew members. Maybe they could tell me more about my father. Maybe they knew Senator Robinson. If he was just a passing acquaintance, a longtime friend of my parents or I was climbing bamboo shoots. Maybe they could help me figure out what my mother and apparently, Senator Robinson, didn't want me to know.

I picked up the address book again and searched for the names in the news clip. I knew that my mother had not kept up with my father's relatives in Holland, but even if they were still alive, it was unlikely they could tell me much about an incident that happened off the New England coast in 1942. My stepfather had not known my mother then, so he wouldn't be much help. I needed to talk to the people who were there--witnesses.

James Barnum was not in the book. Whoever he was, my mother had evidently not stayed in touch with him.

Paul and Ellen Graham were listed, but Paul was crossed out with, 'deceased 3/16/66' beside his name. If Ellen was still alive and she hadn't moved after her husband's death, her address was 12 Front Street in Wickford, Rhode Island.

Coast Guard Lieutenant Edmund Gilmore was the only other possibility. Maybe Alex could track him down with his magic computer on Monday.

I went back to the letters bound with colored yarn and

found correspondence from Ellen Graham going back to 1943. She and my mother apparently wrote to one another three or four times a year about births, vacations, illness, marital problems, plus the usual hopes, dreams and disappointments women seem to share with special friends as they grow older.

It was almost noon when I repacked the trunk and returned it to the closet with everything except the news clipping and address book. I was surprised that my mother hadn't saved any of the follow-up news stories on my father's death or the other man who was lost at sea. Maybe she was too upset after the tragedy. Maybe the newspaper didn't run any follow-up; after all, there was a war on...or maybe there was some other reason.

CHAPTER SIX
Wickford, RI
March 1976

The Eastern Airlines DC-6 touched down at Rhode Island's Theodore Francis Green Airport at 1:55 Saturday afternoon. It was a cold, windy day with lowering clouds threatening to fulfill the forecast snow that I could feel in the air.

Wickford is ten miles south of the airport on the west side of Narragansett Bay, a pretty little New England seacoast village with widows walks on the roofs of two-hundred-year old clapboard homes built by the captains and merchant owners of clipper ships who traded goods around the world for their fledgling country.

I turned the rented Ford off I-95 onto Old Boston Post Road into the center of town along the narrow tree-lined streets, past the art galleries, studios and gift shops that delineated the character of the town in mid-1970.

Front Street was down near the harbor, according to the directions given to me on the telephone by Ellen Graham's daughter, Stephanie, and I found number 12 after one wrong turn on a dead-end road. The Graham family lived in a gray shingled Cape with white trim, a modest lawn and shrubs near the house protected from the weight of heavy snow by wooden A frames.

Standing on the front step ringing the bell, I had no idea what to expect. The daughter had been cordial but hesitant on the phone that morning when I explained what I wanted. She had met my mother a couple of times over the years when the two older women had visited and seemed to want to help me. The problem was that her mother had Alzheimer's and was not very lucid most of the time.

Looking back on it, I think I fell in love that afternoon— probably the minute Stephanie opened the door. She was a

45

big woman, almost my height, with broad shoulders and a lush Rubens body filling a beige cashmere sweater and pleated Tartan skirt.

Somehow, I had always gravitated toward so-called glamour women, the New York model type with flawless skin and svelte figures like those whose elegantly posed photographs appear on the covers of magazines like *Cosmopolitan.* Melissa was a good example. My women had to have some brains, a good personality, of course--but dynamite looks had always been more important; an envied trophy clutching my arm for me to display. Until that day in Wickford.

She held a book against her thigh, index finger between the pages to mark her place and pushed the pair of tortoiseshell glasses up on top of her head. "You have your mother's eyes."

She gave me a big, honest smile, the highlights in her own brown eyes and the tiny crinkles at their corners suggesting she did that a lot. Her auburn hair was thick and glossy, parted in the middle, combed straight back from her forehead and reached down to her shoulders. At first glance, she seemed older, but the pale freckles across her cheeks made me wonder. "My mother said I look like my father," I told her.

"We'll let mom decide."

I followed the movement of her wide hips and solid derrière into the kitchen where Mrs. Graham was making coffee. Mother and daughter were alike except for the older woman's gray hair and weathered skin--solid build, perky, with a slight overbite that added character and intelligence to their faces.

Stephanie introduced us and Mrs. Graham began talking about her life-long friendship with my mother while her daughter restarted the coffee with the filter which the older woman had omitted.

"You may be in luck," she had told me on the phone. "Mother seems to live more in the past now than she does in the present."

I stood looking at the two women in the brightly lit kitchen. I had trouble keeping my eyes off the younger woman's well-filled sweater, concentrating on her mother's absorption in relating humorous anecdotes about, my mother, her friend of long ago. Mrs. Graham was dressed in a navy-blue wool knit dress adorned with gold jewelry as though she was going to an afternoon social event.

We sat in the breakfast nook, daughter and mother on one side of the table me on the other. With little prompting, Mrs. Graham began reaching back into her past to relate the circumstances surrounding that night thirty-four years ago when she all but witnessed my father's death.

George van Oudgaarden, my mother's dad, had volunteered his new forty-eight-foot sailboat for service in the recently formed Corsair Fleet whose mission was to cruise the coast scouting for Nazi submarines. My maternal grandfather was in his fifties in 1942 and running his business in New York city, so he assigned the responsibility of taking *Dutch Master* on patrol to his hired boat captain, Pieter Kramers, who was also his new son-in-law.

My father, a professional sailor from Holland, had escaped imminent capture by the Gestapo by delivering the yacht from the Norway yard of Wolter Huisman the previous summer, crossing the Atlantic single-handed in thirty-seven days. He and my mother had fallen in love and married. My grandfather had chosen their civilian crew from local sailing friends of the family.

"We left Newport on a Thursday afternoon to patrol Rhode Island Sound between Long Island and Martha's Vineyard," Mrs. Graham recalled, gazing at the wall above the empty seat beside me. "The entrance to Narragansett Bay and Quonset Naval Air Station where the carriers came in for refit."

"There were just six of you on board?" I asked. "My mother and father, you and your husband, James Barnum and John Andeweg?"

"That was all we needed," the older woman said, taking a sip of coffee from the flowered cup. "Two of us standing four hours on four off watches. It was kind of informal." She smiled at me, then at her daughter. "We were drinking in those days, having fun pretending we were really in the war. Your grandfather stocked *Geneva* gin in the liquor locker— *Olde* and *Junge.*"

"So, my father and this guy Andeweg were standing watch together."

"It killed my husband, you know."

I looked at Stephanie for clarification. "What did, Mrs. Graham?"

"The drinking."

"Dad died of cirrhosis," Stephanie told me. "Mom's been in AA ever since."

Not my mother. She went the same way Paul Graham had. Massive cerebral hemorrhage probably induced by high blood pressure and pulmonary emphysema. Different diseases, same cause.

"Did my father and John Andeweg always stand watch together?"

"Dutch," Mrs. Graham corrected me. "Pieter didn't like it, but that was John's nickname at college. He was Dutch, so was your father, of course, the owner was Dutch, the boat named *Dutch Master.* Andeweg and your mother got along like brother and sister. Pieter didn't like that, either."

"Did Dutch and my father usually stand watch together?" I repeated.

"No," she answered, "only when the weather was bad at night. Like that time."

"They were both missing when you came on deck," I said, recalling what I had learned from the newspaper clipping.

"It was two or three o'clock in the morning, pitch black. The fog was horrible."

"You came on deck and found them gone?"

Mrs. Graham touched her linen napkin to the corner of her mouth. "Your mother did. She woke up first and started screaming."

"No noise, shouts or anything before that?" I asked. "They just disappeared?"

"Like they'd never been on board." The older woman shook her head and frowned, apparently thinking about that terrible experience.

"What are you scowling about, Mom?" Stephanie asked. She'd been leaning back on the bench next to her mother smoking a cigarette, in silent acknowledgment that the conversation must exclude her.

"I never felt right about it."

"What do you mean?" her daughter asked, turning toward her mother. It took a few moments for the older woman to gather her thoughts. "We called the Coast Guard and they conducted a search. Then the FBI took over."

"The FBI!" Stephanie said. "This was a military operation with participating civilians. Why would the Bureau get involved in something like that?"

"The FBI worked federal crimes almost exclusively, I said. --except in wartime when they handle espionage."

"The local police determined these drownings," Mrs. Graham volunteered, "were the result of an accident. All very hush, hush," the elderly woman whispered. "National security and all that."

"Because two men drowned accidentally?"

Mrs. graham shook her head as though she was still puzzled about the circumstances surrounding that night.

"Your mother claimed she heard an engine" Mrs. Graham offered. "They thought spies might have gotten ashore, but the FBI didn't want to scare the people with unfounded reports."

I felt as though someone had just kicked me in the pit of the stomach. "My father and Andeweg might have encountered Nazi saboteurs?" My voice sounded strange and I felt like I was hanging from the kitchen ceiling watching the three people sitting in the breakfast nook, willing myself to keep asking questions in spite of the sudden paralysis in my mind. "That's why they went off in the dinghy?" the man at the table managed to ask.

"The FBI wouldn't tell us," Mrs. Graham said. "That's what it looked like." She stared up at the wall again, twisting her cup around on her saucer. "I heard one agent ask another why the Germans hadn't killed us all."

"Oh, my God," her daughter said, bringing her hand up to the string of pearls at her throat. Stephanie looked at me, obviously surprised at her mother's revelation. "I've never heard any of this."

"They interviewed us separately at the War College in Newport and made us promise not to tell anybody anything." Mrs. Graham poured fresh coffee into our cups from the flowered china pot in the center of the table. "I don't suppose it can hurt now."

"The FBI thought Nazi spies killed my father and Dutch?" I asked.

"We talked about it afterwards, trying to make sense of their questions during our interrogation." She shrugged at her coffee cup which she held with both hands in its saucer. "I think they decided the men saw the Germans rowing ashore in some kind of small boat."

"And tried to intercept them?"

Armed Nazi agents rowing ashore, a few miles off the coast? A German submarine?

"Why would my father and Dutch leave the ketch without waking the rest of you?"

"The FBI never seemed sure." Mrs. Graham stared into space as though she was searching for something in the distance of her mind. "We looked all over the place and didn't find anything. Neither did the Coast Guard." She frowned again. "He didn't like him, you know."

Stephanie stabbed her cigarette out in an ashtray and beat me to it. "Who didn't like who, Mom?"

"Pieter." She looked at me. "Your father."

"Didn't like Dutch?" I asked.

Her head bobbed up and down. "John Andeweg, the Coast Guard boy."

The clipping said Andeweg was a recent college graduate, a young Coast Guard officer, part of the crew. Was Mrs. Graham telling me there was bad blood between them? I looked at Stephanie for help.

"Mom, wasn't Andeweg the kid who worked summers for Jared's grandfather?"

"He graduated from Brown that spring," her mother answered," and joined the Coast Guard. They assigned him to *Dutch Master* as a kind of deckhand whenever we went out."

"And my father resented that?"

Mrs. Graham shrugged, then took another sip of coffee.

"Did they argue, disagree a lot?" Stephanie asked.

I was obsessed with learning everything my mother's old friend could tell me but distracted by the lovely woman sitting across the table.

"No," her mother answered. "They were good sailors and worked the boat as kind of co-captains. Your father," she looked at her daughter, "and Jim Barnum took orders on deck from the two co-captains. Kiki and I did the cooking, mostly."

I smiled at that and Mrs. Graham winked at me. Kiki was my mother who hated to cook and always tried to avoid it.

"Why did you say they didn't like one another, Mom?" Stephanie persisted.

Mother glanced at daughter and raised her eyebrows. "Six people on that cramped wooden boat was a pretty tight fit after a few days, Honey...you get to sense things."

"You said, 'he didn't like him', Mrs. Graham. Did my father dislike Andeweg," I asked, "or did they dislike one another?"

"At the end, it was mutual, I think."

"My father was a resistance fighter," I said, as though everyone should have loved him.

Mrs. Graham cocked her head and frowned at her coffee cup. "He was not an easy man to be with." She seemed more alert for a moment, turning her head to look at me, her hand reaching across the table, stopping before it touched mine. "It didn't seem to matter at first. Pieter was tall, blond, handsome—like you. He wooed his Kiki shamelessly, an old-world romantic like the wounded hero that he was."

Stephanie placed her hand on her mother's, drawing it toward her and lowered their entwined fingers to the bench between them. "This isn't what you came to hear," she told me.

"That's OK." I grinned at her like it was an old story I knew by heart. Wounded? Damn my mother! Maybe I could get back to that without sounding like an idiot.

"She was a wonderful dancer and lived to party," Mrs. Graham continued. "The young men cut in all the time, until one night Pieter refused to allow it."

Stephanie couldn't help asking, "She let him do that?"

"I think she was flattered," her mother answered. "The serious man of experience, cavalier European. When he wanted to be."

I nudged her on. "Then they were married...."

The older woman moved her head from side to side at the memories she was watching in her mind. "And so different after that."

"Mom," Stephanie cautioned.

"No, no, it's OK," I said.

Ellen Graham turned her gaze out the window. "It was like he'd won a contest, a prize he could put on a shelf, satisfied that he knew he had done it."

Difficult as it was, this was the closest I had ever come to my parents' brief relationship. *'Go on, go on!'* I thought.

"He made her stop drinking when she was pregnant with you. That's when she realized she'd made a mistake." Mrs. Graham nodded decisively. "I know," she turned to look into my eyes, "she told me."

Stephanie started to get up from the table, eager to end these embarrassing revelations my expression must have told her were a shock to me.

I held up my hand. "Please. I need to know this."

She sat back on the bench but seemed uncomfortable.

"They buried your father in your mother's family plot in Newport, did you know that?" The older woman was staring out the kitchen window at the dark bare limbs of the big maple tree in her back yard. "His parents wanted his body sent back to Holland. With the war on, they couldn't get here, and your mother couldn't ship him home."

"So, they never found Andeweg," I prompted.

Mrs. Graham just kept looking out the window, probably seeing her own past as well as my parents' all those years ago. "The boy had no family. We went to the memorial service your grandfather held for Dutch Andeweg in Manning Chapel at Brown."

Stephanie was frowning at her mother and I started to sense that elderly woman was losing interest.

"Did you ever meet a Charles Robinson on *Dutch Master*?"

Stephanie's head snapped around to look at me. "The Senator?"

"I think he may have known my parents around that time."

"What about it, Mom? Do you remember a man named Charles Robinson during the War?"

Mrs. Graham continued gazing out the window without speaking.

"Are you getting tired, Mother?" Stephanie asked.

"What time is your father coming home?" she replied.

"You've been lucky," Stephanie told me, stroking her mother's arm through the sleeve of her blue dress. "She usually doesn't stay on one subject long, but the farther back she goes the better she remembers. It's the here and now that's the challenge. Dad's been dead for seven years."

I wanted to get a few more questions answered before we lost her and I hoped her daughter would give me the time I needed to do that.

"Did you save any of the newspaper accounts of the drownings, Mrs. Graham? Anything about my father when he sailed to America?"

She pulled her eyes away from the window and looked at me for several seconds as if she forgot who I was, then moved her empty glance to her daughter.

"We can look in her scrap book," Stephanie suggested, "but I've never seen anything like that."

"Were there any newspaper reports of the rescue attempts," I asked Mrs. Graham, "or details about the incident after it happened?"

"Just like Watergate," she replied and tapped her daughter

on the arm, so she could slide out of the bench seat and get up from the table.

The younger woman was pulling my emotions like a magnet and I hadn't trusted himself to look at her during most of the erratic conversation. I turned toward her to see if she knew what her mother meant.

"A cover-up, I think. Mom seems to think the authorities were hiding something."

CHAPTER SEVEN
Wickford, RI
March 1976

The morgue at *The Providence Journal-Bulletin* didn't open until Monday morning. I had packed an overnight bag just in case something like that happened and had no trouble getting a motel room near the airport. I asked Stephanie and her mother to join me for dinner, but the daughter said that wasn't a good idea any more. I was welcome to share potluck with them at home or we could go out for a couple of hours after she made dinner for her mother and settled her in for an evening of TV.

Stephanie made reservations for eight-thirty at The Stone Mill, a pre-revolutionary structure on Frenchtown Road built of fieldstones held together by coarse cement. It had been converted to an unpretentious New England tavern over a hundred years ago, but I wondered how they got away with the wood-shingle roof littered with dry pine needles under the smoking chimney.

We sat at the scarred wooden bar sipping house Burgundy while waiting for our table. Yellow flames reached around split tree trunks in the mammoth stone fireplace and tall white candles flickered on every table, creating intimate penumbrae around the subdued conversation of diners seated before place settings arranged on each round surface covered with white linen.

"'Secret Service' sounds so sinister to me." She was smiling, but I sensed the wariness many people have of cops.

"It's just a job. A lot of it's boring."

"But you like it."

She'd been pleasant, interested, almost teasing as she encouraged me to tell her about the only really good time I remembered when mother and I lived with my grandparents, my warm relationship with Max Coughlin, boarding schools and college. I refused to get into 'Nam, as always, but told her about my work.

And Melissa.

Ever since I talked to her on the phone that morning, Stephanie had seemed aloof, glib, treating me as though I was a nice enough guy but nothing special. There I was dying to get my arms around that lush body and she was probably trying to figure out what pigeonhole to put me in.

But she was pretty good at getting to the core of things which I found out later. That night, I thought she might have needed relief from the disturbing interrogation I had put her mother through, or maybe wanted a better perspective on the man she allowed to conduct it. Without appearing to do so, she probed every aspect of my life past and present. Except for revealing she was a child psychologist, she deflected my own inquiries with short answers and more questions.

When our brandy and coffee was served she seemed more relaxed or had satisfied her curiosity about me as a Secret Service Agent and man. Sensing her passive mood, I began to probe her background almost as aggressively as she had mine. As she spoke, I couldn't help thinking how different our lives had been. She was born, raised and went to school in the town of Wickford from the same house I visited that afternoon. The Grahams had maintained a strong sense of family despite two parents addicted to alcohol and a younger brother, Tommy, headed in the same direction with drugs. She had commuted to Brown University in Providence as did many Rhode Islanders who could get into the Ivy League school where the big girl with glasses fulfilled her childhood ambition to probe the workings of the human mind.

When Stephanie left home for the first time to study for her doctorate at Harvard, she maintained her high-grade point average until Sarni Patel, a classmate from India became attracted to her. She spent so much time tutoring him, sleeping on his futon and paying for his meals in exotic restaurants that she nearly flunked two courses in her second year. As soon as she explained her predicament to Sarni and burrowed back into her own studies, his romantic interest evaporated. The following month she learned that her ex-lover had embarked on a similar relationship with an affluent male medical student.

After that, her single extracurricular activity was demonstrating against the country's growing involvement in Vietnam at Cambridge rallies and Boston marches. Until Tommy was reported MIA in the war. My war.

"Those two events nearly cost me my sanity and my degree," she told me. "I must have an innate attraction for users. I ran into a couple more Sarni's as an intern at Belleview."

"So, you swore off men?" I teased her.

She flashed her little smile again. "Not entirely."

"But no luck."

"No luck at all."

"At least we have that in common." I swirled my second brandy in the bottom of the snifter. "I don't think I intimidate women, though."

"But I intimidate men." Her expression told me the thought had occurred to her before.

"You're an impressive woman."

"You seem to be taking it in stride."

"In my business," I said, grinning to make her realize I was still kidding, "we never give anything away."

"But you think I scare off less hardy souls."

"You're an intelligent, attractive lady.....what do you think?"

Stephanie twirled the stem of her glass between her thumb and forefinger, gazing at the refracted light in the amber liquid.

"I used to invite men out on my boat...."

"Two things in common."

"Most of them didn't know a sheet from a shackle. So I had to tell them what to do."

"We don't like that," I admitted.

"Not from a woman."

"Especially a Doctor of Psychology they feel uncomfortable with in the first place."

The waiter poured more coffee, but we refused another brandy.

"What kind of boat do you have?" she asked.

I described my twenty-eight-foot Bristol Channel Cutter and how Melissa hated sailing.

Stephanie had had a serious affair with a married lawyer in Boston who was an excellent sailor, but that ended in disappointment two years earlier. Since then she'd been warier than ever of close attachments, preferring to cruise solo now, because she rarely found a man who could relinquish his chauvinist attitude to acknowledge her as skipper of her own boat.

"Our love of sailing seems hereditary," she said. "I'm surprised your mother kept at it after losing your father like that."

"It was a good excuse to drink before noon."

Stephanie laughed softly and nodded. "My dad, too. Do drinkers gravitate to sailing or sailors to drinking?"

"Seems to work out both ways, doesn't it?"

"Do you think that had anything to do with the way your father died?"

"Probably not--especially if they had Dutch, that coast guard guy aboard. Our parents were civilians, but on military duty looking for enemy subs nine months into a world war."

"My mother never said they were drinking."

"Mine either. Of course, she didn't tell me any of this."

"What do you think mom meant about a cover-up?"

Right from the beginning, Stephanie seemed to understand how badly I needed to learn more about my father's' death. She allowed me to grill her sick mother when she didn't have to, and sounded concerned about the small part of the puzzle I'd already described. I wasn't used to confiding in people and the Service didn't promote it. I knew if I wanted to see more of that magnificent woman, I would have to start out with an open relationship. I should tell her everything--John Goddard, the Germans, the FBI dragging their feet.

So, I did.

* * * * * *

We were the last couple to leave the restaurant. The parking lot was brightly lit and our breath blew white in the cold air. We kept to our own thoughts on the short drive to her house, then sat in the car absorbing the warmth from the heater before the dash to her doorstep.

"I admire the way you look after your mother," I said.

"How can anyone put their parents in a home when they can still take care of them?"

"Not every parent is as nice as your mother.

'Or daughter as nice as you,' I wanted to add.

"I won't be able to keep her much longer. Last week she left a roll of paper towels on the stove and it caught fire."

"That kind of dedication must make pretty serious demands on your time."

She looked at me with that smile and mischief in her eyes.

"I'm not seeing anyone."

"That's what I wanted to know."

"Washington's a long way from Wickford, Rhode Island."

"Piece a cake."

* * * * * *

I returned the rental car Monday noon and took a seat in the main waiting area of the airport terminal. Making a conscious effort to keep a silly grin off my face was a good feeling I hadn't experienced in years. Striking out in Rhode Island on the hidden details surrounding my father's death was disappointing, but as far as I was concerned, the weekend had been a roaring success.

Stephanie and her mother went to Sunday church service while I jogged through a residential area near my motel, then went back to their house for brunch. We took a drive in the afternoon across the Jamestown Bridge to Conanicut Island, about thirty square miles of rural real estate smack on the west side of Narragansett Bay. Then shunpiked old Route 1 through South County which is mostly farmland and seashore. We stopped at Watch Hill, the southernmost tip of the state that juts out into Block Island Sound. Mrs. Graham stayed in the car while Stephanie and I walked along the hard-packed sand in sunlight that did little to warm the raw day. We had come prepared with heavy coats and ski hats supplied by the shelf of the Graham hall closet, and our gloved hands found one another as we strolled along the deserted beach watching small tireless waves surge repeatedly up the smooth, wet sand, eyes squinting past the sparkling sun dancing on the ocean surface, Stephanie spotting an oil tanker heading east about five miles offshore.

Something good had been happening since Saturday afternoon. I couldn't remember feeling so relaxed with a woman. There were no conscious thoughts about what to say next, no need to impress, no anxiety about where it was going. When we stood on her front door step twelve hours earlier, it seemed like the most natural thing in the world to draw her into my arms, gaze into her eyes for a few seconds of confirmation, then lean in to kiss her good night.

Ellen Graham had been introspective all-day Sunday, unwilling or unable to give me any more information about my parents. Her scrapbook contained no reference to the *Dutch Master* drownings. Nor did the archives of *The Providence Journal*, which I had searched earlier that Monday morning. I snapped out of my reverie long enough to phone Alex Shertinsky down in Washington and ask the questions I'd been saving for him. When I called Alex back from National airport an hour later, his computer had dug up the details on the woman at the Germantown phone number. Irmgard Bauer was thirty-two years old, unmarried, blond hair, 5' 4", 140 pounds. She was in the country illegally, probably working somewhere close by without a green card. Alex said she was a domestic who had run away from the German embassy three years ago. Pay dirt!

Alex also found a James A. Barnum of Fairfax, Virginia who sounded like the *Dutch Master* crewmember who was not in my mother's address book. Born in 1885, which would have made him fifty-eight in 1942—about the same the age listed in the news clipping. Alex told me that Barnum had been a Washington attorney who served as a consultant to the War Department from 1940 to 1951. No further details regarding his personal or professional life were available. I could forget Barnum, though, because the man was among the 95-people killed in the American Airlines Boeing 707 crash at New York's Idlewild Airport in March 1962.

Edmund Gilmore, the coast guard lieutenant in charge of the search off Block Island for my father was a possible source. A thirty-year career officer, he had stayed in the service after the war and retired as a full commander to Islamorada in the Florida Keys in 1972 at the tender age of fifty-five. He was a definite possible. John Andeweg would have been an excellent source of information if he had not gone missing when my father drowned.

One of the great things about working for the government was in exchange for the best years of your life, they would hand you a nice, comfortable, early retirement. Counting my time in the Corps, the Service would pension me off in 1987 at forty-five. But I probably wouldn't make it if I screwed up this extracurricular investigation. It surprised me that I wasn't worried about that. Maybe I could find something interesting to do in Rhode Island.

CHAPTER EIGHT
Germantown, MD
March 1976

Spitting snow was driving in from the northeast and I leaned into a stiff wind blowing across the long-term parking lot at National Airport. A layer of wet flakes had adhered to my Camaro, swirling into the car when I opened the door to toss my overnight bag on the back seat and get behind the wheel. Germantown was less than an hour away and there was nothing to go home for. The snow wasn't sticking to the highway, so the driving was fine, but I stayed on the Virginia side of the river to avoid the city until I hit I-495.

The naked limbs of gray trees spread into the falling snow where Route 270 runs along Seneca Creek State Park. I didn't have a whole lot of confidence in that trip, but without all the resources and manpower of the Service behind me, I could only cover so many leads—not that I had that many, but I felt that Bauer had to be checked out. I never understood how those private 'I's' in the paperback detective novels caught their man in two hundred-fifty pages. Sometimes it took a thousand-man law enforcement agency years to track down a fugitive. Luck maybe, or a clever writer. Not having to put up with guys like Burnett and Talbot.

I followed the big green interstate signs and got off at the Germantown exit. Hockley Street was a narrow road on the outer edge of the city, scrubbed, sans litter in typical Teutonic fashion, lined with older model cars parked in front of a tight sequence of multifamily dwellings. Three seventeen was a brown, wooden triple-decker with dirty white paint chipping off the trim under its peak roof. I found a parking spot a half block down from Irmgard Bauer's apartment house and sat in the early dusk waiting for darkness.

There was no way I could conduct an effective one-man stakeout, so I would have to get Henzler to move if he was in there. If he wasn't, Irmgard would have to decide between deportation and telling me where he was hiding. I checked my piece and got out of the car, taking a pair of cuffs from the nylon bag stashed in the trunk. The snow had stopped but it was getting cold and I turned up the collar of my wool pea jacket before stuffing my bare hands into the side pockets.

I strolled along the sidewalk opposite the three-story edifice, studying the glass door protected by metal rods that opened onto a tiny foyer. An alley with a couple of cars parked in it ran down the left side of the building, the right side of the apartment house abutted the one next to it.

A few people hurried past, heads lowered between hunched shoulders, thinking about the warm rooms waiting for them at the end of their day.

I slipped my right hand through the slit in the lining of my jacket pocket to touch the cold steel of the four-inch Magnum, crossed the street and peered through the glass side-door of 317 as if I belonged there, and checked the tags on the mailboxes. 'Bauer, I.' lived in apartment 212.

A couple of trash dumpsters sat in the rear of the building surrounded by cardboard boxes and discarded furniture. There was no back door. The alley was unlit, so I tugged the inner door on my way out to see if it was locked and was back on the sidewalk in seconds.

It was five-thirty when I climbed into the passenger seat of my car from which I could see both approaches to 317 without getting a kink in my neck. It was darker on that section of Hockley. Kids must have knocked out the street lamps with well-aimed rocks or pellet guns. But I could look into the dark alley and lighted entrance of Bauer's building to pick out a short heavy blond woman or Kurt Henzler if they left—more from the description Ed Dekins gave me than the fleeting recollection of the security guard at the Senator's condo.

The usual times people come and go from their homes are six to nine in the morning going to work and four to six in the evening when they return. Since I could not sit there around the clock, I planned to stay for another hour, then come back in the morning with a weird hat, glasses, mustache and rented car.

I could hardly believe it when a hefty woman who fit the description of Irmgard Bauer walked out of her building at ten of six, heading toward the center of town. She could have come home before I arrived and was going to the grocery store. Out on a date or an early movie. Maybe she was going to meet Kurt Henzler. I got out of the car and followed her down the opposite side of the street for three blocks, where the shabby residential neighborhood turned into strip malls ethnic grocery stores and medical clinics. She turned off Hockley, took a couple of side streets, then went into a restaurant-bar called *Der Linden Haufbrau.*

I paced up and down in the cold for a while, until a half dozen people approached, then walked through the door with them as though I was part of their group. The bar was overheated, brightly lit and smelled of beer, sausage and sauerkraut. The decor was probably authentic because it didn't look cheap or forced. Customers talked in loud voices in the wooden booths that lined a long wall under a mural of buxom Aryan girls carrying mugs of foaming liquid gold. their colorful dirndls, and scoop-neck blouses revealed mounds of healthy flesh as they served laughing young men with blond hair and flashing teeth in green lederhosen who looked like overgrown children in costume. Crossed rapiers and fencing masks adorned the rear wall between upright beams the size of railroad ties.

The place was filling up for a busy evening and I could pick out snatches of German from the hearty murmur of the local crowd. The people I came in with had been seated and several heads turned to size me up as an obvious stranger. I took an empty stool in the middle of the bar and ordered a draft from a muscular youth who might have posed for the mural. I drained half the glass like a real drinker before swiveling around to take in my surroundings. Bauer wasn't in the bar, but an archway led to a dining room, most of which was hidden from view. I finished the beer and ordered another. When the young giant slid it in front of me, I asked if I could get a single in the dining room or have my meal served at the bar. As I had hoped, the giant told me to check with one of the waitresses. Walking through the archway intent on picking my quarry out of the room full of diners, I nearly knocked Irmgard Bauer with her tray of schnitzel all over the floor.

I decided to order the bratwurst plate in the bar. After my meal and settling my bill with the bartender, I learned that the kitchen closed at eleven.

There were days in the scorching jungles of Vietnam when I had dreamed of lying nude in a Connecticut snow bank melting it down with the spread-eagled heat of my body. Standing in a doorway up the street from *Der Linden* freezing my tail off for three hours made me think about those sweltering temperatures of *Dak Pam*, selectively pushing all the other lousy memories out of my head.

The plump blond waitress left the restaurant at eleven-twenty with two other women. I followed them on foot along the side streets until Bauer turned off on Hockley alone. I let her go another block before crossing the road and come up behind her.

"*Fraulein* Bauer?" I asked in a sharp German dialect. She stopped and turned but I couldn't read her expression because I had picked a dark stretch of sidewalk to confront her.

"*Ja?*" she answered. Her voice was uneven, and she took a step backward. "*Was wollen sie?*" [What do you want?]

I ignored her question regarding my identity, asking instead for her own ID, switching to the tough timber of police all over the world. "*Zeigen sie ihren Ausweis, Fraulein.*"

"*Wer sind sie?*" she pleaded. "Vhat do you vant of me?"

"NIS," I told her, three letters that make illegal aliens quake with terror. I flashed my Service badge just long enough for it to flicker in the dim light. "Your Green Card, *Fraulein*

Bauer, if you please."

"It... it is at my home."

"You're supposed to carry it on your person at all times." I paused a beat. "If you have one, *Fraulein* Bauer."

"I haff at my house," she said. "I vill go to get now."

She turned and began jogging toward her apartment building, but I caught her in three steps and linked my arm with hers. "I'll just come on up with you." I looked down into her troubled face, squeezing her arm with my own pressing against her ample breast through the fabric of her winter coat. "If you can't find it, maybe we can work something else out."

"*Nein, ne in!*" she said, half shout, half whisper, pulling away, running toward the dim alley beside her building.

I grabbed her arm again, digging my fingers into the soft flesh above the elbow. "You might not have a problem if I come up and help you look for it, Irma. Otherwise...."

"You haff no right to do this," she whispered.

I leaned down and spoke into the blond hair that covered her ear. "You have no right to remain in the United States, *Fraulein.*"

She burst into tears, jerked her arm free and ran into the alley, then fumbled with the key to her building while I hung back. She pushed through the thick glass door protected by metal grating and I let her slam it locked before I began rattling the handle. "Bring it down now, Irma or I'll be back tomorrow with a warrant," I yelled after her, as she scampered up the stairs behind the safety of the thick wooden inner door.

"You've had your chance!"

I ran back to the car and slouched down in the driver's seat, a little warmer after the exercise, but that wore off in the first ten minutes as I waited to see if I had flushed anyone out. If Henzler was in there he'd move fast if he thought Immigration was coming for Irmgard in the morning. If he wasn't there, she might go to him and I could follow. Or she might use the phone to call his hideaway and he'd bolt. Then she'd run. If they both took off, I'd have to pick them up and give them to the FBI. I hoped that would not happen.

At three o'clock in the morning a man with a suitcase came out of the side exit of Bauer's apartment house and threw his luggage into the trunk of one of the cars in the alley. I eased out of the Camaro and sprinted to the corner of the building, peering around it into the halflight to see the shape of well-built man who fit Henzler's description slip a key into the car door. I pulled my snub and ran low along the side of the shadowed wall into the alley. Henzler was halfway in the car when he heard me behind him. His head snapped around as he reached into his coat with his right hand.

This was the same perp who killed John and shot me in the back eight weeks ago. I would be damned if I was going to let the Kraut hit me in the front. Henzler was the width of the alley away as I pushed off from the wall of the building using it like a big sprinter's block, going in low, slamming my shoulder into the door panel, crushing Henzler's thick neck between the edge of the window frame and the car roof. The sissy passed out and I nearly joined him as the pain in my shoulder surged down my right side and my arm went numb. I holstered the snub before I dropped it, keeping pressure against the car door, holding Henzler's inert body pinned between it and the chassis.

By the time the tingling began to leave my good arm my breathing was almost normal. I cuffed Henzler's hands behind his back and retrieved his gun from the seat of the car where it fell when I hit him. The big sucker was still gasping for air, and I did not intend to carry him, so I left Henzler stretched out on the ground while I transferred his suitcase from the trunk of his car to my Camaro. The German was conscious when I came back, and Irmgard Bauer was standing inside the glass door of the side exit with her flannel bathrobe clutched around her chunky figure.

"*Ich geniesse diplomatische immunitat,*" [I have diplomatic immunity.] Henzler mumbled from the oil-stained asphalt.

"You cannot arrest me."

"You're not under arrest," I told him as I helped him stand on his feet. "I'm taking you back to your people."

Henzler scowled at me.

"Well, maybe not right now. We wouldn't want to wake *Herr* Ambassador up too early, would we?"

Irmgard was standing behind the outside door. I walked up to it so she could hear me through the solid glass, but she retreated until her back pressed against the inside wall and I had to shout anyway.

"Sorry about INS." I shrugged with my palms held up to show there were no hard feelings. "You better get your fat ass out of here after you tell his friends what happened."

* * * * * *

The Bureau would be less than ecstatic about my initiative against their orders and making them look like the fumblers they were. So would Burnett. Unless I produced new evidence that tied Henzler to John's murder, they'd probably chew me out and hand him back to his embassy. The chips I had earned at the Senator's home were dwindling fast.

I drove around the city running through my options, the German slouched uncomfortably in the passenger seat beside me, hands cuffed behind his back. If Irmgard Bauer hadn't seen me take the clown away, I might have been tempted to take him out for a sail into the Atlantic. Or drive him up to a dumpsite in New Jersey I heard the Mafia use to dispose of their trash. I hadn't thought like that since 'Nam, but I did that night. Finally, I decided to take a chance that would tick everyone off, but one they could not back down from--if it worked.

The night crew at the Secret Service forensics lab in the bowels of Treasury did not see many live perps, but they were getting near the end of their watch and swallowed my half-truths about Henzler with few questions. They took his prints and mug shot and entered them into NCIC, the nationwide database, National Crime Information Center—as a suspect in an old counterfeit scam from my caseload. A ballistics tech logged in Henzler's gun and would hold it for comparison tests, but it was not the Lugar he had used at the Senator's condo. Before leaving the building, I penned a note to Alex Shertinsky and gave it to the Protective Service guard at reception.

* * * * * *

Roger Talbot was not happy to see me walk into his office at eight o'clock in the morning pushing a handcuffed man in front of me who was protesting the violation of his diplomatic rights. Talbot's expression turned rancid as I made the introductions, then he picked up the phone and placed a couple of calls before digging a folder out of his file cabinet and leading the way into a conference room down the hall.

"You were supposed to stay out of this," he said, sitting down at the far side of the narrow table.

"Hey, I saw the guy in a restaurant--what was I going to do, let him walk?" I pushed Henzler into a seat opposite Talbot and took the chair beside the German.

"You could have called us."

"At midnight, twenty miles away? The perp was paying his check.

"These are lies!" Henzler protested.

"OK, so listen to his version," I said, reaching over to unlock the cuffs.

The German threw me a hard look and began haranguing Talbot about his rights for the next hour, while the FBI agent stalled for time by disputing his embassy function, quizzing him about the shooting, Knopf, Berger and where he'd been for the last month.

A man in his sixties stepped into the room and Talbot introduced me to Assistant Deputy Director Frank DePrete. He was short for an FBI agent with graying red hair going thin and a drinker's complexion. His pinstripe suit looked expensive but pulled tight across his expanding paunch and needed pressing. DePrete took the chair at the head of the table as Judith Silverman from State joined us with an effete little man wearing a double-breasted suit and thin mustache.

Ms. Silverman acknowledged me with a cool glance as she introduced Hans Dietrich, First Secretary from the German embassy. DePrete was the senior man, but when they were all seated, Judith took over the meeting.

"Why is Mr. Henzler being held?" she asked Talbot.

"He's not," the FEEBE replied. "Agent Coughlin brought him in without realizing his status and we asked him if he'd like to volunteer information." Talbot leaned forward, hands clasped on the table. "He was free to go anytime he wanted."

"*Quatsch!*" [Bullshit!] Henzler shouted. "This is a lie!"

"Shut up, Kurt," the First Secretary admonished in German

"Is he accused of anything?" Judith asked.

Talbot surprised me by saying 'yes' as he opened his folder, placed the ridiculous I-dent-a-kit sketch of Kurt Henzler in the center of the table and began reciting the charges of murder, attempted murder, assault on a federal officer and unlawful entry.

Henzler picked up his portrait and laughed at the vague resemblance, then showed it to Hans Dietrich. Talbot winced as the first secretary protested vociferously in heavily accented English.

I tried to deflect their attention from the sketch and possibly trap them into some kind of inadvertent admission.

"There's pretty strong evidence that other people in your embassy were involved, too."

Judith Silverman said, "Explain that please, Agent Coughlin."

I addressed my remarks directly to Dietrich. "Gunter Knopf went back to Germany on one of your military flights the night after John Goddard was murdered. He took a crate with him under diplomatic seal. A crate big enough to hold the body of George Burger, the man I shot in the Senator's condo."

"This iss preposterous!" the first secretary sputtered. And turning to Judith, "I vish to register our formal complaint of these insulting allegations."

"Then where's Berger?" I asked. Dietrich moved to the edge

of his chair, his spine going stiff as he tried to regain his diplomatic aplomb. "He hass valid visa as member our legation. Vee do not account for his vhereabouts."

"You will if he's accused of a crime, Mr. First Secretary," Judith said.

"You haff no proof."

"We have an eyewitness who saw Knopf and Berger committing a robbery," Judith told him. "Agent Coughlin can verify their possession of weapons at the scene where Goddard was murdered."

Dietrich said, "One of your government police."

I pointed to the copy of Henzler's I-dent-a-kit sketch on the table. "The condo security guard couldn't give the artist a good description from memory, but said he'd have no trouble picking our friend here," I nodded at Henzler, "out of a lineup."

"I protest," the dapper German said without conviction this time.

"What," I asked him, "our accusation of your hit squad or the suggestion they acted with the knowledge of someone in your government?"

Assistant Deputy Director Frank DePrete ran a palm over his reddish hair then spoke for the first time since the introductions.

"That's enough, Coughlin." He turned to Judith. "I think we've gone as far as we can this morning."

"Fine," she said. "We'll remand Mr. Henzler to the custody of the First Secretary," nodding meaningfully at Dietrich, "who I'm confident will make him available to us for further questioning."

"He took my fingerprints and photograph," Henzler said.

Dietrich addressed DePrete, "I demand their return."

All eyes turned on me and a flicker of acknowledgment crossed DePrete's face. He realized what I had done and why but asked me anyway. "Where are they?"

"In the system." I turned to Henzler. "You forgot to mention your gun." Then told DePrete, "Ballistics is setting it up for comparison to the slugs they removed from John

Goddard and me."

I caught Henzler smiling. DePrete frowned at Dietrich.

"What's a diplomat doing carrying a gun?"

"For protection from your American criminal gangs," Henzler said.

"Is it registered?" Talbot asked.

Henzler started to speak but the First Secretary placed a hand on his arm and stood up, gave a wordless half-bow that would have surprised no one had it been accompanied the click of his heels. The representative from FRG Embassy preceded Henzler out of the room.

"You shouldn't have held him," Judith said to Talbot.

"He ran before," I argued.

She swiveled on me. "And taking his prints, his picture? Did you book him for carrying the gun?"

"No!" I was tired and starting to feel it. "How the hell are we supposed to find out what this guy's up to? He's no damned diplomat!"

"Was it a Luger?" Talbot asked me.

I shook my head. "Heckler & Koch P7."

Judith asked, "What the hell are you doing in this, Jared?"

"I happened to be there."

She ignored that and turned to the senior FBI agent. "How long will it take to draw up formal charges?"

"They'll be ready first thing in the morning," DePrete answered.

Judith retrieved her handbag from the chair beside her.

"Do you have any hard evidence on Henzler?"

"Nothing except the condo security guard's ID," Talbot answered. "And that's shaky."

"We might have more after they run his prints and photo through the system," I said.

"It won't put him in the Senator's condo," Talbot told me.

I knew that. But Henzler was no virgin. Now that he was in the NCIC Alex could match him to other criminal databases around the world, even learn his affiliations with international subversive organizations.

Judith put her notebook in her handbag while looking at

me. "This is the man you didn't see, right?"

I nodded my affirmation. "He shot me from behind. He was the truck driver, so the guard got a look at him when they went out through the gate."

"Get him," Judith ordered Talbot. "We'll bring him with us when we visit the ambassador tomorrow morning. Ask them to line Henzler up with some of their other huskies."

"You think you can get him to waive D.I.?" I asked her.

"I'm going to try. Or we'll throw him out, *Persona Non-Grata.*" She looked at me with one of her cryptic expressions. "It may depend on what we learn from running his prints."

Frank DePrete spoke for the third time. "The Director wants kid gloves on this."

I started to say something then changed my mind. What good would it do?

DePrete stood up and pushed in his chair. "PNG would satisfy us.

I mumbled, "Shit!" and stalked out of the room.

CHAPTER NINE
Washington, DC
April 1976

The sprawling facade of Treasury on 15th and Pennsylvania had always given me a feeling of reassurance, its Ionic columns and Georgian architecture the source of my authority and justification of lonely assignments in remote field offices across the country.

That night as I passed the south portico overlooking Pershing Square, I felt alienated from this home base and everything it represented. Maybe the eerie glow of streetlights struggling to penetrate the darkness in the little park and the freezing rain on the wooden benches had something to do with it.

The taxi turned onto 'G' Street and let me off in front of headquarters at 1800. As I climbed the slick granite steps and flashed my I.D. to the uniform at the desk, I realized it wasn't the weather that made me uneasy. Burnett had told me to stay out of this and I was doing exactly the opposite. DePrete probably phoned him five minutes after he found out what happened the night before, and there was no doubt in my mind that Ken's secretary had been calling my apartment all day.

After my session with the Germans, FBI and State that morning, I had stopped at MacDonald's for breakfast and gone home to bed with the good sense to unplug the phone as soon as I walked in the door. There were too many unanswered questions circling around those Germans to drop this now. If Burnett wanted to chew me out, I was going to make him find me first.

It was six P.M. when I stepped off the elevator on the seventh floor, passing the last few stragglers of the homeward-bound staff of Alex Shertinsky's ISS day shift.

The plump computer genius broke into a smile behind his beard and waved me into the cracked green leather Government Issue sofa against the wall opposite his desk.

"You're giving me more business since you've been off duty," he began in his precise British version of English, "than some of your peers working real cases."

I hung my wet raincoat in back of the door and took the proffered seat. "This could be a real case very soon."

"Or get us both brought up on charges."

"You're right." I looked Alex straight in the eye. "Maybe I shouldn't be asking you to do this."

"You were busy last night."

"You got my note?"

"And this morning."

"Geeze, Alex, the Russians would pay a million dollars for your grapevine." He let his ready smile spread again.

"Maybe they have."

Fat chance. East German machine guns had cut down his brother and sister in their futile attempt at escape over the Berlin Wall in the early sixties, displaced Jews trying to join their sibling in England.

"Anything turn up on Henzler?"

"Ah, ha! Now things start to get interesting." He unlocked a metal file cabinet next to his desk, extracted a sheet of green bar paper and handed it to me.

"Interpol lists Henzler's fingerprints as belonging to one Gerhardt Walter Hoffmann of *Furstenwalde, East* Germany, purported member of the notorious *Baader-Meinhof* gang."

"Pay dirt!" I read down the printout absorbing the details.

"Description fits."

"Hoffmann was one of the prime suspects in the 1972 attack on U.S. Army headquarters in Heidelberg."

I looked up. "A commie terrorist on their embassy staff?"

"Do not leap to conclusions, my friend. West Germany is almost as tough on terrorists as Israel. They rounded up most of the *Baader-Meinhof* people last year. They're in jail awaiting trial."

"Then what's this guy up to?"

"They're a left-wing gang with previous support from East Germany and the Middle East. With their leaders out of the game, I would think they'd be looking for new angles."

My tone was incredulous. "Senator Robinson?"

"The document," Alex said.

I stuffed the folded printout into my jacket. "Somebody pretty high up in the West German government slipped Henzler and his two pals in here."

"Maybe this will convince the FBI to hold him."

"Maybe."

I needed one more thing. Alex kept smiling so I kept talking. Alex didn't want a great deal of explanation in case this inflating balloon did blow up in our faces. He'd figure things out for himself and say either, 'yes' or 'no.'

The big Brit was silent and I changed the subject. "What did the Bureau dig up in their investigation of John Goddard's murder?"

The grin faded from Alex's face and he lowered his chin to peer at me over round wire-rimmed glasses. We sat without speaking for a couple of moments until his thick hands pushed at his desk, twirling his high-backed chair and rolling up to the main computer terminal behind him.

"If I can find a roundabout," he said, punching in a series of commands, "that will hide my request from the main system access log...."

Alex worked at his keyboard for half an hour before turning and asking me to close the door to his office. "I'm not going to print any of this, so you'd better look at the screen over my shoulder to get what you want."

The case file number and title of Talbot's investigation into the killing of John Goddard and related burglary scrolled up the green-tinted display terminal: the FBI interviews with the Senator's neighbors, the condo security guard and me; my description of Gunter Knopf; the guard's poor recollection of Kurt Henzler; locating the stolen truck in Maryland; the report from the Bureau's forensics section; and Talbot's polite follow-up session with First Secretary Dietrich of the German embassy after our initial meeting.

When he came to the fingerprint analysis I stopped him.

"Hold it right there, Alex."

"Hmmm, that is rather odd, isn't it?"

"Has to be a mistake, right?"

"Let's see," he scrolled back to the initial request for a match on five different sets of identifiable fingerprints found in Senator Robinson's condo: one belonged to the cleaning lady, another was mine, a third belonged to Mary-Lee Bradley, a federal judge the Senator was seeing and the fourth to a house guest from the previous weekend. The fifth and most prominent set of finger prints were Senator Robinson's.

I straightened up from leaning over Alex's chair and watched him frown at the data. "They asked the computer to match five sets of prints and it came back with six?"

"One clearly for Senator Robinson," Alex was rubbing his hands together over the keyboard like a concert pianist before playing Beethoven's Symphony 3 in Carnegie Hall. "The sixth is so close to Robinson's, our fingerprint guys tagged it "unknown," but added a footnote that the sixth set must be Robinson's twin."

"Robinson doesn't have a twin."

"No one has two sets of fingerprints!"

Alex ignored me for the next ten minutes while he hunched over his terminal, typing in a series of codes that flashed information across the screen too fast for me to follow. Finally, he leaned back in his chair and folded his arms.

"It seems that your good Senator Charles Robinson did indeed have two sets of fingerprints in the NCIC file."

"That's impossible!"

"Practically speaking," he admitted. "But when the Bureau asked the computer to match the Senator's prints it came up with two different identity reports."

"So they were really the two sets of same prints under two different names?"

"That appears to be the case."

"What names?"

"His own, naturally. I can't get the other one."

"For god-sakes, Alex, why not?"

"Because all I have is their access transaction history." He swiveled his chair away from the computer to look up at me.

"The FBI didn't put the second name in their report—-and erased the original data on the second identity from the NCIC database."

"How the hell can they do that?"

"They own it, Jared."

* * * * * *

I picked up a pepperoni pizza and six-pack of Pabst on the way home. Before I left him at Treasury, Alex dug into the exhaustive investigation the Bureau conducted on the Senator after he announced for the presidency: Charles Norris Robinson was born in Lusten, Minnesota in 1920; he excelled at the local high school in grades and sports; graduated from Brown University in May 1942 as a first lieutenant in the army A-12 program; took ranger training at Fort Campbell, Kentucky with the 82nd Airborne; and shipped out to the Pacific theatre in July.

My antennae went up at the coincidence that the Senator was in the same class at Brown with John Andeweg, my father's Coast Guard crewman. They might have known one another, but according to the report, young Robinson was halfway around the world when my father, and presumably Andeweg, drowned that August in Block Island Sound.

Senator Robinson collected quite a few medals in the war and survived some of the toughest fighting in the Pacific. He was awarded the Bronze Star for holding rear guard for his retreating platoon in Guadalcanal, earned a Purple Heart in New Guinea and Oak Leaf Clusters in the Philippines. He was wounded again on Kwajalein in the battle for the Marshall Islands in February of 1944. He had recuperated to win the Silver Star on Mindanao and the Medal of Valor on Okinawa in 1945 where he lost his left eye. Somewhere along the way the British Admiralty made him a Knights Commander of the Victorian Order, which must have an interesting story behind it because England had their hands full in Europe in that war and didn't have much presence in the Pacific.

Senator Robinson had been orphaned in 1937 when his parents and younger sister were killed in the crash of the Hindenburg. The only other family he had was an aunt and uncle who died while he was away in the Pacific. At the end of the war, he spent six months in a Hawaiian army hospital.

Quite a war record for a twenty-six-year-old kid—-a lot of dead-end personal history, too. An ideal background for a young man with political ambitions, but the Senator hadn't stopped there. When he was discharged from the army in 1945, he enrolled in Columbia Law School, established residence in Virginia after graduation and at the age of thirty-five used his election to the State House of Representatives as a springboard into national politics.

Never married, he dated plenty of respectable women over the years, had two long-term relationships, no vices and not a hint of scandal. The Bureau seemed to have interviewed everyone he'd known since law school, combed through his financial data and verified practically every day of his adult life. I had never seen any security check that complete. But this background check was for a man running for the presidency of the United States and was probably standard.

It was only nine o'clock when I was wrapping the leftover pizza in tin foil when the phone rang. I stood there in the kitchen looking at it like it held a message of doom, wondering how smart it was to keep avoiding Burnett and his inevitable reprimand. I thought about fighting back, going over his head—taking it to the Senator. After all, it was his aide the Germans killed, his home they violated. Shouldn't he want Henzler nailed to the wall? I answered the phone with more confidence than I felt. It wasn't Burnett.

"We met with the German ambassador this afternoon," Judith Silverman began without prelude. "He won't waive D.I. on Henzler."

"What'd the Bureau find when they traced his fingerprints?"

"Suspected terrorist a few years back but nothing else."

"Geeze, practically an Eagle Scout, huh?"

"Jared, we have no more proof on that now than they did then. The civilian guard from the Senator's condo couldn't make a positive ID." I listened to cigarette smoke being exhaled across the phone line. "We have no reason to hold him without creating a huge diplomatic flap that State is not prepared to tackle."

"How'd a suspected terrorist get on their embassy staff?"

"That's their problem," Judith said. "Dietrich seemed more upset about that than we were." I slouched back against the counter perched on a kitchen stool, running my fingers through my hair, frustrated, resigned, yet screaming inside for some way to extract retribution for this blind injustice being perpetrated by the system.

"So now what?"

"We slapped him with PNG on the spot. He leaves at four o'clock tomorrow afternoon on Lufthansa."

"How about the other guys--Knopf and Berger?"

"We can't charge Knopf or take his visa because he's already out of our jurisdiction. You shot Berger and we assume he's dead."

"So Henzler and Knopf get away with killing John Goddard."

"If Henzler ever comes back we can arrest and prosecute him just like any other criminal." Judith's voice had lost its usual edge as if acknowledging the inequity of the situation and her inability to do anything about it.

"And Knopf?"

"We can refuse him diplomatic status, but he's free to come back any time he wants as a private citizen. If he does, the Bureau can pursue it.

* * * * * *

I did not know what I expected to gain from following Kurt Henzler to the airport. Probably the meager satisfaction of seeing the bastard get the only punishment we were able to inflict. Maybe to make sure the Bureau didn't sneak him into their witness protection program.

It was noon by the time I found a parking space on

Reservoir Road, a half block from the German embassy
where I could see cars coming out of their driveway. I turned
on the radio and waited. This was not like me. Chilling my
buns in a cold car when I could be stretched out on a hot
beach somewhere. Why was my attitude changing suddenly--
fighting the system, risking my job, going off half-cocked,
trying to prove...what?

I had never thought about the right or wrong of Vietnam, I
just went when my country told me to go. Later, I realized
the war was a mistake, but knew I would probably have gone
even if I'd known that then—despite the nightmares that
occasionally woke me sweating and screaming at the
horrible deaths I had seen and inflicted.

Harry Chapin came on WCAP with his new song, 'Circle'
and the lyrics wrapped around my mind as though he wrote
them just for me:

All My Life's a Circle,
sunrise and sundown;
the moon rose through the
nighttime, 'til the day-
break comes around.
All my life's a circle,
I can't tell you why; the
seasons spinin' round
again, the years keep rollin'
by. It seems like I've been
here before, I can't remember
when; I got this funny feelin'
that I'll be back again.
There's no straight lines
make up my life, and all
my roads have bends;
there's no clear-cut beginin',
and so far no dead-ends.
I found you a thousand times,
I guess you've done the same;
But then we lose each other,
just like a children's game.

> As I see you here again,
> The thought runs through my
> mind—our love is like a circle,
> let's go 'round one more time.

What the hell was I doing sitting in a freezing car on a gray winter day waiting to make sure a killer was thrown out of the country? I'd been on a treadmill ever since I could remember, going along, putting up with whatever happened, not making waves. Never insisting that my mother tell me more about my father, what he was like, the way he thought; if she loved him, how he lived his short life. If I'd be proud of him--if I had grown up to be like him. Maybe I finally realized I'd been too accepting about having a ghost for a father. Annoyed at my mother for not telling me more about him when I was younger, then brushing me off later as though the subject wasn't important.

This was the first opportunity I ever had to learn about the man who gave me life. It would probably be the last. Melissa ran my life for three years, deciding that she'd move into my apartment, where we went to dinner, who we would invite to parties, how often we had sex and when she would move out. She tried to tell me what to think about issues, how to get ahead with my career, finally urging me to find a better one that paid more to match the prestige of her ascending status in the Department of Justice.

I knew she saw other men when I was out of town on extended assignments and suspect she had not been faithful to me. Except for 'Nam, getting shot in the Senator's bedroom was the closest I had come to buying the farm. Maybe my subconscious had understood at last that I had to get some kind of game plan of my own for my future.

Which brought me back to Stephanie Graham who hadn't been out of my thoughts for more than ten minutes since Saturday afternoon. I had been infatuated before, in lust with plenty of women and had thought I loved Melissa. But I had never experienced the knee-shaking impact of the combined physical attraction and mental empathy I felt for this captivating female from the minute she opened that door in Wickford, Rhode Island. As casual and unlucky as I had been in previous relationships, I wanted to be with Stephanie, to have her feel the same way about me that I did about her. To love me. I hadn't had much of that and wanted it badly from this magnificent woman I had known only three days.

Ed Dekins walked out the wrought iron gates of the embassy and turned up the collar of his uniform coat against the chill wind as he nodded in the direction of a black Mercedes nosing out behind him and into the traffic. The green Ford that had parked down the street about an hour ago began to follow the Mercedes. I took up the rear of the procession as they headed west, crossing the Potomac into Virginia toward Dulles International Airport. When they arrived, the two cars double-parked in front of Lufthansa Airlines. Henzler got out of the Mercedes with a carry-on bag and started for the terminal. Roger Talbot jumped out of the Ford and caught up to him before he could enter. The FBI agent grabbed Henzler's arm at the bicep and twirled the German, so they stood face to face. Talbot said something that made Henzler frown. Then they both walked into the building.

He might be a pain the ass, I thought, as I drove past the terminal, but no question about it--Talbot would strap that kraut in his seat and wait until the plane took off.

CHAPTER TEN
Washington, DC
April 1976

Agent Paul Hunsacker was parked in front of my apartment when I returned. Burnett wanted to see me forthwith, so we rode in an agency car to the Washington Field Office in the Potomac Electric Power Building on 21st and Pennsylvania.

Paul is ten years older than I am, but the best friend I had in the Service. We had been stationed in Houston for three years together and his wife Ginny had treated my previous girlfriend like the daughter she never had.

I listened to Paul's well-meaning counsel that I was ruining my good record and career with reckless behavior but responded with only innocuous phrases. The older agent became silent when he realized, I would not tell him anything that Burnett could interrogate him about later. Which was probably why our boss had sent Paul to pick me up in the first place.

It was getting dark and colder as we crossed the street from the parking lot to the WFO, then stood together in the heated lobby waiting for the elevator to take us up to the fifth floor. Paul inquired about my wound again but made no further attempt at conversation. Other agents and staff personnel greeted me with the same muted welcome as I walked across the big open room filled with government-issue desks, many with computer terminals on trial for their potential efficiency in agent use accessing several of the same websites Alex did.

I was in the soup and the word was out. Nobody wanted to get too close until they knew if I was going to get canned or hung. I could not envision any other options.

Ken Burnett's corner office was small and with the exception of a badly framed print of Wyeth's 'Girl in the

Field,' no better furnished than the room outside. He was on the phone when I knocked on his open door and he motioned to one of the metal chairs with green padding in front of his desk. I glanced at the customary photographs of the president and William Simon, Secretary of Treasury on the pale green wall over the heavy-duty filing cabinet with its combination lock the size of a fist; the sun-faded colors of an American flag hanging in the corner on its wooden staff.; a gray metal bookcase with perfectly aligned manuals, reference, and law books completed the familiar inventory. Was this what Melissa had wanted me to work for?

Burnett hung up the phone and gave me his hard look. "I guess I don't have to ask how the wound is."

"It's coming along."

"Good enough to disobey my direct order."

"There's an all-points out for the guy, what was I supposed to do, buy him a beer?"

Burnett was sitting on the edge of his chair, his back stiff, the palms of his hands pressing down on the top of his desk. "You could have called in. Haven't you learned anything about backup?"

I tried to conceal my anger. "The Bureau's ignoring this and you're helping them do it."

Burnett leaned back in the chair and ran his palm over the thin sandy hair that started halfway back on his scalp. I knew I had broken enough rules to get my head handed to me and Burnett was fingering the lanyard on the guillotine.

"You're not going along with us, are you?"

"I want John Goddard's murderer."

"You got him," he spread his hands out in a smug gesture of helplessness. "They sent him home."

"Why did they do it? A suspected terrorist and cohorts breaking into the home of a U.S. Senator?" I started to lose my patience and Burnett seemed to like that. "Who's behind it, Ken? Why?"

"A German conspiracy against Senator Robinson to keep him from running for president?" His tone was mocking, and he seemed to relish my frustration. "A foreign Watergate this time?"

"Stranger things have happened. Why isn't anyone else interested in finding out why?"

"The Bureau's satisfied," he said. "The Senator's satisfied. And I'm satisfied."

"Well, I'm not, Ken."

"Aside from the minor issue you're forbidden to act on this, where could you take it?"

"I don't know. There's got to be something."

"Not for you there isn't." Burnett lifted a Manila folder from the pile on the corner of his desk, opened it and extracted several sheets of paper. "Since you've recovered so quickly from your injury, there doesn't seem to be any reason for you to stay out on sick leave."

Resisting him openly would do no good. "I told you I didn't need two months."

"Report to Doctor Bromley for a checkup on Monday." Burnett grinned as he shoved the papers across his desk. "Report to your new duty station next Wednesday."

Great Falls, Montana. I tried to smile back like it didn't matter and walked out of his office.

* * * * * *

Several things bothered me about moving to Montana. One of them was leaving Senator Robinson in the hands of a bunch of clowns who didn't believe he might be in danger. Another was the problem it would present in pursuing my exhilarating incipient relationship with Stephanie Graham? How would I continue probing the mysterious circumstances of my father's death?

I began walking home in the gray afternoon whose temperature was frozen in the mid-twenties. My brain felt tired, needing a rest from thinking about the kind of future I'd have after getting exiled to one of the most dead-end duty stations in the country. I tried going back in my life to see if I could figure out what had brought me to this abysmal juncture.

I think I was in limbo half the time because I don't

remember much of my childhood except the major incidents that no one could forget, and isolated events that stayed with me for no reason at all.

Like the time I had an attack of diarrhea in the middle of our third-grade play, running off the stage with shit dripping down my leg in front of all the other kids and the whole audience, my mother joining in the laughter to reduce her own embarrassment.

The rich smoke of Papa van Oudgaarden's Cuban cigars I inhaled with pleasure, sitting on his lap, pressing my face into the old man's wool vest. His chauffeur carrying me out of his funeral mass at St. Steven's Cathedral when I became hysterical amid one thousand mourners described by *The New York Times* as 'top financial executives, old-moneyed socialites, friends and enemies of one of the last holdovers from the nineteenth century robber barons.'

When I broke my leg climbing over a picket fence the day my mother married again in Connecticut and could not come to the hospital with me because she had to leave on her honeymoon.

The way Max Coughlin showed me affection until he and mother separated. I was twelve years old when she told me not to get upset, reminding me that Max, the only male parent I ever had, was not my real father.

Boarding school is still a blur with most of the guys, classes, football and baseball games blending together. Wrestling was different for some reason. Maybe because it was one on one or that I was particularly good at it, a harmless way to release my frustration in the rest of my life. My mother said she did not like violence, so she never saw me wrestle except the first time I won the state championship. She told me she could not understand how I could humiliate that poor other boy like that. I remember my opponent, almost every point and hold that day.

I believe that my mother and I started growing apart during those prep school years. She seemed intent on hanging on to Frank, her third husband, but unable to keep from engaging in behavior that eventually drove him away.

He liked to go to parties and drink just like she did. The problem was my mother couldn't hold her liquor and began to embarrass Frank when they were out. He was in sales, which required him to travel a lot and my mother started drinking alone. I came home some weekends to scenes that were very uncomfortable. Sometimes I had to put her to bed.

When Frank was home she nagged him right in front of me about being away more than he had to, never taking her out any more, being unfaithful and any other demeaning accusation that occurred to her. Whether Frank was there or not, mother and son ended up arguing, and I usually took the early bus back to West Hampton on Sunday afternoon before she got out of bed.

I learned about her second divorce through a rare letter that placed the blame on everyone, including me--but not herself.

I could remember 'Nam if I wanted to relive twenty-months of heat and blood and death. Why dwell on that, except for the buddies I lost and will never forget.

By the time I entered college I was three years older than most undergrads, out of my class, living off-campus; alienated from almost everybody else at Georgetown because of the war.

I was always amazed when I heard people tell about all their little childhood experiences like they took notes. I knew where I grew up and with whom, but could not remember the details. That was probably why I felt so isolated, even then. Unable to get my personal life moving and only feeling sure of myself in structured organizations like the Corps and the Service. Could I cope with life without that kind of external discipline?

As I approached my apartment building I realized there was not much time before I had to leave for Montana. If the old Coast Guard guy in Florida would see me, that would kill the rest of the week. When I got back, packing and making arrangements to be away from Washington for even a few months would keep me busy.

* * * * * *

Lieutenant Commander Edmund Gilmore, U.S. Coast Guard, (Retired) sounded surprised at my interest in an incident that happened back in 1942, but when I talked to him on the phone he seemed willing to supply whatever information he could.

"Oh, I remember that pretty well," he said. "We didn't lose many men in the Corsair Fleet and I was always puzzled about your father and that other fellow."

"In what way?"

"Little things. Of course, we got shut out of it after the FBI took over, but I kept a personal log in those days that might refresh my memory."

"If I come down there, would you show it to me?"

"Why not? You're with the Secret Service, right?"

I assured him that I was, but my investigation was part personal and part government business. Gilmore seemed hesitant about that and wouldn't share much detail about it on the phone but agreed to meet on Thursday at his house in the Florida Keys.

When I called Stephanie, she said she'd love to sail with me in the Keys on a long weekend. She'd have to move some things around and line up a caretaker for her mother; teased me about not giving a girl much notice but sounded like she really wanted to go. We made plans to meet at Miami airport Thursday afternoon, talk to Edmund Gilmore in the evening and go aboard the charter boat that night.

Stephanie seemed as curious as I was about what Gilmore would have to say and I was glad she would be there when I talked to him. Her mother and father had always spoken openly about the circumstances surrounding my father's death and I had told her everything I knew about it. I thought she might be able to ask Gilmore questions I would not think of.

The thing that really excited me was her ready agreement to drop everything and go cruising with me on two days' notice. No hedging, no pretense, no ego, just 'yes.' The last time I remembered feeling that good about a date was in junior high. This relationship was starting off like the odds-on favorite in the Kentucky Derby, which was not the way things usually happened for me.

* * * * * *

Miami Airport was noisy and crowded with midwinter vacationers in garish shorts, wide-brimmed straw hats and every hue of Caucasian skin from the pale-faced arrivals, exuberant with anticipation of in-flight cocktails and two weeks of sun-basked leisure stimulated by the deep tans of departing month-long visitors. Little children screamed and ran circles around their parents struggling with carry-on luggage, college kids gathered in animated groups planning future activities or relating recent experiences.

Stephanie Graham walked through the moving press of people as bright and lovely as a fresh-cut orchid. An ironic smile made the corners of her eyes crinkle and told me she was just as surprised as I was that we were doing this. She wore a pleated white skirt and double-breasted navy jacket with gold buttons and strands of white beads around her neck. Later, I could not remember what we said as she took my arm, walking along the concourse to the baggage carousel and the rental car counter or driving south in the air-conditioned Oldsmobile down the Dixie Highway.

We were glad to be together and looking forward to our weekend sail, so I decided not spoil things by telling her about going to Montana. As important as my interview with Gilmore was, I suddenly wanted to get it over with so Stephanie and I could get out on the water. We followed Route 1 south in the tropical heat of the late afternoon, through Key Biscayne with expensive homes and tended lawns of dense grass glimpsed between the gates of high stone walls, past the broad green fronds of tall palm trees hanging immobile in the stagnant air.

By the time we reached Key Largo, the landscape had turned flat and tan, parched by the unrelenting sun beating down on weathered bait shacks surrounded by sandy topsoil, gaudy souvenir shops, the worn neon signs of happy-hour bars and low-priced restaurants featuring fried fish and barbecued specials.

We entered the little town of Islamorada on Upper Matecumbe Key and I handed Stephanie the directions Gilmore had given me to his house when we spoke on the phone. They led to a white stucco cottage with blue shutters on the north side of the island overlooking Florida Bay. A sprinkler nourished the tiny lawn in a programmed arc, spilling over a white picket fence to darken the cement sidewalk. The street was lined with neat houses that suggested mature couples adjusting their lives to awkward freedom after their grown offspring had begun their own cycle of family responsibilities.

The retired Coast Guard officer met us on the front porch where he checked my credentials before admitting us to his air-conditioned home. His baldhead was mottled brown with pink splotches that were peeling from exposure to the sun. He wore sharply creased khaki trousers and a white short-sleeved shirt that looked like it had been starched and ironed.

"Kinda strange diggin' into this after all these years," Gilmore said.

"I just ran across the old news clipping about my father's death," I explained, "when I was going through my mother's papers."

Commander Gilmore introduced his wife who offered us iced tea in their Florida room whose curtains were drawn against the bright sunlight.

"How'd you find me?" Gilmore wanted to know.

"The NCIC data base."

"You authorized to use that for personal inquiries?" Gilmore asked.

"I told you on the phone—it may have some bearing on a case I'm working on, too."

Gilmore took a sip from his iced tea. "What case is that?"

This was not the way I had expected this meeting to go. The old man was putting me on the defensive and hadn't given me a chance to ask a single question.

"It's government business, Commander." I shrugged my shoulders and tried my disarming smile like that would be the end of it. "You know how that is."

"A place to hide things."

Was this the same man who promised to be cooperative on the phone? Mrs. Gilmore sat on the small sofa next to her husband, her gray head bent over her moisture-beaded glass, poking the ice around with her finger, obviously uncomfortable in her pale-yellow room with its conch shells and silver fishing trophies lined up on homemade shelves.

Stephanie hadn't said a word since we sat down in the two armchairs across from the sofa but now tried to salvage what was rapidly becoming a dead-end meeting by jumping right to the core of the matter.

"Commander, you did investigate the drowning of Jared's father, didn't you?"

Mrs. Gilmore looked at her husband with a silent signal urging him to be gentle with their female guest.

"We didn't get far," Gilmore answered. "The FBI took over the next day."

"Wasn't that unusual?" Stephanie asked.

"Not during the War. Espionage was their bailiwick."

"But this was an accident," I said.

"Two unexplained drownings," Gilmore reminded me.

Stephanie took over again in her mildly curious tone. "So why was the FBI interested?"

Gilmore looked at me. "Why are you interested?"

"My mother never told me much about my father. The circumstances surrounding his death, how he died or lived, for that matter. I want to learn whatever I can about him.

"I checked with Mr. Kenneth Burnett, your boss in Washington who says you're on medical leave, gonna be transferred to Montana next week."

Stephanie shot me a look under raised eyebrows. There goes the week-end, I thought. I said, "Some things I can't tell you."

"Guy named Talbot called from the FBI after I talked to Burnett. Told me the file on your father's death was still classified and you weren't cleared for it."

"You told me there were things about the drownings you didn't understand—can't you tell me what they were?"

"I don't remember."

I leaned forward, elbows on knees, hands clasped in front of me. "Commander, please! You said you kept a log."

"This is important to us," Stephanie said. "My parents were on that boat, too."

Mrs. Gilmore put her hand on her husband's forearm. "There must be some way you can help them, isn't there, Ed?"

She was still a pretty woman, trim and pleasing in her beige Bermuda shorts and sleeveless blouse, quiet, a military officer's wife, respectful of his responsibilities and judgment. But it was obvious in that split second that they had a good relationship based partly on his regard for her kindness and compassion.

Gilmore sighed and placed his empty glass down on a straw coaster on the table beside him. "I won't talk about anything after the FBI got into it. Understood?"

I agreed to that.

Gilmore said, "I had more questions than answers then and still do."

"Like what?" Stephanie asked.

"Why didn't we find what they must have gone off in the dinghy to look for?" Gilmore began ticking each item off on his fingers. "Why didn't they wake up the others before they left the boat?"

I started to interrupt but the retired Coast Guard officer stared me down, raising his voice a notch and kept on talking.

"Two life jackets were missing from the boat--why wasn't your father," he inclined his head at me, "wearing his when we found him? We didn't find it during our three-day search. Why didn't we find Andeweg if he was wearing one?" He held up his right hand indicating the five pregnant questions that had puzzled him over the years. "And if he wasn't wearing his life preserver, why not and where was it?"

"I don't suppose there's any way of coming up with the answers now," Stephanie said.

"Couldn't do it then," Gilmore admitted.

"What about the espionage Mrs. Graham mentioned?" I asked him.

"What about it?"

We were getting into the area Talbot had warned him to stay out of and he was clamming up again. "We came all the way down here, Commander, because you said you suspected things about my father's death."

"You came down under false pretenses," he shot back.

Stephanie stepped in to deflect his reluctance to continue. "Why would the FBI think it was espionage?" She looked over at Mrs. Gilmore. "There was no evidence of that, was there?"

"The FBI didn't think it was espionage. Your parents, the crew of *Dutch Master* thought they heard a sub out there. And we—the Coast Guard, started looking for it."

"Until the FBI came on the scene," I said.

Gilmore just stared at me. I regretted lying about this being partly official business, but that was done.

"If it wasn't an FBI theory," Stephanie said, "surely they can't object to you telling us what you and the crew thought."

The old Coast Guardsman ran his hand over the top of his peeling head and glanced at his wife. She lifted her eyebrows and looked directly at him. "He's trying to learn about his father, Ed."

Gilmore nodded at me as though he had finally decided to give me what I asked for but knew I wasn't going to like it. "They thought they heard a big diesel engine that night off in the fog after they woke up and found the two men missing."

I couldn't help leaning forward again, prodding him for the rest of the story. "A German U-Boat?"

"That's what they thought."

"Why the hell would my father and Andeweg go chasing a Nazi submarine in a twelve-foot dinghy?

"We couldn't come up with a reason," Gilmore paused,

looking at me with a mixture of embarrassment and accusation. "Unless one of them wanted to get to the sub and the other was trying to stop him."

* * * * * *

We pulled into a barbecued chicken place for a silent dinner on the way back to Tavernier Key, then picked up groceries for the weekend at the IGA on the edge of town. The implications of Gilmore's story had killed our enthusiasm for conversation. We were both afraid to explore the possibility that my father had been a German spy.

But he was a resistance fighter! And the Bureau didn't seem sure about espionage or anything else after they took over the investigation. Had they discounted the spy theory or pursued it? There'd been several landings of German agents on the east coast in World War II that were common knowledge then and now. Why had they clamped a lid on this? A lid that was still screwed down tight after thirty-four years.

I drove the rented Oldsmobile to the north side of the island, so we could watch a gigantic red sun settle in behind long purple clouds above the distant horizon of the Gulf of Mexico. We parked beside a boat dealership that was closed for the night. An evening breeze stirred the lingering heat of the day and we rolled down the windows, each pressed into the outside corners of our seats.

"I didn't know this was going to be a two-night stand," Stephanie said.

"I beg your pardon?"

"What's this about Montana?"

"I was going to tell you about that."

"When, after you slept with me?"

I couldn't keep the damned grin off my face. "Was I going to do that?"

She smiled right back at me. "Not now, you're not."

I burst out laughing and couldn't stop, losing control when I saw her reaction—-laughing right along with me.

After we did stop, I gave her a tissue from the glove compartment to wipe her eyes and turned in the seat to face her. I held her hand in both of mine and told her how ridiculous I felt telling her my feelings toward her after so little time. I explained the problems I was having at work and explored my limited options. I would not give up my apartment in Georgetown or sell my boat. One way or another, Montana would be a short visit.

"I wish I didn't have to hear about it from Commander Gilmore," she said.

"I didn't want to spoil the weekend."

"Of course not."

Another spasm of laughter, brief this time.

We had missed the sunset and Stephanie stared out over the water at the darkening clouds off in the distance, back-lit with the receding light of the lost day. "Is prevarication a habit you picked up in the Secret Service?"

"I didn't lie to you."

She cocked an eyebrow at me, withholding judgment. "You did to Gilmore."

"Sometimes we need to be less than honest to get the job done."

Her smile was back again. "Like not telling me about Montana."

"It's not the same thing."

"Everyone seems to have their own criteria for what they will or won't do to get what they want," Stephanie told me, "deciding where the line should be drawn."

We sat there staring out at the bay until Stephanie leaned over and kissed my cheek. "Am I making you uncomfortable?"

My laugh felt forced, but I answered truthfully. "Damned right!"

"Good. Important relationships have to be honest." Her eyes and teasing grin were giving me another chance. "Let's get checked out on the boat."

We each stayed with our own thoughts on the drive to Pirate Harbor Yacht Charters. That exchange bothered me. I did not lie all the time. How could I be an effective agent if I treated every bad-check passer or counterfeiter with total honesty? Told them what evidence we had so they wouldn't trap themselves, didn't mislead them into giving up their pals.

Kurt Henzler would be going about his business up in Washington now if I had played it straight with Burnett and the Bureau. If I hadn't held back with Judith Silverman or tricked Irmgard Bauer. People in business cut corners for a lot weaker reasons than putting criminals away. Husbands cheat on wives, everybody fudges their income tax. Why was Stephanie making me feel so guilty?"

I had chartered from Phil Jackson a couple of years ago so our checkout at the dock was minimal. With any luck, we'd get more sailing in two days than I had the last time in a week with Melissa.

In '74, I had wanted to cruise out to Key West to visit Hemingway's retreat home and stomping ground, but Melissa found an exclusive resort on Duck Key where Presidents Truman and Nixon used to vacation. She couldn't get a reservation at their five-star restaurant until three days later, so Duck Key was as far as we got.

After getting our groceries, ice and gear on board, we sat on opposite sides of the cockpit leaning against the cabin housing with a nightcap of Barbados rum listening to crickets rubbing their legs together in the darkness beyond, the violet hue of fluorescent lamps flickering above the boats bobbing gently at the wooden dock. A cool breeze drifted across the water, moving the ragged fronds of weathered palm trees battered over the years by tropical storms, canting in the darkness over the far end of the narrow harbor.

My mind and body were exhausted. I found it impossible to comprehend the speculation that Gilmore had grudgingly offered about my father, much less verbalize it. I must have dozed off for a while, because I remembered no thought or motion until feeling the soft warmth of Stephanie's lips on my mouth.

"See you in the morning," she whispered, and before I could respond went below to crawl between the sheets of the 'V' berth forward.

CHAPTER ELEVEN
Hawk Channel, FL
May 1976

Stephanie roused me out of my bunk with a cup of cold orange juice before dawn and we kicked out of the little charter basin under auxiliary power into the narrow channel toward a humongous red sun lifting over the horizon. Sailing up to Key Largo we stopped to anchor and snorkel through John Pennekamp State Park. Porkfish, sergeant majors, parrotfish and four-eyed butterfly fish with their strange colorful tail design swam around us as we explored the prehistoric form and texture of the only living coral reef in the continental U.S. Stephanie was awed at the sight of the thirteen-foot bronze statue of Christ standing among the giant coral heads in thirty feet of ocean water and said she was glad I had not warned her about it.

We motored into Largo Friday evening, showered and ate grilled pompano, Caesar salad and key lime pie for dinner at the marina. We were back on board in separate bunks before ten.

The next morning, we sailed up to Biscayne Bay for a swim, lunch and an afternoon spent reading in the shade of an awning rigged over the boom to protect our northern hides from the relentless rays of the Florida sun. I got horny seeing Stephanie's oiled body in her black bikini stretched out on those white cushions two feet across the cockpit. She was reading Doctorow's new book, *Ragtime*, propped on her belly and kept pushing her tinted reading glasses up when they slid down her nose.

Saturday night I charcoaled steaks off the stern barbeque and we ate them aboard with rice and salad, watching the setting sun escape the residual heat of a perfect day. I had anchored outside 'No Name Harbor, and the tide turned the sloop away from the lights on shore.

When dusk settled, we drank coffee in the open cockpit. I stretched out on the padded bench propped up by the cabin housing, Stephanie nestled against me gazing at the billion pinpricks of light in a black velvet sky. I knew she could feel my growing erection pressing into her side.

My voice was hoarse. "Stephanie...."

She smiled, turning to clasp her hands behind my neck, drawing me into her musky aura, our lips grinding hard, painfully together. My hands grasped her full hips, pulling her belly on top of me as she lifted herself to make it easier. Our clothes came off in frenzy, her body surprisingly firm and sinewy beneath my touch.

"Right here in the open?" she asked.

"There aren't any bugs," I said.

The first time was rough, nearly violent, neither one of us able to press hard enough, push deep inside and around each other, mesh our slippery bodies sufficiently close together. A cool breeze came with a wind shift to dry the perspiration on our skin as we lay back drained and semi-conscious on the narrow cushion of the cockpit seat, murmuring euphoric, unintelligible gratification.

Our appetites for one another seemed impossible to fill that night, but successive couplings became gentler, more considerate, committing ourselves without words to something we did not yet understand or try to articulate.

How do those things happen, I wonder? We stumble through most of our lives looking for the right person, true love, a best friend, a life companion, seeking, rarely finding, settling for less, sticking it out or not, through a disillusioned existence.

After Melissa, I had almost resigned myself to that. From what I had seen, few people find the uncompromising love and devotion that seems to be the only source of happiness for men or women. Stephanie's parents? Edmund and Mrs. Gilmore? Paul and Ginny Hunsacker.

That night under that infinite star-speckled sky I honestly believed we might be one of the rare few. Was it the sex? Her quick forgiveness of my innocent deceit--the ability to bring me up from the depression I felt at being responsible for John Goddard's death? To soften the renewed impact of the bad relationship with my mother, the frustration at my ignorance about my father? Would I ever know what happened to him?

We hoist anchor at 2130 to begin a forty-mile beat that would get us back to Tavernier about noon on Sunday. As we rounded Key Biscayne, the sloop heeled in the ten-fifteen knot breeze, parting the dark water with a ribbon of green phosphoresce on either side of her bow.

We were still in Hawk Channel, south of Old Rhodes Key at 0230 hours Sunday morning when I became concerned about the running lights of a power boat a mile or so off our port quarter. The lights had remained at the same distance for an hour, matching our progress tack for tack.

I shot a relative bearing and during the next thirty minutes confirmed that the powerboat had not budged: they'd been running the same course and speed for over an hour, our chartered sloop under sail, making five knots under main and Genoa. Motor boats cruise at fifteen to twenty. This was not a fishing party coincidentally tracking our progress. What was a powerboat doing poking along on our tail at sailing speed?

Up to that point, I thought the weekend had been great. Stephanie brought me back to the present. "Do you think they could be boat-jackers?"

We were tacking in toward Old Rhodes Key and the faint glow of shore lights in the distance. I could turn the engine on, but that wouldn't do much good if the stalking craft wanted to catch us.

"I doubt it, Steph. What would they want with a beat up thirty- foot sailboat?"

"They can't tell that from where they are."

"Right. So, they'll have to get closer before they realize we're not worth stealing. Or maybe they're just having engine trouble."

"Is that why they're zigzagging all over the ocean trying to crawl up our wake?"

I had the wheel and Stephanie was sitting on the starboard bench peering at the compass course inside the binnacle.

"Jared, don't minimize the potential problem in this to make me feel better." She poked the front of my parka with her finger. "If we're in danger, I want to know from what and how much."

"Sorry."

She picked up the binoculars and studied the distant running lights, taking a couple of minutes to calm down.

"Maybe they're drug smugglers mistaking us for their rendezvous."

"Could be."

"Or want this innocuous boat to transfer a shipment inshore."

All of those scenarios were credible.

"They wouldn't just let us go if they did that," she said.

We were both thinking of the isolated horror stories we had heard about whole families found slaughtered on their drifting boats down in the islands, murdered for their cash and electronics. Yachts gone missing, discovered abandoned months later on Central American shores, their owners and crews assumed murdered, dumped in the ocean, never to be seen again.

"I'm going to call the Coast Guard," Stephanie said.

"Maybe that's them out there, thinking we're running drugs."

She turned to go below to use the VHF radio. "God, I hope so!"

I could see her standing at the foot of the companionway ladder speaking into the mike on emergency Channel 16. "PAN, PAN, PAN, this is the yacht *Seamist*, Bravo Charlie Delta three-seven-six-niner calling the U.S. Coast Guard, come in please."

The CG station in Miami answered immediately. Stephanie explained our problem, gave them our location and described our boat. The easy Southern drawl of the Coast Guard operator asked her to stand by and left the air for several minutes.

"Steph!" I called down to her, "our friends are picking up speed and closing the gap.

"They must be monitoring Channel 16, too."

She called the operator again and I could hear the apology in the radioman's voice as he told her they had three cutters working an activity offshore between Miami and Fort Lauderdale and several patrols on the other side of the Keys in Florida Bay. Busy night, he admitted. They could get out to us in an hour or so. The powerboat in our area was not theirs.

I told Stephanie our RADAR reflector was secured to the backstay and we couldn't get it down under way, so they could track us wherever we went. I left the helm, leaned down the companionway and snatched the mike out of Stephanie's hand.

"Coast Guard, this is Jared Coughlin, skipper of the *Seamist*," I said into the open mike. "I'm a United States Treasury agent, badge 4071, TAD Miami. I'm carrying a weapons bag to my new assignment, so we can probably hold these turkeys off and do some damage until you get here." Stephanie shook her head in feigned amazement.

"Tell your guys to give me a full ID before they come roaring in here, got that?"

The young Southerner began stuttering about authorization and his commanding officer as I signed off.

I couldn't believe she was able to laugh in these circumstances. "Liar, liar, pants on fire!"

I didn't believe I could join her. "Do you want me to tell the truth, now?"

"Point taken."

Stephanie turned off our cabin and running lights before coming back on deck, then took the helm and started the engine. I hauled the mainsail down and told her to make a 100° course change that would take us out to sea--the last direction our pursuers would think we would go. The powerboat had closed the gap after our first radio transmission but seemed to be hanging back again since I talked about being heavily armed.

"Did you bring your gun?" she asked.

"I am not a complete fake," I answered.

"Maybe I'll get a chance to see you in action." She pulled me close in the darkness kissing my cheek, still clutching the wheel. "Save my life."

This was some woman, I thought, as I got the snub out of my duffel, checked the load and stuffed three magazines in my pocket. If those guys wanted this boat they would get it. One .357 Smith & Wesson revolver was not going to slow down a couple of machine guns. Stephanie probably knew that but seemed calm and ready to do anything that would give us the best chance of surviving whatever our adversaries had in mind.

Knowing the Coast Guard could show up in an hour, plus the uncertainty about my arsenal might make our pursuers decide it wasn't worth it—whatever 'it' was. But all of my training had taught me that the most common, common denominator among practitioners of the drug trade was their unpredictability. If those clowns decided to take a run at us, we would be out-gunned, out-manned and underpowered. We would need a diversion.

I stuffed our sleeping bags with pillows, towels and clothing then tied them with marlin to shape necks, heads, arms, waists and legs. I realized the makeshift dummies wouldn't fool a glaucoma victim from the five-yard line. If the powerboat came that close it would probably be all over anyway.

"They're speeding up!" Stephanie called down to me.

I dragged the dummies topside and looked off to starboard where she was pointing.

"Going around in a circular search pattern. Damn! They must have heard our transmission on 16 or decided to come in on our RADAR blip--they have to be nuts, keeping at this with the Coast Guard coming."

"They know they'll never get away with stealing this boat," she said. "It'll slow them down and the Coast Guard will pick them up on RADAR."

"They must think we're someone else, like you said."

"Don't patronize me, Jared. They heard you on the radio."

I propped one dummy against the pedestal guard in the cockpit with a line running down into the cabin and rigged a halyard around the neck of the other dummy, securing its feet to the grab rail on the cabin housing while I explained my harebrained scheme to Stephanie. She didn't like it any better than I did but admitted she couldn't come up with anything else.

A powerful searchlight on the speeding motor yacht caught the radar reflector suspended from our backstay and suddenly our entire boat was bathed in harsh light. Our pursuers were still a good quarter mile off, crashing through the darkness without running lights, but I could see the high profile of their phosphorescent bow wave swing toward us as they thrust their blinding, white beam in our direction.

I shoved Stephanie down the companionway ladder before me and we fell together against the port settee. "Did you set all this up just to get into my draws again?" she asked.

"Is it working?"

"Not now, sailor-boy." She gave me a rough hug and I could feel the tension in her body.

"I think I'm falling in love with you, Jared Coughlin." She held my face between her hands and kissed me on the mouth. "I want to make sure you know that."

A burst of machine-gun fire shattered the windows and portholes in the cabin housing above our heads. I pushed Stephanie down on the cabin sole and gave her the bitter ends of the halyards hanging through the center hatch, scrambled aft to poke the snub out the companionway then looked over my shoulder at her in the darkness.

"I'm a little nervous," her voice was a shaky.

"Me too."

"Don't scare me."

"You said you wanted to know the situation."

"I take it back."

The powerboat was circling about a hundred yards off, anxious to get in for the kill but still wary of the arsenal I referred to on the radio. They waited another three or four minutes that seemed like hours until the boat's engines roared, and they came speeding at *Seamist* on a course that would take them thirty yards off our stern with machine guns firing.

No matter what they show in the movies, aiming an automatic weapon from a high-speed boat pounding across the water depended far more on luck than skill. They scattered some rounds across the deck but didn't do anywhere near the damage as their first run when they had shot broadside at a slower speed.

I was waiting for a break in the attack. When it came, the boat was closer and I popped my head up over the sights of the snub, squeezing six rounds off at the constant circle of their big spotlight. Our boat was sitting relatively still in the water bobbing slightly, so I had a good platform to aim from and was not surprised when the spot went out and the boat sped away into darkness.

If I had a better weapon I would have used it. So the men on the powerboat could be pretty certain now that my arsenal consisted of mostly a pistol. I ducked below again, moving forward through the main salon to the 'V' berth in the bow, giving Stephanie a couple of hollow words of encouragement on my way as I crawled out the forward hatch onto the port catwalk. The powerboat had sped off from our starboard quarter and would probably come back that way. If they did, the cabin housing would shield me from their fire as I lay with my face pressed into the non-skid deck.

I felt exposed up there reloading my snub, out from the false security of the fiberglass hull, but more in control. The night breeze ruffled my hair and carried the increasing sound of their powerful engine running down from the north. This time they probed the darkness with the feeble beams of two flashlights, slowed down when they found us, then pumped at least four magazines of ammunition into the hull of the sailboat.

In the middle of that attack I pounded the cabin top and

Stephanie yanked the halyards, which ran through a block at the top of the mast down to one dummy propped against the doghouse, and the other one crouching in the cockpit. The movement jerked the dummies upright, and when she let go the halyards they fell to the deck.

In the receding illumination of their flashlights, I prayed that our unknown attackers would think they had killed or wounded us. The powerboat circled closer and slower, sweeping the dim beams of their lights over the two dummies. Suddenly, the helmsman gave a short burst of power to her double screws and slammed broadside into the side of our boat. Two crewmen were poised to jump onto our deck while a third held the flashlights on the inert dummies.

A high-pitched yell of warning went up from one of the men as I caught him square in the gut with my first shot. The second boarder dropped to his knees and swung his machine pistol toward the flash of my gun just as I dropped him with two hits in the chest. The last crewman was trying to point a flashlight at me and shoot at the same time. He took one in the throat and went down like a fifty-pound anchor. During the four seconds this was going on, the helmsman was shouting his lungs out, hitting the throttle, gunning the yacht away from *Seamist* at top speed.

My central nervous system sent tremors through my arms and legs, soaking my torso with sweat. Blazing guns and shouting voices coming at me out of a dark night catapulted my mind back into the jungle where attackers in black pajamas popped up from dense foliage to kill a buddy three feet away then fade back into the void.

I poked my head through the forward hatch and called down to make sure Stephanie was all right. She sounded weak and shaken but had not been hit. I wanted to rush below to crush her against me, but slumped back on the deck, not sure that my legs would carry me.

The light wind felt good as it dried the shirt clinging to my chest. I replayed the last two minutes in my mind and another kind of chill shot up my spine. The warning cry by the boarder who realized they had been tricked by a dummy was not in English, but German. Those men in the powerboat were not risking their necks getting shot or captured by the Coast Guard for this old tub, a botched drug rendezvous or an attack on rival smugglers.

The Coast Guard showed up an hour and a half after the action. Two enlisted men came aboard the sloop to wait for a tow and Stephanie and I were transferred to the patrol boat. They wrapped us in wool blankets and gave us steaming cups of coffee before treating us to a high-speed ride back to their station in Miami.

During the time it took the Coast Guard to reach us, we held one another in the shattered cockpit, shivering in the night air and the aftermath of our frightening ordeal. Deluged by her relentless questions, I admitted the attack could have been prompted by my harassment of the Germans. Or their effort to put me out of the game— whatever it was.

I felt her stiffen at the realization that we might be assassination targets of some foreign conspiracy, but managed to convince her that revealing my suspicions to the Coast Guard and DEA would be pointless: the assailants I shot had fallen back onto the powerboat, which the Coast Guard would probably not find; except for the bullet-riddled, blood-splattered hull of the sailboat, there was no tangible evidence of the attack or its perpetrators.

In spite of our story, the Drug Enforcement agents kept us up most of Sunday asking questions and verifying our identities. They impounded the charter boat for some obscure reason, which meant I would lose my security deposit, and unless Mr. Jackson had a good marine lawyer and a lot of luck he would probably be engaged in futile litigation to recover his property from the U.S. government for the next ten years.

At the airport, Stephanie and I held hands in the waiting area next to her gate, staring out the plate-glass window at several Eastern jets refueling and loading baggage.

"I might not get a chance to see you again before I leave," I said, my eyes intent on the baggage handlers on the tarmac below.

"What do Navy wives do when their husbands are off on a cruise?"

"Wait."

She squeezed my hand. "I hope we can be more inventive than that."

When her flight was called, she leaned in and gave me a long, soft kiss, then placed a finger across my lips.

"See ya," she said with that little smile; picked up her carry-on bag and walked through the door to the boarding ramp without looking back.

CHAPTER TWELVE
Washington, DC
May 1976

Ken Burnett was bullshit. DEA had contacted him at home on Sunday to verify my identity, so he knew about our encounter with the powerboat. He refused to speak to me when I called from the airport, but Annie, his secretary, told me to get my tail in there for a three o'clock meeting that afternoon.

I sat outside Burnett's office for an hour, gazing across the open floor of agency people at their desks, on the phone, writing reports, engaged in brief conversations as they moved toward the close of another work day. Annie gave me the nod a few minutes before four, an unreadable expression on a face that was normally a good barometer of her boss's mood.

Burnett didn't waste time on amenities. "What the hell's got into you, Coughlin?"

I sat in one of the chairs in front of his desk as Annie closed the door behind me.

"A spotless six-year record," he went on without giving me a chance to answer, "fucked up beyond repair in two months."

Burnett was in a foul temper, but for some reason seemed to be restraining it. He stabbed an index finger at a Pendaflex folder on his desk. "Jeopardizing your career for some screwball idea that doesn't make sense to anybody but you."

"It doesn't make sense to me," I said. "Maybe that's what I have to do, make sense of a senseless killing."

"John Goddard. And your father's disappearance."

Gilmore's check on me had inspired Burnett to drag out my personnel file. Or did the Bureau initiate that? "I don't see how that's any of your business."

Burnett folded his arms over his cheviot sport coat and a little snort escaped his lips as he leaned back in his chair. The Service owns your ass," he answered. "Everything about you is our business."

"Before I was born?"

"Before Christ was born! Especially when you're digging up classified information."

"From World War II?" I asked him. "About two men drowning off the coast of Rhode Island?"

"You know better than that."

"What, to question the U.S. government?"

Burnett leaned forward in his chair, eyes narrowed, shoulders hunched, clenching his fists on the file folder. "There may be bigger issues at stake here than your curiosity about the circumstances surrounding your father's death."

"You ordering me to ignore my family history, now?"

"Orders don't seem to impress you anymore." His mouth tightened, his anger threatening to run away with its leash. "I warned you off the Germans and you danced around that. You're not a team player, Coughlin."

I could tell he regretted his next statement as soon as it came out. "That could get you in a corner where the Service can't protect you."

"Like the Florida Keys."

He forced himself not to respond to that, but his lips compressed harder as he glanced at the bucolic Wyeth print on his wall, giving me more time to think than if he had flung back a threatening answer.

"I can't get into much trouble in Montana," I said.

Burnett did not speak for a couple of seconds, throwing a hard stare at me, controlling his wrath until he could get his voice working again. "You're not going to Montana."

I cocked my head at him and figured it was his turn to wait. The Service probably had duty stations more remote than Great Falls, but I couldn't think of one. Maybe I was canned.

"You're back on protection for Senator Robinson." He pulled a sheaf of papers from under my file and tossed my orders across the desk.

"Special request of the candidate," he snarled. "Dismissed."

No wonder Burnett was pissed. Not only had I evaded his plans to banish me to the boondocks, but my orders read, 'Permanent Duty Station,' and were signed, William E. Simon, Secretary of Treasury. 'Permanent?' Till the election in November? To President Robinson if he makes it? No question, the Senator was behind this.

Protective details for politicians are made up of a Special Agent in Charge and sixteen agents selected from Secret Service offices around the country for thirty-day tours. They work a hundred twenty-five hours a week in twelve-hour shifts, a dollar an hour overtime, no days off for the month. Two seventeen-man teams are assigned to a protectee rotating month-on month-off between the detail and their permanent duty stations. Contrary to popular belief, this was not the most popular job you could pull in the Service.

My original assignment a couple of hundred years ago, was to Detail 'A' that had pulled the first tour with Senator Robinson from the middle of February to mid-March. The orders I held now were cut for me to join that same detail for their second tour on April fifteenth after a one-week refresher course at the Special Agent Training facility in Beltsville, Maryland.

Popular or not, U.S. Secret Service protective duty is probably the most heads-up law enforcement job in the world. It was originally set up as a bureau within the Treasury Department in 1865 after John Wilkes Booth assassinated President Lincoln with a single-shot derringer in Ford's Theater despite special police guards. Congress didn't give us the authority to protect the Chief Executive until Leon Czolgosz assassinated President McKinley with a .32 caliber revolver at a reception in Buffalo, New York in 1901.

Before that, presidents were pretty much on their own. Andrew Jackson survived an attempt on his life in 1835, and James A. Garfield was murdered in 1881 by Charles Guiteau with a .44 caliber revolver as the president was walking to the Baltimore & Potomac Railroad station in Washington.

I had always thought that the legislature figured they'd better start making the top job a little more secure. McKinley was the third president assassinated in less than fifty years, and the office of president was a position to which many congressmen aspired.

Since the Service had been on the job, four U.S. Presidents had been the targets of attempted assassinations. In 1933 Giuseppe Zangara fired five shots at FDR, killing Mayor Anton Cermak of Chicago as they rode in a Miami motorcade. One Special Agent and an assassin were killed when Puerto Rican Nationalists tried to assassinate Harry Truman at Blair House in 1950. John Kennedy was gunned down by Lee Harvey Oswald in '63. And Lynette 'Squeaky' Fromme tried to kill President Ford just last year.

The week I spent retraining at Beltsville was exhaustive, covering every conceivable situation except the two that agents feared most: the high-powered telescopic rifle and the surprise in the crowd. The only advice they could give about those threats was, 'concentrate on the attempts you can prevent and put yourself in harm's way around the protectee as much as possible, hoping you'll catch the long-range slug instead of him.' Not reassuring for the protectee or agent, but like most of my peers, my response to that aspect of our duties was, 'no job is perfect.'

On Super Tuesday Senator Charles Robinson took nine of the eleven states holding primary elections. Two other candidates were still in the running, but the Senator had acquired over 850 of the 1,105 delegates needed to win his party's nomination at their convention that summer.

* * * * * *

"The strangest bloody clearance file I've ever seen." Alex Shertinsky placed a small piece of veal between his bearded lips in the left-handed inverted tines manner affected by Europeans. His half-closed eyes reminded me of a purring cat savoring a special delicacy, waiting for my reaction to what he had told me.

Alex had tracked me down in Beltsville during my retraining week insisting that I call as soon as I returned to D.C. Buying him dinner at Brighton Grill would be nice, he suggested, as some new information he had gleaned on 'our friend' was quite astonishing.

Except for the dual set of fingerprints, our original research made sense. The Senator had been in the public eye for twenty-five years and recently vetted backwards and forward by the FBI, DAR, CIA, VFW, ACLU and every other acronym in the country. Senator Charles Robinson was Mister Clean.

"The summary report seemed OK to me," I said.

"Precisely their intention," the big man explained between mouthfuls. "The report looks credible; the backup is cods wallop."

"How'd you get hold of it?"

Alex peered over a fork-load of asparagus and Béarnaise sauce. "You don't really need to know that, do you?"

I gazed around the restaurant, recognizing several faces that appeared regularly in *The Post* and *Time*. A table of men in evening clothes occupied the center of the room. Banquettes with distinguished and young female heads inclined together in the soft candlelight.

"Why, then?"

"My insatiable curiosity," he replied with an irreverent glint in his eye. "The report was too symmetrical." He resumed eating, his attention torn between his two compulsions: gourmet food and information gleaned through computer hacking.

"Every vetting summary has inconsistencies, one or two unanswered questions, nothing important, just loose ends not worth binding up," Alex told me. "Senator Robinson's doesn't have any," the big head shook back and forth. "Not in the report."

"And the documentation?"

"Replete."

"Like what?"

Alex finished chewing his veal and paused for effect, knife

in right hand, fork in left, wrists resting on the edge of the table.

"Your Senator Charles Robinson has no living relatives, friends or acquaintances prior to his admission to Columbia Law School in 1946 when he was twenty-six years old." He sipped his wine. "None."

"That's impossible."

"Like a character in a Pirandello play who suddenly appears on stage without warning or precedent to interact with the established cast."

"No neighbors, high school or college friends, army buddies, girl friends?"

"Lusten, Minnesota was a tiny fishing village on the shores of Lake Superior in 1920 when the Senator was born. The kind of place from which youngsters move away. His parents are deceased, their friends and neighbors all passed on or whereabouts unknown "

I shook my head, nudging my plate aside with its half-eaten steak, the red juices congealing around the edge of the cold meat.

"According to the Feds."

"The high school had a fire in 1946, contained to a records room next to the principal's office," Alex continued, shrugging his wide shoulders, acknowledging my expression of disbelief, "destroying most student academic and personal information."

"College?"

"Apparently a loner, worked his way through, lived by himself in off-campus digs, didn't join a club or frat house as you Colonials call it."

"He must have had a girlfriend. Didn't the Bureau turn up anyone I can talk to?"

"They couldn't seem to find a soul with all the moving around after graduation, the war just on for you Yanks."

Alex signaled and gave our waiter his order for apple torte and coffee before continuing.

"Remarkably unlike his extracurricular activities at Columbia: university-wide graduate council, law review, debating team."

"Like two different people."

"With two sets of fingerprints," Alex reminded me.

"Maybe the war mixed up his records, changed him...."

"Into someone else?"

"Geeze, Alex, it all sounded so convincing."

"There's no guarantee it's not true," he warned. "Just because it looks cooked, doesn't mean it is--unless you can prove it."

"I know, I know."

It was nine-thirty and I was getting brain dead. My training schedule for the past week had begun at four a.m. daily, ending at midnight. I had trouble staying awake driving in from Beltsville.

"There's more," Alex said, leaning back with a smile of anticipation as the waiter placed dessert before him. "His army transcript is all paper."

"Isn't everybody's?"

"Not with orders signed by untraceable or deceased officers. The soldier missing from group photographs. Every assignment brief and circuitous, placing the man on the periphery of each unit to which he was attached. Decorations recommended by commanders killed in action, presented by general officers who wouldn't remember him if their proverbial lives depended on it."

"Isn't there anyone who can verify the early years of his life?"

Alex's mouth was full of torte, so he just shook his head.

"I can't believe there isn't a single person in the entire country who knew him!"

"Someone did," Alex said. "Under whatever name he used with the second set of fingerprints."

"They would have recognized him when he became a national figure."

Alex drained his coffee cup and patted his mouth with his linen napkin as the waiter placed the leatherette folder containing our check near his elbow.

"The years, his white hair, the beard--don't forget, he lost his eye at the end of the fighting."

I was exhausted. "How the hell am I going to find someone who knew him before 1945?"

"You're the policeman, Jared."

"I know, I know."

"There's a good fellow." He smiled and slid the oblong maroon folder across the tablecloth.

"Do let me know what happens. Perhaps we can meet next time at *Maison Blanche*."

"Shertinsky, if the Service had to feed you every week instead of paying you money, Congress would renege on our budget."

* * * * * *

I finished training on a Friday, the second week of May. When I arrived at National Airport that evening after my dinner with Alex, the terminal was crowded with frustrated businessmen and government employees whose flights for a weekend home were delayed by high winds and thunderstorms moving across the northeast corridor. After I finally moved to the head of the line at a bank of pay phones, it took me almost ten minutes to track Stephanie down at her Boston office. She sounded tired and distracted.

"You're working too hard," I told her.

"A teenager whose family I've been counseling tried to commit suicide."

"Aw, Steph, that's a shame. Is he OK?"

"She," Stephanie corrected "Thirteen. Her mother's a heroin addict, her boyfriend's been raping the girl."

"The bastard!" I said. "Thirteen years old?" They ought to castrate the fucker."

A fat man behind me whined, "Hey come on, buddy, that's public phone, you know?"

I turned to the man and pressed the mouthpiece against my chest. "Shut up, fats," then stared the man down until he looked away, blushing.

".... no father in sight," Stephanie was saying when I put the phone back to my ear, "the mother's in jail and Cindy's headed for a foster home or institution when she gets out of

117

the hospital."

"How's she doing?"

"They took fifteen stitches in each wrist. It's not her physical condition we're worried about."

"That is rotten, Steph."

"Gotta run, Jared. I have to do a current workup on Cindy for the Department of Social Services. Whether or not she's still a danger to herself will determine if the State sends her to a foster home or Bridgewater."

"You take care of yourself, hear me?"

CHAPTER THIRTEEN
Detroit, MI
June 1976

I reported to the Detroit office of the Secret Service the morning of the 14th fitted with a new earphone cast from a mold by injecting warm plastic into my ear. Thin wires ran from it, under my collar to the walkie-talkie clipped to my belt, back down my sleeve to a flesh-colored mike under my cuff. On duty, this unit would keep me in touch with the Command Post and other agents on the detail.

At six o'clock the next morning, the headlight beams of the lead chase car swept out of the darkness, across the security shack outside the chain link fence of Butler Aviation. A yawning guard checked us through the gates and onto the field where private, corporate and cargo planes are serviced at the backside of Detroit International Airport.

We confirmed the I.D.'s of a pre-checked Ground crew and baggage handlers who dozed or smoked in a van waiting on the outer perimeter of the designated parking spot for the chartered DC-3, then began our own patient wait for the inbound flight. Ten agents sat inside four cars parked at different angles on the tarmac watching all approaches to our position. Parallel lines of yellow ground lights converged at the ends of distant runways, as an occasional commercial jet took off or landed.

Murphy was back at CP coordinating our group, the agents at the Detroit Hilton suite reserved for the Senator's breakfast meeting were checking hotel staff and eye-balling out-of-town supporters. Several humps were scouting the Ford assembly plant on John R Road where Senator Robinson would address almost 1,000 union workers that morning.

A couple of charter buses with 'Robinson for President'

banners affixed to their sides rolled up beside us at six-thirty, followed several minutes later by a Chrysler Le Baron, Ford Granada and Chevy Impala, each with a triangular Robinson Campaign sign strapped to its roof. A couple of agents checked bus drivers, local politicians and auto execs, combing through each vehicle until word came down from the Control Tower that CANDY--less an acronym than an abbreviation for 'candidate,' had landed and was taxiing toward us.

Paul Hunsaker was agent in charge of the Detail, but he didn't need to say a word. Drivers stood by their doors facing away from the inbound plane, scanning the approaches from the access gates and buildings of the Butler terminal. Four agents gathered at the foot of the portable ramp searching the gray light of dawn in every direction of the compass.

Hunsacker stood by the open right front door of the lead car talking to CP on the special frequency boosted and scrambled by the power pack under the back seat. Another hump was poised with his hand on the partially open trunk of the follow car. I stood behind the 'war wagon,' the last of our three chase vehicles. Beneath our two left hands were eight Uzi submachine guns, four Remington .870-gauge pump shotguns, a case of tear gas grenades, canisters of mace, back-up handguns and enough ammo to support the the next *Charge of the Light Brigade.*

Several agents put on sunglasses and all of us unbuttoned our coats, pressing them to our bodies against the warm breeze as the ground crew waved the big DC-3 into its parking spot. The ramp was rolled up against the massive silver fuselage and an agent on 'B' Detail swung the door open, exchanging salutes with Hunsacker, who spoke the words, "arrive, arrive" into his mike.

A big blond agent was the first person off the plane, followed by Senator Robinson trotting down the aluminum steps, thick white hair blowing in the wind, his single blue eye taking in everything around him, then locking his attention on his Michigan aides and the representatives of the automobile industry. The four agents at the ramp formed a loose phalanx around the candidate as he conferred with the local dignitaries.

During that conversation on the tarmac, Senator Robinson's glance lifted above the shoulders of the group to catch my eye. He nodded with an almost imperceptible tug at the corner of his bearded mouth, walked away from the others and climbed aboard the lead bus surrounded by four Secret Service agents. Hunsaker signed the log of Detail 'B', accepting protective responsibility for Senator Robinson and told Jenkins they were pushed.

The last of the political campaign contingent hurried from their cramped night of fitful sleep on the plane, through the mild spring air into the buses. Their doors closed and the lead Service car swung out in front of the motorcade. When the follow car had pulled in between the first and second bus, I grabbed a Uzi out of the trunk, slammed the lid and jumped in the back seat as the driver turned out to take up position behind the little convoy.

It had only begun. The watching, searching, scrutinizing every person, thing, reflection, shadow and movement around us. But with any luck the next thirty days would go just as smoothly as the last few hours. Most of them did.

* * * * * *

Over the next month, I adopted a routine of nocturnal phone calls to Stephanie from hotel rooms scattered across the country. Our expressions of longing, affection and disappointment at our inability to sustain our intimate relationship in more convenient proximity were frustrated by our inability to plan our lives with any certainty or timetable. During those long-distance conversations, Cindy Farrell, Stephanie's teen patient who had attempted suicide became a regular topic of discussion. It sounded as though the girl had progressed from another emotionally disturbed patient to Stephanie's primary case, consuming a great deal her time in Family Court, with the Department of Social Services and interviewing potential foster parents.

"Do you get paid for all the time you spend on a case like that?" I asked in a phone call from LA.

"No," she said. "It's *pro bono*. You can't leave a child with her problems stranded in the system."

"*You* can't."

"We haven't been able to find an appropriate foster home. Both the judge and DSS want her institutionalized for her own protection."

"Doesn't that make sense?"

"As a preventive measure, yes. And she'll get therapy. But it won't provide the family environment she needs to purge the self-destructive demons she's been fighting for years."

* * * * * *

Senator Robinson flew back to Washington from Frisco on American Airlines so he could vote on a nuclear arms treaty with Russia and attend to other legislative business. We made his reservation in a phony name, checked all passengers visually as they boarded the plane and drove him to the foot of the ramp at the last minute. The candidate and two aides occupied four facing seats in first class, with Bob Murphy across the aisle, Hunsacker and I in the last two seats of the small curtained first class cabin. Two other humps were back in coach.

Thirty-thousand feet over Wyoming, I was gazing down at a layer of cumulous clouds reflecting the glaring sunlight when the Senator walked down the aisle and asked Hunsacker if he'd mind switching seats. Paul was on his feet so fast you'd think his boot camp D.I. had ordered him to recite the specs of the M-16 rifle.

The Senator took his time fastening his seat belt while I sat there like a white-knuckle flier, waiting.

Senator Robinson gave me a nod and a reassuring smile through the snow-white beard, then stretched his long legs out under the seat in front of him, leaned his head back, folded his hands in his lap and closed his eye.

After a few minutes, he asked, "How's it going, Jared?"

"Fine, sir."

"No problem with the wound?"

122

"No, sir. Thank you for asking."

I had been working his protective details for three months and assumed he hadn't made any reference to the incident at his condo previously to spare me the taint of favoritism. This was the first time he'd mentioned it.

"I understand you caught one of the men who broke into my home," he said.

"Yes sir."

"And chased them all back to Germany."

I had been facing straight ahead and turned to look at that rugged profile, the strong, placid features under the black eye-patch.

"I doubt John Goddard would call that justice."

"He was a gentle man, Jared. Not a grain of vengeance in his body."

My voice was hoarse, and I spoke before I could think. "Well, there is in mine!"

Senator Robinson didn't reply for several moments. Then: "'Justice,' Mister Webster wrote, 'is the great interest of man on earth.'"

Neither of us spoke until I said, "Thanks for bringing me back from exile."

"It seemed the least I could do." He turned his head toward me and opened his eye. "Is it keeping you out of trouble?"

An image flashed through my mind of two medieval knights with sunlight glinting off their heavy armor, visors down, lances lowered, charging at one-another in slow motion on big, padded horses, the tall grass bending beneath unshod hooves.

"What document were the burglars looking for?" I asked him.

Something flickered behind that cold blue eye, but other than that he betrayed nothing. Senator Robinson faced forward again. "I have no idea."

"The Germans were looking for it and some key in your condo."

The Senator seemed comfortable with long pauses. Probably discovered they were just as effective getting people to blurt things out in politics as they were interrogating witnesses.

"What are you after, Jared?"

"The truth, I guess."

He had closed his eye again and smiled without opening it.

"A modern-day Diogenes."

"The old Greek with the lantern?"

"He was a cynic, you know. His purported quest for an honest man was a public relations stunt to emphasize his contention that neither the truth nor a man of total candor could be found."

"Maybe he didn't look hard enough."

"As the cliché goes," he said, "it can hurt sometimes."

"I think we need to know it."

"In spite of the consequences?"

"Yes."

"Should a woman confess her single infidelity to her husband?" he asked.

I looked out the window at the fleecy clouds, wondering if this was really his argument or he had absorbed some of Stephanie's integrity by remote osmosis.

"Should the government disclose all its secrets to the public," he continued, "for the world to chew on?"

"We have to be selective."

"Who would you have do that?"

"Someone who can see the big picture," I said. "Someone we can trust."

"Yes." Our eyes locked. "Someone we can trust."

* * * * * *

Stephanie picked me up at Rhode Island's Green airport with Cindy Farrell, legs curled beneath her, pressing herself into the far corner of the back seat.

She seemed small for thirteen, with pinched, nondescript features peering out from long brown hair hanging down the front of a new gray sweatshirt with "Harvard" stenciled in crimson on the front. Stephanie introduced us and the girl extended a listless arm to touch limp fingers to my proffered hand, but did not respond to my greeting.

"The ruling came yesterday," Stephanie told me. "In the absence of suitable foster care, she was going to Bridgewater."

I reached to rub Stephanie's knee, smiling. "So, Dr. Graham to the rescue."

She glanced in the rear-view mirror. "We made the decision together, didn't we Cindy?"

"Hard choice," the girl muttered, staring out the window.

I couldn't help frowning. "How long does this... arrangement last?"

"Until everyone agrees that Cindy is ready for permanent foster parents."

"Or I screw up again," Cindy offered.

"You're not going to screw up--oh, everybody screws up once in a while. Just so long as it's not a major screw up."

"Get her one of those 'damn I'm good!' bracelets," I quipped.

"Hey! Great idea," Stephanie said. "How 'bout that, Cindy? As a reminder."

The girl didn't respond so we engaged in our own conversation, catching up on other news and planning our weekend activities until we arrived at Stephanie's Wickford home.

I was introduced to Mrs. Mackenzie who cared for Stephanie's mother in her absence and reintroduced to Mrs. Graham who did not remember me. Stephanie took off the blue blazer she had worn over a beige turtleneck and paused with her hand on the knob of the hall closet, watching Cindy pull her sweatshirt over her head and toss it on a cane-bottom chair in the hallway.

"How about that discussion we had this morning?"

"What?"

"You know what."

Beneath the sweatshirt, Cindy wore a tie-dyed-tee shirt a size too small, knotted in front exposing three inches of midriff and clinging to her surprisingly mature breasts, whose hardened nipples showed through the thin material.

"Oh, yeah," Cindy said, with a distressed expression. She retrieved the sweatshirt from the chair and started up the stairs to the second floor.

"I wasn't referring to that part of the discussion," Stephanie called after her.

"OK, OK!" Cindy said without breaking stride, then disappeared around the upstairs banister and slammed her bedroom door.

"Nevertheless," I told her, it seems you bought a job of work on this one."

We had gone out for pizza that Saturday night, seen the movie 'Rocky,' and were lying under the sheet of the wide bed in my hotel room, heads propped up on pillows, the tip of Stephanie's cigarette glowing in the darkness.

"None of my cases are easy," she said.

"But you don't take them all home."

"I've tried to explain that."

It wasn't that Cindy Farrell's case was so unique, Stephanie told me. The prognosis for most children in comparable circumstances is they can either be helped to lead fairly stable, productive lives or are so emotionally impaired that they will probably not. In her professional opinion, this girl was borderline. Her only hope was therapy, a strong sense of family support and a constant effort to rebuild her total lack of self-worth.

Few of even the most qualified foster parents could provide that and fewer could handle the specter of suicide, ensuing guilt or constant anticipation of disaster. After spending hours with Cindy at Bridgewater following her mother's arrest for selling drugs, Stephanie concluded that committing this child to an institution would not only exacerbate her low self-esteem but inflict further emotional trauma that could prove irreparable.

"You think you can erase the aftereffects of forcible rape permitted by her own mother?" I asked her.

Stephanie blew a stream of smoke at the darkened ceiling.

"Never. The best we can do is help her deal with it; understand that it was not her fault. It was her mother's addiction, not her mother that allowed that man to abuse her."

"What about the ignored 'no-bra' confrontation you had with her earlier this morning?"

"Cindy is totally confused about sex. She knows rape is wrong and unpleasant, but it made her mother happy or the heroin men gave her did. So, she realizes sex can get things. That's all she has and wants to keep it ready in case she needs to use it again."

"Geezes, the poor kid."

We were occupied with our respective thoughts while Stephanie finished her cigarette.

Then I asked, "How long do you expect this to take?"

"No one can predict that."

"I mean, until she's OK to go to a foster home."

"I don't know."

"Months, years...?"

"Could be."

∧ * * * * *

I drove Stephanie home in her car at two in the morning, returning for breakfast at nine o'clock. Cindy was still upstairs sleeping when mother and daughter left for church.

I was reading the Sunday paper in the living room when I smelled it. At first I wasn't sure what to do. This was Stephanie's problem, not mine. Then the remote beat of the music I began to hear after the women had left became louder and was turned up periodically until I could feel the vibrations in the air.

If this was going to take years, I thought, I was going to be involved whether I liked it or not. I got up and walked to the foot of the stairs.

"Hey, Cindy! How 'bout turning that down!"

She didn't answer so I yelled up again. When my third call produced the same result; I moved halfway up the staircase and tried once more. Nothing, except louder rock music and the sweet smoke I had smelled in the living room. I climbed the remaining stairs and walked to the closed door from which the booming sounds were emanating and the smell of marijuana strongest.

I banged on the door.

"Cindy!"

There was no response for several moments during which I knocked and called more gently. The music stopped. A few moments later Cindy opened the door.

"What?" She was about five-feet-five inches tall, her long brown hair pulled back from her narrow face in a pony-tail, her thin torso draped in a man's faded flannel shirt.

I tried to smile. "Good morning."

"What do you want?"

"How 'bout a little less woofer, turn the tweeter down to six, huh?"

"Oh, you're so hip."

My smile wasn't working. "Just turn it down, OK?"

"Who died an' left you king?"

"And let me have the grass."

"Up yours!"

She started to shut the door, but I stopped it with the palm of my hand and stepped into the room. It was a mess: dirty clothes, music tapes, miscellaneous candy wrappers, a couple of dirty dishes, empty Coke bottles and other debris scattered over the bed and floor. I spotted the plastic bag of grass on the bureau and took it.

"Hey! That's mine," Cindy whined.

"Not anymore," I said, walking out of her room. "Let's see what the management has to say about this."

"Bastard!" she screamed and slammed the door.

CHAPTER FOURTEEN
The United States of America
July 1976

During that last week in June I joined Detail 'A' in Seattle as the Senator began crisscrossing the western states by bus from Oregon to Georgia, campaigning in any town where his local people could promise a crowd of two hundred voters. We traveled into Kentucky and Tennessee, around clear blue lakes created by the TVA, through rich farmlands of green tobacco leaves and white cotton bolls.

The buses made a brief stop at the Hermitage, the home of Andrew Jackson where the Senator shook the hands of tourists from all over the country. The fourth of July found us in Pulaski, the birthplace of the Ku Klux Klan, where Senator Robinson delivered an electrifying speech against racism which received national coverage for a week and increased his popularity in the polls by eleven percent.

On that 200th birthday of the United States, the entire nation joined in the celebration of the most successful democracy the world has known. Solemn memorials and reenactments of battles from Concord to the Carolinas commemorated the defiance of British rule by a rag-tag, untrained civilian army, under-staffed, lacking the basic weapons and supplies for waging war, culminating in wresting victory from the most powerful nation on earth.

Two-hundred-fifty tall ships sailed into New York harbor past the Statue of Liberty and up the Hudson River as thousands of people on the banks and rooftops cheered the spectacle. Brilliant fireworks lit the night skies from Caribou, Maine, to San Diego. Over 10,000 immigrants became U.S. citizens in mass ceremonies held in major cities. Practically everyone caught the bicentennial spirit in organized festivities on sandy beaches, rural fairs, parades and backyard barbecues. Even protest groups who chose this event to demonstrate against an imperfect government were proof of its strength and their freedom. I believed that I was just as patriotic as any other American, but the legitimate euphoria stimulated by the legends of our past made me wonder what had happened to my country recently. According to Senator Robinson, we had been too successful in the Second World War. During those four-years a nation of diverse interests shaken by a staggering depression had been galvanized into an unbeatable juggernaut, conquering half the planet and saving the other.

After 1945 the United States had taken everything for granted, surrendered victory to conquered and allied nations, finally ripping itself apart over Vietnam. He says they used to be a country of 'doers,' then started complaining about everything, producing less and demanding more. Like nothing worked and nobody cared. If we didn't change our attitudes and national course by the end of the century, the Senator claimed, some historian will write a book entitled, *The Decline and Fall of the United States.*

We continued east past rolling hills of bluegrass spotted with cattle grazing in the sunshine on to the foothills of the Great Smoky Mountains. I could not stop agonizing over Senator Robinson. He looked good on paper, he sounded good in person, he made sense to everyone and the whole country was buying it. Except me. If things kept moving the way they were going, the man would win his party's nomination the following month, get elected president in four and start work in the Oval Office in January. Unless the people who had tried to kill me, assassinated him.

If they didn't, what kind of leadership would the voters get from a man whose life seems to have started at twenty-six years old and has been living a lie ever since?

All that turmoil had been floating around in my mind ever since I came back on duty ten days earlier, my conviction the Germans were plotting to interfere in the presidential election because of something Robinson knew about or possessed; and my corked-up anger at the complacency of Burnett and the FBI who refused to acknowledge the possibility of the threat.

It was one o'clock in the morning when the Senator retired to his room in the Maxwell House after delivering the last of several speeches in Nashville. The night air was hot in the state capital, which sits on the Cumberland River, the city a pleasing combination of rural and urban influences with antebellum homes, the Grand Ole Opry, the classical architecture of its universities, plus a proud reputation as the Athens of the South.

By the time we got there, I decided I had to confront the Senator or go out of my mind. I was barely under control when I greeted the humps outside Robinson's suite and knocked on his door.

Senator Robinson was the most difficult man to read that I had ever met. When he opened the door, there was no surprise on his face, no look of impatience or question about what I wanted. Not a hint of annoyance at my late-night visit. He gave me a half smile that ruffled the white beard near the corners of his mouth and welcomed me inside with a sweep of his arm. Like he knew why I had come.

He liked his privacy despite of his public aspirations, and no campaign meetings were held in his suite. The living room was small and neat with a white Shantung sofa and matching wingback chairs. A floor lamp between them cast a pale circle around both, leaving the rest of the room in shadow. A light shone through a door to the right, illuminating the spread turned down on a double bed. The Senator was in his shirtsleeves looking fresh and alert, cuffs buttoned, tie snug against its collar.

He offered me a Coke which I declined, and a seat in one of the armchairs which I accepted. Senator Robinson sat on the sofa just outside the rim of light and waited.

Now that I was there, I didn't know how to begin and felt like a fool, gazing helplessly around the darkened room, rubbing my palms down the tops of my thighs.

The Senator scrutinized me, his brow furrowed with

concern. "Perhaps the aftereffects of your wound have not dissipated to the point where you are fully fit for active duty. If there is anything I can do, Jared...."

This was as good an opening as I was likely to get. "You can tell me what's so important about some key and document that somebody tried to kill me for hassling the Germans who want it."

The Senator made no response, no protest, just that level stare. He said, "This goes back to the break-in at my condo in February."

"John Goddard's murder would be a better way to describe it."

"Of course." His expression didn't change.

"And the photo of my mother," I said, "in your bedroom."

He shook his head, like we had covered that ground before but didn't offer a rebuttal.

"You believe the attack in the Florida Keys was an attempt on your life, I understand."

I realized that I wouldn't have to fill in much, because somebody, probably the FBI, was keeping him posted.

"You believe they were German agents?" he asked.

"They weren't drug runners."

"You think all this is tied to some key the burglars were trying to steal from my home and I know what it is."

"Geeze, Senator! I try to stop them in your home, they snuff John and try for me. I talk to Gilmore, the old Coast Guard commander, I nearly get killed by so-called smugglers. Every time I rattle the cage on this, somebody tries to take me out. Damned right, I think you know about it!"

His face showed concern for the first time since I walked into the room. He stood up and walked over to the small refrigerator in the corner. "Are you sure you won't have a Coke?"

"No. Thank you."

He peeled the plastic wrap off a thick-bottomed hotel glass-and poured the cold drink before sitting down again.

"Maybe I should take all this to the *Washington Post*," I

said.

The Senator pursed his lips for a second, then nodded his head. "Perhaps you should."

This sunovabitch was like a toy Shmoo, that two-foot high inflated plastic toy made with a weight in its round bottom that brings it back to vertical no matter how hard you push it.

"They could start in Lusten, Minnesota. Maybe find something besides your birth certificate. An old fishing buddy, childhood sweetheart. "

"I'd be delighted. I went back there after my discharge to do just that. All my friends seemed to have been scattered around the country by the war."

"With no forwarding address or relatives to help you locate them."

"I wasn't tracing missing persons, Jared. I just went home for a few days to see who was around after being gone for a long time."

"And everyone who ever heard of you had evaporated when the Bureau checked you out after you announced your candidacy."

"That's not true," he said.

I held a hand up in mock apology. "Beg your pardon, Senator. Everyone who knew you, had evaporated. Plenty of wags claimed to remember the skinny blond kid who used to live on Sturgeon Drive and was running for president."

He shrugged and took a sip of his cola before responding. "I can't help that, now, can I?"

"Unless you set it up."

"Why would I do that?"

"I don't know yet, Senator. But your history is too thin and uncorroborated to be true. No high school records because the school burned down," I started poking my finger at the upholstered arm of the chair to emphasize each accusation. "Parents killed in the Hindenburg crash when you were seventeen."

"That's all documented, my boy," he was getting annoyed. I hoped he would lose that damned control and let something slip. "What do you want, an eye witness to my every move, forty, fifty years after the fact?"

I was probably going to get myself canned from the Service, but I couldn't swallow all his patronizing bullshit. "I'm not your 'boy,' Senator. And yes, I would like to talk to one person who knew Charles Robinson prior to 1945."

His eye closed for a couple of seconds and he looked as though he was getting tired. Good.

"Your army records are an elaborate paper trail of some phantom who dashed from island to island up the coast of Asia performing heroic feats of bravery, scooping up medals as he went." I took a breath to see if this was getting a rise out of him. Nothing. He should have thrown me out in the hall for talking to him like that. Maybe he wanted to see where it was going. So did I.

"Your college transcript is almost a duplicate of a member of my father's crew. A picture was taken of you with my mother aboard my grandfather's boat, but you claim you didn't know them."

"That was not your mother in the photograph I gave you. How could I have known her?"

"Because the first half of your life is a goddamned lie, Senator! Where were you all those years? Who the hell are you, anyway?"

"I believe that's enough Agent Coughlin."

"Did you know John Andeweg?"

"Not well. We took some classes together in college. He was killed in the war, I think."

"You deny knowing my parents in the summer of 1941?" I was purposely repeating myself, getting impatient.

"You've studied my life history fairly thoroughly. As you may recall, my A-12 unit shipped out to the Pacific Theater two weeks after graduation."

I had had it with this bastard. I leaned forward in my chair but didn't raise my voice. "I think you're full of shit, Senator."

Senator Robinson put his glass down on the cocktail table and stood up. "Then don't vote for me."

* * * * * *

Ken Burnett telephoned from Washington at 5:30 the next morning. At 5:35 I was out of a job. Tom Jenkins knocked on my door ten minutes later to pick up my snub and shield. I didn't know how much Ken had told him, but despite his expression of sympathy, it was obvious he thought I was wrong and the Service was right. I was on the outside now and the ranks were closing.

It was July 6th, my birthday. There was nothing to do but go home.

CHAPTER FIFTEEN
Annapolis, MD
July 1976

Until a couple of months ago I thought the best things about my job were being in the action, four weeks' vacation and the early retirement option. Working twenty-seven days a month was not supposed to be part of the package. Neither was four years in the White House standing under a microscope or getting ulcers trying to protect POTUS from every loony tune and merry melody he'd be exposed to in his travels around the world.

On my flight back east, I started thinking about the box I'd jumped out of. At the rate I'd been going, I would have gotten one or two days sailing that summer. None, if I spent my free time chasing the elusive conspiracy surrounding Senator Robinson. Never, if the Germans got lucky. The whole thing was crazy---there I was worrying about protecting CANDY and I was the one getting shot at. It had turned into exactly the kind of situation my type 'B' personality always tried to avoid. One of my character traits that made Melissa decide to leave. I didn't want to live to work, I wanted to spend time on my boat with someone special. Go cruising down Maine, Nova Scotia, even farther someday. See if the amazing vibes I was getting from Stephanie Graham would turn into the permanent commitment I'd begun to hope for.

Eight hours ago, I had no idea when or if I was going to get *Dutchman* ready to cruise that year. On my 'best things' list, my 28-foot Bristol Channel Cutter was a close second to perfect sex.

She was in wet storage at the Annapolis Marina and now I had little else on my agenda but puttering around, getting her ready to cruise.

I used to sail the Chesapeake every spare minute I could find. With Melissa when fair weather coincided with a lull in her social calendar and alone when it didn't. One summer we took separate vacations and I sailed *Dutchman* singlehanded 150 miles down the Bay non-stop, then out into the Atlantic, gunkholing up the Machipongo Islands off the Delmarva Peninsula. The temperature stayed in the high eighties most of the time, tempered by brisk winds out of the southwest. Clear skies, sunny days, and cool nights crowded with more stars than I ever imagined were up there. It was probably the finest two weeks of my life. I still remember the way Melissa looked at me when I told her I only got off the boat once and spoke maybe fifty words to six people the whole time I was gone.

* * * * * *

I walked into my apartment, dropped my bags on the floor and opened the windows to let the summer breeze replace the musty air trapped inside. Then slumped on the chair beside the phone and picked it up.

Stephanie listened without interrupting until I was finished.

"Are you OK, love?"

"Yeah. I guess I provoked it."

"Subconscious wish-fulfillment?"

"Am I being analyzed?"

"Are you going to pay me?"

"No."

"Then that was just an offhand comment."

"On the mark, though, huh?"

"So now what?" Stephanie asked.

"Who knows? My best thinking comes from messing around on the boat."

In the spring, I would usually sand and varnish Dutchman's bright work, strip and grease winches, service her engine and perform a hundred other annual maintenance jobs to get her in shape for the summer. This year I had neglected her completely, except for instructing the yard to sand and paint her bottom and launch her.

"Want some help?"

"You get that lovely tail down here for the weekend, Pal, we'll take a run across the Bay."

"Can I bring Cindy with us?

I hesitated. "Geeze, Steph, I haven't seen you in weeks."

I could hear the smile in her voice. "She's not too fond of you, either."

"I'm crushed."

"You are the 'pig that squeals.'

"Not bad."

"Neither is she, Jared."

"No comment."

"She's just a little girl, she won't get in the way. I'm sure she's never been on a boat or any place like Annapolis. She'll love it--it'll be great therapy. Would you mind, Jared?"

I was torn between my desire to please this wonderful woman for whom I cared deeply and my need to be alone with her after weeks apart. With no sex for an eternity. Maybe the kid was a heavy sleeper.

"Fine, fine."

* * * * * *

The first shuttle out of Boston on Saturday touched down at National Airport at 7:30 on a brilliant summer morning. Our mutual anticipation of days together sought release in a prolonged embrace at the arrival gate bringing smiles to the faces of arriving passengers forced to step around the two lovers and thin girl standing a few feet away.

"Hello, again, Cindy," I reached out to shake hands.

"Hi," the girl said, looking down at her new sneakers, scuffing the polished tiles, hands jammed in the pockets of her jeans.

Stephanie tried to pry Cindy's right hand out. "Come on, you guys are going to be living in tight quarters the next few days."

Cindy pulled her arm out of Stephanie's grasp and looked up at her. "You said I was gonna get my own room."

138

"I'll make you walk the plank" I said, "if you don't behave."

"Jared!" Our eyes locked, a half-smile of challenge on both our faces.

"Law of the sea." I looked down at Cindy before she could respond. "No fancy trial, lawyers or easy jail time. We do flogging, keelhauling, hang 'em from the yardarm, lotsa neat stuff."

"What's keelhaul?"

"We'll talk about that." I picked up their luggage and turned toward the wide corridor leading toward the down escalator to the baggage carousels. "But you don't have to worry, 'cause I think you're going to be a first-class sailor."

When we arrived at the marina parking lot Stephanie shouldered her bag, picked up the picnic basket she had brought and watched Cindy struggle with her new nylon roll bag. I lugged their sleeping bags and miscellaneous boat clothes to the gate above the dock and piled everything into a two-wheel cart. I began pushing the cart toward the ramp, then stopped and turned to Cindy. "Do you know what 'Zero Tolerance is?'"

"Another one of them sea laws?"

"Exactly. Only this one is very serious. Aggressively pursued by the Coast Guard and rigidly penalized by the Drug Enforcement Agency."

Stephanie interrupted me. "Jared is this necessary?"

I held my hand up palm out without taking my eyes off Cindy.

"The Coast Guard can come aboard any boat for no reason at all and if they catch you with as much as a roach, they take your boat, impound it, arrest and fine the owner."

"Ah, they can't do that," the streetwise teen argued. "That's illegal search."

Stephanie spoke up. "No, Cindy, it is the law. If you take as much as a single joint on Jared's boat, he could lose it, never be a federal agent again, get fined and go to jail."

Cindy's grin was ear to ear. "Yeah?"

I frowned at Stephanie. "I don't think this is going to work."

Stephanie picked up Cindy's bag, grabbed her by the hand and started off toward the marina rest rooms.

"Hey!" Cindy yelled, "what y'gonna do, strip-search me?"

"You're damned right I am," Stephanie said, dragging the girl behind her.

I was still laughing as I unloaded the gear in the handcart onto my boat.

When they came aboard, Cindy snooped around below for a few minutes, then scrambled up in the 'V' berth, put on the earphones of her Walkman and began reading a comic book she extracted from her roll bag.

Stephanie gave the cutter a critical inspection topside and below, at the end of which I received her warm hug of approval. We put the sails on, I ran up the engine, then called below to invite Cindy to help steer the boat under power. Stephanie had to go down to repeat the invitation over the volume of the Walkman but my offer was refused.

We motored out of the harbor, rounding up to a westerly breeze to hoist canvas as soon as I felt the short chop of open water. Half an hour later, Cindy climbed up the companionway ladder and threw up on the cockpit sole. Stephanie admonished herself for letting her stay below in the still air where the motion of the boat was greatest, then settled her in the corner of the lee cockpit seat with a bucket and fistful of saltine crackers before cleaning up the mess. The girl was seasick during the entire three-hour sail to Eastern Bay but recovered as soon as we dropped the hook in Warehouse Creek.

Only a few boats had stopped for their noon meal in the warm afternoon sun in the shallow cove bordered by wooded marsh. Lunch was late and terrific. We set up a table in the cockpit under sparse cotton clouds in a washed-blue sky. I uncorked a bottle of white wine to go with Stephanie's heaping platter of chilled Chicken Caesar Salad and fresh-baked French bread. She had brought peanut butter and jam sandwiches for Cindy, who took them to the foredeck with a couple of throw-cushions on which she later fell asleep while Steph and I lingered in the cockpit over lunch.

We avoided the topic on both our minds until halfway through the meal, when Stephanie's irrepressible curiosity nailed it to the mast.

"Do you have any idea what you'll do now?" she asked.

"Who knows?" I took a forkful of salad, chewing slowly to give me time to think. "Take the summer off. cruise Maine with the love of my life."

"The love of your life has certain obligations," she said. "So, do you, I think."

I gave her my martyr grin. *Dutchman* moved beneath us in the water, straining gently on her anchor rode, a pleasant motion urging us to take her to sea.

I looked south through the mouth of the cove at a lone sail on Eastern Bay. A 30-foot powerboat nearby revved her engine before rattling its anchor chain back into her hold, and I thought of the attempt on our lives in the Florida Keys. I knew that if I backed off right then, whoever was after my hide might leave me alone. And probably succeed at whatever scheme they were hatching for Robinson. I might learn about it eventually along with the rest of the world. Or not. The only way anyone was going to stop what was going down before it happened was for me to find out what the hell it was.

Stephanie told me she had some news the last time we spoke on the phone, but anxious as I was about my own dilemma, I forgot to ask about it. She reminded me of that with her question about my plans.

"You discovered something about Andeweg?" I asked. Stephanie had been trying to learn if John Andeweg, who drowned with my father and seemed to be a connection between my parents and Senator Robinson. They had been in the same class at Brown University and Stephanie knew a woman in the alumnae office.

Alex had not been able to tap into the records at Brown because student data before 1960 was not on computer. Stephanie had promised to ask her friend to check the microfiche records for John Andeweg.

She took a sip of wine, then compressed her lips and

shook her head before answering. "Martha called a few retired professors Robinson and Andeweg had, plus other alumni who took the same courses. Most of them remember Andeweg, but Robinson must have been a real loner."

He still is, I thought.

"Nobody remembers a kid who turned out to be a U.S. Senator?"

"Oh, everybody knows him now and readily claim they were classmates, but no details, no pals, no vivid recollections or anecdotes like you'd expect."

"What about their academic records?" I asked.

"You're going to love this." She paused, making sure we had full eye contact. "Except for different majors, their electives were identical."

I was a little slow on the pickup. "What?"

"Charles Robinson's concentration was political science and John Andeweg was an engineering major. Both took the same distribution courses."

"They sat in the same classes?"

"Yes, they did," Stephanie said. "Brown admitted only four hundred freshmen in 1938. They took three years of German together."

"German!"

"A lot of kids did," she explained. "It seems that Brown recruited a whole slew of German scholars to the faculty who were anxious to get out from under the Nazi regime in the late 1930s. Some students tried to meet them halfway on the language barrier."

"They must have known one another!"

"Four hundred is a lot of kids."

"But the same classes. What, fifteen, twenty students per?"

"Probably knew of one another," Stephanie admitted "but friends?" She was playing devil's advocate and I knew it.

"Why not?"

"Robinson took a room off campus. Andeweg joined *Sigma Nu,* lived in the frat house. The Senator was a better student, made dean's list three years in a row, graduated magna cum laude. Andeweg's grades were average."

"Did either one of them play sports?" I asked.

"Andeweg," Stephanie answered, "was first-string catcher on the varsity baseball team. Sock and Buskin drama club, student council three years running."

"How about Robinson?"

"No sports, no extracurricular activities, no participation in student affairs or fraternities. When the war broke out, he enlisted in an army program called A-12, an on-campus officer's candidate unit. Andeweg joined the Navy program."

"It's hard to believe they were in the same classes, walking around the campus for four years," Jared said, "and never spoke."

"Oh, one thing." Stephanie shook a Lucky out of her pack, lit up and tossed the match in the water. "Andeweg worked on the Brown radio station during his sophomore and junior years."

We were stabbing in the dark and I knew it. "Anyone remember Robinson from that group?"

She exhaled a stream of smoke and shook her head again, her thick auburn hair brushing her shoulders. "I called two men who did most of the work, one was Sarnoff, son of David. Ran RCA?"

"No soap?"

"Things were hectic," Stephanie explained. "The kids created the first college radio station in the country by hooking up crystal sets and receivers to the gas pipes and radiators connecting their rooms. They called it the 'Gas Pipe Network,' messed at it between classes, all hours of the day and night. Except for a handful of organizers, it was a pretty transient operation."

"Shit! The Senator sounds like a goddamned phantom."

"I don't think Brown would alter their records just because some government bureaucrat asked them to."

"Be different if it was Yale," I said.

Stephanie wanted to know what I meant.

"That's where Colonel Bill Donovan recruited OSS agents during World War II."

"You haven't kept up," Stephanie told me. "According to

The Brown Daily Herald, good old Brown's college was a spawning ground for the CIA during the height of the Cold War and Vietnam."

"Then anything's possible."

"We're groping, though."

I knew that but ignored it. "What about the yearbook?"

Stephanie opened the thermos, concentrating on the steaming black liquid as she poured the coffee. "My friend says Andeweg's in it. Charles Robinson, however, evidently did not make the photo session."

"Dammit! So all we have is his bio listing."

Stephanie put her cup down on the table and leaned back against the cockpit combing. "Not quite. It seems that without the picture, the printer must have omitted his listing.

CHAPTER SIXTEEN
Chesapeake Bay, MD
July 1976

After lunch, we sailed out on the Chesapeake, reaching down the bay until late afternoon when I tacked back into Eastern Bay and came into the dock at the little town of Claiborne. Stephanie volunteered to walk up to the grocery store to get provisions for Sunday while I topped off on diesel, water and ice.

Cindy had remained topside during that afternoon sail, curled up in her corner of the cockpit with her Walkman headset glued to her ears, but was not seasick. When Stephanie asked her if she would like to go shopping with her, Cindy claimed she was tired and had retreated below to the 'V' berth forward.

I finished refueling and walked the boat to the end of the dock where I had made arrangements to tie up for the night. A gentle breeze blew through the open hatches and I decided to stretch out on a bunk in the main salon to wait for Stephanie's return. Cindy had opened the door of the hanging locker amidships to close off the two compartments and I assumed she was taking a nap.

I dozed off, and later could not remember what I had heard first, Stephanie's greeting from the dock or Cindy's scream in my ear. When I jumped upright, the girl swung her fist in a roundhouse punch that must have carried every ounce of her ninety-eight pounds with it, landing square on my nose which immediately began gushing blood down my chin onto my bare chest and the khaki shorts I had unbuttoned before lying down.

Cindy grabbed me around the neck, smearing her face and front with my blood, then pushed me back on the settee and continued screaming. I could see that her tee shirt was pulled up around her neck, her tiny bra unhooked, hanging from a shoulder exposing a pert, red-tipped breast streaked with my blood. Stephanie rushed down the companionway ladder and stopped.

"What in blazes is going on here?" Cindy ran at Stephanie, throwing both arms around her waist, half screaming, half crying a mixture of hysterical gulps and unintelligible words.

I stood holding a handkerchief to my nose as my unbuttoned shorts slid down my hips. "The friggin' kid's nuts!"

Stephanie wrapped her arms around Cindy, tried to pull her shirt down over her chest, then looked at me. "Why don't you go up to the men's room and clean up."

"I was sleeping. The little bitch attacked me!"

Since her initial expression of incredulity, Stephanie became composed, her tone and attitude noncommittal. "We can talk about this later."

"Later!" I wagged a bloody finger at Cindy. "That little street monster's trying to frame me as a god-dammed' child molester!"

"I'm gonna tell the cops," Cindy sobbed into Stephanie's waist.

"Come on, Cindy," Stephanie said, leading her forward to the head. "Let's get you cleaned up and find out exactly what happened."

I shook my head. "Geezes!"

When I returned, she and Cindy were seated on the starboard side of the dinette table, and I slid into the port settee opposite them.

"So, somebody's lying in their teeth," Stephanie said.

After the combatants had cleaned up and changed clothes, Stephanie made each of us tell our version of the incident in the presence of the other. Then I went for a walk while Stephanie heated the take-out spaghetti and meat sauce she bought and Cindy sulked with her Walkman in the 'V' berth.

"Why do you think Jared would do that?" Stephanie asked her during dinner.

"Cause he's just like all the rest. They get off on young

pussy."

I made a sibilant noise with my lips.

"Jared, why do you think Cindy would go to such great lengths to make me think you tried to rape her?"

I had been staring into the food on my plate that I had not touched. When I looked up, my eyes were narrowed. "Stephanie, I'm probably ten seconds from throwing the two of you off this boat and saying the hell with you and us."

"Maybe that's what she wants. Is it Cindy?" The child had been eating ravenously. She shrugged.

"To pay you back for telling me about smoking marijuana, the embarrassment of making me search your bag before you came aboard."

"Why in God's name didn't you say that in the first place? What the hell are we in here, therapy?"

"Were you trying to get back at Jared, Cindy? It's a pretty normal reaction."

"Normal!" I shouted. "So's child abuse, according to her."

Cindy stopped eating and looked at me with disgust. "You believin' him?"

"I think you tried to hurt Jared without realizing what a horrible accusation that is."

Cindy looked down at her clenched fists in her lap with no response. Then a tear fell on them and she said, "Well, it ain't too great getting" pronged by every old guy that comes along, either."

"I am sure it is the most dreadful thing that could happen."

Cindy's head snapped up with red eyes shooting pure venom at me. "An' I'm tellin' the cops soon's we get back t' Boston!"

When I had realized what Stephanie was doing, I folded my arms and leaned back against the settee. Now, I sat forward.

"Cindy, you'll ruin my life."

"Then you shouldn'ta done it!"

Stephanie held her finger up to silence me. "Cindy, you're starting to believe your own... fantasy."

"It's true!"

"Well suppose it is," she said. I started to speak, but Stephanie motioned me to be quiet.

"What do you think is going to happen after you turn Jared in to the police?"

"They'll arrest him and throw him in jail."

"And how about me?"

"What do you mean?"

"Well, this alleged attack was made by my boyfriend while you were in my care....

"Oh."

"And what do you suppose would happen to you?"

* * * * * *

It was still light when we finished dinner, but Cindy immediately crawled onto the 'V' berth and swung the locker door out closing off the forward sleeping compartment from the main salon.

Stephanie and I washed the dishes in silence, then carried a bottle of brandy, glasses and coffee out to the cockpit.

"You had me going there for a minute," I said.

"I'm sorry. There wasn't time to explain. If I had, she would have seen two adults lined up against her again."

"But the little tramp was lying!"

"She is not a little tramp, Jared."

"Well, then she's nuts, and the sooner you send her back the better."

"Do you think I treat people who are in good mental health?"

"No. But you don't bring them home to work their insanity on your friends." I hadn't touched my coffee but drained the brandy from my glass. "What if she decides to go to the police with this nutso fabrication in spite of the consequences?"

"I would refute her story."

"Sure, after the press gets their slimy teeth into it and runs my picture on network news with some talking head claiming an ex-Secret Service Agent molests little girls."

"She won't do that."

148

I poured myself another brandy. "Were you surprised she pulled that terrific rape act on me?"

"No. I certainly didn't expect it, but she hung around gangs that settle insults with guns and knives. Slash and shoot one another for a jacket, a gold bracelet."

"Then I was wrong. That kid doesn't belong in a mental institution, she belongs in jail."

"She's staying with me, Jared."

"What?" I gestured at the salon below with my drink hand and spilled brandy on the cockpit sole. "After what she tried to pull on me?"

"I am not in the habit of committing my patients to an institution because of one minor relapse."

"Minor! Lady, you got your degrees of magnitude screwed up. Y'know, I oughtta report *her* to the cops and let you corroborate that!"

Stephanie reached out and stroked my arm. "C'mon, love, let's not talk about this anymore tonight, OK?"

The dusk had come and gone and we sat under the sparse lights on the dock casting weak shadows nearby, accentuating the black bay to the south.

"I'm getting drunk," I said.

She snuggled up and put her head on my shoulder. "A little."

I spoke distinctly so I would not slur my words. "She'll have a hold on us, you know."

"What do you mean?"

"She can go to the cops with that story any time she gets ticked off at either one of us. Say it's been going on for months."

Stephanie frowned but said nothing.

"Women accused a shrink in Washington of rape and they yanked his license. Anything like that in Boston?"

"Yes," she said. "Hollywood, famous women, assistants to high-profile big shots, accusations going back ten, twenty years.

"You gotta get rid of this kid, Steph. She's bad news."

As soon as we went below, Stephanie stepped out of her

white shorts and unbuttoned her pink blouse in the main salon with an impish grin on her lips. I had not turned on the interior lamps, and the ambient light from the marina created a soft ethereal glow in the cabin. I encircled her waist with one arm, grinding the length of our bodies together from thighs to teeth as my free hand worked between our chests unfastening the remaining buttons on her blouse. Despite our urgent passion we restrained the lust-born erotic fantasies in lonely nights of the recent past to savor the luxurious pleasure of slow, varied foreplay on the double bunk.

Seconds before we were ready to consummate the act, we heard mewing in the forward compartment. Cindy might have become unsettled by some benign nightmare or recrimination, the movement of the boat in the water and strange noises of lines and rigging in the night. Stephanie pushed off me, sprang off the bunk and threw her clothes on. I looked down at my rigid appendage and screamed an obscenity.

The malicious little brat stopped crying when Stephanie went forward to comfort her, then returned to inform me that she had better sleep with the girl in the 'V' berth. I slammed the double berth extension back to its single position despite her profuse apology.

Our first real argument lasted almost an hour. When Cindy refused to return to Annapolis by boat, Stephanie suggested driving back to the airport in a rented car. I tried to convince them both that the girl would not be sick if we took *Dutchman* straight back under power. I lost both arguments without a "modicum of understanding or graciousness," according to Stephanie.

I phoned a taxi to take them to a car rental agency while Stephanie packed their bags. I attempted to mitigate the friction by insisting that Stephanie take the keys to my Georgetown apartment from which she could give Cindy a quick tour of the nation's capital the following afternoon. We parted with a silent buss on the cheek.

I beat back to Annapolis into a fifteen-knot breeze under a

cloudless blue sky, the bright sun warming my bare torso, experiencing a mixture of loneliness and anger at not sharing the day with Stephanie as I tried to erase the tension that had crept into our burgeoning romance during the past eighteen hours.

It wasn't the kid's fault, I realized. The poor little thing had her own problems. From birth no doubt, or the horror that began when her child's body started to mature. But that was the responsibility of some state agency, a foster home equipped to handle a girl with a history of sexual abuse. Neither she nor we deserved to have Cindy Farrell dropped onto a couple of people trying to start their own lives together.

Especially with all the disturbing questions I had about Senator Robinson and my father. Sure, Stephanie had every right, maybe even felt an obligation to counsel Cindy professionally. But the kid obviously wasn't ready, emotionally or otherwise, to interact in a social environment she'd never experienced before.

By the time I secured Dutchman in her slip at the marina, offloaded my gear and driven to Georgetown, it was almost eleven o'clock. I used the spare key I kept in the car to enter my apartment and found the living room couch made up with sheets, a light blanket and pillow. I assumed that Stephanie and Cindy were sleeping in my double bed behind the closed door to my room and wondered if that was the kid's idea or hers.

At six a.m. Stephanie pulled up the shades in the living room and opened the windows with more noise than necessary. She perched fully dressed on the edge of the couch, kissing me awake.

"Let's not do that again," she said, as I sat up to take the proffered cup of steaming coffee.

It had rained during the early morning hours and a moist breeze lifted the curtains at the open windows. The room felt cool despite the bright sunlight creeping across the carpet without the strength to warm it.

"Agreed." I glanced at the closed door to my bedroom

before sipping the hot liquid.

"She's glued to cartoons on the tube, Stephanie told me. "Grinding Corn Flakes into your percale sheets."

"Terrific."

My bare leg protruded from under the blanket and she ran her fingernails up and down the blond hair on my calf. "Give her a break, Jared, you're a grown man, she's just...."

"I know, I know: 'a little girl.'"

She stopped stroking my leg. "Why can't you forgive her?"

"I have. It's the next time I'm afraid of, when she gets mad at me again and goes to the police without warning either one of us. The most difficult thing to forgive is the disruption of my once a month time with the woman I'm falling in love with. Dropping you off on some strange dock to find transportation back to Georgetown. Arguing with you about some troubled kid we have no control over. I have a problem forgiving her making me sleep alone within fifteen feet of you."

"That's very selfish."

I placed the cup of coffee on the night table and tossed the covers aside, swinging my legs off the couch.

"I'm sorry if you feel that way. I have a few other things on my mind right now and I was looking forward to a little R & R with my best and only girl." I stood, picked up the empty cup and saucer and brought them into the kitchen.

When I returned, she was standing. "Well, Cindy Farrell is on my mind. She is no more disruptive to our relationship than your obsession with Senator Robinson."

"But possibly a tad more important."

"That depends on your point of view."

"Steph, we've never had an argument like this until that kid showed up. She's been fifty percent of every long-distance phone conversation we've had recently. I admire your dedication, but isn't there supposed to be some danger when a therapist gets too involved with a patient?"

She folded her arms and looked away. "Not with a child."

"Well, it's getting dangerous for us."

"Is that an ultimatum?"

My heart sank, but I was convinced our affection would sour if we endured many more days like the past two with that disturbed kid.

"You don't have to stop counseling her. Take a break from your work when I break from mine."

"Oh, thank you, Jared, for at least letting me keep my patient!"

"I didn't mean it that way. Can't you place her in a foster home or institution where she belongs, give us a chance to deepen the affection I hope we have for one another?"

"She won't be going to a home or institution."

"Oh?"

"I'm having the temp custody extended. She's going to be living with me."

"For how long?"

"For the time being."

"Thank you for letting me in on that little turn of events."

Stephanie ran her fingers through her thick auburn hair, still damp from the shower. "Maybe we ought to take a break from each other for a while."

"Yeah," I said, "you can go back to Wickford, take your precious Cindy with you, pull your little bungalow over your head and watch life pass on by with your mother."

Her head jerked back as though I had slapped her. "Jared!"

I just stared her down for a couple of seconds, watching her search the hard expression on my face. Then I turned away, padded toward the bathroom in my underwear and shut the door.

When I came out twenty minutes later she and Cindy were gone.

CHAPTER SEVENTEEN
Washington, DC
July 1976

I pulled on running shoes, shorts and an old Georgetown tee shirt, then headed up 34th to the bike paths in the Archbold Parkway, running hard for three miles under the scorching sun that soaked the gray shirt with dark perspiration, the red bandanna around my forehead unable to keep the droplets of sweat from stinging my eyes. Despite my resolve, I could not purge my mind of the disturbing incident of Saturday evening, Stephanie's reaction to Cindy or the enigma surrounding Senator Robinson and my father all tangled together.

During my cool-down walk back to my apartment, I was even more confused about what my next move should be and was seriously doubting if I should make one. I was no longer a Secret Service Agent. Senator Robinson was not my responsibility. I would have all I could handle trying to salvage my romance with Stephanie, get a job.

I spotted the tail halfway down 39th Street--two male Caucasians in a gray '74 Buick sedan. At first, there was no way to tell if they were Burnett's idea, guys from the Bureau or more Germans. Whoever they were, they seemed pretty casual about it. A single car, no deception, just keeping track of where I was going. Maybe they wanted me to see them, to show me they wouldn't tolerate any more interference from a civilian and were ready to pounce if I kept sniffing around.

I assumed that the Service and Bureau were working in tandem under the Senator's orders or on his behalf. Either way, the U.S. government was hiding something significant that would probably derail the campaign of the leading presidential candidate if made public.

That secret seemed to involve a key, some document, a

country the United States defeated in the Second World War and coincidentally, the death of my father. I found it hard to believe that two federal law enforcement agencies under the current administration would conspire to get a bogus politician elected president. Or cover up the murder of an innocent man and grant a Nazi hit squad open season on my life. If the top cops weren't holding hands with the Germans, how did those foreign nationals know so much so fast about my inquiries and whereabouts? A pipeline from the US government to a friendly embassy was not unheard of, but interfering in the election of our chief executive was hardly the activity of a friendly nation.

I realized there might be no connection between the Feds and the espionage elements at the German embassy. The Eastern Block krauts could be running a scam of their own against the Senator and the whole country. Maybe I was getting too close to finding out what it was. There seemed to be more than one game being played on the same field. I didn't know the purpose of the contest, what players were on which team or who was opposing who. I certainly didn't know what the score was.

The gray Buick crawled past me and the clown in the passenger seat was grinning, even though he continued looking straight ahead. Not one of our guys, I hoped. What the hell was I thinking about? I didn't have any guys any more. The Buick pulled in next to a fire hydrant down from my apartment and one of the men got out of the car and lifted the hood. I walked past my building which must have confused my tail, because the man got back in the car that just sat there.

Walking down the sidewalk, sweating from every pore in the hot sun, I suddenly felt exhausted. I didn't want to play games with those baby sitters, I wanted them out of my life, time to get my jumbled thoughts together, maybe say the hell with everything after all. I looked up and realized I had walked to the edge of campus and was staring across the quadrangle at Dahlgren Chapel.

I must have sat there in the subdued light of the cool nave

for a couple of hours. I did not go to church often or know any formal prayers but did believe there was a Supreme Being that ran things. We had a pretty good conversation that day. The responsibility I felt for the death of John Goddard was the big issue, but I kept losing my concentration, drifting around to the Senator. Stephanie. And riding a one-man posse that was screwing my life up.

Half my mind wanted to take out my savings, toss my gear on *Dutchman* and sail off to Tahiti. That part resented the obligation I felt to see the people who killed John pay for their crime; and to Stephanie because I could not run off and leave her. The other half realized it could never live with the rest of me if I didn't make sure the country knew the real man behind the phantom they seemed determined to elect to the presidency of their country. And every gene in my body was screaming to learn what had really happened to my father.

Now that I was out in the cold, I should take what I had to Bob Woodward and Carl Bernstein at *The Post*--let them do the same thing on this they did with Nixon and Watergate three years ago. But what did I have? A bunch of groundless accusations by a disgruntled ex-government employee. The Washington press had been inundated with so-called tips on political corruption ever since.

The *Post'* won the Pulitzer Prize, but no responsible reporter would look into anything without hard evidence. The Germans broke into the Senator's condo, not his party headquarters.

God didn't say much about all this or maybe He did. Because when I walked out of that chapel there was no doubt in my mind what I had to do.

It was late afternoon when I walked down the steps of the chapel and started for home. I didn't spot the Buick until the driver turned north on 38th Street. They had not even bothered changing cars. With that kind of arrogance, it had to be the Bureau, and the message was clear: they'd be on my ass like stink on shit.

Inside my apartment, I ripped off my malodorous

running gear, showered, then tossed clean underwear and warm clothes in a nylon roll bag, listening to the messages on my answering machine while wrapped in a damp towel. The one from Judith Silverman convinced that me that I was not a paranoid idiot.

"... not sure what it means, but I thought you'd better know. Gunter Knopf came back into the country through customs at Logan International in Boston three days ago. I lodged a formal protest with Dietrich at the German embassy, but they claim no knowledge. He wasn't PNG, so we didn't catch up with it until yesterday. Now he's disappeared."

That could have been the end of the message except for the sound of whispering tape and Judith dragging on a cigarette, blowing the smoke against the telephone mouthpiece in her office at State. "I told Burnett and Talbot," she continued," but they don't seem concerned." Her voice lost its usual confidence. "It's probably nothing, but Gunter Knopf is on the loose somewhere in the U S of A, and I thought you should know."

If Kurt Henzler, AKA Gerhardt Hoffmann, was *Baader-Meinhof*, Knopf probably was too. Back here to dig around for the elusive key again. Or worse, if they still believed the Senator had it. Dammit! That was all I needed.

I threw on a pair of sun-faded Levi's, polo shirt and Topsiders, grabbed the .45 semi-automatic Colt from the back of my bedroom closet shelf, slapped a full magazine in the butt and jammed a box of shells with two spare magazines into the bag.

Packy Papadopoulos was maître d' in a Rosslyn restaurant, who lived in the apartment building behind me. My penchant for souvlakia and Packy's for married women had led to an arrangement which Melissa found extremely distasteful, except when Packy treated her like a queen in his culinary establishment. On occasions, Packy found it necessary to find an alternate exit for his women and/or himself other than the front door of his own building. In those circumstances, the escapee(s) would climb to his roof, cross onto my building via two extended fire escapes, use a dupe of my key to open the rooftop access door to the interior, walk down the stairs and out the front door of my building. Packy had insisted that I keep a key to his building also, just in case Melissa came home unexpectedly some fortuitous afternoon during one of the illicit dalliances to which he assumed I was just as prone as he.

I rummaged through my bureau drawers until I found it, pulled a White Sox cap down low on my forehead, climbed up to the roof and out the front door of Packy's apartment building. After walking several blocks, I was sure no one was following, and took a cab to the Greyhound Bus Terminal. I used my bank card to withdraw the limit from an ATM, then boarded the 10:30 bus for Annapolis.

* * * * * *

When I motored *Dutchman* out of the harbor at one o'clock in the morning, all I had on board to eat was a box of crackers and a can of peaches. I needed distance between me and the District in case they started hunting in earnest, so I sailed down the Chesapeake, stopping in at Onancock Creek on the eastern shore of Virginia, anchored off a sandy beach inside Ware Point where I slept until noon, then took on fuel, water, ice and groceries from the general store.

Beating down the bay for the first hundred miles took me thirty hours, even using the engine when I lost the wind. Out on coastal waters, the next five hundred miles should have been downhill with the prevailing south westerly's. If the forecast held, it would take four days of round-the-clock sailing to get to Boston.

Even if they figured out what I had done, they would have a difficult time finding me out there--the Coast Guard had trouble locating bigger boats than *Dutchman* when they didn't know where to look. If they thought I might be fifty miles out on the ocean, the Feds and the Germans would probably leave me alone.

A gigantic red sun dropped behind the Virginia mainland as I rounded Cape Charles. The wind picked up out of the southwest and *Dutchman* began sliding up the coast on a broad reach at a good six knots. A long swell began to heave the rippled surface in the lingering twilight, breaking lazy whitecaps for miles around on the empty sea. I engaged the autopilot, snapped the tether of my safety harness on the windward jackline, then walked forward to set the whisker pole on the number one jenny.

I kept watch at night, napping in the cockpit during the day when other boats could look out for me, waking up every couple of hours to check my course, adjust the auto pilot and scan the magnificent barren ocean.

The rumb line for the Cape Cod Canal took me 63 miles off the Jersey coast on a clear night with the lights of Atlantic City glowing on the distant horizon. The next night, I crossed the New York shipping lanes under overcast skies, dodging the dark outlines and towering running lights of container ships and supertankers gliding to and from the busiest port in the world.

The Senator had over 1,700 delegate votes going into the Convention, 600 more than he needed for his party's nomination. With almost eighty percent of the delegates behind him, his last opponent had dropped out of the race three weeks before. The nominating process would be a formality. Senator Robinson would oppose the incumbent president in the general election on the first Tuesday in November. Unless the unthinkable happened. Again.

The previous day NOAA weather had announced a surprise nor'easter. As *Dutchman* passed Montauk Point on the tip of Long Island with a hundred miles to go to Boston, the barometer fell like a piano from a ten-story window. I shortened sail, secured loose gear below and dogged the hatches. Half an hour later, the temperature dropped twenty degrees and black clouds carried sheets of rain down from the east.

By noon Monday, the convention had been called to order. My favorable breeze backed to fifty degrees and increased to gale-force winds. *Dutchman*'s bow plunged into seven-foot waves, rising again with seawater cascading aft along both catwalks. I turned on the engine and the little cutter pounded into the heavy seas under storm jib and trysail, barely making headway against the angry elements. Her twenty-eight-foot wooden hull struggled up each mountain of water, her single propeller beating air as she slid down the other side, losing almost as much ground as she gained, like some amphibian Sisyphus.

A nor'easter usually lasts three days and I began to worry that I would not arrive in Boston until the convention was over. From my advance briefing the previous month, I knew the Senator would not arrive at Hynes Convention Center until Thursday night to deliver his acceptance speech. Until then, he would rest in his suite, polish his presentation and confer with his aides. As dictated by tradition, he would be out of the public eye, inaccessible to strangers from Monday, right up to a fund-raising banquet in the hotel on Thursday evening. That's when both of Senator Robinson's seventeen-man protective details would go to work in earnest.

Despite Burnett's casual response to Knopf's re-entry into the country, I knew the Service would tighten security around the Senator--especially since Judith Silverman claimed that both Germans had disappeared. The Bureau might try to find them, but there was still no threat on the candidate's life or proof of conspiracy. Since they hadn't believed me during those past months, it was unlikely they would set up a special task force now, because they did not think they had anything to point it at.

But I did. Gunter Knopf would not come back to risk criminal charges for John Goddard's murder unless he had a specific job to do. A job that had to be related to unfinished business or they would have sent someone else. Showing up ten days before the convention meant his business would take place then and involve Senator Robinson.

The visibility was so poor, it didn't matter whether I stood watch or not--if a tanker was going to run me down, I would feel it before I saw it. I had put hot soup in a thermos before the storm hit but consumed it in the first twelve hours. Cooking in those conditions would leave me scalded or scraping food off the overhead, so I lived on cold sandwiches and milk. I dozed in the cockpit by day, huddled against the cabin housing to avoid the stinging spray and behind a lee cloth in a bunk below during the black hours of interminable night. Every couple of hours I forced myself to estimate my position on the sodden chart, but other than using the depth sounder to make sure *Dutchman* wasn't being blown onto the lee Connecticut shore, I could not tell where I was.

The storm finally began to abate on Wednesday noon, and Block Island loomed on the gray horizon under dark scudding clouds. I was exhausted from lack of sleep, bracing against the violent motion of the boat and wrestling the helm for hours at a time when the auto pilot faltered. There was no way I could navigate Buzzards Bay and the Canal in that shape. At four o'clock in the afternoon, I pulled into Great Salt Pond on the southwest side of the island, picked up a mooring off Champlain's dock and collapsed on a bunk with salt spray caked on my unshaved face and a week's body odor trapped inside my foul weather gear.

All I could see was the blond head half-submerged in the water, the crinkled fingers of the hand clawing toward me from the sodden sleeve of a black knit sweater. A white circle of light pierced the night, playing across the surface of the heaving ocean, creating a misty penumbra in the dense fog.

As I leaned down to grab the extended hand, the arm thrashed beyond my grasp, jerking the head beneath the water. Something just beyond the rim of light was dragging him under into the darkness, out of my reach. The head bobbed back above the surface, blond hair plastered against his forehead, a wild look of fear and anger flashing in the pale blue eyes. He looked directly at me for the first time and his gaze seemed to shift from his immediate predicament to something far more significant as it stabbed my heart with a force that sapped my strength.

The outstretched hand seemed paralyzed beneath mine, my mind straining to decipher a wordless message from another world. Finally, his head was pulled beneath a wave followed by the rigid arm in dark wet wool, his claw-like hand

slipping silently below the surface.
   "Dad!" I screamed, "Dad!"

* * * * * *

Groping down over the edge of my bunk, I fell sprawled across the cabin sole, dazed and sweating inside the layers of wool shirts and foul-weather gear. I crawled to a sitting position on the damp floorboards and leaned against a settee in darkness, knees bent, bearded face buried in dirty hands and cried like a frightened child.

* * * * * *

I woke before dawn and wolfed down a can of hash, four eggs, stale bread and coffee in *Dutchman*'s cockpit, watching a huge orange sun lift into a sky of vibrant blue beyond the cliffs of the island. The storm had cleared the midsummer haze off the Rhode Island coast and a light southeasterly skittered cats-paws around the other yachts moored in the harbor. The breeze would die before noon and I would never make it to Boston in time for the fund-raising banquet that night or the Senator's acceptance speech to the convention delegates. I made sure *Dutchman* was secure, packed a duffel, then pumped up the Avon and rowed to the marina for a hot shower and the Block Island ferry.

CHAPTER EIGHTEEN
Boston, MA
July 1976

When I got off the bus from Providence I called the CP in the Boston Copley Plaza and the radio operator patched me through to Paul Hunsacker at the Hynes Convention Center.

"Am I hot?" I asked him.

"Not particularly," Paul said. "He's got other things to worry about."

"The krauts?"

"Yeah. All we have is the artist's sketch. With a good disguise, we're dead."

"That's why I need to get inside tonight. I saw him. Know his face, bulk, stance, walk, mannerisms."

"Gee, I don't know, pal."

"Where will you be?"

"Portal three. Employees, press."

"Perfect. I'll look different, show you a card and walk through."

"I don't know, Jared. Be my ass."

"You think I'm a threat?"

"Of course not."

"Could I have a better chance of spotting the kraut?"

Paul was a conscientious agent who had been assigned to Mrs. Kennedy in 1962 because he was an expert skier. He'd been riding chase that November in Dallas. His sigh was audible. "OK, OK. It starts at eight, so seven-forty-five would be good. I'll be on the left."

I spent a couple of hours that afternoon using my powers of persuasion. First in a Boylston Street tailor shop convincing the proprietor to alter the worn suit I had purchased at a Salvation Army shop by six o'clock that evening. Then persuading the owner of a Newbury Street hair salon to squeeze me in between appointments to dye my blond hair black. The matching brush mustache and thick, non-prescription glasses I bought in a theatre costume supply store, plus a third-hand Hasselblad and Nikon SLR cameras hanging around my neck transformed my physical appearance into a nondescript, free-lance press photographer. A generic photo ID press card from a hole-in-the-wall print shop in Boston's South End completed my thin ruse and might even have justified Paul issuing me a legitimate press pass for the convention.

When I stood before Paul in a noisy, jostling line of workers and other authorized personnel that evening, my friendly agent took a couple of seconds to acknowledge me with a flick of an eye, peering into my black-rim glasses, inspecting the contents of my canvas case, and cameras before passing me through the metal detector.

I moved toward the linen-draped tables crowded together in the huge ballroom, joining a thick stream of excited members of the Senator's political party who had contributed $500 each to his campaign coffers. Three Secret Service agents stood at each entrance checking invitations and two humps from the bomb squad roamed the hall with Labrador retrievers trained to sniff out explosives. There must have been thirty agents in the room who would be joined by another eight or ten escorting the candidate, plus fifteen more in and outside the hotel. The Service did not do much better than this for POTUS, which meant Burnett was taking the German threat seriously. The same precautions would be in place at the convention later that night when the Senator made his acceptance speech.

I knew I never would have gotten within a mile of CANDY without Paul--how in blazes did the kraut expect to get at Senator Robinson in here? If he did, I could have a problem picking him out of the crowded room, especially if he'd gone to the same lengths to disguise his appearance as I had.

I stood against the left wall near the podium with a TV cameraman and several other photographers who also thought that was the best position to watch the entire room.

I began taking inventory of the crowd through the telescopic lens of my Nikon. The room was almost full, and waitpersons started serving the fruit cup.

The Senator made his entrance to a roaring ovation and 'God Bless America' rendered by a live band with a young vocalist who did a pretty fair job imitating the bell-clear voice of Kate Smith. When the prolonged welcome died down, everyone took their seats and the agents at the doors sealed the room. The Senator went to the podium to thank everyone for their contributions, then introduced the members of his national campaign staff at the head table.

Every time I saw that military posture, that piercing look of total sincerity, the white hair, neat beard, the black eye patch--I found it hard to believe that the man was a fraud. But at that moment I knew he was and felt more determined than ever to prove it.

"Please continue serving that expensive Boston scrod," he told the wait staff to the laughter of the crowded room. "Tonight, I'm going to give you loyal supporters something for the hard-earned money you donated to my campaign. A little taste of what the rest of this country can expect in January, something for their money."

The diners gave him another round of applause, and although he said he appreciated it, urged them to continue eating, but asked for their undivided attention and to hold their applause while he gave them a preview of his nomination acceptance speech.

I took photographs during the meal, constantly scanning every table, waiter and other roving person in the ballroom. That's when I spotted Gunter Knopf. I had seen him only once, the day I confronted him in the Senator's home, but I'd recognize that kraut anywhere in spite of the blond wig and waitress get up. He was standing with his hands clasped in front of his red vest on the platform decked out with red, white, and blue bunting, rocking back and forth on the balls of his feet, features a closed mask, seemingly oblivious to the serving activities going on throughout the room. How the hell did he pass clearance to get in here?

Instinctively, my feet began to move in Knopf's direction, but stopped. Here I was fired from the Service, in disguise, violating security, disobeying direct orders from the FBI and my ex-superiors to stay out of this case. The only way the German could get up there was with a valid union card and documentation of several months' tenure as a Boston hotel waitress. He probably got assigned to the head table by bribing the steward.

If I warned Murphy now, he'd hustle the kraut and me off for interrogation. Which could give Henzler, their prime shooter, probably a trained assassin, an open field to the Senator. Maybe that was their plan. If they thought I'd be here to screw things up: put Knopf out in the clear, let me roust him as a diversion, then Henzler could make his move. But how? The detail had the room covered like a summit meeting. Nobody could get a gun in there. If Knopf pulled a knife, the humps standing up there would grab him in seconds. I had to wait to find out.

* * * * * *

"The United States of America is at war," the Senator said. "A war of survival--that we are losing."

The guarded whispers ceased, the clinking of glasses and silverware arrested as his supporters stopped eating and Senator Robinson continued speaking to the hushed room of 2,000 people. "Not a cold war of subterfuge and intrigue. Not a badly conceived and poorly executed guerrilla fiasco in the impenetrable jungles of some foreign land. Not a war of philosophy, a fight against hunger or a battle for outer space. But a war of economics in which American jobs are being ceded to foreign nations."

The room erupted in sustained applause despite his prior admonition as busboys continued clearing tables and I saw Knopf head for the staging area to pick up the next course for the head table. A half dozen wait people were between the kraut and me in the fast-moving line through the food disbursement room and I held my breath until he walked back through the swinging doors into the banquet hall with a serving tray loaded with plates of Boston Scrod balanced professionally on his shoulder as the Senator addressed his audience.

I tried to keep an eye on Gunter Knopf and stay on the lookout for Henzler while waiters, waitresses and bus boys hustled between tables, in and out of the service area, trays at shoulder height obscuring their faces. If Henzler was there, he could be playing the same game Knopf and I were. Maybe I wouldn't spot him until it was too late. My great plan suddenly seemed like a joke. I came here to nail an assassin only I could recognize but couldn't find--was afraid to grab an accomplice I could, and stood there like an idiot waiting for them to do what they came for.

"......solve the problem," the Senator was saying "or surrender without ever doing battle. When I am president, I will use the power of that office to balance our trade agreements with every nation. I will work with Congress to restrict dominant foreign investments in our major industries. To prevent foreign entities from taking over U.S. corporations. Diminish our debts to countries that are beginning to hold our financial future hostage; demand an accelerated repayment schedule of credit extended to governments squandering the loans and misappropriating the financial aid we've given them. Prohibit the wholesale purchase and development of American real estate by offshore interests."

He lowered his voice and seemed to wonder aloud. "If we sell our land and are in debt to the world, what will we have?" He was asking every man and woman in the room, "What will become of us? Of the United States of America? Of our children's children?"

Knopf had served the people at the head table and seemed to be concentrating on keeping their glasses filled with water. I still couldn't see Henzler anywhere.

"As in all wars," Senator Robinson was saying, "we will need to sacrifice. Stockholders cannot continue demanding high dividends. Corporate officers must forego obscene compensation. Workers and unions cannot insist on wage

167

increases that are pricing our products higher than imports right here in our own stores.

"We must bring our footwear and textiles back from Asia. Our electronics home from China and Japan. Our steel back from Germany. We must produce quality automobiles at competitive prices. We must buy American and rebuild America."

The Senator's platform proselytization and his campaign speeches had suggested this sobering theme during the past eight months, but he had never spelled it out as clearly as he did that night. This was the fiery banner of patriotism he would wave for the rest of the campaign. An uncompromising flag of hope he believed would appeal to voters weary of non-issues, vague promises and confused direction. A drastic, sharp-edged philosophy that would propel him into the White House in an avalanche of popular support.

Was this why the Germans were out to get him? How could they know the Senator would take this stand?

Senator Robinson finished his address to an awestruck audience, standing tall and relaxed at the podium, hands gripping the sides of the lectern, his eye challenging the crowd to support or oppose him. A smattering of applause broke the stunned silence of the room and grew, gathering momentum and volume, building to a booming crescendo of approbation as men and women began standing at their tables. There were no cheers or whistles, just the swelling thunder of 4,000 hands beating together in their acceptance of an idea that had moved them, a summons they were ready to meet, a leader they would gladly follow.

Gunter Knopf spoke to one of the busboys who began clearing the head table as the German left the podium and walked through the double doors to the food service area. By the time I reached the serving room he was pushing another set of swinging doors leading to the kitchen. I followed him into the noisy confusion of a dozen cooks preparing petit fours and coffee for the banquet under the supervision of a black chef sporting a van-dyke and the tall, starched hat of his profession. Men and women in food-soiled white uniforms and aprons stirred voluminous stainless-steel pots on industrial stoves, removed trays of pastry from ovens, shouting to one another across tables of cluttered butcher block. I recognized an agent standing against the wall as Knopf disappeared through a wide archway off to the left. This was no time for explanations, so I just said, "Jake " to the hump on duty and kept on walking after the receding waitress.

"Barnes," the agent replied, completing the password of the day with the surname of the main character in Hemingway's novel, '*The Sun Also Rises*,' accompanied by a puzzled expression as he moved in behind me. He wasn't sure who I was or what was happening, nor did he alert our Command Post on his walkie-talkie. CANDY was fifty yards away and in no apparent threat from the kitchen.

The archway led to a large storage area with pallets of boxed canned goods, sacks of flour, sugar and other kitchen supplies. Knopf was jogging down an aisle of stacked cartons toward the wide sliding door of a loading platform at the far end of the room, still wearing his waitress get-up.

The agent caught me just as the kraut threw the lock on the door and Kurt Henzler wrestled a trash barrel in off the outside dock. We both knew that an agent was guarding the service alley to prevent anyone coming in that way until the Senator left the banquet hall and realized we had an incapacitated or dead buddy out there.

The hump beside me still didn't know who I was, so he pushed me against the wall of boxes and raised his walkie-talkie to his mouth while we were still thirty feet from the two men at the doorway. Henzler reached into the barrel, withdrew a silenced Luger and shot the agent in the chest. As the kraut swung the pistol in my direction the agent got off one shot on his way down that opened a neat red hole under the German's left eye.

When I bent down to retrieve the agent's gun, Knopf pulled a metal briefcase out of the barrel and started jogging toward me, unsnapped the clasps and reached into the case.

"Bomb! Blow the whole fucking hotel," he shouted in heavily accented English. I had vowed to lay down my life for my protectee, but that didn't include taking him and hundreds of people with me. I straightened up and held my hands out at shoulder level as Knopf stopped three feet away from where I stood.

"Smart woman," he said, then gestured with the briefcase to the agent at our feet. "Drag him between boxes. *Schnell!* Quick, quick!"

The kraut saw an androgynous news photographer, not a Secret Service agent--small threat to him and his plan. Reaching under the arms of the unconscious man, I pulled him as gently as possible between two rows of canned goods as I heard Knopf kick the agent's walkie-talkie under a pallet. Knopf must have picked up the agent's snub, because I just started to look around for it after dragging the limp body across the cement floor and the Kraut swung the butt of a gun at my head in a wide arc.

When I came to, the old bean felt like Hank Aaron had hit it with a Louisville Slugger. I couldn't have been out for more than thirty seconds, because the blow had glanced off the side of my thick Dutch skull as I turned. I used the stacked cartons to pull myself to my feet and realized I was all alone. The agent's shot must have been muffled by the cavernous storeroom piled to the ceiling with large boxes and noise in the kitchen.

I couldn't find the agent's walkie-talkie, his gun or the Luger, but the metal case Knopf was carrying lay open on the floor. I bent over to get a closer look and my head nearly fell into it. When the vertigo stopped, I knelt down and put my hand in the padded container. It felt like a warming oven. Food! The Senator would consume his dinner after his speech and Knopf was serving him poisoned food.

As I ran back into the main aisle, I noticed that Henzler's body was no longer sprawled in front of the doors to the shipping platform. This was a hit and run operation that wouldn't leave any dead or wounded to let us prove who did it. By the time the Senator felt the effects of the poison,

Knopf would be on his way back to his fatherland. If Henzler was dead, his embassy would probably ship him home in a sealed crate like they did with George Burger.

I ran through the kitchen shoving sous-cooks out of the way, sending dessert trays flying off the counters, knocking a waitress flat on her ass as I pushed through the swinging doors to the serving area, bumping a coffeepot out of a waiter's hand, leaving a trail of angry wait people shouting behind me. Knopf was walking up the steps of the head table platform to deliver the Senator's meal as I burst through the doors into the banquet hall.

The kraut still had the agent's and Henzler's guns, so yelling at the humps on the dais could provoke anything from murder to getting me gagged and hustled away before I could explain what was going on. The guys behind The Senator went on alert when they saw me approach, hesitated when I slowed down, held up my press badge, pointing my Hasselblad camera out at the room full of diners.

Knopf and I couldn't have been out back more than three minutes. The candidate was shaking hands with his national campaign manager as the sustained ovation began to subside, the strength of its previous volume echoing from the walls and chandeliers hung high in the room. Knopf was standing behind the Senator's chair, perspiration on his forehead, trying to control his breathing, holding a dinner plate with a silver warming cover in both hands. I felt like I was moving in slow motion, pretending to take pictures of the audience, my camera pointed away from the Senator, trying to close the gap between me and Knopf before the agents hustled me away or the kraut saw me and pulled one of the guns I was certain he had.

The applause died off and the excitement of a thousand conversations replaced it as the diners resumed their seats to attack their desserts. Senator Robinson sat down at the head table and Knopf stepped forward, lifting the silver cover off the plate before placing the deadly food in front of him.

Then everything happened at once. I dropped the camera,

pretended to stumble forward and lunged full-tilt at the Senator, swiping his dinner plate off the table and him off his chair, then fell on the German assassin, tackling his knees, driving him a dozen feet down the length of the raised platform, the Senator and his dinner pate skidding down the coarse tufts of red carpet that was scraping the pancake makeup off Knopf's closely shaved face. The two humps piled on us as though we were on fire and I could hear other agents rushing the Senator out of the room to the startled shouts of his supporters.

Knopf lay pinned under me with his face in the plate of fish, immobile for a few seconds, then began to struggle like a man infused with superhuman strength. He bucked so hard that he lifted me and the agents off his back, tossing one of them aside onto the floor. Somebody else tried to hold him down and the German arched up on his hands and knees, throwing the man over his head.

With my glasses off and mustache askew, an agent knelt on my back with his snub pressed into the back of my neck. All I could do was watch several other humps try to hold the German still.

Suddenly, Knopf gave a powerful thrust of his shoulders, tossing two more agents in the air. His spine snapped into a backward arch and he lay still, his grotesque features inches from my own, eyes glazed, his face twisted in agony, the white flakes of Senator Robinson's fish dinner clinging to his purple lips.

* * * * * *

Ken Burnett reminded me of a balding Raggedy Ann doll with a loose neck as he shook his lowered head from side to side. We were sitting on wooden folding chairs in the on-site trailer outside the Hynes Center. The low voices of the agents manning the communications equipment in the next room filtered through the thin partition. Murphy, in charge of the combined details assigned to protect the candidate during the convention was seated next to me at a narrow Formica table. Roger Talbot sat across the table beside Mark Lothrop, an eager young man with a ponytail who served as the Senator's press secretary began pumping Burnet for information.

They quizzed me from all angles on every minute from the time I left Nashville to half an hour before, but I did not tell them much more than they already knew. Burnett smiled at the media maven.

Ken said, "You can quote me on the facts, Mr. Lothrop, but we're not ready to go to the public yet with the details of our investigation."

Lothrop held up a miniature recorder and Burnett spoke for posterity. "The Secret Service learned that a right-wing German organization called the *Baader-Meinhof* Gang was planning a violent disruption to the electoral process for the American presidency.

"Based on that intelligence, the Secret Service initiated extreme protective measures for all presidential candidates during the past few months, particularly at the national conventions of both political parties."

Lothrop interrupted, "You mean all the candidates were in danger, including the President?"

"Not with the extraordinary security measures taken by their protective details."

"Then Senator Robinson," Lothrop persisted, "was not the specific target of these assassins?"

"Not according to the information, we had," Burnett lied. "But he is the leading candidate."

"Has this *Baader* group claimed responsibility?"

"No--this is something we think they'll deny, avoiding the outrage of the American people and our full-scale retaliation."

"So, you can't prove who was behind the attack or why...."

"We will," Murphy interrupted.

"International terrorists out to assassinate or abduct a U.S. Senator, our next president," Lothrop said. "You have to know more about that!"

"Keep it up," Talbot gestured at the recorder, "I'll take that tape, and you'll live a solitary existence for a while." Lothrop opened his mouth and Talbot added, "National Security can temporarily override the First Amendment."

The press secretary tugged at his ponytail, then switched his line of questioning. "Agent Coughlin comes up a pretty big hero on this, right? Maybe saving the Senator's life tonight, getting wounded last winter when they burgled his home."

I wondered how Burnett would field that one, but his answer was not surprising. "There are no heroes in the Secret Service, Mr. Lothrop. Our job is to protect the men we're assigned to. Several agents were undercover tonight. Coughlin happened to be in position to do what all of us have been trained to do given the same opportunity."

"Didn't you fire Coughlin a couple of weeks ago?"
Burnett flashed me his good ol' buddy grin. "That's what we hoped the opposition would believe. Agent Coughlin was the only one who actually saw the Germans in person. Evidently Gunter Knopf never left the country as mandated. We're checking into how that happened. When Kurt Henzler slipped back and disappeared we wanted him to think Coughlin was off the job, coax the German out in the open."

"Pretty good," Lothrop admitted. "The media will love it!"

"All part of the job," Burnett said. I nearly threw up.

Lothrop cutback to a subject he hadn't finished with. "Maybe they want to assassinate the Senator because of his stance on reparation."

"I don't think that's on the agenda of terrorists," Burnett said.

"And how could they know that," Talbot asked, "until the Senator's speech tonight?"

Listening to the two lawmen, I thought that despite their rivalry, they sounded like a couple of husbands defending their wife and children. I could have jumped in with my own theories, but then I would be forced to defend my premise that the Senator knew about the key and document the Germans were trying to steal from his condo last February—which I could not do at that juncture with any credibility.

The door of the conference room opened and we all stood as Senator Robinson came in from the CP area.

"I am in your debt again, Agent Coughlin."

"He was just doing his job," Burnett told him.

The Senator's gaze had fixed on me when he entered the room and didn't waver even as he answered Burnett. "I am aware of the circumstances, Agent Burnett."

A peculiar expression came over Robinson's face as though he was torn between appreciation and anger from our last conversation. He seemed to regret getting me fired, but I knew he would not admit having any knowledge of items the Germans intended to burgle from his home.

"You will accompany me to Naushon," he continued, a half-smile replacing the enigmatic look. "Light duty. We all need the rest before the big push toward November."

"Yes sir."

"*Spielen sie Tennis?*" [Do you play tennis?] he asked. Pretty fair German for someone who took it in college thirty-four years ago.

"*Ja, mein Herr, aber ich bin ein bischen aus der Ubung.*" [Yes, sir. I'm a little rusty but need the exercise.] I could feel a wall going up around the two of us, excluding everyone else in the room.

"*Wie war's mit ein paar leichten Spielen auf der Insel?*" [How about a few easy sets on the island?] Senator Robinson asked.

"*Sehr gern, mein Herr.*" [I'd be happy to do so, sir.] If the Senator could find time to play tennis on the island so could I.

Senator Robinson walked around the table, stood directly in front of me and extended his hand. "I suggest you get your hair washed," he said in English, as he grasped my hand and squeezed it in both of his. A warm grin broke through the white beard. "You'll never be anybody's fair-haired boy in that rig.

* * * * * *

I took a taxi to Stephanie's apartment on Beacon Hill. Her greeting was cool, but I apologized for my anger at Cindy spilling over on her and explained that in retrospect I wasn't as angry at the kid was the at the vicious incident.

"If I ever want to ruin somebody's life," I quipped, "I'll ask Cindy for suggestions."

She melted into my embrace with relief, then pulled back. "Don't ever try to run my life, Jared." Her eyes were moist, but her voice firm. "I respect your judgment; I expect you to respect mine. Especially my professional judgment. If we differ, we'll work it out. Or not. Understood?"

When I told her what had happened at The Hynes, she debriefed me as thoroughly as Burnett. But the rewards were infinitely better. She cuddled against me on her couch, rubbing my arm with slow strokes as we watched the Senator deliver his acceptance speech from the high bunting-festooned platform at the convention.

When it was over, we lay on her double bed with the streetlight slanting in through the Venetian blinds on the open window, falling across the sheet in alternate slats of dark and white. Underneath, our bodies were warm and slick with perspiration, touching from calf to shoulder, reluctant to separate after our ecstatic exercise.

"You're still not satisfied," she said.

"Steph, I never had a better screwing in my life."

She jabbed my ribs with her elbow. "That is not what I meant."

I watched the headlights from a passing car ricochet across the walls, a mirror, then the ceiling, brightening the room for several seconds, illuminating the vague shapes of her bureau and dresser, a chair in the corner, leaving behind the gray darkness of early morning.

"It's not over," I told her. "We still don't know what's going on or why."

"The FBI will handle that now, won't they? Tonight, must have convinced them there's some kind of conspiracy going on."

"They might have one working with the Senator."

"Jared, that doesn't make sense!"

"Because we don't have all the answers."

She reached over to the night table for a cigarette, lit up

and smoked for a few minutes without saying anything, inhaling several puffs. Rain began to spit against the window panes as daggers of heat lightening flashed across the sky.

Finally, she spoke without looking at me. "So you're going to get them."

"Do you buy the fact," I asked her, "there's a vacuum in the Senator's past?"

"There seems to be."

"That people in the FBI and Service are covering it up?"

"It looks that way."

"That the Senator and those same people who must know why the Germans are trying to prevent Robinson from becoming president are keeping it hidden from the voters, the press and me?"

She turned her head on the pillow. "Why would they keep it from you? You're one of them. You have top security clearance, don't you?"

"That's my point! They must think I'll force their secret out in the open...if I find whatever I'm digging at."

"Which means they don't trust you."

"Not with this, they don't."

"Jared, what in God's name could it be?"

I swung my legs over the side of the bed, slipped into my shorts and flicked the switch of the lamp on the night table. My duffel bag was on the chair in the corner. I dug around in it for a couple of seconds then came back and put my black-and-white photo of my mother and father down on the bed sheet. Beside it, I placed the Senator's old picture of himself and the woman who resembled my mother.

"Look what happens when I put these together like this." I slid half of my photo over the Senator's, so my mother blocked out the other woman and covered my father with the palm of my hand. Now the two 8x10 glossies merged into a single photograph without my father or Robinson's fiancé in it, just my mother and young Charles Robinson.

"My, God!" Stephanie said. "Except for the unknown woman, both prints could have been made from the same roll, sequential negatives."

177

"The perspective is the same, the lighting, depth of field, grain, their attire. Which means my mother and Senator Robinson had their picture taken together." I nudged the two shots into tighter alignment on the bed. "Everything seems to be the same including the time—the summer of '41, the summer my father drowned."

"In your mother's photo, your parents are leaning against the boom of a sailboat with young Robinson. In the Senator's photo there's just your mother and Robinson. In the print he tried to palm off on me, the Senator and mystery gal are standing in the same pose, the background blurred.

"Any anomalies can be attributed to professional retouching." Stephanie pulled the bedsheet up over her chest and hugged her knees to her breasts. "Oh, Jared, I wish you could leave this alone."

I picked up the photos and sat on the edge of the bed. "Could you walk away from this if you were me?" I shook the prints in front of her face. "If your father's death had so many questions around it? If the next president of the United States is lying about knowing him, the good possibility that this supposedly paragon of virtue is a murderer."

"That's ridiculous!"

"Suppose there's a faction in our government that wants Robinson to be president at all costs but knows he could never get elected if people knew the truth about his past."

She put her chin on her knees and rocked her body back and forth saying nothing.

"Suppose he really is a good man and they're doing all this for insurance. Something like Watergate."

"Nixon was a good man?"

"He wasn't some phantom who seems to have been born at Brown University in his early twenties."

Stephanie gripped her knees tighter now rocking rhythmically on the soft mattress. "What dark secret in his past could be so harmful to his campaign?"

"Who knows?" I tossed the prints back on the bed. "Maybe he wasn't a war hero, that looks thin. If he wasn't, where the hell was he during the war? What did he do?"

I got up and walked to the open window. The brisk night wind was lifting the rain through the blinds, making the love seat damp under the sill. Lightning flashed across the clouds somewhere beyond the Charles River as a violent clap of thunder reverberated through the air inside the room.

"Maybe he was arrested for something," I continued thinking out loud, "served time in jail."

"Bad kid good man," she murmured. "That could do it."

"Or maybe he's not a good man and Commie plants or radicals in our own government are using the FBI to get him elected for some devious purpose. Maybe the krauts caught on and are trying to do us a favor."

"Phish! The *Baader-Meinhof* Gang?"

I turned back from the window to face her. "That's who we think they are. Suppose terrorists aren't behind it--the mafia, white supremacy clowns with government influence who placed the three East Germans in the FRG embassy."

"So, what are you going to do, Tiger?"

I walked over to the bed, picked up the Senator's photograph and studied the open-faced young man looking out at me. "The only place we've been able to nail him down is college."

"My friend in University Hall checked that out," Stephanie said. "There's nothing tangible, not even a picture of him at Brown."

"She didn't check the girl," I pointed to the pretty young woman in the sleeveless blouse. "If she went to Brown...."

"Girls went to Pembroke in those days."

I slipped under the sheets, set the alarm and turned out the light.

"If I find her, maybe I can get her to give me some answers."

CHAPTER NINETEEN
Cape Cod, MA
August 1976

Naushon, the largest of the eight Elizabeth Islands, runs southwest/northeast along the Massachusetts coast from Woods Hole on Cape Cod, between Buzzards Bay and Vineyard Sound. The Forbes family has owned the island since the turn of the century and maintained its pristine condition by prohibiting visitors from coming ashore without permission. Deer and sheep roam loose through the tall sea grass and sand dunes. Several species of wild bird's nest in the stunted shrubbery and the only buildings are a half-dozen weathered summer houses clustered around Hadley Harbor.

The patriarch of the Forbs clan, a major contributor to the Senator's campaign, made the secluded island available to him as a post-convention retreat. Senator Robinson, his executive staff, and most of Secret Service Detail 'A' embarked from Falmouth in the Forbes yacht and two Coast Guard cutters at dusk on Friday evening. It would take less than an hour to transport the party of thirty-seven men and women six miles through the dense fog and treacherous currents of Woods Hole to the calm inlet of Hadley.

I stood behind the radar man on the second cutter watching the scanner sweep over the green land masses on the square screen as the rating called out phlegmatic commands to the helmsman.

"Will it bother you if I talk?" I asked him.

"No, sir. Sandy been drivin' the Hole so long all he needs me for is keepin' us away from movin' targets." The Coast Guardsman pointed at an irregular dense green dot in the wake of the scanner. "Boats like that one, crazy enough to be out in this soup."

"Does this gear pick up everything?"

"Just about. Signal bounces back off any sizeable metal object above the water. Buoys, ships, boats over twenty feet or so."

"Fiberglass boats?"

The Coastie nodded, keeping his eyes on the screen. "Most of 'em have enough metal to bounce off."

"How about wooden sailboats?"

He called out a course correction to the helmsman before answering. "Not unless they hoist a radar reflector."

That confirmed what I already suspected. "Quite a machine," I said and left him to his duties.

The fantail of the small craft was deserted and I leaned on the railing watching the churning wake disappear into the thick white mist surrounding us. I was still shaken by the events of the night before and a discussion I had with Stephanie that morning.

No matter how well trained you are, physical combat is never like you imagine. In 'Nam, I had concentrated on trying to stay alive, zapping Cong before they zapped me. Secret Service agents compared protecting your assigned politician against an assassin to defending your best girl from a gang of hoods. You had a fight on your hands that was more important than your life. Because if you didn't win it, your life would not be worth living. We were like the ancient knights, an instructor at Quantico told us. Most people think the concept of honor is corny, out of date. But agents on protective details put theirs on the line every day for the entire country to see--and are ready to kill or die to keep it intact.

* * * * * *

The rain had softened when I woke up that morning. I lay on my side staring at the curtains wafting in the breeze, waiting for the alarm to go off. When it buzzed I reached out to shut it off as she stirred in the bed beside me. I turned to enclose her warm body in my arms and she snuggled against me until she felt my growing erection, then raised her palms to my chest, pulling her hips away.

Her voice was hoarse with sleep. "I have to tell you something."

"Oh, honey, not now!"

Stephanie scrambled out of bed, grabbing her robe on the way to the bathroom. "Calm down, I'll be right back."

When she returned, she sat cross-legged on the foot of the bed, her robe wrapped tightly around her. "You claim you love me."

I cocked my head on the pillows I had propped against the headboard. "I hope you don't doubt that."

"No. I've just been wondering how much."

I reached out for her hand and took it. "More than anything Steph. I want to be with you. Always."

"What does that mean?" she asked. "Exactly."

Where was this coming from, I wondered. Where was it going?

"We're not a couple of kids," I said. "I think we both know what we've been looking for. That we've found it. Another year or so shouldn't tell us anything drastically new about one another than we know already."

"So, now what?"

I laughed. "What is this? Are you pregnant?"

"Not quite."

"What the hell does that mean? I feel like I'm being pushed into a corner."

"Do you plan on asking me to marry you?"

"Of course, I do!"

"When?"

"As soon as I get this Robinson megillah resolved, find out if I'm going to stay in the Service or what else I can do with the rest of my life."

She extracted her hand from my grasp. "That sounds a bit tenuous."

"Steph, what's the matter?"

"I have to make my own plans."

"You're talking in riddles. What happened to our plans?"

"They don't seem to be very solid, Jared. And your

commitment may not include Cindy Farrell."

I sat up, lips parted, staring at her.

"I petitioned the court to extend custody again. For a year." She spoke quickly to get it all out before I could interrupt.

"Cindy is down at my mother's house, they have a live-in nurse, she's enrolled in school and I may adopt her." She got off the bed and held up her hand. "Please don't say anything we'll both regret. I haven't told Cindy, I wanted you to know."

"Geezes!"

* * * * * *

Stephanie had a nine o'clock appointment at her Boston office. We walked down the hill to Charles Street where she pressed against me harder than usual as we kissed good-bye. Then she turned away toward Cambridge Street, and I started for the garage under Boston Common to get her car.

The rain stopped on the drive down I-95 to Providence, but by mid-morning it had turned hot and muggy with a bright glare shining behind dark gray clouds that hid the sun.

What chance would we have for a happy marriage nursing someone else's psychologically disturbed kid? Average couples had enough trouble making a go of it without dragging some external anchor between them. The girl would not want to go sailing again, that was certain. Would Stephanie leave Cindy for weeks at a time every year all through our lives or give up cruising? Would she expect me to? Cindy and I had gotten off on the wrong foot--could that be changed? I had no experience with children and tended to treat them like small adults. How was I going to win over this troubled kid with all the usual problems of six more teen years ahead of her? What would happen when Stephanie and I had kids of our own? Would she even want them if her life was all wrapped up with Cindy? Could she find enough time for me?

I was glad Stephanie had not let me respond to her astounding revelation, because my mind could still not assimilate the potential repercussions of including Cindy Farrell in our lives, or envision a life without Stephanie

Graham. I shook off these disturbing questions as I turned from the interstate onto the exit ramp to downtown Providence.

I did not know what I expected to find in the Brown yearbooks but had a strong hunch that the photographs of my parents and Senator Robinson were the answer to my puzzle and somehow linked to the items the Germans were so determined to get their hands on.

Stephanie explained that Pembroke had been a women's college from inception with their own dorms, separate from, but affiliated with Brown University until 1971 just five years ago. They had always shared classes and social activities but had separate campuses, administrations and yearbooks. It was a long-shot that the Senator had used an old candid Pembroke photo taken with a college sweetheart who resembled my mother to throw me off the track--but all I had were long-shots. Brown was the only place I was sure Robinson had been before World War II. Where else could I look for the woman? If the Senator had pulled her out of a stock photo file six months ago this would be another dead-end.

There was a single alumni office now located at 38 Brown Street in an elegant three-story example of American Federal architecture, the former home of university Chancellor William Goddard, class of 1846, with an historical plaque dating it back to 1830. Gleaming white pillars supported a deep portico surrounded by an apparently re-pointed red brick exterior, black door and shutters. A pineapple door-knocker of polished brass signifying welcome completed its pre-revolutionary character. I found a parking space on George Street, a block down from Wriston Quadrangle named after Henry M. Wriston, Brown President 1937-55 and advisor to President Eisenhower. Waiting for the alumni office to open, I watched summer students going to early classes.

College kids in long hair, faded blue work shirts, tie-dyed tee shirts and bell-bottom jeans walked across the campus under the elms. Fiercely individual in their common dress and liberal ideals that were different in concept yet similar in conviction to those their parents held when they were young. No matter what they did or thought, they were destined to inherit a world that men like Senator Robinson would shape for them.

What kind of place would that be? Could he really set the country on a different track? A nationalistic course based on economic policies designed to bring corporate managers and workers together in a unified force to compete with other nations instead of each other? How would that jibe with the liberal philosophy of these students and the other political party who would feed and police the world while Americans went hungry, jobless and races antagonistic to one another? Did he mean what he said in his nomination speech? The liberal press had ripped it apart. Now at least, the voters had been given polarized issues to choose between: the status quo of the past thirty years or a strong, self-serving democracy. "America first." Not a bad idea for a change. Could he be trusted to do it if he was the unknown charlatan I thought he was?

After the convention I became more convinced than ever that the people should know the man intimately before they could weigh his promises, evaluate his philosophy or judge his integrity. Would they vote for a man whose early life was a lie?

A young Asian woman opened the black door at eight-thirty and I trotted up the half-dozen sandstone steps as she smiled a warm greeting, holding the screen door open for me. I explained what I wanted, and she escorted me up to the library on the second floor. Framed class reunion pictures were hung on the ivory walls above the winding staircase. One side of the long room consisted of floor-to-ceiling bookcases, the other adorned with photographs of famous alumni.

James Mitchell Varnum, Brigadier General in the Revolutionary Army and Member of the Continental Congress graduated from Brown in 1769. John Hay, class of 1858, President Lincoln's secretary during the Civil War. You would never know it from watching their recent football scores, but John Heisman, 1891, helped legalize the forward pass; and Fritz Pollard, the first black All-American, led his team to the Rose Bowl in 1915. Senator Theodore Francis Green (D-RI), 1887, whose illustrious 54-year career of public service included two terms as Governor of Rhode Island and four in congress; John D. Rockefeller, Jr., 1897; 'Tommy the Cork' Corcoran, 1922, advisor to FDR. That funny little man who wrote for *The New Yorker*, S. J. Perelman, 1925. IBM President Thomas Watson, 1937. Charles Norris Robinson, 1942, U.S. Senator.

He was in pretty good company. Would they be changing the caption under his picture to read, 'President of the United States?' Could he measure up to that job and all the other great Americans on that wall?

The young woman brought me over to the oak shelf containing the yearbooks from the late '30's to early '40's. She told me I could not take them out of the room except to use the Xerox machine on the first floor at ten cents a copy. I should leave the books on the table when I was finished.

I sat down in a cushioned, straight-back wooden chair, slid the Senator's photograph out of my manila envelope and placed it next to the 1938 Pembroke yearbook. Opening the padded white and brown leather cover took me back to an artless time, an era of simple purpose, a unified majority with codes of behavior and respect for accepted values. These coeds with bobbed hairdos' and scoop-neck dresses had been humbled by the Great Depression in which wealthy families had become destitute overnight. They had seen unemployment approach 30%, the life savings of average workers wiped out and proud men beg in the streets. Some of their fathers had committed suicide.

I compared the young woman in the Senator's photo to every Pembroke graduate from 1938 to 1943. Nothing. I pored through the candid shots and group photos of student organizations and activities. Zero. I pulled down the volume titled, '*Liber Brunensis* Class of 1942' embossed in faded gold script across its brown leather cover with the school seal and motto, *In Deo Speramus*. A lofty idea, but I knew I'd have to do more than place my hope in God to solve this conundrum.

I double checked the 'R's' in the formal shots of graduating Brown seniors. Someone had pasted a typed footnote at the bottom of the page indicating the omission of the distinguished alumni, but Stephanie's friend was right--there was no picture or bio of Charles Robinson.

I leaned back on the hind legs of the chair, riffling through the pages, ready to give up. The war was six months old when the book was printed and contained a paradox of posed and candid photographs of varsity sports, student activities and stiff young men in military uniforms.

Now, what? I had no proof of my suspicions, nothing of substance to confront him with. Whoever had submerged the man's past and fabricated his current identity had done one hell of a job.

Suddenly, the face of young Charles Robinson jumped out from a black-and-white photo of Naval Reserve Officer Training Cadets. He was marching in front of a company of young men wearing dress blue uniforms and white hats with patent leather visors. They were parading in ranks with shouldered rifles, looking like a bunch of self-conscious boys playing soldier. Robinson wore a red sash and scabbard, his sword drawn, pointing at the ground before him, its polished steel blade catching the sunlight,

But the caption was wrong, confounding the omission of the man from his yearbook.

Then a heavy curtain of confusion lifted in my mind, the incipient heat of the summer day turning cold in the room as I reread the caption over and over, shivering in bewilderment, disbelief, finally understanding.

'NROTC Company 'C' on parade at Marvel Field, led by Student Commander John B. Andeweg.'

I flipped back to the formal senior portraits and found the 'A's'. Andeweg, John B., his photograph with complete student bio: Engineering major; NROTC Company Commander, Class Secretary, Sock and Buskin drama society; the Cammarian Club, a semi-secret student government organization; nickname, 'Dutch'; aspirations: high-rise construction. Stephanie's friend had looked the two men up in the yearbook; when she inquired about their transcripts last spring without benefit of the photo of young Robinson. If I had checked it myself....

The blond youth in the yearbook pictures was the same person standing next to my mother in the photograph from the Senator's bedroom and the one with the woman who resembled my mother he had used to convince me of my error. That's why their transcripts were similar. No wonder his past seemed so elusive!

Charles Robinson *is* John Andeweg.

* * * * * *

My mind did not begin to clear until I pulled Stephanie's car into the parking garage under Government Center in Boston. It had started to pour again. I called her office in Mass General from the hospital lobby and she agreed to meet me in twenty minutes for lunch. I dashed down Cambridge Street, my raincoat flapping at my legs as I headed for a little Syrian restaurant across from MGH.

Half an hour later, she peeled off her dripping poncho and slid into the red plastic booth across the table. "Are you all right?"

"Senator Robinson killed my father."

"Jared!"

I showed her the Xerox of Andeweg's entry in the yearbook and the old photo the Senator had given me that had started everything.

"They're the same person," she admitted.

A waitress came over and we ordered iced tea, Shish Kabob and salads. The room was filled with the aroma of baked lamb, garlic and the voices of intense men and women in white smocks, interns with pagers on their belts and stethoscopes jammed in their pockets or around their necks. A mural on the wall looked like it had been copied from a pack of Camels.

"Robinson was John Andeweg when he went to Brown," I explained after the waitress left. "He joined the Navy in college when the war broke out. He must have transferred to the Coast Guard after graduation, then was assigned to my grandfather's boat in the Corsair Fleet patrolling for Nazi subs on Rhode Island Sound."

"*Dutch Master.*" She reached across the table and squeezed my hand. "Your father was skipper. Andeweg, your mother, my parents and Jim Barnum were crew."

I had put it all together in my mind on the drive up from Providence but saying the words out loud was harder. "My father went off with Andeweg in the dinghy that night and drowned."

I stopped speaking again while the waitress served our Cokes and Stephanie gripped my hand harder, her face reflecting the pain in my voice. "They recovered his body, but never found Andeweg."

She knew the details as well as I did. "The FBI took over, hushed everything up, then declared Andeweg drowned, too."

"But he didn't. Oh, he disappeared all right. But only he and the Bureau know that. Or why."

Everything was tumbling around in my head so fast, I drained my drink in gulping swallows to slow myself down. "John Andeweg turns up after the war with the name Charles Robinson, a new identity and a manufactured history--including a paper trail that makes him a hero in the Pacific Theater."

Stephanie tried to help me work it out. "Then Robinson starts making his own history at Columbia Law School, the Virginia State Legislature and the U.S. Senate." She hesitated and held my gaze. "When we questioned Commander Gilmore in Florida, he thought either Andeweg or your father might have been a Nazi spy." Realizing we were engaged in an emotional conversation, the waitress, served our Shish Kabob and salads and retreated.

"It had to be Andeweg," I said. "My father was a Dutch national. Hitler invaded Holland in 1940. The Dutch hated the Germans." I took a breath, struggling to slow down again.

189

"My father must have caught Andeweg attempting to signal a U-boat or something and tried to stop him... the bastard killed him."

As much sympathy as she had for what I was going through, her intellect couldn't help exploring every possibility. "How did a twenty-two-year-old Brown student become a German spy?"

"He was Dutch, too, remember. Probably second or third generation. Maybe the Nazis were holding his relatives' hostage in the Netherlands. Or he could have been a German sympathizer--a lot of Americans thought Hitler was great stuff before the war. Charles Lindbergh, Ambassador Kennedy, Errol Flynn."

"Couldn't your father have been a German sympathizer?"

I slipped my hand out of hers and shook the ice in the bottom of my glass. "Our side didn't execute spies by drowning them."

"We were at war," she said. "Our boys were supposed to kill theirs."

"Then why pretend Andeweg drowned? Why not make him a hero, intrepid spy killer? Why did he disappear for five years? Where was he?" I knew she was challenging my theory to make me waver, stop me from doing something that could change our lives. But I was adamant. "He was in the military. They were fighting a war. Why did he resurface as Charles Robinson afterwards?"

"If Andeweg was a German spy," Stephanie wondered, "why would the FBI be trying so hard to keep his secret now that he's almost certain to get elected president?"

A new thought occurred to me. "He could have been a double agent...."

Stephanie sighed and shook her head. "This is all speculation, Jared." Then she asked the question she hoped I couldn't answer. "How can you ever know?"

"Get Robinson to tell me."

"Oh, Jared! Please don't do anything foolish. Can't you take this to the police?" She shook her head, dismissing that immediately. "The press, the opposition party."

Now it was my turn to reason with her.

"Steph, what have I got? A photo of a young man I say is Senator Robinson that resembles the yearbook picture of John Andeweg. All the Senator has to do is deny it's his picture. It looks nothing like him now...are they going to make him shave his beard? He'll claim he was friends with Andeweg at Brown, it was Andeweg who knew my mother who just happened to be in the keepsake photo of his drowned friend. And I can't prove otherwise."

The waitress came to clear our plates and we declined dessert. She made out the check and I paid it as Stephanie made rings on the plastic table with the bottom of her glass.

We sat in silence for a couple of minutes after the waitress had gone, then I picked up where I left off. "If this comes from the other party it could backfire, look like wild-eyed last-ditch mudslinging. What could they prove that I can't? Giving it to them is probably the fastest way to get the whole thing dismissed."

Stephanie began sliding her finger across the rings of water her glass had made on the table, cutting them in half, destroying the imperfect circular patterns. "What are you going to do?"

"That depends."

"On what?"

I reached out for her hand. "On you."

"Oh, no!" She yanked her hand away and hid it in her lap. "I'm not going to help you risk jail or worse doing something dangerous or illegal."

"What should I do?"

She didn't have an answer. We both knew 'nothing' was not an option.

"Let the people elect a murderer and German spy as president? My fault, responsibility? The only person on Earth that can derail this charlatan? "

Her reply didn't have a lot of conviction to it. "If the FBI thinks he's OK why can't you?"

"Because it's not for the FBI to decide. The people are supposed to decide. After they have the facts."

"You're not sure of any of this."

"I'm sure that Senator Robinson is not the man he pretends to be. You don't take on a new identity because you're proud of your past. I'm convinced he killed my father.... I'm positive he knows what papers and key the Germans were looking for in his house, why they tried to assassinate him when they couldn't find them."

She dug a pack of Lucky's out of her lab coat and lit up as I continued. "I'm sure he and the FBI know why we were attacked in the Florida Keys. Why John Goddard was killed."

Stephanie took a long drag on her cigarette and blew the smoke at the wide glass window beside us. She stared at the people walking by in the rain on Cambridge Street, couples hunched in summer slickers pausing to read the *prix fix* menu taped to the plate glass restaurant window. "You can't take on the man who's going to be our next president and the FBI."

I saved my best argument until last, and I believed it like I believed the world was round. "If I don't, who's to say the krauts or whoever won't come after him again? Me. Maybe you." I leaned forward, hands gripping the side of the table, its edge pressing into my sternum. "I'd be a loose cannon they might not want rolling around when the man's in the White House. Maybe there's something I missed or they're plotting a way to control our gridlocked legislative process, maybe create an event that would give me the proof I need to take to the press."

She stubbed her half-smoked cigarette out in the ashtray and leaned back in the booth, then crossed her arms over her breasts and looked out the window again for several minutes. "I won't take part in anything illegal."

"All I want to do is get him alone and confront him."

Stephanie almost jumped across the table. "Kidnapping?" She said it so loud a couple of people turned to stare at us.

"How else can I reason with him?" I lowered my voice hoping she would take the hint. "I have to get him away from his supporters, the Bureau, the Service. Maybe he can explain everything...."

"What if he can't?"

"I'll get it on tape. He's bound to say something incriminating I can take to the media."

We went back and forth like that for another half hour. All I wanted her to do was sail my boat from Block Island where I had left it, to Naushon. She could stow one inflatable dinghy aboard and tow the other. Anchor *Dutchman* close to shore, bring one of the dinghies in for me, then during slack water, run the mile across Woods Hole to the mainland in the other dinghy with an outboard. She'd be out of it. I'd figure out some way to get the Senator to go sailing alone with me and grill him for all he was worth.

By the end of lunch, I hadn't convinced her, but she didn't say no. "Let me think about it."

"We're leaving tonight. We'll only be on the island through the weekend."

"It'll take me, what--ten, twelve hours to get there?"

"You'll probably have to power with the fog and rain."

I was asking her to make a stinking trip, but other than that I wasn't worried. She was as good a sailor as I am. We worked out the details as if she was going to do it. She had to. I had no alternative. She'd take the ferry to Block Friday night, sail all day Saturday and arrive at Naushon after dark. Which was perfect.

"Have you thought about Cindy?" she asked me.

"I can't get her out of my mind."

"Have you come to any conclusions?"

"No, Steph, I haven't. It scares the hell out of me. For us."

Stephanie looked at her watch and got up from the table. "Call me tonight," she said and walked out of the restaurant.

CHAPTER TWENTY
Naushon, MA
August 1976

The caravan of boats picked its way through the heavy fog that obscured the narrow inlet of Hadley Harbor. Senator Robinson, his aides and half the agents in Detail 'A' disembarked from the big motor yacht at the wooden dock. The press was banned from this retreat and the bar had been open on the trip across, so the candidate's staff sounded like a bunch of salesmen coming in for a weekend of golf and awards. There was no course on Naushon, but that didn't discourage them from wearing colorful pants and bright windbreakers with little animals sewn on their shirts.

By the time the Coast Guard cutter put me ashore, the main party had disappeared up the rutted dirt road into the drizzly night. I tied the drawstrings of my hood under my chin, zipped the Uzi into its jiffy bag and pressed the button on my handheld mike.

"CP, CP, Last Man, read me?"
"CP," Murphy responded.
I said, "Last Man secure."
"Patrol Post 4, Last Man."
"Roger, CP. Post 4 out."
"CP out."

An advance team from the Boston office had secured the island three days before. Half the agents on Detail 'A' relieved them at noon, setting up the command post in a first-floor living room of the main house where the Senator was staying. On the topographical map, six smaller homes were strung out in a loose semicircle around the head of the harbor. The main house was a three-story building of late

Victorian architecture with gables and round corner turrets. All the houses were covered with wooden shingles weathered by years of exposure to the hot sun and winter storms.

The Command Post was Post 1 where two agents would handle communications and maintain security from within by roaming the house day and night. Two more agents walked concentric perimeters of the main house which were designated Posts 2 and 3. Post 4 was a man on foot roving the half mile of road around the harbor. The remainder of the six-by-one-mile island was patrolled by a pair of agents circling the outlying roads in a Jeep with a .30 caliber machine gun mounted on the back, and two agents in an All-Terrain Vehicle covering the beaches and off-road areas. These motorized units were Posts 5 and 6. One of the armed Coast Guard cutters swept the north side of the island and the other the south side. Both were linked by radio to the CP, which could patch them into the walkie-talkie frequency for direct communication with each guard post. They were not expecting an invasion, but since Thursday night Burnett was taking no chances--he and Murphy had created a virtually impenetrable security net around CANDY.

Coming over from the mainland I refreshed my memory of the area with the charts on the cutter and during the last two hours of my watch, walked every foot of the shoreline between Naushon and Uncatena Islands. The tiny cove was a shallow with poor holding ground and half-submerged boulders a hundred yards off the beach. No yachtsman in his right mind would anchor there, especially with the forecast of easterly winds, which made that side of the island a dangerous lee shore. If the anchor broke free of the sand during the time Stephanie left *Dutchman* and I went aboard, I would be picking my boat off the rocks in splinters. She'd have to let out plenty of scope on the Danforth anchor and back down with the engine to dig the flukes, so they'd hold for the couple of hours I needed. Assuming she agreed to help me.

The blurred glare of a hand lantern swept down from the

compound in steady strides. The Senator was out for his nightly stroll. He came to the fork in the road, paused at the dock, and leaned on the wooden railing, playing the ray of light over the water below. Great target. They were all the same, inflated egos with delusions of immortality. Fatalists. Dreamers far removed from reality when it came to security. Maybe the human mind couldn't function with the constant thought of assassination.

Thursday night had proved someone was out to get him. That was enough to make anyone think. Senator Robinson stood at the head of the harbor for several minutes, a formless shadow behind the beam of light as though he was waiting. He must have known whose post this was. I stood hidden by the darkness, thinking about the last time we had spoken, the Senator using our mutual fluency in German to challenge me to a tennis match, pulling me toward him with the double barbed hook of language and message.

Was he taunting me, warning me off? Or compelled to expose a sliver of his terrible secret, like the man on the edge of the cliff in Poe's *Imp of the Perverse*, driven to thoughts of his own destruction. The light moved along the path to Nonamesset Island. Burnett had told us that CANDY still insisted on these solitary walks in secure areas, but to keep him in sight. I followed at a distance that kept his light visible, then walked off the road into a copse of bushes when the Senator started back, waiting there until he disappeared up the road to the house.

I couldn't help thinking about what I was risking, asking Stephanie to help me. Talk about anchors! During the past six months she'd become the mooring that was keeping my life from going adrift. I had never experienced the unguarded relationship we had right from the start. The way I could depend on her, count on her insight, on any response she made to be in my interest. I still had trouble seeing things the way she did, like everything was black and white, the correct runway marked with landing lights. The line drawn sharp and straight which she would not cross. Nothing was that simple, was it?

I closed my eyes and could smell her scent, the subtle fragrance of her perfumed soap mingling with her musky odor when I kissed her breasts, the clean residue of shampoo as I nuzzled her hair. I could almost feel the warmth of her fleshy thighs, the acid taste of her juices on my tongue, the tips of her fingers on my cheek. I heard her laugh at something silly. At me. Herself.

I admired her concern for Cindy Farrell in spite of the threat I was convinced she posed to our happiness. Her need to give, to heal, to experience life and all its emotions. I saw her become one with *Dutchman*, squinting up at the luff of the jib, driving the boat down Chesapeake Bay, fingertips guiding the varnished tiller.

I felt like a blind man shuffling his way along the dirt road, holding my arms in front of me, then stabbing a beam of light into the black mist to get my bearings. How would Melissa have reacted to this? Fighting the system, jeopardizing my career, maybe my life? Asking her to get involved.... Melissa would have jumped off this runaway train months ago.

If Stephanie said 'no' tonight, and I did something else, we'd be finished. If she said 'yes' and found out what I really had planned, I'd lose her. Life is not black and white. I could not confront the Senator in an open forum. I could not walk away from what I knew. If I confided in Stephanie she'd try to stop me, probably tell Burnett. Was Senator Robinson worth it? Exposing the man who would be president as a fake, a liar, a murderer? Avenging my father? How could I not do this? How could I look in the mirror again if Robinson won the election and subjected the country to some foreign conspiracy?

The fog absorbed the beam of my flashlight, swallowing the white shaft in its wall of gray. I could barely see the berm of the road where the damp earth met the coarse grass and followed its ragged line back to the dock. A dull glow appeared from the direction of the houses, rising and falling as it moved toward me. I snapped off my light, unzipped the jiffy bag and stood still, invisible in the oppressive darkness.

When the light was twenty feet away, I said, "Who goes?"

The light stopped and pointed upwards, casting angular shadows on the pale features enclosed in the hood of a camouflage parka. "Fisk."

I gave him half of the night's password. "Dusky."

"Donna," Fisk answered. "You're pushed, Coughlin." We stood together in the monotonous drizzle, complaining about the weather, the boredom of protective details, his thirty days away from his wife and kids, the unmowed lawn of his home in Cleveland. We didn't talk about the assassination attempt, my lone forays against Burnett's orders or the perception the other humps must have of my strange relationship with Senator Robinson.

I couldn't blame them. First, catching a slug in the man's home, then disobeying Burnett's orders to stay off the case. Next, sounding off to the Senator who had me fired. Going under cover on my own in defiance of all the rules, but probably saving the Protectees life, then getting invited to play tennis in a language nobody understood. As far as the rest of the humps were concerned, I was a loner. They wanted nothing to do with me off the job and barely trusted me on it. The first might sidetrack their careers, the second could cost them their lives.

My billet was in the last of the gray shingle houses that made up the Forbes compound on the rise of land above the harbor. A couple of humps who had just come off watch were sitting on the front porch shooting the breeze as I climbed the steps. I stood there for a couple of minutes listening to them talk about the Montreal Olympics and Nadia Comanici, the fourteen-year-old Romanian kid who had just taken the gold for gymnastics. They did not invite me to join them.

The screen door opened onto a faded oriental carpet that ran down the center of polished floorboards to the back of the house. A single bulb with a shade of frosted glass hung from the ceiling. My vision adjusted to the soft light as I stood in the foyer breathing the musty smell of stale flowers and oiled wood in the damp salt air.

Three more humps sprawled on furniture worn from years of gentle use in a large sitting room off to my left. They had the lights turned low and their conversation stopped as I looked in through the archway. One of them called out a greeting, told me there were sandwiches in the kitchen and where my room was. I waved at them, picked up my sea bag and trudged up the wooden staircase. Whatever happened the following night, the Service was no longer an option for me.

My room was empty. A low-watt table lamp shed a cone of light on the upper half of the chenille spreads on the twin beds. I stood on a braided rag rug taking in the prints of old English hunting scenes in heavy frames scattered across the yellowed wallpaper, beige shades on rollers pulled down to the window sills behind country curtains, a mismatched pair of painted bureaus, a secretary and several caned chairs. An open suitcase lay on the rumpled bed of my on-duty roommate

I tossed my bag on one of the chairs and stripped off my foul weather gear. There was no phone in the room, but I noticed a black rotary unit next to a vase of wilting flowers on a table at the top of the landing. The operator cut in to assist my long-distance call after I dialed the Rhode Island number. I did not think Burnett would monitor my phone calls.

"Hi." I said. "It's me."

"Hi, 'me'." Her voice was lazy, coarse with sleep. I detected a note of resignation in it.

"Sorry I woke you."

"S'OK. Makes me feel like a young intern again."

"Made your mind up?"

"About you?"

I held my breath for a couple of seconds. "Yes."

"You're determined to do this with or without me, right?"

"There's no phone in the room, so I'm calling from the upstairs hallway."

"Aren't you?"

"Yes, Stephanie, I am."

It was her turn for silence. When she spoke, her voice sounded stronger like she'd sat up in bed and turned on the light.

"OK," she said, the resignation gone. "I'll do it." I realized I'd been holding my breath when it rushed out all at once, making a plosive noise against the mouthpiece she must have heard.

"Stephanie...."

"You owe me." I could sense the teasing in her voice, that little smile.

"Name it." Then immediately regretted the implication.

"We'll talk." She hung up.

* * * * * *

On Saturday night, I was tired and stiff from playing three sets of tennis that afternoon with Senator Robinson whose lean body exhibited toned legs and arms covered with light blond hairs, except for a three-inch patch of smooth skin on his left forearm, the superimposed tattoo of an American eagle that practically obliterated it.

He had a smashing serve, a devastating backhand and despite his crooked right elbow, cleaned my clock in all three sets.

For some reason, I had hoped our ambiguous relationship would make things easier, give me an excuse to avoid what I might have to do that night. We played hard and did not talk much, two opponents gauging each other, me wondering about the incongruous American eagle on Robinson's forearm, the Senator seeming to figure something out himself, maybe afraid of what I knew, regretting taking me back.

Under ordinary circumstances the other humps would have ragged me about brown-nosing, trying to get a job on the White House staff, stuff like that. As it was, they seemed even more distant, half resentful, half respectful. Murphy offered to shorten my watch that night if the afternoon match had exhausted me. I didn't care about the other guys' reaction to one of them standing part of my tour, but I had to be on my post when the Senator took his walk.

* * * * * *

A thin drizzle started after I came on duty for the eight to midnight watch. The persistent fog felt like someone had stuffed me in a black sack of seamless velvet. I felt sick and confused by all I had learned and what I was about to do.

No wonder people had lost their sense of values, with all the venal men in high places as poor examples. Senator Robinson, for example, who had their confidence and would surely betray it. They had no one to look up to anymore, no great men to emulate. Where had all the heroes gone? Nathan Hale, who regretted having only one life he could give for his country. Washington, the conquering general who refused to be king. Franklin, Jefferson, Hamilton-- Lincoln, struggling under the weight of severe depression to keep the nation intact and abolish an evil practice. Daniel Webster, John Calhoun and Henry Clay who shaped our democracy during the first half of the nineteenth century. Fredrick Douglass, a freed slave, writer and champion of black suffrage. Builders, leaders, men of purpose, integrity.

Did the United States deserve its greedy egotists who gained public office and positions of influence by default? Were our citizens responsible for these self-seeking hedonists or did unscrupulous politicians and bureaucrats' lower public expectations, weaken our moral fiber through their poor example? Had the entire country progressed beyond rebellious outrage at immoral behavior? Do we elect crooks and brigands or does opportunity make the thief?

By 10:15 I was pumped up, not tired, outside myself, like I used to get before a wrestling match or night patrol into the thick Asian jungle, feeling my arms and legs obeying unprocessed signals from a brain that was running on instinct. The dull glow of a flashlight probed the mist from the direction of the compound, bobbing down the dirt road toward the harbor. I stood beside a stunted tree where the road forked around the inlet. The dark form behind the light walked straight and tall like a soldier on parade.

When he was twenty feet beyond me, I called out, "Dutch!"

The Senator broke his stride and his head gave a little jerk before he pulled it back and kept walking. That told me all I needed to know. Then Robinson stopped and turned, shining the white beam on me unzipping the jiffy bag as I closed the distance between us, pointing the Uzi a foot above the light.

"So you figured it out," the Senator said, his strong voice resigned, tinged with annoyance.

I stopped a couple of feet in front of him.

"Not all of it." The muzzle of the machine pistol touched the flashlight. "Turn it off."

He did, and we stood together in the darkness listening to water lap the pilings beneath the dock.

"What now?" he asked, his tone washed of its previous emotion.

"Turn around and keep walking the way you were going. You can follow the road by touch if you stay in the wheel rut."

We had walked about 500 yards, well out of sight of the compound when I told him to turn the light on again. I found the path down to the beach at the northwest tip of the island, and we moved down the incline, stepping around rocks and exposed roots of the scrub pine that lined both sides of the narrow track.

Stephanie had taken the 7:15 ferry from Point Judith to Block Island that morning. If all had gone well, *Dutchman* had slid between the fog-drenched jetties of Great Salt Pond at ten a.m. towing my inflatable dinghy and outboard and the one she rented from Champlain's Marina. The seas had been calm all day, but the current ran against her in Buzzard's Bay, so the fifty-mile trip probably took close to thirteen hours. The plan was to drop the hook in the cove between Naushon and Uncatena, tow the rented dinghy ashore with mine, then run across Woods Hole to the mainland with the outboard. Simple.

"I presume this is going to look like an accident," the Senator said.

I had all I could do to keep my finger from pulling the trigger. "The way you killed my father?"

The Senator breathed a deep sigh but did not answer. The man was hard as steel and just as cool, standing in front of a loaded gun gripped by the frustration and anger he must have known I felt at that moment.

The beam of my flashlight swept over the Avon on the beach, and I told Robinson to drag it into the water. We got into the inflatable and he rowed while I used the hand-bearing compass Stephanie had wedged under the seat. I had heard stories of yachtsmen searching a crowded harbor for hours in fog like this for a boat rigged with a bright anchor light. I could not afford that tonight. Despite the coordinates she'd left to help me find *Dutchman*, it took me twenty minutes to spot the pencil flashlight she had taped to the mast. We climbed aboard the sloop and tied the Avon to a stern cleat.

The Senator knew his way around a boat or I would have had my hands full. Robinson seemed resigned to whatever his captor had in mind and did exactly as he was told. A chill breeze had picked up from the west, so we hoisted sail, raised anchor and began to ghost through the night like a black snake. We could not see ten feet, but neither could the Coast Guard--hear us or pick up my wooden hull on radar. If I could keep off the rocks as we sailed through the Hole, we would be out in the ocean in a couple of hours.

"You're pretty good at this," the Senator said.

"Family trait."

The current was coming off slack, going with us. I had memorized the compass headings and distances from buoy to buoy through 'The Strait' and 'Broadway.' I had to concentrate, but it was no great navigational feat. Senator Robinson probably knew that, too.

We heard Gong '1' off the eastern approach and eased sheets for the broad reach down Vineyard Sound.

"I don't suppose there's any way to deter you from this," the Senator said.

"Will you confess to murdering my father?"

"I did not kill your father."

"Will you tell the truth to the voters?"

He hesitated, his voice subdued when he said, "I cannot do that."

"Pull out of the election?"

"That would throw the country into turmoil."

I said, "So will this."

"What do you hope to gain by it?"

I was stumped for a second. I knew the glib rationale I had used on Stephanie would not be good enough for this man.

"Satisfaction." A word burst into my mind that I hadn't acknowledged before. "Revenge, maybe."

"Then what?"

"Nothing, if I'm half the actor you are. Oh, a little hassle, some bad press. Probably get fired again."

The wind backed a point and I told Robinson to bring in the jenny. "Don't forget, I probably saved your hide last week. Who'd believe this was anything but poor judgment. Once you confess to the truth."

"You're prepared to live with that...."

I couldn't help laughing. "It doesn't seem to bother you!"

The Senator leaned forward on the cockpit seat opposite me, looking like a crazed pirate in the reddish glow of the binnacle that shook me a little, but not my purpose. I could not stop.

"You're responsible for the deaths of my father, John Goddard, two Germans and maybe a Secret Service agent." Now I was having trouble with my voice. "Burger, the German I killed, the men I shot in Florida, Henzler, Knopf." I shook my head, hardly able to believe that I could not arrest this man and see him tried for my father's murder and whatever devious scheme he was planning. "You disregard your own safety, mine and everyone else's. Is covering up your sleazy past to win the presidency really worth all that?"

"You want everything for nothing, don't you? No risk, no unpleasantness." Robinson was getting angry again. "Yes, innocent people die, and that does bother me a great deal."

The high-powered engine of a Coast Guard patrol boat

could be heard in the distance. They must have discovered both of us missing. I shifted the Uzi on my lap as I looked off into the fog. Then turned back to find that single eye riveting my attention.

"I've had to make some hard decisions that no one wanted to handle. Do you want to do that?"

We were well out in Vineyard Sound now, the waves deeper, stronger, surging in from the open water. *Dutchman* was heeling to starboard. I engaged the auto pilot, picked up the Uzi and flicked off the safety. The Senator was a stubborn old bastard and my options were limited if Robinson did not cave in. Even as I stood there, I did not know if I had the guts to throw him overboard and watch him drown.

"You're a fake and a murderer, Senator. The country will be better off without you."

The companionway hatch slide open behind me with a bang, and Stephanie shouted, "Jared, no!" She was standing on a step in the companionway halfway up the ladder, tears of anger and betrayal glistening on her cheeks in the pink light. Everybody had their own agenda. She had brought both inflatables into the beach, left one for me, then used the other to return to *Dutchman*, towing the second dinghy to some remote anchorage before stowing away below.

None of us moved for several moments as we listened to the sound of the bow cutting through the water, passing along the sleek hull, gurgling beneath the transom. All this, and she was going to screw it up. The tension dropped from the Senator's shoulders as he realized he was saved.

I gestured with the gun barrel. "Sit over there with him."

She stood where she was, looking at me. "I thought I knew you."

"Do it!" I screamed.

Her expression made me want to reach out and hug her, whisper in her hair. I leaned forward and slapped her face so hard she rocked back on the step, grabbing the side of the hatch to keep from falling backwards. She stopped crying but did not put her hand to her cheek. The look she gave me was pure disgust. She zipped up her foul weather jacket, climbed into the cockpit and sat beside Senator Robinson.

"I'll figure out what to do about you later, "I told her.

"You'll have to kill me, too, Jared." She folded her arms across her chest. "However, you've justified this to yourself, it is murder." She put her hand on the Senator's arm. "I'll tell the police." Then shook her head. "The FBI."

I ignored her and lowered the muzzle of the gun. "OK," I told Robinson. "Now you can save two lives." I checked the compass heading and sat down on the opposite seat.

"Give me one good reason, John Andeweg, why you both shouldn't develop a bad case of accidental drowning just like my father."

1941

CHAPTER TWENTY-ONE
Newport, RI
June 1941

Mr. George Van Oudgaarden sat on the veranda of the Ida Lewis Yacht Club holding a brass telescope to his eye, watching his new boat sail around Adams Point into Newport Harbor. He wore white flannels, a double-breasted blue blazer with brass buttons and his family crest in gold thread sewn into the handkerchief pocket. His white yachtsman's cap resting square on his head carried a silver anchor above the polished black visor glistening with gold braid.

"Let's hear it now," the Vice Commodore, who was similarly attired, called out. "Hip, hip, hooray!"

The family and guests who were gathered around Mr. Van Oudgaarden overflowed the railed wooden porch onto the green lawn that sloped down to meet the stone retaining wall, a barrier against flood water. Many of the men reflected the traditional yachting uniform of their host, regardless of whether they had ever set foot on a boat. Their women, for the most part, wore calf-length summer dresses with wide belts and floppy brimmed straw hats with colored ribbon circling the crown.

"Hip, hip, hooray!" they shouted with raised champagne flutes. "Hip, hip, hooray!"

I stood on the dock in a pair of white ducks and polo shirt, squinting into the afternoon sun glaring off the water. The club steward adjusted the brim of his long-billed Block Island fishing cap and glanced at his two dock boys fingering the lines on new fenders of woven hemp.

He said, "Don't let her paint touch, mind you." The boys nodded and shortened their grip on the fenders.

"He's going to sail her up to the dock," I said.

"Naw, he ain't," Steward answered, hitching his khaki trousers up. "He's got a lee shore, 10 to 15 knots a wind."

The big ketch had dressed ship, her international code flags and pennants running from stem, up her fore-stay to the top of her main mast, across triadic to mizzen, down her back-stay, forming a pyramid of fluttering color above the white sails and hull.

"He's sailing her in," I repeated.

"Damnation!" Steward cursed, picking up one of the coiled ropes at our feet. "Look alive, boys! Maybe that furriner crossed the pond, but he ain't gonna pile Mr. V's new boat up on my dock!"

He'd plow more than the dock and we both knew it. Tied to the gas wharf, ten feet beyond the transient berth was the varnished transom of Mr. John D. Rockefeller's sixty-foot Chris Craft. If our transatlantic skipper misjudged his landing, and we couldn't stop his momentum with a bow spring....

"He might have engine trouble," I said.

"Then he should take all that laundry down." Steward jerked his head at the colorful display flying from the rigging of the ketch, "and hoist 'Q'."

I agreed with him. If his engine didn't work, he should request permission to anchor. If the engine was working, Mr. Van Oudgaarden's delivery captain must be a crackerjack sailor or a dangerous show-off. Either way, I didn't like him or his sailing judgment and hadn't even met him.

The crowd behind us had figured out what was happening and became quiet. I picked up a dock line and turned to look at Mr. V, who was standing now, not visibly anxious, but very interested. He held my gaze and smiled, nodding his head a couple of times. I got the message: 'do not let that man embarrass me in front of my friends.'

The sleek ketch turned head-to-wind, lowered her main, then fell off and bore down on the club again under jib and mizzen. A hundred yards off the dock, he rounded up to the wind again and dropped the mizzen. Not bad without a crew. Now, the hard part.

"You boys keep those fenders between her hull and the dock no matter what," Steward said. "Dutch," he grabbed my arm, "he don't have a spring line rigged!"

The man at the helm could be seen clearly now, his blond hair ruffled by the wind, standing bare-chested in a pair of blue shorts, his skin bronzed by the ocean sun. He held up a coil of rope attached to a stern cleat, then pointed at us. Seasoned sailors don't yell at one another, especially in front of an audience. He wanted us to grab his stern line and wrap it around a bollard to arrest the forward motion of the boat. Twenty-five tons of boat going at that speed would probably part the line or pull his stern cleat out of the deck. Steward sliced his hand back and forth at waist level in a distinctly negative signal, then held his own coiled line up and pointed at the yacht's bow.

"Come 'round again," he growled under his breath, "and get a spring up there, Mister!"

The captain waved his arm in the same negative motion and jabbed his finger at his chest. "I'm the master of this vessel," he seemed to be saying, "you will obey my orders!"

Steward glanced at me shaking his head. "We'll never stop his forward motion with that stern line. Can you scramble aboard, Dutch, and throw a line on both bow cleats?"

The concept was simple: an after-bow spring secured to a forward cleat on a boat and attached to the dock amidships would not only prevent the boat from moving forward but pull the length of the hull into the pier. It was a professional docking procedure that could make a novice helmsman look like an accomplished yachtsman.

I glanced over my shoulder at Mr. 'V,' who was gripping the wooden railing hard enough to leave dents. His daughter, Marijke stood at his side with her arm looped through his. "I'll give it a try," I told Steward.

The ketch was twenty yards off the dock when the skipper let the jib sheets go. Too much way on, I murmured, taking the bitter end of the one-inch rope in my teeth. *We'll never stop her*, I thought.

Steward was taking a turn around the iron bollard bolted

into the dock when the delivery skipper broke the rule, yelling his Nordic lungs out for someone to take his stern line. The dock boys ignored him, intent on their assigned task. Steward was watching me concentrating on the big pole-like bowsprit sweeping inexorably toward me on dead aim for the varnished transom of Mr. Rockefeller's pristine yacht. Two Filipino boys in white jackets had been clearing the remnants of lunch from the after salon of the big Chris Craft when they saw the bow sprit of the ketch bearing down on them. They stared in wide-eyed horror before their trays crashed to the deck as they scampered away from imminent impalement.

The bowsprit past, I grabbed the port gunn'l and took a belly dive onto the fore-deck as Steward played out the line behind me. The wind shook the jib with a vengeance, its sheets lashing above my head like angry whips as I dug my tennis shoes into the teak surface, propelling my body forward on burning knees and elbows, expecting to hear the sickening crunch of wood on wood at any second.

I was still three feet from the cleat when I took the line from my teeth and looped it over a forward horns of the cleats, pulling the bitter end to slide me closer so I could complete the round turn and figure eights. When Steward felt the tension, he took up slack and snubbed down on the bollard, putting twenty-five tons of moving boat on the rope in my hands. Somehow, I managed the round turn, placing the strain on the cleats. The six-foot bowsprit, the circumference of a telephone pole, stopped less than eight inches from the Chris Craft's transom.

It's amazing how the human mind can leap from one problem to another. The skipper let the jib halyard go and the sail dropped down the head-stay on top of me. Lying there on the fore-deck, I was relieved that we had managed to prevent Mr. V's new custom ketch from running up the backside of his club member's yacht. But I wondered if the white strands under the bloody rope burns on my palms were bones or ligaments. And whether I'd ever be able to use them again.

Somebody pulled the heavy canvas off me.

"Imbecile!" a harsh British/Germanic accent shouted behind me. "You disobey my specific wish! You board this boat without permission!"

I rolled over on my back and tried to sit up, but I couldn't put the palms of my hands down on the deck.

"Getting your filthy blood all on my sails!"

He looked like an angry blond god standing above me, tanned legs matted with curly golden hairs spread apart, balled fists on narrow hips. "You almost cause me accident, no? Vhat is your name?"

"Andeweg," I told him, still struggling to get up, my hands feeling like over-inflated basketballs ready to burst. "John Andeweg."

"Who is your superior?"

Anything to get this guy off my case. "Mr. Van Oudgaarden."

"Vel, John Andeweg, I am protesting your unseamanship behavior to Mr. Van Oudgaarden who is also my superior!"

Steward had finished securing the dock lines and stood on the dock beside the boat looking at us. Mr. V was coming down the steps of the veranda, his cheering retinue close behind him. From their vantage point, this fiasco must have looked like a three-point landing.

"Remove him," the god instructed Steward and walked off to meet our employer.

"Welcome to America," I groaned at his retreating back.

Marijke was torn between concern for my bloody hands and the blond god. Mr. V solved her dilemma by having Gregory, his chauffeur, drive me to the hospital with carte blanche instructions to provide me with the best medical care at their disposal.

The damage wasn't irreparable, but I spent a couple of hours under local anesthetic while a hand surgeon sewed my flayed palms back together. After the doctor told me I'd have limited use of my hands for a couple of months, all I could think of was the bad luck that would prevent me from sailing that beautiful new ketch.

In my freshman year at Brown, I answered an ad in *The Providence Journal* for a boat captain. My father had taught me to sail an 'E' Scow when I was seven and I'd been sailing Lake Michigan ever since--so I was certainly qualified for the job. But there were still a lot of men out of work from the Depression, and I always suspected that Mr. V hired me because I was a poor kid with the same ethnic background as his--no family, working my way through college.

He had a thirty-five-foot Herreshoff sloop then, which I scrubbed, polished and helped him sail for three years. That summer of 1941 would be my last, and I'd been looking forward to the new ketch as much as Mr. V had. I came away from the hospital loaded with painkillers and both hands wrapped in bandages.

Gregory drove me back to the servants' quarters in the four-door black Packard Clipper sedan, then helped me change out of my bloody whites into my good slacks and jacket. He even had to tie my necktie. How in blazes was I going to tie a bowline?

The party was out in back of the main house with a live band playing under a green striped canvas tent. A hundred or so guests sat around the pool, stood in clusters near the bar or had wandered down the sloping lawn with drinks in hand to gaze at the sparkling ocean. A late afternoon breeze was blowing in off the water and several couples were dancing in the shade of the tent to 'Stardust,' the current Tommy Dorsey hit.

Mrs. Van Oudgaarden came up behind me and touched my elbow. "Gregory told me the surgeon said your hands will be fine."

She had caught me watching Marijke and her partner dancing. "The doctor called Mr. V?"

"My husband called the hospital." She was a tall woman with dark hair and angular features. "He thinks a great deal of you, John."

"Thank you for saying that."

"It's true."

I turned my bandaged hands up in front of me. "I guess I'll

be spending the summer in Providence this year."

She placed her finger on my wrist. "That's all taken care of."

"I can't help him sail your new boat with these."

"He's hired Pieter Kramers until your hands are healed."

"Who?"

"The delivery captain." She looked out at the blond god dancing with her daughter. "He's agreed to stay the summer."

Great. No job, no hope of getting one with these hands and I had sublet my room on Benefit Street. I was disappointed that I had been replaced so easily. "I can move out of my room over the weekend, if that's OK."

"John! You're staying right where you are. Pieter will do the work and you'll help however you can."

The band had stopped for their break and Marijke was running toward us, towing Kramers by the hand. She was tall and dark like her mother with creamy skin and blue eyes that yearned for happiness. The breeze pressed her yellow dress against her body, swirling around her thighs and she was breathless and flushed when she stopped before us.

"Did you know he fought the Germans?"

"No," I said. Kramers was standing beside her, their hands still clasped in the folds of her skirt.

"He was in the army, then joined the resistance when Holland surrendered." She noticed my bandages. "Are your hands all right, Dutch?"

"They're fine."

"Good." She turned to Kramers who was tamping tobacco into his briar pipe. "Tell them about your escape, Pieter."

I studied the blond man as he spoke in his harsh accent. We were about the same height and build, light-haired, but he was harder, leaner--in his early thirties, more confident than my twenty-two years. He had an annoying mannerism of jerking his head from side to side like a seagull, but he looked right at me as he talked, smirking, which pulled on the red scar at the corner of his sunken eye.

"The *Boche* place a price on my head, posters vit my

picture and vould shoot ten men every day I did not give up." He shrugged, puffing on the brown pipe as he made a gesture with his hand that was again entwined with Marijke's. "The Van Oudgaarden boat had been completed at yard vere I had verk, so I took delivery yob."

Mrs. Van Oudgaarden asked, "Then they didn't shoot anyone?" Kramers looked puzzled. "Oh, I am sure they got tired of that." He turned and grinned at Marijke. "They do not shoot me, anyhow."

Marijke tossed her head back laughing as she scooped two champagne flutes from the tray of a passing waitress. "Here's to our gallant hero," she called out, raising one glass in the air and handing the second to Kramers. They drank their wine looking into each other's eyes under the disapproving stare of her mother.

"I think you've had enough of that, Kiki," Mrs. Van Oudgaarden said.

"Please, mother!" Marijke laced her arm through Kramers'. "I'm a grown woman."

"Then try to behave like a lady," her mother replied. Marijke rolled her eyes at me as Mr. V joined us just in time.

"What's this, what's this?" He laid his hand on my shoulder. "Shouldn't you be resting, my boy?"

"I feel fine, sir," I lied.

"Good, good." He turned to Kramers who had released Marijke's hand and was sucking on his pipe. "We'll have to get you settled in, get your things off the boat."

"That's all taken care of, Daddy. I've had Francis move him into the guest suite in the west wing."

Her parents exchanged looks which their daughter interpreted correctly. "Pieter is our guest," she said, "not a servant. The only reason he's staying is to help with the boat until Dutch's hands get better."

"Fine, fine." Her father was used to capitulating to his strong-willed daughter. "We'd love to have you stay with us, Mr. Kramers."

"Call me Pieter, please," the Dutchman said.

"Pieter, then." Mr. V reached out and shook his hand.

"Welcome to our home."

* * * * * *

That was not my best summer. Without the use of my hands I couldn't row a dinghy or pull the starter cord on an outboard, much less haul a sheet or take the wheel on the ketch. I went out with Kramers a few days after he arrived and couldn't even brace myself when the boat heeled in the bay. Kramers told Mr. V he was afraid I'd hurt my hands if a sudden squall came up and I was grounded after that.

July dragged by with me on the beach trying to concentrate on Steinbeck's new book, *Of Mice and Men*, while the Van Oudgaarden's entertained their friends on *Dutch Master*. When they didn't invite people for day sails on the bay, Mr. V and Kramers took a bunch of men out for club races or an occasional regatta. The owner had to attend several meetings in New York that month, which left Kramers free to take Marijke for long sails on Rhode Island sound, from which they rarely returned until after dark.

Gregory drove me to the hospital a couple of times a week to get my bandages changed, the stitches removed and learn how to squeeze a rubber ball. I didn't see Marijke as much as I had in previous summers when it was me she'd get to take her sailing or come pounding on the gatehouse door, rousing me out of my loft at seven in the morning for an early set of tennis. I thought things would pick up in August when my hands got better, but everyone seemed locked into a routine by then and I wasn't part of it.

Mr. V made sure I was a member of his crew whenever he took guests out or raced, but Kramers had established himself as skipper of *Dutch Master* and shouted his harsh orders at me like he did at everyone else except our employer. The only way I got to sail with Marijke was when I went aboard early to polish brass before she and Kramers came out to the mooring with a picnic basket. They couldn't very well ask me to leave, but I'm sure Kramers wanted to.

One day Kramers and Marijke came out in the launch with Julia Bettencourt, a friend of Marijke's. She'd made plans to pair me up with Julia for a day sail up the East Passage into Mount Hope Bay and out the Sakonnet River. Julia was a flighty brunette who after coming out in the Debutante Cotillion had rejected college for the Junior League and a heavy social calendar. She was amenable to a lazy day of sun and cold beer on her friend's yacht, but clearly not interested in the hired help of one of her peers.

Before we put the sails up, Julia produced a Kodak Brownie and asked me to take a picture of the two girls hamming it up together. Then they draped themselves around Kramers standing at the helm and I shot a half a roll of the three of them, plus several posed pictures that Marijke wanted of her and Kramers alone. When I handed the camera back to Julia, she said, "Oh, I have only one more frame on this roll. Dutch, why don't you get up there on the cabin top with Marijke and Pieter so I can get all three of you?"

Pieter had stripped down to his blue rugby shorts and was leaning against the furled sail on the main boom, his tanned arms folded across his hairless chest. Marijke wore a green wraparound skirt and sleeveless blouse with a gold barrette holding her dark hair away from her face.

She jumped up beside Kramers. "Come on, Dutch, get up here!"

The bandages had come off my hands the week before and I'd been working on the engine in a pair of old khaki pants and frayed dress shirt stained with oil. I didn't feel like getting my picture taken and said so.

"Come on, come on," the girls insisted. "Clark Gable you ain't," Marijke reached her hand out to me, "but I want my whole crew in this."

I climbed up and stood on her left, trying not to look as uncomfortable as I felt, with Kramers stiff and unsmiling on her right, the Ida Lewis Yacht Club on the shore behind us. Julie urged us to crowd closer together and snapped the picture quickly, so she could load another roll of film before we left the mooring. Marijke enjoyed the irony of her two suitors posing together and her impish expression showed it. Later, when I looked at the stilted photograph that Julie Bettencourt took that afternoon. I saw it as an omen of the events that would happen to the three of us through the following year.

During the first weeks of August, Marijke and Kramers came out to the boat alone and I became their crew, stuck on the helm with the two of them sunning themselves forty feet away on the fore-deck, out of my sight behind the cabin housing, the sweet aroma of his pipe tobacco carried aft on the summer breeze. In spite of my love of sailing, after a couple of those trips, I rowed ashore when they interrupted my chores without Kramers having to ask me. As a matter of fact, it was the worst summer I can remember. I don't think I minded losing my dreams about Marijke as much as I did losing her friendship. What chance did a penniless twenty-two-year-old college kid on financial aid, working a summer job have against an intrepid war hero, single-handed transatlantic sailor?

It was after Labor Day when everything really fell apart. I was going back to my senior year at Brown, so I would not return to my summer job the following year. Mr. V held a farewell party for me beside the pool, Steward came with some of the dock boys and small boat sailors I'd befriended at the yacht club during the previous summers I'd worked on Mr. V's boat. His regular crew were invited: James Barnum, a Washington attorney I'd played chess with in quiet harbors; Paul Graham and his wife Ellen, who brought their three-year old daughter, Stephanie. Gregory and the rest of the servants were encouraged to toast my health and future prosperity after graduation in the spring.

Mr. V gave me a warm speech and a bronze sextant which I still have. His wife blinked back tears as she kissed my cheek. And Marijke couldn't look me in the eye when she broke away from Kramers' side to give me a brief hug good-bye.

The party broke up about 9:30, and I was packing when Marijke came up to my room in the gatehouse. She had the decency to be embarrassed but didn't apologize.

"I'd almost forgotten," she said, "you're a senior this year."

"Finally!"

She sat on the edge of the bed and I kept putting clothes in the suitcase beside her. "We might not see you anymore."

"Guess not."

"We didn't have as much fun this summer, did we?"

"I didn't."

She wore a sleeveless dress of white linen in attractive contrast with her long brown arms, hands resting on her lap, her fingers twisting a lace hankie. "I'm sorry, Dutch." I held a folded shirt above the open suitcase. "I don't suppose there's anything I can say," she continued. "I'm not going back to school."

She was a junior at Sarah Lawrence. "Why not?"

"It doesn't seem important any more. Pieter says America will be dragged into the war in Europe whether we want to or not."

"Mr. Roosevelt disagrees."

"He was there, Dutch. You have no idea what it's like."

I stopped packing and looked in her eyes.

"When is he going back?"

"He's not. Daddy made inquiries about getting him a job at the Brooklyn Navy Yard."

I went back to my packing. "So, you'll be seeing him in New York."

"He's a wonderful man, Dutch...kind, brilliant and very brave."

"He's what, ten, twelve years older than you are."

"He's forceful and disciplined. That will be good for me."

"You don't need someone to tell you what to do, Marijke."

"Maybe I do," she said. Then sat there staring at her wrinkled handkerchief. Suddenly, she jumped off the bed and threw her arms around my neck. "I have to go."

I could smell the gin on her breath and held her away from me. "Marijke, are you OK?"

"Of course, I'm OK," she said, dabbing the handkerchief at her eyes. "Good-bye, Dutch. Write to me, will you?"

"I don't know Marijke. What will I say?"

"Then don't!" she cried and ran from the room.

"Marijke!" I shouted.

She flew down the stairs and out of the gatehouse. I followed as far as the front door and stood there watching her white dress floating across the lawn in the darkness.

"Marijke!"

"Marijke!"

CHAPTER TWENTY-TWO
Providence, RI
October 1941

Back at school everyone was talking about the war in Europe. The German army had conquered Poland, Denmark, Norway, Finland, Belgium, Holland and Luxembourg. France surrendered after the devastating defeat of the combined French and English forces at Dunkirk. Paris was declared an open city, and on *Juin 14*[th] the German's marched into the capitol to minimal resistance and few shots fired.

Luftwaffe bombers were terrorizing London in the Battle of Britain, dumping tons of explosives in offensive raids, killing 500 civilians a day. Hitler staged a massive attack on Russia, sweeping across 600,000 square miles of the Soviet Union to the outskirts of Moscow.

Incredible rumors began to filter back to the west of mass executions of Polish and Russian civilians, prisoners of war and Jews by Nazi soldiers. That summer German submarines torpedoed three American warships. Although President Roosevelt claimed those disasters would not affect U.S.-German diplomatic relations, Secretary of War Stimson drew the first number for America's peacetime military draft. I buckled down to my senior engineering thesis and jerking soda at Thayer's Drug Store.

Getting into a training program at one of the big firms like Stone & Webster or Bechtel was my immediate goal, but jobs were still scarce. I thought I might have to work day labor for a year or so in some small construction firm, if I could get that. The war could change everything.

Then Marijke called me one Friday afternoon from the Biltmore in downtown Providence.

"Since you didn't write," she said, "I thought I'd visit."

I tried to sound casual. "Great. What's the occasion?"

"Isn't this homecoming? Big doings at Brown's College?"

We were playing Columbia and the whole school had pinned its hopes on Bob Margarita who was leading the country in punt returns.

"Kind of last minute, isn't it? Suppose I had a date?"

"Do you?"

"No."

"That's swell," she teased, "'cause I'd make you break it if you did. What time do the festivities start?"

With a couple of drinks Marijke was always the life of the party. We showed up at the frat house at seven and didn't leave until last call. The jitterbug was starting to replace the Charleston as the hot dance of the season and Marijke showed us all the latest steps that originated in the nightspots of New York City. The walk down College Hill to the Biltmore cleared her head a little and I screwed up my courage to ask about Kramers.

"Let's not talk about that old fuddy-duddy tonight," she answered. "This'll be our weekend, our last fling."

I tried to press her on that, but she wouldn't budge. After she sneaked me past the desk clerk up to her room, I forgot all about it.

Margarita set a 233-yard single-game rushing record the following afternoon and we beat the Big City Blues by thirteen points. That Saturday night, the whole campus went crazy, including Marijke and me. After hopping from one frat house to another until the wee morning hours, Marijke snuck me up to her room again and we drank from a flask she produced from her suitcase.

We talked about the first two summers we'd spent together in splendid intimacy, but not the last one. The winter phone calls, our silly letters, the times I'd gone up to Sarah Lawrence, the weekends she'd come to Brown.

We had always behaved like brother and sister, had never gone much farther than long kisses and frustrating gratification that Marijke lead me up to then down, laughing, the repetitious instances so inane that I couldn't help laughing myself.

That night was different.

We'd been awake all night, probably the most euphoric eight hours I had spent in my life. We lay under the sheets, our bodies warm and slick, still entwined, reluctant to return to reality. For a few moments that morning, I had hopes that my dreams had come true.

It was almost dawn when she said, "He wants to marry me."

I felt as though I'd been pushed off a cliff. "Oh?"

"You could wish me congratulations."

I sat up on the edge of the bed. "No, I couldn't do that."

"Happiness, then?" she pleaded.

When I turned to look at her, she was sitting up in bed, eyes brimming with tears. I guess I was able to smile despite my dashed hopes that began to crush me into black depression.

"Happiness."

She buried her face in her hands, shoulders shaking with muffled sobs; the sheet had slipped from her breasts making her look like some forlorn child from a seventeenth century Italian painting.

"Marijke, what's wrong?"

"I'm OK!" She willed her emotions under control, touching the corner of the bed sheet to her eyes. "I'm in love with a good man, aren't I?"

"I don't know. Are you?"

"Yes!" she shouted at me. "Yes, I am, goddamn you, Dutch Andeweg!"

Women!

* * * * * *

I was never able to figure out what she was trying to prove that weekend or what I could have done to make things turn out different. I tried to concentrate on my studies after she left but wasn't having much success until the first of December when Mrs. Van Oudgaarden sent me the announcement of her daughter's marriage to Pieter Kramers.

The Japanese bombed Pearl Harbor on the following Sunday. We declared war on Japan the next day and on

Germany three days later. I forced Marijke into the back of my mind. I had other things to think about.

A month before graduation, the C.O. of my A-12 Naval unit sent a runner to get me out of class with instructions to report to him immediately. When the department yeoman brought me into the Commander's office, James Barnum, Mr. Van Oudgaarden's friend and crew-member was alone in the room seated behind the CO's desk.

He was a tall angular man in his mid-fifties with graying hair and horn-rimmed glasses. When we raced Mr. V's boat, he served as navigator, a precise master of geometry with a relaxed demeanor who inspired confidence and respect in the crew. I had lost countless chess games to him on extended cruises when we'd been forced to wait out bad weather in remote harbors. On the boat, he wore the baggy khaki trousers, frayed Brooks Brothers' shirts and worn tweed jackets affected by the scions of old moneyed families who had nothing to prove.

That day his attire consisted of a tailored three-piece suit of pinstriped flannel, starched shirt and four-in-hand club necktie. We engaged in small talk for a couple of minutes until Mr. Barnum said, "I have come to ask you to volunteer for a military mission for which you are uniquely qualified, Dutch."

At that point, I believed the man was a successful Washington lawyer and amateur yachtsman. I had no idea what he was talking about or how to respond. He must have read the confusion on my face and began to explain.

"In time of war, some of us are called upon to serve our country in rather extraordinary ways. A Colonel William J. Donovan, who reports directly to President Roosevelt has asked me to act as counsel to his new agency, the Office of Strategic Services."

Volunteer for a mission for an agency I'd never heard of, run by an army officer who answered to FDR? I was going to be commissioned in the Navy when I graduated the following month.

The A-12 section was squeezed into the basement of Sales

Hall. The CO's office was small and cluttered. I was sitting in a wooden chair across the desk from Mr. Barnum. Shafts of spring sunshine from the narrow windows near the ceiling warmed my legs.

"What did you mean," I asked, "when you said I was uniquely qualified?"

"Allow me to proceed at a certain pace, Dutch." He smiled, but I had never seen him this serious before. "The mission to which I referred has a high priority on our agenda for the war in Europe." Mr. Barnum clasped his hands and leaned forward in his chair, forearms resting on the edge of the desk. "It could be dangerous. It might require physical...violence."

The room felt chill despite the sunshine and I found myself wishing I was back in class. "Are you asking me to volunteer for this mission based on that?"

"I said we would proceed at a pace. If you refuse the assignment as I have described it so far, we will terminate this conversation and no one except the two of us will ever know it took place." He paused. "If, however, you believe you have the capacity to accept this responsibility, I will tell you more."

"Until I do refuse."

He smiled again. "That is correct."

"I joined the Navy prepared to fight a war, Mr. Barnum. Let's hear the next part."

It was simple. Four Nazi spies had been landed by U-boat near Amagansett, Long Island. They were set up to collect information on defense installations on our northeast coast for a planned invasion of the United States. The shortwave radio code they were using to transmit data to Germany had been broken by OSS cryptographers who were intercepting the Nazi messages, substituting disinformation and relaying it back to Berlin. The FBI had come to believe that a fifth spy had entered the country by other means. This agent was apparently free to travel in the U.S. He was scheduled to rendezvous with a German submarine off the New England coast during the summer to deliver annotated maps of our coastal defense systems and reports of the radio messages which would tell the enemy we had broken their code and alert them to our disinformation ploy.

In April '42 the invasion of the United States by Adolph Hitler's Third Reich was a real concern of our government and civilian population. Batteries of aircraft searchlights had been installed around east coast cities. Blackouts were enforced in major metropolitan areas. Civil Defense volunteers with triangular insignia on white helmets and armbands searched the night skies with binoculars from the roofs of office buildings.

Beside the four spies under surveillance on Long Island, a U-boat had landed three agents in Sullivan, Maine where they were captured by the FBI that had been alerted to the strangers in town by the suspicious son of the local sheriff. On the west coast, a Japanese submarine had shelled an oil refinery in Elwood, California.

Two pairs of Nazi spies had come ashore at separate locations in Florida. One of them, George Dash, turned himself and his fellow agents in to the FBI. When interrogated, Dash gave the location of the Long Island group and the means of entry into the country used by the fifth agent.

"The mission I mentioned," Mr. Barnum said, "is determining when this agent is ready to make his move so we can prevent him from delivering his information to the U-boat."

"Then you know who he is?"

"We think we do." Mr. Barnum offered me a Lucky from the green pack, which had been resting on the desk beside a glass ashtray. I declined, and he lit up.

"Why not arrest him?"

"Because he may be working with others we don't know about. They could be holding the material for him until the last moment, so it doesn't get seized if we capture him. If that were the case, the information could still find its way to Berlin by another route and we would never know it."

"Why is learning the delivery date so dangerous?"

"This man is not a frightened George Dash or some other born-in-America German whose sole credential for espionage is fluency in our idiom." Mr. Barnum's eyes locked on mine before he resumed. "This man is a trained killer." He let that register for a couple of seconds. "You would need to be with him, keep him under surveillance, search for his maps and message transcripts." He paused again, drawing deeply on his cigarette. "You may be required to prevent him from getting them aboard the U-Boat."

I was afraid to repeat the question he still hadn't answered. "What makes you think I'm so right for this job?"

"Are you inclined to take it?"

"I've never done anything like that."

"Few of us have."

"Can I think about it?"

"Whether or not to fight for your country?"

He was right. I was in the Navy. If my ship got torpedoed I wouldn't get a chance to think about that. How about the marines getting shot in the south Pacific? The G.I.'s they left on the beachheads in Tunisia? Nobody was giving them a choice. I was afraid of two things--I could get killed and that I would fail.

"Would I get special training?"

He looked relieved. "You'll start hand-to-hand combat school the day after tomorrow in Quantico, Virginia."

I hadn't realized how badly he wanted me to do this. "Your mental agility displayed during our games of chess have impressed me no end." He stubbed out his cigarette and swept the pack off the desk into his pocket. "When you return, I'll brief you on the details and trade craft, as Donovan calls it."

"I'll miss graduation. My sheepskin."

Mr. Barnum rose from his chair and picked up a thin briefcase of soft brown leather from the corner of the desk. "I'll see that it gets mailed to you."

"You still haven't answered my question." I had remained seated and was glad that I had. "Why me?"

He pushed his glasses up on the bridge of his nose and scowled. "The man we suspect of being the fifth Nazi spy is Pieter Kramers."

CHAPTER TWENTY-THREE
Newport, RI
April 1942

When I rowed out to *Dutch Master* Marijke was in the cockpit, reclining against the cabin housing in the shade of a canvas awning stretched across the boom. She wore a black scoop neck bathing suit with her hands clasped around a towel draped over her knees that were pulled up on the cockpit seat cushions. Perhaps a few pounds heavier than last summer, but her skin looked tan and healthy, her face radiant. Our greetings were subdued as I tossed my sea bag and 30 caliber Springfield rifle onto the catwalk. She eyed the weapon soberly and we were both reminded that this was not a pleasure cruise. That was our first meeting since our Home Coming Weekend and we experienced some initial embarrassment and coolness toward one another.

During my briefing in Quantico, Mr. Barnum told me that Kramers had quit his job at the Brooklyn Navy Yard after learning that his access to classified information was restricted. During the past few months he had applied for work at shipyards from Norfolk to Bath, Maine, eluding his FBI watchers on several occasions. Mr. Barnum had decided to keep closer tabs on Kramers and attempt to precipitate his delivery contact by suggesting that Mr. V volunteer *Dutch Master* for duty in the new Corsair Fleet with his son-in-law as captain.

Kramers came up through the companionway, his pipe clenched in his teeth and stood in the cockpit wiping his hands on an oily rag.

"Ensign Andeweg, our young naval commander," he said while I was still in the dinghy. "Do not confuse your position with mine."

"Our responsibilities are spelled out in your written

orders," I said. "You make the sailing decisions; I make the military ones."

Kramers leaned over, picked up the rifle and threw the bolt back, laughing. "You are going to sink a German submarine with this?"

I climbed aboard and took the rifle from him. "Maybe I'll shoot some spies."

The red scar on his left temple had healed to a thin white line, and the glass prosthesis which had replaced his missing eye looked more natural when he squinted. "You will do as I say on this boat."

"Here come the others," Marijke said.

Mr. V and the rest of his crew were standing in the club launch as it motored across the harbor toward us. None of them really thought we would encounter Nazi submarines but they were taking the patrol seriously, believing that the presence of this civilian/Coast Guard effort would deter German espionage attempts from the sea. They were doing their part in the war and it was exciting.

Paul and Ellen Graham came aboard with James Barnum as Kramers took Marijke's hand and helped her to her feet. The towel fell away from her bent knees as she stood, revealing a very pregnant midsection.

"Do not have my child while I am gone," Kramers said, kissing her cheek before handing her into the launch. But she did.

During that fifteen-day period, we settled into a routine of four-on-eight-off watches with the Grahams on one shift, Mr. Barnum and Kramers on another and Mr. V and myself on the third. Our patrol group consisted of a Coast Guard picket boat and four Corsair yachts, whose assigned duty stations covered 600 square miles of Rhode Island and Block Island Sounds from Cuttyhunk Island to the Connecticut border.

Our mission was to observe the eastern approaches to the two most important strategic naval installations on the New England coast: Quonset Point Naval Air Station on the west shore of Narragansett Bay in Rhode Island and the combined facilities of the New London Submarine Base and Electric Boat Works in Groton, Connecticut, located across the Thames River from one another in Connecticut. A similar Corsair group was responsible for the western approach from New York harbor to Montauk Point, Long Island.

On that first patrol, we saw no signs of German submarines or Nazi spies and the trip was more like a pleasure cruise than guard duty. *Dutch Master* was a dream to sail and the winds blew steadily out of the southwest under sunny skies and a zillion stars.

Scheduling problems for our replacement yacht extended our first two-week assignment through early July. On the sixth, Mrs. van Oudgaarden called us ship-to-shore to inform us that Marijke had given birth to an eight-pound son. Mr. V uncorked bottles of champagne at eight o'clock in the morning and we toasted the health of his new grandson. It was the only time that I ever saw Kramers lose control of himself because of alcohol or anything else. I guess it was excusable under the circumstances.

Despite our uneventful cruise and the happy announcement from Newport, the war news imposed a somber atmosphere aboard the ketch. In his six o'clock evening broadcasts from New York, Gabriel Heatter's staccato voice reported the British surrender of Singapore to the Japanese after a two-week siege; the fall of Corregidor and capture of 42,000 American and Filipino soldiers in one of the worst military defeats in U.S. history; and the sinking of an American cargo ship by a *Nazi* U-boat in the mouth of the Mississippi River which resulted in the deaths of twenty-seven merchant seamen. Heatter's standard opening over the Mutual Broadcasting System, 'Ah, there's good news tonight...', was suspended during most of that summer.

CBS war correspondent Edward R. Murrow issued equally dire reports from London: thousands of Canadian troops had died on the beaches of Dieppe in a daring commando raid into northern France; eleven thousand Russian soldiers were killed and twenty-nine-thousand wounded when the Nazis overran the Soviet Black Sea naval base of Sevastopol;

the Desert Fox, Field Marshal Erwin Rommel, plunged sixty-miles into Egypt in captured Allied tanks, scattering British forces demoralized by the fall of Tobruk; and *SS* storm troopers executed 1,300 civilians in the town of Lidice in reprisal for the assassination by Czech resistance fighters of Gestapo Officer Reinhard Heydrich, 'The Hangman of Europe.'

After that initial cruise, *Dutch Master* went out on ten-day patrols every other week with a different crew, depending on the civilian jobs and other responsibilities of our core contingent. Kramers and I were always aboard, sailing the ketch in grudging tandem with local yachtsmen and acquaintances of varied experience. Between patrols, I made frequent excursions out to the yacht to search for the material Kramers was expected to cast adrift for retrieval by a Nazi sub. My efforts were futile through the remainder of the summer until five days before our patrol that was scheduled for the end of August.

When I removed the floorboards in the head one afternoon, I found a waterproof packet wedged above the bilge between the outer hull and interior liner. It was sealed with the same black electrical tape we kept in the boson's locker, so I opened the bulky glassine envelope and examined the contents by flashlight on the lid of the marine toilet. Inside, just as the FBI had suspected, were naval charts of coastal Rhode Island and Connecticut with superimposed drawings of the locations of anti-submarine nets and mines that spanned the entrance to Narragansett Bay and the Thames River. Supplemental sketches of the docks at Quonset showed the carrier *Wasp* being refit with new aircraft, several destroyers nestled together at the Newport Naval Base and the location of our submarine pens in New London. Four exposed rolls of 35-millimeter film and a couple of dozen pages of coded transcript completed the package. I replaced the floorboards, jammed the bulky envelope under my belt, took a spool of black tape from a ditty bag and rowed ashore

* * * * * *

When I telephoned Mr. Barnum at his home in Washington, he didn't seem surprised at my discovery. He asked me to take the train to New York that night and meet him at Belleview hospital the following morning where he would be taking his annual physical examination.

A secretary came out to the admissions desk and escorted me up to the sixth floor where Mr. Barnum awaited me in a small windowless consultation room with a red-haired man he introduced as Special Agent Frank DePrete of the Federal Bureau of Investigation. I placed the glassine packet and the roll of electrical tape on the desk. DePrete picked them up without looking inside, walked to the door and passed them to a man waiting in the outer room.

The agent was a couple of years older than me, shorter and better dressed. He wore a brown double-breasted suit with a starched white collar, dark green tie and French cuffs. My Coast Guard officer's uniform looked like it had been slept in, which it had.

When Mr. Barnum and I were seated, he inclined his head toward the agent and said, "They rounded up 158 German aliens in the City last week."

"We raided the German-American Vocational League on East 86th and got their membership roster," DePrete said. "Some other documents in code."

"The same code the spies in Amagansett are using," Mr. Barnum added, "the one we broke." He was sitting on the edge of his seat behind the tiny desk, his back stiff, hands grasping the wooden arms of the chair.

"One of the documents referred to the man you're watching." DePrete was standing to the side of the desk, arms folded across his chest with his shoulder touching the wall, but not leaning his weight against it. I was sitting on the opposite side of the desk like a sick patient, dreading the bad news that I knew I would hear.

Mr. Barnum reached for his cigarettes and cleared his throat. "Their plans have changed, Dutch. Kramers will not simply pass our defense material onto the U-boat. He's going back to Berlin to interpret it for them."

I felt relieved. "Then all you have to do is capture him, right?"

DePrete nodded. "We could do that, yes."

"Then someone else would deliver comparable information," Mr. Barnum said, "whom we might not catch. The Germans would still find out their Amagansett operation had been compromised."

"Which could have happened anyway, I said, if you had prevented Kramers from delivering the packet to the U-boat as originally planned.

"Colonel Donovan believes we have a greater opportunity than that," Mr. Barnum continued. "Secretary Stimson and the President agree."

I felt nauseous again, as much from being manipulated by my own people as what they were going to ask me to do. Yet I needed to hear it. "Which is...."

"Kramers is a Dutch national," Mr. Barnum interrupted, "his mother German. As you know, he was in the resistance movement in Holland."

"But really a Nazi agent," DePrete added. "The Dutch found him out, shot him in the head and tossed him on the front steps of the German administrator in Rotterdam."

"The Germans patched his wound," Mr. Barnum said, "and figured that Kramers was the ideal agent to take advantage of Mr. Van Oudgaarden's boat delivery. They sent him here to assess our defense systems and verify the Amagansett operation. The rest you know."

"He's going back to Berlin," DePrete said, "to work with German Intelligence on their invasion plans for America. If we let him return with sketches of Quonset and Groton, and Amagansett message reports, he'll help them devise an invasion plan with all the knowledge of our weakness and defenses."

"Only a handful of Nazis in occupied Holland have ever seen Kramers," Mr. Barnum said. "No one in Germany knows exactly what he looks like."

I was maybe three seconds behind them, but my stomach

started turning cold and I could sense it coming, especially when he used my Christian name.

"John, if we had a man inside Admiral Canaris' staff," I heard Mr. Barnum say, "feeding them erroneous information, making them think we have a stronger defense system than we do, getting word of their plans back to us...."

I could pass for Pieter Kramers under the circumstances they described. We were both blond, looked roughly the same age, about the same build and height. I spoke Dutch, my family language, enough German. except...."

".... wouldn't have to waste our resources," Mr. Barnum continued, "changing our defensive tactics, rebuilding elaborate alternative deterrents. If the Germans believed our northeast coast was well-protected, we could shift men and equipment from defense to offensive units, start whupping their tails, save thousands of lives." He had trouble meeting my gaze in the silence that followed.

"You didn't come here for your annual physical today," I told him.

He shook his head and seemed to crumple inside his expensive suit, looking older and more tired than I'd ever seen him. "No, John, I did not."

"We could send you out on a battleship," the FBI agent said, "you could get wounded or killed."

The older man whirled on him. "Shut up, Agent DePrete!"

I glanced around the room and noticed the padded leather chair in the corner, the wooden cabinet with its stack of narrow drawers, a device that looked like an elaborate pair of binoculars attached to a sturdy arm folded against the wall. A white chart with a big black 'E' at the top and a diminishing alphabet under it.

"This is a sacrifice that your country has no right to ask of you," Mr. Barnum said.

"But you are asking." I almost felt sorry for the man. "Aren't you, sir?"

* * * * * *

I left the hospital and walked around the city. The sidewalks were filled with summer whites and khaki uniforms, sauntering along in pairs and groups, laughing, whistling, ogling girls who were willing participants in the harmless pursuit of what literally might be the last fling some of those boys would ever have.

I wandered down Broadway to Washington Square, a scuffed grass oasis with broad shade trees dwarfed by the office buildings of lower Manhattan. I sat on a wooden bench, oblivious to the noise of congested summer traffic. A colored nanny in a white uniform rocked a carriage on the other end of my bench watching the pair of old men across from us playing cribbage. Garrulous late teen and early twenty-year old kids in uniform strolled past, holding hands with thoughtful girls. Two nurses sat at a picnic bench under a leafy oak with several soldiers, some with crutches leaning against the table, a few in wheelchairs, others with casts or bandages wrapped around their heads. My gaze drifted up to the inscription on the lintel of the granite arch across the way, a remark uttered by our first president: "*Let us raise a standard to which the wise and honest can repair.*"

As I trudged back toward Belleview the sun dropped behind the skyline, its lingering heat rising off the cement sidewalks enveloping me and late workers straggling out of their offices. Crossing 42nd Street, I closed my left eye to see what it would be like and discovered the meaning of the phrase blindsided. It was better when I cocked my head to the left but learned that the peripheral vision of a one-eyed man is reduced by roughly forty percent. Now I knew why Kramers had that habit of swiveling his head from side to side.

Mr. Barnum was waiting in the same examining room when I returned, sitting behind the little desk much as he had almost seven hours earlier. An empty pack of Lucky Strikes lay crumpled beside a half-full ashtray.

"I knew you'd be back," he said.

"There didn't seem to be any place else to go."

He pursed his lips and almost said something but decided against it. Then he picked up the phone and dialed a two-digit number. "Your patient is ready, Doctor. Will you join us, please?"

Dr. Samuel Gillespie walked into the room ten minutes later with Agent DePrete. The ophthalmic surgeon was in his early thirties, short, balding, and visibly uncomfortable. He asked me to sit in the leather chair, darkened the room and produced a chrome cylinder from the breast pocket of his smock that he used to probe into my eyes with a thin beam of light.

Gillespie straightened up and put the instrument back in his pocket. "I can't do this."

The only light in the room was from a small shaded lamp on the corner of the desk. DePrete stood by the door, his features in shadow. "We've been all through it, Doctor."

"I'm trained to save people's sight," the surgeon shouted, "not take it!"

"His mission will save thousands of lives," DePrete answered.

"Would you rather feel guilty about all those deaths?"

"I'd rather not mutilate a healthy body."

"There's a war on, Doc. A lot of people have to do unpleasant things."

"Not decent people. Not any means to an end, surely. That's not our way."

DePrete looked at his watch. "Doctor, you've been chosen to help us because you're good at what you do and frankly, because you're shipping out with the army next week for Hawaii, which will minimize our security problems." DePrete took a step closer to the physician and pointed a finger at his chest. "Now, you can perform this operation and go off to save the sight of hundreds of boys in the Pacific who could use your wonderful skills," he lowered his voice, "or by God, Gillespie, I'll have you shipped into a forward combat unit where all you'll do is pick shrapnel out of your ass between amputations!"

The physician looked at Mr. Barnum who said nothing, then at me. "You are doing this of your own volition?"

"I suppose so."

"Dammit, man, enucleation is not something to be taken

lightly!" The surgeon brushed past DePrete, flicked on the wall switch, and the harsh fluorescent lighting flooded the room. "It cannot be reversed. If you should injure your other eye, it gets diseased...."

"What are the chances of that happening?" Mr. Barnum asked.

Gillespie shrugged. "In peacetime, a normal civilian life— three, five percent. Combat, whatever crazy mission he intends to undertake? Much higher."

DePrete changed the subject. "He has to be back in Newport tomorrow.

"Impossible!" Gillespie said. "This isn't like pulling a tooth, it's a shock to the body, a chance of infection."

"Give him antibiotics," DePrete said. "He can rest on the train."

"He'll need to be fitted for a prosthesis," Gillespie persisted.

"No, he won't," DePrete said, turning to me. "If he gets caught with an American-made glass eye, he'll wish he were dead and get his wish."

Now that he had me, the agent seemed to want to test my resolve. "You're both blue-eyed, you'll have to use Kramers'."

The doctor jammed a fist in the side pocket of his smock and reached for the doorknob. "I'm doing this under duress."

"Me, too," I said.

CHAPTER TWENTY-FOUR
Rhode Island Sound
August 1942

The plan was to wait until Kramers contacted the sub, restrain him and take his place. Simple. Mr. Barnum would be part of the crew, and although he was a fifty-seven-year-old desk man, he would be armed, prepared to restrain Kramers while I went off to the U-boat. Then he and the others would take him back to DePrete in Newport.

The rest of the crew could not be told anything until the German sub showed up. Their ignorance would lessen the chance they might react to Kramers in a way that would make him suspicious. Marijke was recovering from childbirth and would be spared the trauma of seeing her husband arrested at gunpoint as a Nazi spy. The fallacy in all this was that we did not know Kramers' plan. How he would rendezvous with the sub or what steps he might take to incapacitate us while he made his escape.

The first thing wrong with our assumptions was Marijke's insistence on going on that patrol. The inactivity of the past six weeks and the constant demands of her new son were not her idea of an exciting summer. Her husband did everything except refuse to take her but must have figured that making too big an issue of it might look odd. Mr. Barnum and I could say nothing.

The second awkward moment occurred when Marijke quipped that the gauze bandage over the infection in my eye made Kramers and I look like twins. Neither one of us appreciated that and none of the others laughed. I think Marijke had a few drinks before she came aboard and was elated at the prospect of ten days away from the tedium of her maternal responsibilities.

We left Newport at two P.M. in bright sunshine on August

23rd, with Kramers and I as co-captains and Mr. Barnum navigating. Marijke, Ellen and Paul Graham made up the remainder of the crew. While Kramers was busy getting the ketch out of the harbor. I went below and looked through his sea bag for a handgun, then removed the firing pin from my Springfield rifle. I hadn't found any weapons hidden on the boat when I replaced the sealed packet of altered maps three days earlier, so unless Kramers had one on his person or stashed one away since then, Mr. Barnum would be the only man on the boat who was armed.

The weather turned lousy that night. Fog so thick that it dripped from the sails and lifelines as we ghosted through two raw days and nights of light winds and intermittent rain. Moisture drenched our faces, gathering around our necks and seeped under the collars of our slickers. Everything was damp below, including bunks and blankets. On watch there was nothing to do but stare into the gray veil that enveloped us, too uncomfortable for polite conversation, impotently alert for other vessels that we would probably hit before seeing. Blowing the fog horn would only alert any quarry that was out there.

Marijke came on deck with the Grahams on the evening of the twenty-fifth, all in good spirits, each with a glass of clear liquid in hand. Kramers had the helm. I stood by the starboard shrouds listening for the sound of an engine, peering into the solid mist that I hoped would not reveal a dark shape bearing down on us.

"This is not a time to drink," Kramers told the off-watch crew.

"Oh, Pieter," Marijke said, "don't be such an old fogey! There's nothing else to do."

"I will not have my crew drunk," he said.

"Now, now, Old Skipper, no one's drunk," Paul Graham said. "We're just upholding one of our time-honored American traditions called The Cocktail Hour."

"Your American traditions will lose the war."

The venom in Kramers' voice made me turn to look at him. He was standing behind the wheel in glistening oilskins, gripping the varnished wheel as though he were battling gale force winds.

Ellen Graham tried to ease the tension. "Oh, nonsense! A little drinkie before dinner never hurt anybody."

Marijke accepted a cigarette from Paul, raising her head from his cupped hands when it was lit. "Don't make such a big deal out of everything, darling husband. We're not a bunch of your resistance lackeys."

Kramers' face puckered with rage as he reached forward, slapping the glass out of his wife's hand and into the water. *"Du werden auf disem Schiff das tun, was ich befehle!"* [On this ship you will do as I instruct.]

We all stared at him. Under stress, multilingual people tend to revert to their native or preferred language. The Grahams didn't realize it, but Marijke and I knew that he had shouted at her in German, not Dutch. She began yelling back at him, probably shrugging it off as an inadvertent lapse into one of the many tongues of Europe in which Hollanders become fluent. I asked my grandfather why that was so and he replied, "Because no one else is going to learn Dutch."

But Kramers quick outburst in German registered with me. If German was that easy for him to yell in, maybe DePrete was wrong about him being unknown in Berlin. Maybe that Nazi sub would be carrying me right to my own funeral.

"Andeweg!" Kramers called out. "Take the helm."

I moved aft and took the wheel. "Calm down, will you?" I said. "Nobody's behaving badly but you."

He glared at me, then turned and went below. Two minutes later, he came through the companionway hatch with his arms full of liquor bottles and began tossing them overboard.

"Hey!" Paul Graham grabbed Kramers' arm to stop him and the Dutchman shoved him so hard that he hit his head against the cabin trunk. The women protested in unison as they examined the lump on Paul's skull, but our angry skipper kept flinging the bottles into the water.

"There," he said. "End of discussion."

Mr. Barnum had been sleeping in one of the forward

berths but awakened by the shouting, appeared at the foot of the companionway ladder. "Gentlemen," he admonished. "And ladies." He smiled and rubbed a hand over his long face. "The sun will shine tomorrow and we'll all feel much better."

No one responded.

"Perhaps some hot food will raise our spirits, then. May I be of assistance to our lovely cooks?"

The women went below and Paul followed.

Kramers walked up to the bow to stand lookout. That guy didn't make it hard to dislike. Punching his lights out would be a pleasure.

In bad weather Kramers and I stood the worst watch together. That night, we came back on deck at midnight. Dinner had been a sullen affair despite Mr. Barnum's attempts at small talk. The Grahams had taken their trick on deck while Kramers and I slept. Marijke must have dug out her silver flask, because when we relieved Paul and Ellen, she was still up, and they were all pretty giddy. Kramers shrugged into his oilskins and life jacket then went up to the bow again without a word.

He must have heard it before I did or had a prearranged schedule. Two hours into our watch he went below into the darkened cabin. He turned on the red night-vision light above the navigation table, made a calculation on the chart and called up a course change. I came 'round to our new heading and was adjusting the mizzen sheet when I sensed, rather than heard him at the wheel behind me.

If I hadn't started to turn he would have caught me square on the back of the head with something very hard and heavy, I'd have been out for good. As it was, my knees collapsed, and my chest slammed down on the push pit, my mind dazed, with no motor control over my arms or legs. I felt my feet being lifted up, then my body pushed over the lifelines into the water.

The cold ocean stung the raw flesh behind the bandage on my empty eye socket and sharpened my wits, but not before I swallowed a lung-full of water. The worst nightmare of any singlehanded sailor is falling overboard and watching your perfectly balanced boat sail away from you faster than you can swim. Once you're in the water the only thing that can save you is grabbing onto a knotted rope streaming from the stern for that purpose. But I wasn't sailing solo and we hadn't rigged one. By the time I stopped coughing and got my arms working, *Dutch Master's* stern light was disappearing into the night fog.

But the dinghy was trailing after it on fifty feet of line. I thrashed my way back into the boat's wake just in time to reach out to the twelve-foot inflatable boat, clutching at the smooth, wet rubber pontoon of the little skiff, fingers desperate for a handhold on the wet rubber, finally grabbing the slack three-strand lifeline hanging from bow and stern of the boat, flinging both arms up over the gunn'l, hanging there catching my breath.

Salt water filled my sea boots and oilskins, intent on dragging me off the dinghy down into thirty-fathoms of ocean. I started to yell for help but realized that if I woke the others Kramers might hurt them. The only hope I had of hanging on against the pull of the sea was to strip my clothing off right down to my underwear which nearly took more strength than I had.

When I slipped back into my life jacket I was able to hang on to the transom with one hand, resting, as my body trailed behind it on the surface of the buoyant salt water. Minutes later, I felt the dinghy being pulled toward the ketch and changed my grip to the starboard-side of the boat hoping that Kramers would not see me.

I could feel the little boat being pulled alongside the ketch to allow Kramer to climb in. He shoved off from the ketch, digging his oars in deep as he pulled away from *Dutch Master* that sailed on untended, perfectly balanced, her dark shape and running lights fading silently into the mist.

I tried to kick my legs under the surface of the water so Kramers wouldn't notice my weight slowing him down, but he was too good a seaman. When he rested on his oars to listen for the sub, the drag of my body arrested the momentum of the dinghy like a drogue. I felt him ship one of the oars, stand up and step to the rear of the little boat. He was coming after me with an oar and would kill me by bashing or drowning or both. At that moment, I heard the deep pulse of a heavy marine diesel engine and knew that if I swam away to avoid him he would escape.

Kramers was standing in the skiff peering over the port side wielding the oar. I slipped out of my life jacket and dove under the dinghy, coming up behind him on the starboard side amidships. Grabbing the gunn'l with both hands, I lifted my chest up onto the rail and pushed down as hard as I could. Kramers was leaning over the stern looking for me with the oar raised above his head and the violent motion threw him off balance into the drink.

Now his bulky oilskins and boots filled with water and encumbered his movements. I swam around to the port side of the dinghy still trailing *Dutch Master* and approached him from behind. I had never killed a man before, but they had taught me several ways to do it at Quantico. This was the enemy. Worse. A Dutchman, traitor to his country, responsible for the deaths of innocent civilians, men and women in the resistance, then posing as their hero. He had deceived his own people and now us, ready to give the Nazis the information and assistance they needed to invade the United States.

He had deceived Marijke, too, and things might have been different between us if he hadn't. A quote I had read somewhere flashed through my mind. I tried to suppress it but could not: '*The last temptation is the greatest treason; to do the right deed for the wrong reason.*'

Kramers sensed me behind him as a narrow beam of a search-light muted by fog swept across the water to our left, then went out. He turned toward me in the water, the glint of steel flashing in his hand. I raised my arm to ward off the knife and tried to kick him in the groin. The blade slashed my bicep and the water prevented my leg from getting enough power into it. Kramers' water-logged clothing restricted his lower body movement, but the life jacket was keeping his arms above the surface, so he could stab or cut if I got in close.

He didn't want to yell at the sub because our crew on ketch might hear him and use the radio; I couldn't shout for the ketch because the Germans would hear me. All he had to do was fend me off until the U-boat found us. The engine sounded closer now and the beam of the searchlight pierced the darkness off to our right.

I dove under water again but Kramers started turning as I went down and was facing me when I surfaced, kicking toward me, the cutting edge of the blade in the palm-up position of a trained knife fighter. I swam away from him, diving deeper this time and felt the half-inch line of the dinghy painter passing beneath me. I grabbed the line with both hands and shot to the surface on the same side of Kramers I had submerged on. He had turned again, expecting me to come up on the other side so I was behind him, his back to me.

I crossed my forearms making a looped garrote out of the slack dinghy painter and tossed it over his head. He dropped the knife as I pulled the rope tight around his neck, trying to force his fingers between the wet hemp and his throat. I braced my knee against the small of his back, took a deep breath and pulled us both down into the water, jerking the line with all my strength against the buoyancy of his life preserver until his writhing torso flattened against my chest and his twisting head ground matted hair into my cheek.

His body went limp just as the air in my lungs gave out and I kicked up to the surface. I hauled him back to the water-filled dinghy, hanging on to it with one hand, holding Kramers under the surface with the other. I rested for a few minutes, watching the spotlight trying to penetrate the fog in the opposite direction. I could hear Marijke screaming into the night behind me and the muffled throb of the big diesel engine ahead.

If the sub didn't find me, I could stay right there and tell Mr. Barnum that I couldn't find it. The mission would be half complete. Then what would be the point in losing my eye?

My life jacket was floating in the dinghy and I put it on, then removed the glassine packet from where Kramers had stuffed it into his belt under his oilskins. I was exhausted and could use some extra buoyancy, so I removed his life jacket and put it on backwards.

I dug his glass eye out of his face, put it into my empty left socket as Dr. Gillespie had shown me and started swimming toward the German submarine.

CHAPTER TWENTY-FIVE
Berlin, Germany
September 1942

The transatlantic crossing took eighteen days. Except for pausing to torpedo a crippled British merchant vessel off the Azores, I experienced surprisingly little stress surrounded by fifty German seamen in a Nazi U-boat. The officers and crew left me to myself, having no respect for a spy and traitor, even one who was working for their side. I did get a chance to practice my German on a couple of the younger boys, an exercise I took seriously, designed to emulate trying to pass the inevitable tests I'd encounter when we landed.

In retrospect, the hours we spent stalking and sinking the British cargo ship were good practice, too. I watched helplessly as the German crew tracked the defenseless merchantman, jockeyed for a shooting angle and fired a pair of torpedoes into the limping hulk. I was not allowed on deck when they surfaced and didn't see it happen, but I could hear the chatter of machine guns and cheering through the steel hull. As long as I live, I will carry the black-and-white movie in my mind of those imagined dying British sailors floating in an oil-slicked ocean. That incident reminded me that I might see, and even be forced to participate in similar events during the months ahead. Or would have to stand by some equally atrocious event without protest in order to maintain my cover.

We landed in the occupied French port of Brest where I was met by two young German naval officers who were less friendly than the submariners. They appropriated my glassine packet and locked it in a leather briefcase that one man held on his lap as our train rattled across Brittany and northern France.

Before her surrender, France had been under siege for

only a few months, but the country and people seemed beaten. Fields and forests between *Fougeres* and *Argentan* were scarred and blackened by artillery shells and fire. The railroad station in the city of *Nogent* was rubble. In the years to come, Allied bombers would wreak infinitely more destruction on this German-held nation, but compared to Newport, Rhode Island, it looked to me like the battlefield of the hundred years' war. Red flags with the ubiquitous *Hakenkreuz* [swastika] flew from every building

Paris was relatively unscathed structurally, but her spirit seemed dashed by armed German soldiers in the streets, in olive drab uniforms, trucks and tanks with black swastikas painted on their sides rolling down the *Champs Elysees*. On the road to the airport we passed through road blocks manned by black uniformed *schutzstaffeln* [Gestapo] troops I would come to know as the feared *SS*.

From the time of the torpedo incident 700 miles off the Bay of Biscay until our plane landed in Berlin, my mind had been replaying images of those poor murdered English sailors and I began to wonder if I would be able to pull it off. I probably would not have made it if it hadn't been for Admiral Wilhelm Franz Canaris, Chief of *Spionage Abwehr*, the Intelligence Bureau of *Oberkommando der Wehrmacht*, the Nazi military high command.

He seemed distracted during our first meeting in his Berlin headquarters at 74-76 *Tirpitz Ufer* but understood the implications of my doctored charts and defense reports on the northeast coast of the United States better than anyone else in the room. Several officers sat around a long, polished conference table in the gray wool uniforms with the black-and-silver insignia of the German army.

I had arrived in Brest three days before on *U.203*, the *VIIC* submarine that had picked me up in Block Island Sound and transported me across the Atlantic. *Obrest* [Brigadier General] Hans Oster had interrogated me for two days. During the staff meeting which followed, he stood next to a wall chart of New England, tall and sparse with a monocle on a black ribbon glinting against the narrow chest of his tailored uniform. He was a handsome, sharp-featured man in his early fifties whose tapered fingers gripped a wooden pointer in one hand and a Turkish cigarette in the other, making effete gestures that belied a history of indiscretions with the wives of fellow officers. Oster summarized his evaluation and conclusions of our debriefing sessions to the *Abwehr* executive staff.

"*Ihre Abwehr ist besser als wir dachten*," he summarized. [Their defense is better than we thought.]

His conclusion, based on my verification of the Amagansett messages, was that our artillery, troop, fortifications, submarine nets and mines presented a formidable challenge to an attack from the Atlantic Ocean. American coast patrols would make even a token invasion extremely risky." Oster used the pointer to indicate the Thames River on the Connecticut shore.

"With the possible exception of their New London submarine facilities." he added.

The exact opposite was true. *Hauptstrumfuhrer* [Major] Alfred Helmut Naujocks, a young *SS* officer demurred, voicing Hitler's desire for even a token attack on the U.S. "*Der Fuhrer wunscht, dab der Krieg nach Amerika erweitert wird.*" [The *Fuhrer* wants to invade America.] Naujocks proved to be an unscrupulous intellectual gangster who carried out sleazy tricks for Hitler, Himmler and Heydrich. I learned later that this repugnant muscle-man had led the *Gleiwitz* Operation, a ruse in which German prisoners in Polish uniforms were murdered during the fake attack on a *Gleiwitz* radio station to give the impression of Polish violence, providing an excuse for Germany's invasion of Poland. Although vastly overstated by the press, this conniving sociopath basked in the assertion of the Fourth Estate that he was "the man who started World War II." He had also participated in the *Velno* Incident, kidnapping British agents on Dutch soil, giving Germany a pretext to invade Holland.

The men around the table glanced at one another with noncommittal expressions at this reminder that their leader wished to invade the United States. Admiral Canaris spoke for the first time during that two-hour meeting. "If we try and fail now, it will prove we cannot invade America."

The *Abwehr* Chief was seated at the head of the table--a small gentle man a few years older than Oster with prematurely gray hair and bushy brows over pale blue eyes as unfathomable as the man himself.

"What about the New London sub base?" Naujocks persisted. "We could run U-boats up the Thames to launch torpedoes and a commando raid that would do serious damage to their submarine fleet."

Oster nodded in apparent agreement with the *SS* officer. "That would give the American newspapers something to write about, *wurde es nicht?*" [wouldn't it?] He turned to where I was sitting on a mahogany bench against the wall. "We discussed that at great length, did we not, *Herr* Kramers?"

"We did." I stood up to address them in German, still wearing the second-hand trousers, submariners' turtleneck and tweed jacket they had given me in Brest. "The area is patrolled, only by civilian yachts. They have fewer mines and nets there to reduce the danger to their own submarine traffic."

"What is behind this Long Island?" the Admiral wanted to know.

"Long Island Sound, *mein Herr.*"

I was supposed to be a Dutch national and my German wasn't expected to be perfect. A few of them winced at my accent, but I didn't care as long as they didn't realize it came from an American college and not Holland. "Long Island extends about ninety miles west to east along the coast and twenty miles from the island to the mainland, sir."

"Large enough and deep to contain anti-submarine destroyers?" Canaris asked.

"*Ja, mein Herr.*"

"But you saw no evidence of that."

"*Nein, mein Herr.* I could not patrol the area myself, but our agents on shore reported no activity of that nature."

"Does it not seem strange," Admiral Canaris asked his staff, "that the Americans patrol and fortify this entire stretch of coast but leave one critical naval facility so vulnerable to attack?"

"To invite an attack," Oster said, "of the kind we have planned."

Naujocks was skeptical. "Are they so devious, these mixed-race Americans?"

"They proved themselves in the Kaiser's War twenty-five years ago." Canaris' remark created an uncomfortable silence in the room. Then Naujocks redirected the same question at me.

"I'm not sure," I answered. "Sometimes they act like emotional children playing at soldiers. Others...they can surprise you."

Oster moved his pointer to the mouth of Thames River on the wall chart, tapping the tip on the General Dynamics Electric Boat construction pens on the north bank.

"What do you think they are doing with this? Allowing it to seem undefended?"

"I don't know," I said.

"*Verdammt!*"*[Dammit!]* Naujocks snapped. "You were not asked what you know, Dutchman, what do you conclude?"

"I think they're bluffing to draw you into a heavily armed attack force in a narrow estuary. The failure of a sea invasion would strengthen Allied determination and have the opposite effect on the German population, including the army."

That was the first time I used the trade craft skills James Barnum had taught me in Quantico or realized why our chess games had convinced him that I could handle this assignment. Later, Admiral Canaris told me that Naujocks had intuitive reservations about me from the beginning and was purposely testing me in front of the *Abwehr* staff.

The Admiral turned in his chair at the head of the table and scrutinized me for several moments. "I too, surmise that this is a ruse to trap our attack force in heavily defended shore batteries on the Thames.

"Work out a plan for the mission, *Hauptstrumfuhrer*," he told Naujocks, holding my gaze. "Boats, men, equipment and training. Schedule the attack for the end of the year," a smile flickered across his lips, "December 7th might amuse our *Fuhrer*."

The officers around the table laughed in appreciation and I joined them.

"Hans," Canaris addressed his second, "confirm the Amagansett reports through our Boston source."

"*Ja, mein Admiral*," Oster replied.

"And use the Dutchman," Canaris ordered Naujocks, turning to me again as though we shared a private joke. "*Herr* Kramers will accompany your commandos to New London."

* * * * * *

Being undercover for almost three years in the capital of an enemy nation, working day to day within their intelligence division was a matter of getting into the part or losing my sanity. It wasn't like doing '*Hedda Gabler*' for Sock and Buskin, but remembering how our drama coach at Brown encouraged us to submerge our identity did help. Yet nothing could have prepared me for impersonating the character of Pieter Kramers before an audience of Nazi butchers. It was certainly the most difficult role I ever played--there were no intermissions and I was never offstage.

Hauptstrumfuhrer Naujocks rarely stopped testing me. He continued to grill me about our east coast defenses and specifically the mine placements in the approaches to the aircraft carrier facility at Quonset Naval Air Station. He could not believe that our Corsair Fleet of private yachts crewed by unfit civilians was supposed to prevent German U-boats from getting into Narragansett Bay.

Naujocks became obsessed with striking not only the New London submarine pens, but the sitting-duck carriers in for refit at Quonset. Hitler was right. If the Germans could attack the U.S. mainland and attack two of our most vital naval installations,: they could cripple up to one fourth of our naval power; decimate critical repair facilities; force the navy to pull ships away from offensive duty in both European and Pacific theaters to defend our east coast. In addition, a German victory would inflict immeasurable harm on the morale of our civilian population and fighting men.

During my *Abwehr* tenure, I learned that Hitler did not attack England because of false intelligence which convinced him of a formidable defense. My job was to make sure he believed the opposite of the United States.

Admitting that New London had less protection than the rest of the coast made the larger lie more credible--that German ships could waltz into the Thames and lay a barrage of firepower on both River banks. But if Oster was able to refute the falsified Amagansett messages through some Boston cell I'd never heard of, Canaris would know our defenses were weak, Naujocks would get his wish, and my life as a spy would be short. Plus, they'd realize we were feeding them disinformation through Amagansett and we'd lose that advantage.

The only way I could think of to avoid this imminent disaster was to let Mr. Barnum know what was happening and hope he could figure out how to prevent my data from being contradicted by Boston.

Most of the world was aware of the various resistance groups that fought the Nazis in the occupied countries throughout Europe. These heroic men and women were patriots to the most of general public who would support them in any way they could. Few people realized that similar resistance groups of German citizens operated inside Germany itself. Unlike their counterparts in other nations, these courageous anti-Nazis were considered traitors to their country and its visionary leader. Any resistance to the Nazi Party, the Third Reich or Adolph Hitler encountered by 'loyal Germans' was generally related by their quarter-million internal security informants to the various state police forces led by the nefarious *Gestapo*.

Mr. Barnum had told me how to get in touch with a

resistance cell in Berlin. The night after I threw my cryptic message in the trash receptacle near the *Bahnhof Zoo* I was accosted by a skinny prostitute as I walked to my rooming house smoking my briar pipe.

"*Ich habe keinen Platz,*" [I do not have a place.] she confided, linking her arm in mine, "you will take me to your room?"

She was a lovely teenage girl with long black hair, dark eyes and seductive smile.

It was nine o'clock, and I had just left Naujocks at his *Abwehr* office. We trudged through a driving snow down a deserted side street on the outskirts of the central district, a pair of lovers going home from dining at a nearby restaurant. After the British had bombed Lubeck and other Baltic seaports, Berlin imposed a blackout that cast the city in darkness. I could feel the girl's body shivering inside her thin coat. I hadn't had a woman for almost a year but clamped my teeth on the stem of my pipe and told her I wasn't interested.

She snuggled her head against my shoulder. "I could change your mind, *Herr* Pieter Kramers."

I stopped walking and looked down at her face. "How did you know my name?"

"I know more than that," she teased.

My resistance contact was Anna Rosenthal. After we turned the heat up and the lights on behind the drawn shades of my third floor sitting/bedroom, she became very businesslike.

"We will get a message to your Mr. Barnum in one week through Boulogne and London," she assured me. "A reply will come by the same route."

"I'm not sure I'll get one," I said. If Barnum could help me, the response would have to come to Hans Oster to convince him the information I'd brought them was accurate.

Anna was sitting on the edge of the worn sofa, her thin arms folded across small breasts, hugging the skimpy coat to her body. "You will need to send other messages."

I agreed with that.

"Then I will have to stay."

"Here? Tonight?"

"As your woman," she said, patting the cushion beside her. "To live here."

It did not sound like a good idea for a double agent spying inside Nazi intelligence headquarters to have a member of the resistance for a roommate and I guess my expression showed it.

"How else will we meet?" she asked.

"On the street like tonight. In a bar."

"Where we can be observed by the *Gestapo*."

"Don't they have anyone else they can send, change the lineup once in a while?"

Anna rose from the sofa and walked across the faded rug to the iron radiator beneath a washed out copy of a pastoral scene by some old master. She rubbed her hands together over the meager heat, seemingly transfixed by the painting. "This is the job they have given me," she whispered. "If you ask for someone else, I would have to...." She turned around and there were tears brimming in her eyes. "Please. I have nowhere to live, no food."

"But you're in the resistance. Won't your friends help you? There must be some other assignment."

"Not for me." She unbuttoned her coat and reached down the neck of her sweater into her brassier. When she withdrew her hand, it held a black patch of cloth with a yellow star of David and the word, *Juedin.* "Even the resistance will not let us do more than the most dangerous courier runs."

"And you want to live with me."

I was sitting on a wooden chair next to a table with the only lamp in the room and she scurried across the rug to kneel at my feet. "*Bitte!*" [Please.] she begged, "The *Gestapo* believe I am a prostitute and you are a traitor to your Holland." She wiped her cheek with her sleeve. "They have no respect for either of us and will think it natural that we are together. It will be safe." She clutched my pants leg and pressed her cheek into my thigh as she began to sob in abject desperation. "*Bitte, bitte!*"

During the past few weeks the incredible rumors that had leaked out to the west were confirmed by snatches of guarded remarks I overheard on the streets and shops and restaurants of Berlin. Hitler had devised a Final Solution to the Jewish 'problem,' which would cleanse Europe of this infectious race. Thousands of Jews were classified as *Untermenschen*, [sub-humans], who disappeared from their homes during the night, were herded together in railroad boxcars like cattle and shipped to concentration camps in *Auschwitz*, *Buchenwald* and *Theresienstadt*, where men, women and children were stripped naked, gassed in concrete bunkers, incinerated or shoveled into mass graves. Without personal knowledge, few believed these rumors, especially Jews, who thought they were propaganda to force them to flee from their homes, shops and possessions.

Anna had visited a girlfriend overnight the previous spring, returning to her parents' apartment the next morning to find her family gone, her home ransacked, and her father's store looted. She had been on the run ever since, forming an uneasy liaison with the German underground in a desperate attempt to avoid selling her body to soldiers for food and shelter.

"I suppose we could try it," I said.

She began to laugh and babble through her tears and I wondered if I had just endangered my mission and my life. She was barely seventeen years old, and that night I believed she would probably make a mistake that would get us both lined up in front of a stone wall. I had no idea how she would repay my reluctant act of kindness or what she would sacrifice to do it.

* * * * * *

Admiral Canaris sent for me six months later. He rose from behind his desk when I entered his office, greeted me cordially and closed the door behind me. It was past midnight and most of his daytime staff had gone home. The *Abwehr* worked around the clock and the turned-down bedding on the iron cot in the corner bore truth to the gossip that its Director rarely left the building.

He offered me tea and set a kettle of water on a hot plate. We stood together in the center of the dimly lit room waiting for the water to boil, the little man in his blue naval uniform with ornate shoulder boards and wide gold stripes on the sleeves looked up at my face, unintimidated by the disparity in our height.

The Admiral lit a foul-smelling *Gauloises* and invited me to smoke my pipe. Then he asked, "How are you getting along with *Hauptstrumfuhrer* Naujocks?"

"Fine, sir," I lied.

I had been working with Naujocks at the *Brandenberg* Training Company, a crack sabotage and special forces unit made up of *Balts* and *Volksdeutschen*, foreign nationals of German descent who were fanatically loyal to Hitler.

"He's very thorough," a smile flashed across his lips. "Ambitious, too." Canaris held his palm over the spout of the aluminum kettle that emitted a weak stream of vapor. "He is disappointed that his commando raid on the United States has been cancelled."

I didn't know that and said so with appropriate surprise. "*Oberst* Oster received a transmission from Amagansett informing us that our Boston source has been compromised. *God bless James Barnum!*

"And just in time." The Admiral smiled again as though we were playing a harmless parlor game, then turned to attend to his whistling kettle. "The Boston cell had originally reported that the entire east coast of America is virtually undefended." He continued speaking with his back to me as he made our tea. "Imagine what a disaster Naujocks raid would have been if we believed that."

I muttered something innocuous around my pipe-stem as Canaris handed me a Dresden cup and saucer. He beckoned me over to a low couch against the wall opposite a picture of the *Fuhrer*, which was required in every office in his military command. This was not the traditional framed portrait, but a candid black-and-white blowup of Hitler going aboard the old battleship *Schlesien*, which Canaris had skippered. The

Admiral sat in an arm chair facing me with his back to his *Fuhrer.*

"Tell me how you did it," he said.

"What?"

"Hans Oster has an independent method of checking the Boston cell. It has not been compromised. Amagansett has."

I know I didn't handle that part of the session well. I don't think the cup rattled on the saucer, but I could feel the perspiration running down my sides. I expected half a dozen *Gestapo* in long black leather coats to burst through the door at any second. Maybe he was bluffing. I took a sip of tea and did the best I could to grin. "Then he must know the truth."

"He does."

I waited.

"Was it the girl?" Canaris asked.

"What girl?"

"The *Juedin* who lives with you."

Barnum must have been crazy to send me in here. A naive college kid dumb enough to let the damned establishment make him half blind and send him into the heart of the crack intelligence organization of the *Nazi* high command.

"Admiral Canaris, I may have made a mistake with the prostitute," I forced another grin, "but I don't have a social life here and I do have needs." I put the tea down on the table at my elbow. " It rattled on the saucer. "As for the rest of it, I don't know what you're talking about, sir."

Canaris reached back to place his own cup and saucer on the corner of his desk. "In 1935, shortly after I was appointed to this post, I was touring the Rhineland when I ran into an acquaintance from Berlin. *Obergruppenfuhrer* Reinhard Heydrich was a neighbor in *Schlachtensee,* who came often to my house for dinner as *Frau* Canaris and I went to his. As *Kommandeur* of the *SS,* Heydrich was in charge of the Chancellor's racial cleansing program and urged me to accompany him to a field at the edge of the town to witness his work."

The pale eyes of the old man seemed to focus inward, and

his ruddy complexion lost its color. "A squad of soldiers with fixed bayonets had marched a hundred or so Jews from their homes and forced them to dig a large pit in the center of the field. The Jews were standing in front of the pit when we arrived in Heydrich's staff car. The *Kommandeur* gave the signal to his *Oberleutnant* and a *tabsfeldwebel* [corporal] pulled a tarpaulin off the back of a truck to reveal two men kneeling behind a 50-caliber-machine gun."

Canaris drew a deep breath and continued in a voice hoarse with emotion. "The *Oberleutnant* issued the order and the gunners opened fire, raking the Jews from left to right and right to left until not a man or woman or child was standing. Some were only wounded, and the soldiers moved forward with their rifles and shot or stabbed into the pile of bodies. When they stood back with their wet bayonets the grass was dark with blood."

The pale eyes became moist as his story poured out in its rough monotone. "A group of townsmen who had been standing near the truck were prodded forward by a couple of soldiers. The *Oberleutnant* instructed them to throw the dead bodies into the pit and shovel dirt on them. The men refused. The *Oberleutnant* glanced toward the staff car and Heydrich nodded his head. The platoon leader again gave the machine gunners the order to fire. Heydrich thought it was great sport." The Admira*l* shook his head. "My neighbor!"

I didn't understand what was happening, but this was not an evil man. He was the enemy though and suspected that I was an American spy. I sat there and listened.

"That was the beginning for me. Or perhaps the end. In 1940 I learned that our glorious *Fuhrer* had given orders to dispose of our mentally ill through euthanasia. Our sick. Germans!"

The Admira*l* was silent for several minutes. I didn't dare move. His eyes lost their liquid quality and refocused on me. "I have opposed this madman for ten years. Longer than De Gaulle, Churchill, Stalin or your FDR. There are others who feel as I do. That Adolph Hitler will destroy Germany and subject her people to a thousand-year penance at the hands of an outraged and vengeful world."

He reclaimed his cold tea from the corner of the desk. "We will not permit that to happen."

I could not believe it. The Chief of *Abwehr*, the powerful intelligence arm of the *OKW* an anti-*Nazi?* An adversary of Hitler at the highest level of military authority, privy to secrets and planning strategies the Allies would die for?

What in God's name had I stumbled into?

CHAPTER TWENTY-SIX
Berlin, Germany
November 1943

After that strange conversation, certain data became more accessible to me and I found ways to make sure it was valid. I told Barnum that Canaris thought we were sending disinformation from Amagansett but seemed to be distributing some of our messages intact.

Anna couldn't carry copies of classified military documents around Berlin, nor could she memorize the complex troop strategies and numerical data Oster was able to make available to me. So we devised a direct link with a member of the resistance named Fabian through a 'gas pipe network, the same system devised for the original Brown student radio station in 1936. Students discovered that gas pipes and electrical wires could double as antenna for low-power radio frequency currents, and 30,000 feet of transmission lines were strung all over campus through underground steam tunnels and over rooftops, connecting dormitories and fraternities with transmitters built into their heating or lighting systems. Any radio within 100 feet of a heating pipe could pick up the broadcasts.

I built two crystal sets out of copper wire and a stolen microphone. Instead of a book code, Mr. Barnum borrowed an idea from the British who used the opening bars of Beethoven's Fifth in BBC broadcasts to Europe to communicate the Morse code letter 'V' for victory. An OSS cryptologist at Quantico had shown me how to use music to encrypt data with the governing sharps and flats of each tune the key to unscramble the message.

When I wanted to transmit, I attached the copper wire to the gas feed of my gas-fed fireplace heater and played a popular German song on the gramophone into the open mike. Fabian jotted down the message from his crystal set attached to his radiator hooked up through city piping, and surreptitiously connecting wires twelve blocks away. He recorded the raw data, and had it smuggled to London for deciphering. Anna's job was to drop and pick up transmission schedules to send and receive messages from Fabian or deliver changes I made in the code key.

At first, it was unbelievable to me that members of Hitler's high command could be actively plotting to overthrow him and working against the *Nazi* war machine while not only part of it but running it. *Zentralabteilung*, the inner sanctum of the *Abwehr* known as Department 'Z' was the facade behind which the conspirators in Germany's most determined anti-*Nazi*/Hitler movement operated. For that reason alone, Canaris would not compromise it. Even though there were suspiciosns about the Admiral's loyalty to Hitler, no one dared to confront his power and status without proof. Since Canaris was an extremely intelligent man apparently born to intrigue, there was none.

Although Oster left certain large-scale strategic plans where I could see them, I never had access to battle plans or tactical information that could cause the deaths of German personnel. Despite the fact that it would rattle us badly, I realized Canaris did not want an expeditionary force to attack the U.S. mainland because it would be a logistical nightmare: a suicide mission that would invoke violent retribution from the angry Americans and make the ultimate plan of their *Shwarze Kapele* [Black Choir] infeasible.

I remained assigned to Naujocks, who on Hitler's direct order, continued searching for a way to land a large attack force on our east coast. I pursued my work with feigned imagination and enthusiasm but came under increasing scrutiny by Naujocks for suggesting ways that sabotage expeditions into the Norfolk, Maryland and Gulf state coasts could fail. My negative comments were ignored, and those trial incursions were met with surprisingly swift capture.

I was working late one night when Naujocks came into our deserted office in *Brandenburg*. A short man in his late twenties, who wore a peaked SS cap indoors and out to conceal his premature hair loss, Naujocks leaned his hands on the edge of my desk, the lamp on its corner the only light in the darkened room.

"So," he said. "You are a lover of Jews."

"I can take them or leave them."

Naujocks threw his head back and laughed as though I had uttered the hilarious punch line of a clever joke.

When he stopped, his expression became cruel. "You have taken one of them."

I didn't respond.

He leaned farther over my desk and I could smell the alcohol on his breath. "Filth!"

Naujocks stood erect, tugging at the hem of his black tunic. "One way or another," the *SS* man hissed, "one way or the other." Then he turned, placing his feet with exaggerated care as he walked across the room.

On my way to the bus that night four hulking teens in brown shirts and swastika armbands jumped out of a car and beat me with wooden clubs until I fell to the street bleeding and battered, finally unconscious, my right arm broken from shielding their blows to my good right eye.

Toward the end of my stay in the clinic, Oster sent me a securely wrapped package by special messenger. The heft of it and some wary instinct made me wait until I got home to open it. Inside was a Mauser 6.35 pistol with three loaded magazines.

My arm was still in a cast several weeks later when Anna and I were walking back to our flat from a late supper at a neighborhood *Wirtschaft*. Naujocks pulled up to the curb of the darkened street behind the wheel of a little humpback *KDF-wagen*. "Is this the *Juedin* you are fucking?" Anna gripped my arm harder but we kept walking.

It was almost curfew and the few pedestrians on the sidewalk hurried along to the relative safety of their homes, consciously ignoring the SS major harassing two civilians.

Naujocks slipped the clutch, and the car moved slowly beside us. "Get in the car with me, *Juedin* and we will go where I can examine your...papers." He threw his head back and laughed. Anna stopped and released my arm, immediately resigned to certain rape and possibly worse at the hands of the black uniformed bully.

"Don't do this, Alfred," I warned him.

He hesitated for a second at the tone of my voice, then shouted at Anna again to get in the car. Before she could move, I pulled the Mauser out of my sling, leaned down to the window, put the muzzle into his ear and cocked the hammer with an audible click. Naujocks stared straight ahead through the windshield, frozen, his black gloves stretched so tight around the steering wheel, I thought he would break it.

"If you ever terrorize this young woman or me again," I promised, "I will kill you. On the spot. Or later, when you least expect it." None of us spoke or moved for almost a minute. "Now get the fuck out of here."

* * * * * *

That incident drew me into a conspiracy into which Canaris either insinuated himself, was drawn into out of expediency or ignorance of its co-conspirators. It began after midnight on Thanksgiving Day, November 23, 1944, a date seared into my memory, on whose anniversaries I have wept unashamedly for the past thirty-one years, my ambivalence shifting between a thirst for revenge and appreciation--when the dreaded pounding of rifle butts on our door reverberated through my apartment. A half-dozen black uniformed *SS* goons burst into the room, dragged Anna and me naked from our bed, shouting, *Juedin Hurensohn Arschloc* [Jew whore, asshole] as they pushed us down the stairs of my apartment building and loaded us on a truck.

The back of the tarpaulin-covered vehicle was crowded with equally frightened men, women and children, some as naked as we, others in nightgowns or wrapped in blankets. The slat benches along the sides were full, so we squatted on the cold metal floor wedged among a dozen silent people who had no seat either. An old man gave Anna the worn suit coat he had thrown over his pajamas. Some of the women were crying, clutching their whimpering children to their breasts. The truck made several more stops, gathering its night harvest until its hooped-canvas pen could hold no more.

Anna was weeping more for me than herself, blaming my predicament on her stubborn insistence to live with me almost two years ago. I hugged her thin body under the old man's coat, and she responded with much of the same desperation that had engulfed her when she crawled into my bed one freezing winter night those long months ago. We had become lovers out of a primal need for comfort amid the constant danger of our work and her mere existence, but without romance or love. I had a deep affection for this brave girl who had done nothing to be hounded by these ruthless killers other than being born to an ancient religion. I tried to comfort her as much as I could, reminding her that although the Germans didn't know it, I deserved this ride more than anyone else on the truck.

We were taken to a freight yard outside the city where at least a hundred other unmarked vehicles with similar cargoes waited in the freezing air by an empty loading spur. As a pale sun rose above the long horizon of factories and warehouses, a locomotive backed an interminable string of wooden boxcars into the siding, the white smoke from its funnel trailing behind it. An *SS* guard pulled down the tailgate of our truck and ordered us to get off. I moved slowly, still naked, cold and cramped from the painful journey. A guard smashed the butt of his rifle against my ribs to speed me up and I whirled on the man who had already turned his attention to someone else. Two young Jews pinned my arms and moved me back into the crowd.

"Do nothing to anger them," one of them said. "They will shoot you here and a dozen of us as example."

Anna recovered me from their grip and guided me back into line. This was it, I thought. No accusation, no interrogation or trial. They weren't going to torture me for information, get me to reveal the damage I'd done or give them Canaris and Oster. No firing squad, just a train ride, and merciless labor until we dropped, or sudden death. Neither James Barnum, Frank DePrete, nor anyone else would ever know what happened to me. I could break and run and end it there. Then Anna would be alone.

There were countless queues long and slow, terminating at boxcars all down the rails as far as the eye could see, with an *SS-Stabsfeldwebel* and armed noncoms checking their clipboards. The lines stopped for several minutes when they had filled one boxcar and rerouted people to the ramp on the next.

The sun rose higher and I could feel its meager warmth on my shoulders, incapable of taking the deep chill out of my bare skin. There would be no sun in the boxcar, just the chill breeze forced through the gaps in the wooden planks as we rushed across the countryside. I didn't know how far it was to the nearest concentration camp or wherever they were taking us, but all we had to look forward to was a miserable train ride and hard labor or an indiscriminate bullet. Despite being spared the harsher agony I would endure if they realized I was an American spy, I felt no relief at having escaped it. For the first time in my life, I understood how debased and hopeless a human being could feel when misjudged or persecuted for no valid reason by unconscionable bigots.

Black-uniformed thugs prodded us up a wooden ramp into a boxcar that gagged me with its stench of manure, vomit and other malodorous smells. More than one hundred men, women and children were forced into an area that would ordinarily accommodate thirty cows. Everyone was pressed firmly against one another back to back, nose to nose, shoulder to shoulder, parents holding small children in their arms to prevent them from suffocating at their knees, older kids crushed beside them, faces raised up in an effort to breath. It was impossible to sit or lie down. We would stand jammed against one another for however long it took to get to our destination. A final jostling of bodies crushed Anna against me and the huge slatted door slid shut and was locked from the outside, sealing us into a gray half-light of cold moist air thick with the stink of vomit and human fear combined with residue of cattle droppings and urine. The low murmur and whimpering which could not be stemmed by the guards now grew to a cacophony of high-pitched cries in German and Yiddish, mingled with the hysterical sobbing of women and children joining the similar wails of terror and outrage from the cars ahead and behind us.

The stuttering shots of a machine gun pierced the noise of human misery, sending bullets and splinters of wooden slats into our packed car. The screams hit crescendo as a half-dozen people near the far wall slumped against their neighbors, bleeding from gunshot wounds. A second volley achieved similar results and the screaming stopped. We could hear the laughter of the guards outside as the train jolted on its tracks, jamming us closer together. After several more false starts the locomotive crept forward, dragging its train of human misery, gathering speed as it left the freight yards, the rough road-bed jolting the planks of the uneven floor against my feet up through my entire body.

A biting wind streamed through the slatted sides of the car and one-meter oblong 'windows' crossed with barbed wire, causing young and old alike to gasp and shiver against the next cold body in a futile effort to achieve an absent warmth. At first, we thought standing against the walls was the best position in the car and tried to rotate old people and kids to the outer perimeters. When the rough planking began to rub their skin raw, men took the outside position, giving access to others who leaned against them. I forced my way through the packed mass to where two dead bodies had been shoved in a corner and stripped their clothes off. They were soiled and still wet with blood but would provide some warmth, and cover Anna's and my nakedness.

People who carried luggage were cursed for the space it took, arguments arose about whether to prop the dead shooting victims against the side of the car or lie them down and stand on them; where to defecate and how to share some of the meager food a few women had brought. In one sense, that first day is a blur of inhuman suffering experienced and observed, that to this moment I cannot recall the entire canvas, yet can remember every detail, every obscenity, every beating, every death, every degradation--and it had not yet begun.

The weak afternoon sun slanting through the narrow windows told me we were heading southeast. I estimated the train averaged about eighty-kilometers an hour, stopping frequently at small stations, switching junctions and crossings. When darkness came, the turns, stops, and switchbacks obscured my fragile sense of direction and we could have been heading for any point of the compass. The black night must have dropped the temperature another ten-degrees Celsius, bringing an audible undercurrent of misery overlaid with fervent prayers in Hebrew and the strong, sweet voice of a Cantor that had a calming effect on all.

We had nothing to drink for eighteen hours. When we stopped at a station the men near the windows raised women and children to beg people on the platform for water. A loud male voice from the car ahead implored a group of travelers for a pail of water until a shot cracked through the night and all were silent.

"*Kein Wasser!*" A voice shouted for clean water at which two SS guards sauntering past our car began laughing.

Anna hadn't made a sound since shortly after the locomotive jolted to life that morning. I had draped her arms around my neck and I tried to shield her frail body from the pushing and shoving and sharp elbows as best as I could. and the agitated human cargo crushing against us. For nearly twenty-four hours she seemed catatonic, arms listless, still hanging over my shoulders, body slumped against me, her legs unable to bear her own weight.

We had been stopped at a switching junction for hours one night, and sometime before dawn, just as the train started to move, a railroad worker appeared from beneath our car and handed up a calabash full of water. "Throw the goatskin off after you get moving," his urgent whisper told us. "It's a bullet in the head if they catch me." He spoke in German, so we had not moved beyond the border.

Most children, the elderly and some women got a mouthful. One mother was punched in the face by another when she tried to force some down the throat of her dead infant. When the bag came close, I grabbed it and poured a little into Anna's mouth. She swallowed greedily but seemed only semi-conscious.

Those incidents and others like them repeated themselves for a day and a half. Old people and children died beside us and slid to the floor where we first tried to avoid stepping on them, then removed our shoes using their corpses to soften the pain in our feet and legs from the vibrating floor. We saw several locomotives pulling twenty, fifty strings of empty boxcars like ours heading in the opposite direction and concluded that this was a shuttle line exporting Jewish workers to factories and assembly plants. But where? Where were the thousands of people who had ridden those jam-packed cars in our direction just hours or days before us? What did they need so many people for? Old women, babies?

Our car crept through a crossing where a boy sat on a shaggy mule. A few of the men shouted questions asking where we were, where we were going. The boy's answer was indistinct above the noise of the train, but he was not speaking German. Polish, some people said., "What the hell were we doing in Poland?" Just before he receded beyond our line of sight, the boy drew a finger across his throat and the meaning of that gesture sustained arguments for days. The unanimous interpretation was that we were done for. But in what way? Cooped up in a concentration camp for the remainder of the war? Subjected to the same brutal treatment we had already experienced? Forced to work at hard labor or semi-skilled jobs eighteen-hours a day?

The train passed a station and stopped in an open field in mid-afternoon of the fifth day. I had dozed but not slept since the night before we were rousted out of our beds a hundred years ago and was exhausted. I remember hallucinating, dreaming I was back on Narragansett Bay at the helm of Mr. Van Oudgaarden's boat, a cold, brown bottle of 'Gansett beer in my fist, beating into a fresh breeze, the wet salt spray drenching my bare chest.

The doors crashed open. "*Ausleeren! Ausleeren!* [All out, empty the car.]"

A wooden ramp had been shoved up against the threshold and *SS* guards with rifles at the ready shouted and waved us down its incline. Those leaning against the door were off-balance and blinded by the bright sunlight when it slid open, some tumbling, slipping down the frost-coated ramp, others instinctively drawing back away from the gaping opening back into our claustrophobic cocoon.

Two guards started beating an old man and woman who had fallen out, another raised his rifle and shot three or four people standing in the doorway, all the while shouting for us to get out of the car immediately. Weak, dehydrated, slipping in stocking feet on feces, urine, vomit, the blood of several suicides and around dead bodies, it was almost impossible to move quickly or without falling. A few people had gone mad during the trip and wandered aimlessly among us in silence or screaming bizarre nonsense, abandoned or grasped by frantic relatives who led them down the ramp to a blazing rifle muzzle.

Anna and I were at the far end of the car and I knew they would kill her if she remained unconscious. I propped her up in a corner forcing her body to support its own weight, then slapped her face with the palm and back of my hand as hard as I could. All she did was slide down the rough planks and mew almost inaudibly at my efforts that failed to reach her. I had less than sixty-seconds to bring her around. I grabbed her shoulders and slammed her against the wall. "Anna! Anna!"

Whether the release from the constant pressure of that human mass, the cold, fetid breeze blowing in from the open doorway or the harsh methods I used to wake her, her eyes opened. Most of the people had left the car amid occasional shots and I encircled her tiny waist with my arm, my own knees nearly buckling as I urged her forward through the corpses.

"If you can't walk they'll kill you," I said in her ear. "Do you understand me?"

Her hair was foul and tangled against my lips. I slapped her again and repeated the warning just before we reached the threshold of the box car door. Her eyes blinked at the bright sunlight, and I warned her once more. A guard yelled at us and raised his rifle. I dropped my arm from Anna's waist but grabbed a handful of skirt at the small of her back and started walking us down the ramp. She stumbled but gained her balance and her head jerked back as though I had slapped her again as she absorbed the scene before us.

Halfway down the incline, I released my hold on her skirt, and she continued unsteadily to the ground on her own, where a guard pushed us toward the end of an interminable queue that was already shuffling along a dirt road trampled through the field by similarly debased souls from previous trains. A large sign contradicted the treatment we'd undergone during the past five days and instead of reassuring me, convinced me that none of us would ever leave this place alive. "*Juedin Willkommen zu Gross Rosen. Du Sie gehoren hier.*" [Welcome to Gross Rosen, Jews. You belong here.]

The interminable march to the camp under pale sunlight entailed more of the same: shootings, beatings, death from dehydration, exhaustion, hypothermia, heart attacks and insanity. When a soldier kicked a woman who had fallen, her husband tried to strangle the armed guard with his bare hands. Not only was he beaten to death by a half-dozen SS troopers, but they forced two other prisoners to drag his broken body up to the front of our ranks, drew their pistols and indiscriminately shot several men, women and children in the back of their heads.

There was no doubt in my mind that Alfred Naujocks was responsible for Anna's and my plight. If I hadn't humiliated the bully by sticking a gun in his ear we wouldn't be in this predicament. Anna would have been raped that night and sent home. I would have been humiliated and Naujocks

271

would not have felt the need to exact this revenge.

I pulled Anna into the midst of the column and tried to support her weight with one arm or the other to the best of my ability, under the circumstances. I was not in very good shape myself and doubted whether Anna or I would last the day. Watching the unconscionable treatment, the Nazi thugs imposed on other people, I was certain I would be unable to save either one of us from whatever fate awaited?

CHAPTER TWENTY-SEVEN
Bergen-Belsen, Germany
December 1944

Despite the abusive treatment, most of the thousand or so prisoners transported with us from Berlin marched through the double gates of the series of chain-link fences and guard towers surrounding the complex. Anna was pulled from my grasp and shoved into a group of young women being assembled on the slush covered surface of the *Appfellplatz,* [Parade ground] whose perimeter was lined with low wooden buildings. Behind these, wood-framed barracks called *Blocks* stretched out to the east as far as my eye could see.

The place was teeming with adults and children wearing the broad-striped gray and black *Konzentrationslager* [Concentration Camp] trousers and jacket uniforms, .unescorted or marching together under the supervision of *Kapos [Jews working for the Germans],* in mismatched clothing that looked worn, but warmer than the calf-length uniform overcoats of prisoners standing at attention in ranks, shoveling snow, pushing wheelbarrows or performing other maintenance tasks.

New arrivals were separated by age and sex, including children, except for infants, who remained in the arms of their mothers. The SS-*Ausfehr* [Gestapo guards] arranged clusters of frightened humanity in a wide circle around a white flagpole from which the ubiquitous red, white, and black *Hakenkreuz* [Nazi symbol] waved in the wind. With the exception of crying children, and the occasional wail from a hysterical woman, we were all subdued, whispering questions or reassurance to a neighbor.

They kept us at attention for an hour or so, then a thickset *SS-Hauptsturmfuhrer* in black dress uniform marched to the base of the flagpole. "*Sichentkleiden!*" [Undress] he shouted].

273

People stared at the Gestapo captain as though he had spoken Chinese. We looked around, some fumbling with shirt buttons, others unlacing shoes, most just frowning, shifting from foot to foot.

"Undress now!" he repeated, slapping his swagger stick against his leather boot. *"Schnell! Schnell!"* [Quick]

With that admonition, guards began roaming among the groups, prodding people with their *Gewehr* rifle muzzles, slamming the wooden stock into kidneys of men who had not removed their hats, women and children who were not stripping fast enough. Finally, we all stood naked, shivering so hard our teeth rattled, our clothes in mounds at our feet, averting each other's darting glances, hands trying to cover private parts from the prying eyes of laughing guards.

A young *Ausfeher* standing before the ranks of old men yelled for the attention of the officer at the flagpole. *"Hauptstrumfuhrer* Vogel! Look at the *Wurm* on this one!"

He dragged a bearded old man with stringy *tits* in front of his group, jabbing the Jew's hands with his rifle gun-sight to pry them away from their vain attempt to cover an incredibly long penis that hung almost to his knees. Several other guards gathered around laughing, making obscene comments as the *SS* officer walked forward to join the fun. Two guards held the old man by each arm as another lifted the limp organ with the tip of his rifle.

"Enough!" *Hauptsturmfuhrer* Vogel said, nodding to the *Ausfeher,* who continued to hold the penis up. Then to the old man, "How dare you bring that rotten piece of *Schweinefleisch* [Pork] in here. He lifted his swagger stick above his head and brought it smashing down on the penis that began bleeding from a gaping wound. The old man let out a piercing shriek, then slumped in the grasp of the guards who were holding him. Vogel returned to his position by the flagpole amid the laughter of his men and the murmur of prisoners.

"Achtung! Bergen-Belsen is an *Erholungslager [Recreation camp]* specially designed for people who can contribute to the war effort. If you work hard, you will be treated well.

Some of you will work in factories nearby, others will perform tasks here in the camp."

I could sense a feeling of relief among the men around me, but from what I had just seen and endured during the past hundred hours, did not experience it myself. I discovered later that Vogel's lie would have been true six months ago, but recent losses on the Eastern Front had forced the Nazis to start closing *Auschwitz, Belzec, Sobibor,* and other *Vernichtungslager* [Extermination camps] in Poland. So they were shipping them here and the gas chambers and crematorium at Bergen-Belsen were working overtime.

Vogel's welcome speech was intended to assure us that we had nothing to fear as long as we obeyed the rules set down by our *Judenrat,* a council of Jewish elders who administered routine schedules and orders to save German manpower and absolve them from direct involvement in certain functions. These *Kapos* were invariably drawn from criminal, and the worst elements of Ukrainian, Polish, and Jewish population.

When *Hauptsturmfuhrer* Vogel had finished, he marched back to his office followed by most of the armed guards. A Camp Elder walked to the flagpole carrying a wooden stool he climbed on as his fellow *Kapos* materialized around us.

"You will obey our orders and endure your stay here or I will have you shot," he began. "Any attempt at escape will be met with immediate execution of your family and those in your *Block.*" His name was Moshe Saperstein, and he spoke without emotion, but great conviction. I would learn later that despite his absolute power over every other prisoner in the camp, his own life hung on the thread of our cooperation.

"Remove all valuables from your clothing and baggage," he continued, "give them to the *Kapos* who will pass among you and issue receipts for reclamation when you leave."

The prisoner-guards took our *Reichsmarks* and scant possessions while begging for cigarettes as they pried gold wedding bands, diamond rings and watches from our wrists. Saperstein told us that we would be given medical exams, but we stood in place freezing for another hour before each group was marched off one by one and I lost sight of Anna in the confusion. I prayed to God they would pick her for some relatively simple task that would not break her brittle spirit, but suspected that young, attractive women would be raped and ultimately discarded unless they were clever and strong enough to service their captors with enthusiasm. I doubted Anna would have the stomach for that.

My group was marched single file into a long building containing a maze of rooms in which we passed men in white jackets who wrote in ledgers at tables, but rarely looked at us. Finally, I was shoved into a side room where an *Obershutze* [Senior non-com] seated at a desk asked my trade, and I told him lathe operator hoping to get assigned to one of the factories I'd heard about. He sent me out a side door to where a *Kapo* pointed to a concrete building that I prayed was not one of the rumored extermination chambers.

My assemblage was composed of men and older boys in fairly good physical condition, but I could tell we had all not passed the medical exam as we were run through a painful de-lousing process we didn't need. A *Priviligierte* [Prisoner with privileges] lathered us with some astringent salve, then shaved off all our body hair. Next, our scalp and facial hair were shaved off with clippers, except for a single patch on top identifying us as prisoners. The hot shower would have been welcome if, yet another prisoner hadn't scrubbed harsh soap into our salve-sore bodies with a hard-bristled brush as we tried to swallow as much of the scalding nectar as possible.

Previously, only *Auschwitz* tattooed numbers on prisoner's forearms, but it seemed that the practice had accompanied the population from that hellhole when they were transferred to other camps, and from then on, our names were relinquished to mere digits in the official records of the Third Reich. At our last stop in that dehumanizing process, worn, ragged steam-cleaned *Pyjamas* were thrust into our arms regardless of size and we had to make the best exchange we could of the striped *KZ* uniforms among ourselves back out on the cold *Appfellplatz.*

Somewhere between the beginning of the de-lousing process and receiving our Zebra-Suits, our group had been reduced by about a third by a process called 'selection,' in which a doctor or anyone in authority could send us up the chimney. If some of the fittest men in the camp didn't make it through the first afternoon, what chance did the others have?

When we were dismissed in front of our *Block,* some of us pushed ahead and ran inside to grab the blankets of the men who had not passed their physical. My billet, *Hutte 47,* stood worn and shabby at the west side of the camp: gaps between the weathered planking, no insulation, narrow tiers of bunks pushed together, scarred with initials, names and Hebrew words, a small wood stove, a single bare light bulb, and if lucky, one used blanket folded on each straw mattress.

I wondered about the men who had occupied this corner of hell before us. It was dark by the time were settled, when our *Hutte Altere* [Elder] informed us that we had missed dinner and locked the door of our *Block* behind us. It turned bitter cold that night, and I was glad for even one thin blanket. We hadn't known where to get wood for the stove, so some men crawled in bed together for warmth. One man who slept alone without a blanket froze to death. Our conversation that night after role call meandered from hunger, wives, despair, discipline, escape, children, fortitude, vengeance, hope, suicide, sweethearts, and extermination. We slept.

* * * * * *

Hirschberg, our permanent *Kapo,* woke us before dawn for *Zahlappell,* [Roll call] clomping up and down the tight aisles yelling "get up" in German and Yiddish, banging a baton he'd made from a solid oak limb against bunk supports and the stocking feet of men alike.

Roll call, we learned, was the most feared event of the day by common prisoners and *Judenrat* alike. At the whim of the Nazis, it could last for ten minutes or ten hours, during which all prisoners including *Kapos* had to stand at attention. That was the time when the entire camp was told what their fate would be for the next twenty-four hours. If someone was missing, of course, those members of the *Judenrat* deemed responsible would be shot on the spot before the entire company. 'Selections,' and other punishment would be carried out through the day while the surrounding countryside was scoured for the escapee. One veteran told me that a woman missing at roll call that summer had been the cause of nearly fifty deaths in one morning, only to be found hanging in a latrine that night.

"What a joke on the Nazis!" he said.

If all were accounted for, work parties were assigned, sick, debilitated, elderly and dying prisoners were selected from the ranks for the gas chambers and crematorium, whose smoke and stench of burning flesh wafted among us daily. All were regularly assured however, that the monstrous furnaces existed solely for those who became too sick or weak to work or stupid enough to require repeated beatings, torture, or consistently fell from attention at roll call. Terror was a standard *SS* implement.

'Stay healthy,' the veterans advised us. But after a few meals of thin soup and crust of bread or a half-cup of gruel, I couldn't see how that would be possible. Yet the majority had done it. And it was not long before we understood a philosophy of survival embraced by many: look out for yourself alone; every other prisoner is a competitor for life; have no sympathy for them. This accepted philosophy was rationalized by the contention that weaker individuals were going to die anyway, so all the determined survivors were doing was shortening their miserable existence. What should they do, let them have full rations and die with them?

Or, if *Hauptsturmfuhrer* Vogel and his *Schutzstaffeln* guards were in the mood at a particular *Zahlappell*, they would declare a day of games. One event was called *Fechten*, in which two prisoners were armed with stout clubs and forced to beat each other until the loser couldn't stand up. Another variation was a race in which contestants ran between two rows of prisoners who had to hit them with clubs as hard as they could or run the gauntlet themselves.

The worst event I heard about entailed naked men, women and children enclosed in a pen the size of a tennis court with dogs trained to bite arms, legs and genitals.

At my first *Zahlappell*, I realized our contingent on the train had been reduced by more than half. I tried to see Anna among the ranks of women prisoners several groups away but couldn't, and my effort earned me a bash on the back of the head from Hirschberg's stick, which nearly brought me to my knees.

My second day began with a brief roll call, then breakfast from a huge metal pot set down before us by two emaciated women with downcast eyes from a kitchen *Kommando* [worker]. They ladled small portions of cold meal into wooden bowls that our *Kapo* instructed us to file by to collect. When I took mine, I had the urge to ask the woman if she had seen Anna but knew that was ridiculous. There were no spoons, but that didn't prevent us from emptying our bowls like wolves, licking the sides until forced to return them, then sucking our fingers for the last remnants of the sour gruel.

Hirschberg formed up the seventy-three remaining inmates of *Hutte 47* and marched us to the main gate where we were counted; there, Hirschberg signed his number and his life for our custody. Four more work *Kommandos* closed in behind us. When all was in order, the gates were opened, and over two hundred prisoners marched out in the custody of five *Kapos* and one teenage *SS-Shutze* armed with a *Sturmgewehr MP44*. The temptation to overpower our guards and flee through the woods was strong, but impractical—it would mean the deaths of a hundred prisoners and eventual capture from an armed, mechanized search team. So much for escape.

We walked through snow-covered fields and woods in our thin street shoes that were sodden in minutes, numb at the core in spite of our coats, knitted toques and mittens, exhausted from lack of food, just trying to keep pace with the *Kapos*. How the hell did they expect us to work?

We turned a corner of the compound heading west, passing near wooden carts heaped with pale, skeletal corpses. Several *Sonderkommando*s [Death workers] supervised by stocky *SS-Ausfeherin* were throwing bodies into the massive pit dug in the hard earth. One of the female guards watched us trudge by, gloved fists planted on broad hips, a mean look on her bloated face. Her arm whipped out pointing in our direction as we came abreast of the sordid detail.

"You!" she yelled at us. The veterans remained facing front, but several new men including myself looked, but didn't answer.

"*Blonde!*" she shouted again, her outstretched finger jabbing the air in my direction. "What *Hutte?*" I was the only man with blond hair in my file, so I answered. "Forty-seven." She nodded, then noticed one of her prisoners faltering with a heavy male corpse. She clubbed the worker with a truncheon, grabbed the dead body by its feet and flung it in the pit. As we marched away, someone behind me muttered, "*Dummkopf.*"

Our destination was a long brick building in a forest about three kilometers from the *KZ*, camouflaged from all sides, even to planted trees covered with snow on the flat roof. The *Kapo* of another hut ordered his *Block* inside where they would assemble hand grenades in the relative warmth of the factory. Our *Kapo* that was supervising a similar prisoner group continued leading their charges down a snow-packed road to factories beyond. A German civilian in a bulky loden coat, hat and gloves emerged from the end of the building that looked like the office, beckoned to Hirschberg without a word and disappeared around the corner.

We followed the *Kapo* to where the civilian waited behind the building at a wide excavation shored by wooden planks. Two-wheel wooden carts stood at the edge of the hole with piles of picks and shovels in the cart beds. Hirschberg ordered us to take the tools, climb down into the pit and dig. It didn't take long to figure out that the factory was being enlarged and since the bombing by Allied planes had become so intense would be built underground.

We dug wet dirt from the bottom of the partial excavation and tossed it up to the ground above where other workers shoveled it into wagons, then hitched rope harnesses across their chest and, pulled the carts through a rutted mud path to the trees and emptied it. Others fashioned wooden pegs to replace the nails they didn't have, gouged holes with blunt chisels to secure planks, mixed mortar with sticks and spread it on foundation bricks with pieces of wood or bare hands. Our noon meal of bits of suet and bread in greasy water had been brought from the compound and was cold. It began to snow in the afternoon, but we worked nonstop through dusk until Hirschberg formed us up on the road again, counted, then marched us back to our *Block* in the compound.

We all collapsed under blankets, two to a bunk, shivering in the acrid sweat on our bodies from the hard work and forced march. Several men slept immediately and would have lost their evening meal to the rest of us if a broad-shouldered man with wide-spaced eyes, and a large head had not intervened.

That night Aaron Levi shamed us back into the human race and set the tone for the way we would try to behave toward one another from then on.

"No!" he shouted through chattering teeth, striding up the narrow aisle between the rows of tiered bunks with a blanket clutched around his shoulders. "We cannot become the animals they are. We cannot do their work of killing Jews for them." He continued to pace, his huge eyes piercing our conscience. "We endured three centuries of oppression in Egypt, Moses led us out with the help of God, the Maccabees took Jerusalem, then Hadrian massacred us scattering survivors to the winds." He willed his big body to stop shivering and braced his shoulders under the blanket. "We have endured countless persecutions through the ages and did not turn against one another. History will judge the evil scum who commit these atrocities. And us. "We have always been strong in adversity. Strength is self-discipline. Strength is obeying the laws of God. Strength is living with honor." His large head nodded as though he was agreeing with something in the future he could see. His final words were almost inaudible. "And courage is dying with dignity."

Most of us were sleeping, but the lights were still on, low voices talking, the sound of a man crying, several arguments about Aaron's speech. The door of the hut banged open against the wall, and three *SS-Ausfeherin* [Camp guards] strode into the room in a swirl of snow driven by the bitter wind. Each carried a thick wooden baton they hit against our bunks as they moved slowly up and down the aisles. One of them was the mean-looking, fat-faced female guard from the burial *Kommando* who yelled at me that morning. When she came to my bunk she stopped and whacked my feet with her baton. "*Machen!*" [Get up]" she shouted, "*Schnell, schnell!*" [Quickly]

I got up and she prodded me out the door behind the two other women who had similarly appropriated a prisoner from their bunks. They marched us across the *Appfellplatz* into the crowded room of a barracks near the east fence where we were greeted by the shrill yells and obscene catcalls of more than a dozen female *SS* guards.

The first thing I noticed was the blessed heat which was probably 20 Centigrade, the warmest I had been since the night Anna and I were dragged from our beds in Berlin a few days ago that seemed liked months. The room was small, partitioned off from similar quarters in a building that was not much better than ours. Except for the larger potbelly stove to heat the smaller area and two bunks to a tier instead of four. The room had the same smell of unwashed bodies as our hut, plus the odor of menstrual fluids and vaginas which had probably not been douched for weeks, if ever.

"*Sich entkleiden!*" [Take off your clothes.] my ugly antagonist ordered. Aaron and I stood in a common area between two rows of bunks encircled by some of the women gawking, others lying on mattresses half-undressed, laughing at us. I took my coat off as ordered, resigned to what they wanted and started to unbutton my jacket. A big kid in his late teens with a row of tight black curls that had grown back quickly, a look of intelligence on his handsome face, followed my example. Aaron hadn't moved, and one of the *Ausfeher* who had fetched us began jabbing his kidneys with her baton, repeating the order to take off his clothes. Aaron just stood there, facing forward with his hands stuffed in his overcoat pockets.

"*Sich entkleiden!*" the guard yelled again angrily and swung the stick viciously against Aaron's right kidney. The big man grunted, arched forward, then turned, grabbed the baton from her hand and stood there with the club, looking around defiantly at the silent women, a tinge of sadness dimming his large eyes. My original tormentor they called Gert, seemed to be the senior rank and I was staring at her for a reaction. The way I had learned to twist my neck to let my eye see as much as possible caught a movement at the back of Aaron's head. The sound of the shot made me jump a foot as Aaron toppled against the stove, his dark blood leaking from the black hole in his closely shaved skull.

The door to the barracks opened, and an *SS*-Corporal looked in, laughed and closed it. The slack-features of the female troglodyte holding the pistol didn't change as she swung it at me. "Undress!"

By the time I had, Gert was lying nude on her mattress, the spectators clapping and chanting lewd taunts for the show to go on, Aaron forgotten. Gert's mouth opened in an intended smile revealing gray and broken teeth, arms flung open, black hair in their pits, shapeless dugs, and a wide patch of black fur descending from the rolls of fat around her waist to the raw gash between her wide-spread legs. I would have to get this over with or be sick and end up on the floor with Aaron.

I mounted the beast, gagging on her foul breath, my eyelids pressed tight, praying for an erection. I didn't know what the boy was doing, but the raucous shouts of the women around me seemed to be taunting two acts being performed at the same time.

I felt a sharp blade at my jugular and opened my eye to a wild expression on Gert's face that told me she would slit my throat if I did not perform satisfactorily. Somehow, even in my exhausted state, scared stiff, revolted by the moist slab of slimy jelly beneath me, I became hard. Feeling it, Gert grabbed me, impaled herself and began writhing like some crazed reptile. I held off as long as I could, pumping to meet the awkward thrust of her buttocks, then at the end, pinned her arms with feigned passion to shift the knife away from my neck. I sensed she did not have an orgasm and probably never did, so I rolled off onto the floor and scampered away from her reach. The spectators were applauding wildly, and Gert was still prone on the bunk gasping, so I grabbed my clothes and got dressed.

When the kid finished his chore, we were ordered to carry Aaron out of the hut and lay him beside it. The boy must have done a better job than I did, because his woman told him to take Aaron's coat. They escorted us back to our block and left.

I lay in my bunk crying for Aaron, myself and every other miserable person alive or dead in that hell on earth. There was no question in my mind that I would die there. From malnutrition, TB, typhus or the whim of some *SS* sociopath like Gert. I wondered how long I would last. A week, three months? Where was God that night? I'd ignored Him most of my life and was sure He was doing the same to me then. I started to say the 'Lord's Prayer,' but choked on the words, "thy will be done, on earth...." Was *Bergen-Belsen* His will?

That was the longest day of my life.

* * * * * *

When Hirschberg called my number at *Zahlappell* the next morning I thought I had been selected. My knees buckled, and I would have fallen if the men beside me hadn't propped me up. I could have run then, and they might shoot me, plus another fifty prisoners as an example. Or go along. Dying then would prevent the pain and misery I would endure as long as I survived the bitter cold, debilitating work, incidents like the night before. My mind rebelled in comic relief with the thought that I would probably be the first man in history executed for being a lousy lay.

Walking unsteadily, head down behind the *Kapo* leading me, I could not help picturing my final moments, standing naked with 200 other pathetic souls crushed together in a concrete bunker as the capsules of prussic acid were dropped through holes in the ceiling. Death would follow in three to fifteen minutes.

The *Kapo* led me up some wooden steps and knocked on a door. I looked around and realized we were standing in front of the Camp *Commandant's* office. My God, I thought, Naujocks must have found out I was a spy! I whirled away from the terrible torture that awaited me, but the *Kapo* grabbed the back of my coat as I tried to jump off the porch, just as *SS* Shultz opened the door. They both pulled me inside.

Shultz led me through an anteroom full of *SS* and prisoner clerks, down a hallway to a large well-furnished office at the rear of the building. *Kommandant* Rudolf Franz Hoess sat behind a polished mahogany table. *Hauptsturmfuhrer* [Captain] Vogel stood behind him facing a man seated across the desk whose back was to me as I entered the room. *Obersturmbannfuhrer* [Colonel] Hoess had been recently transferred from Auschwitz, where at his trial at Nuremberg after the war, boasted personal responsibility for exterminating three million Jews.

Oberst [Brigadier General] Hans Oster stood and turned from the table when he heard us enter the room and I nearly fell on my knees. I hadn't seen a gray *Wehrmacht* uniform since the day before we had been forced on the train and I wanted to hug him. Without warning, my *Abwehr* superior stepped forward and whipped me across the shoulder with his swagger stick. "*Schmutzig Spion!*"[Filthy spy.]

I cringed from the blow, then stood immobile, willing myself to stifle my hilarity while trying to absorb the terse exchange between a Brigadier-General of the German Army and a Lieutenant Colonel in the *Waffen SS [Regular army]*.

Technically, the former outranked the latter by two grades, but the insidious powers of the SS gave Hoess more authority, particularly inside a camp where even an army general could disappear. Whatever cock-and-bull story Oster had given Hoess, he wasn't buying it. But the *Abwehr* held certain powers, too. Although the *Kommandant* promised to lodge a protest with Himmler, their mutual superior since Canaris' demotion, he agreed to release me to Oster's custody. I later learned that the war was finally going badly for the Germans and if they lost, Hoess' history would place him at the mercy of not only the Allies, but the *Wehrmacht*, the legitimate army of the Third Reich.

My euphoria at hearing the *Kommandant*'s capitulation was tempered by Anna. Oster purportedly wanted to take me back for questioning as a Dutch spy, yet in spite of the threat it could present to my freedom, I claimed that my courier had more information about our underground contacts than I did. Oster did not seem pleased at my insistence that he take Anna with us--if she was still alive; but he knew the SS kept meticulous records and asked Hoess to let me see them.

Three Anna Rosenthal's were listed on the camp roster, and prisoner 753421's number was closest to mine. Unless her status was outdated, she was assigned to one of the *Sonderkommandos*. Good God! Had she survived that? Hoess was further irritated by Oster's request for an escort to find her but yielded and ordered *Hauptsturmfuhrer* Vogel to accompany us.

Vogel marched us across the *Appfellplatz* in silence, between rows of empty *Blocks* to an isolated area at the far end of the camp where hundreds of naked men, women and children were freezing in line outside a low cement structure with *Ausfeher* holding their rifles at port arms. A large sign bore the German '*Dusch*,' [Shower] in addition to the word for 'shower' in Hebrew, Polish and French, plus several Slavic languages I didn't recognize.

The *Hauptsturmfuhrer* led us around the structure to an enclosure surrounded by a wooden fence extending from the rear. He gave us a malicious grin as he opened the gate on a sight that I will see in my mind every night for all eternity. Old men dragging gassed corpses from the chamber with meat-hooks and nooses, emaciated children sweeping blood and excrement across the threshold. Women and girls searching the dead for gold teeth, bridgework, diamonds and rings hidden in body cavities, removing teeth, eyeglasses and the last remnants of hair classified as raw materials. Several younger men pulled the plundered corpses up a ramp and threw them in wagon where they were stacked like logs for their final journey to the crematorium. Whether this work detail knew it or not, they would be thrown into that wagon in sixty days when the Nazis deemed their efficiency had slacked off.

Anna was on her hands and knees among the bodies, working a pair of pliers and a metal pick inside a woman's mouth. I stepped around the corpses and leaned down to whisper, "Anna, we're going home."

She didn't stop what she was doing or look up. "No, I cannot leave."

"Anna, it's me, Pieter. I've come to take you home with me. You must come now."

Tears began streaming down her cheeks and she shook her head frantically, probing wildly, harder into the gaping maw. "I cannot leave until I finish! Not until I finish!"

I dug my fingers into her shoulder. "Anna! Look at me. It's Pieter. I've come to take you home."

"No!" She did look up. Her eyes were dull slate, filled with pain, sunk in purple rings, gazing inward. "When I am done with the last," she whimpered. "Then I can rest. But not yet, Pieter. I have too much work to do." She had not taken the pliers or pick out the mouth and returned to her grisly task, trying to make up for lost time.

"Get on with it, *Herr* Kramers," Oster called out behind me. He hadn't moved from the wooden gate, Vogel was standing near the wagon talking to the chief *Kapo* of the *Sonderkommando*.

I grabbed Anna's wrists, yanked her to her feet and pried the tools from her fingers. Her eyes stretched wide and she threw her head back screaming like a madwoman. I raised my arm at half-cock, threw a short jab at the point of her jaw and she collapsed in my arms. She must have weighed less than forty kilos but felt heavier as I carried her out of that abominable Gahanna from which I prayed she could recover.

CHAPTER TWENTY-EIGHT
Eiche, Germany
January 1945

Despite the bomb-craters pocking highways, Oster's chauffeur drove the 200 kilometers toward the ravaged city of Potsdam south of Berlin in four hours, compared to our three-and-a-half-day train ride to *Belsen* a billion light years ago.

In the fall of 1944 the war had turned in our favor, yet was far from over. The Axis powers were still winning battles and Germany's new jet-propelled rockets were exploding on London. But General Patton had taken Sicily and the Russians had liberated Smolensk. RAF Lancaster bombers and American Flying Fortresses were making high-altitude precision bombing raids, paralyzing Nazi industry throughout Germany and occupied northern Europe. Two American divisions stormed the beaches at Anzio, driving the Germans sixty miles up the Italian boot.

General MacArthur had pushed off from New Guinea in the Pacific theater, recaptured the Bismarck Archipelago, the Marianas and the Marshall chain in a series of bloody island battles north of the Philippines.

The previous November, another of the frustrating pitfalls that had lain in the path of prior attempts at a coup to unseat Hitler threatened to derail the current plan. The entire *Abwehr* station in Ankara, Turkey--two married couples, defected to the Allies with all of their codes, documents and sources. Plans for a negotiated surrender were nearly terminated when Hitler blamed that damaging incident on the man who had secretly opposed him for almost a decade. He fired Canaris three days later, combining all German intelligence agencies under the direction of *SS-Reichfuhrer* Heinrich Himmler, who had compiled a 160-page report on the suspected subversive activities of the Admiral, including his behind the scenes involvement in the July 20th assassination attempt on the *Fuhrer.* The fatherland's Master Spy was awarded the *Eisernes Kreuz* [iron Cross] for valiant service and assigned to head up the Department of War Economics.

At three o'clock on the afternoon of our resurrection, Oster's driver wheeled the *Wehrmacht* gray Mercedes into a cleared lot next to the Admiral's new office in Eiche, near Potsdam. Anna and I were huddled in a corner of the back seat sleeping. Hans woke me, we left Anna to her restless coma in the care of the *Unterfeldwebel* and walked into the partially demolished brick building.

Admiral Canaris had apparently moved into his predecessor's office without changing a thing. It was larger than his cubbyhole on *Tirpitz Ufer* with a broad desk of polished wood, comfortable black leather furniture and a wide oak conference table which stood on a maroon carpet of deep pile. The traditional portrait of the *Fuhrer* dominated the long interior wall and heavy maroon drapes half drawn across the opposite windows creating a more sinister atmosphere than his room in Department Z.

"You survived, I see," he said.

"Thanks to you, *Mein Admiral.*"

He gestured at the leather couch and I sat on it; Oster took a wooden chair.

"You can thank Naujocks for saving your lives," Canaris said with his ready chuckle. "If he hadn't had you beaten up, we would not have kept you under surveillance. I might not have learned of your situation in time."

I balanced a cup of tea on the leg of an old pair of flannel trousers deciding not to mention stuffing a pistol in his ear. They had found a clean army shirt and sweater that fit, but no shoes, and I was conscious of my stocking feet on the pile rug.

"Aside from the fact that he probably put our names on the *Konzentrationslager* list in the first place."

Oster seated across from me shrugged under his

impeccable uniform, incongruous in the simple wooden chair. "We were able to track you down before the monster could swallow."

In spite of the close call or maybe because of it--I couldn't help grinning. "My savior won't be too happy to see me again."

"He will not see you," Oster replied.

"We did not save your life out of pure altruism." Canaris was sitting behind his desk, hands clasped at the ends of arms thrust forward in his naval uniform jacket, displaying the broad gold stripes of his rank on the smooth surface.

I waited. Nothing could be as bad as standing in that *Appel.* I looked at Oster and recalled the freezing cold endured just an incredible nine hours before, hearing my number called out for what I believed was my 'selection.'

"From now on you will work for us," Oster said.

"Against my own country?" The words were out of my mouth before I could think. "You'd better put me back in that camp."

"No, no," Canaris said.

Oster referred to a conversation we had in the car.

"You have contributed quite a bit to the Allied forces."

"I thought we were going home." The words put a lump in my throat.

"We cannot just book you with a travel agent, *wahr?*"

"Naujocks will find out you took us from *Belsen.* He'll be tracking us down."

"But will not find you."

"What do you want me to do?"

Canaris smiled. "First, some questions and honest answers between spies."

I had to remind myself that even though these men may have allowed me access to classified military data and saved my life, they were the enemy, not my friends.

"Did you kill Pieter Kramers," Canaris asked "or do the Americans have him in custody?"

"I am Pieter Kramers."

I hadn't seen Canaris much in the past year but he seemed

depressed at that meeting, tired, older. The tide of war had finally turned against Germany on all fronts and I'd noticed a general pessimism behind the bluster of the military. Resignation, relief in some.

Oster spoke to the Admiral as though I were not in the room. "We could let the *SS* extract the information, but then he would be of no use to us. Or let Naujocks take him out and shoot him. Send the girl back to Hoess."

"He should answer our questions," Canaris said. "Take part in a mission his leaders would endorse and perhaps live to see the end of the war."

If what they said was true, I should at least know what their deal was. Even though they claimed to be anti-*Nazis* and seemed convinced I was a double agent--admitting that I was an American spy to the Chief of German Intelligence did not come naturally.

Canaris turned to me. "What is your true name?"

"John Andeweg."

"Where is Pieter Kramers?"

"Dead."

"You killed him?"

"Drowned him. With a garrote."

"Were you chosen for this assignment because of your missing eye or did that come later?"

"Later."

Canaris appraised me for several seconds, then said to Oster, "No wonder we are losing this war."

The setting sun streamed through the parted drapes creating highlights in the gray hair of the little man behind the desk, as Canaris began a story I did not digest easily.

"A group called the *Schwarze Kapelle* [Black Choir] has conspired against 'The Little Corporal' since 1938. Its members are in the highest ranks of the military, the government, industry and civic leaders. Germans who are convinced that the *Fuhrer* and his ruthless *Nazis* are destroying our country. Our purpose has been to thwart their efforts in every way possible without harming the German people or our nation."

"We do not commit *verrat*," Oster said. "We are patriots, not traitors."

The Admiral sat back in his chair and gripped both hands on the edge of the desk. "But we are viewed as such by almost everyone and watched by *SS* informers."

"If they know who you are," I asked, "why don't they arrest you?"

Oster twirled his monocle on its cord and a sunbeam threw refracted light onto the dark-paneled walls. "The *SS* believe in watching a man until all his contacts are known, then arresting the entire network.. Instead of taking one man and letting his unknown associates slip away...if the man should die prematurely during interrogation."

The Admiral's next statement shocked me. "There have been assassination attempts on Adolf Hitler which have failed."

I found that hard to believe. "And they let you remain free?"

"They shot the men who tried it," Oster said. "They only suspect who the other conspirators are."

I allowed my expression to show my skepticism.

"The members of our *'Black Choir'* are not without power," Oster insisted. "Several are Generals who command the armies. Even if rank and file soldiers remained loyal to the 'Little Corporal,' could he afford to purge his most experienced officers?"

"We are honorable men," Canaris said. "At first, we planned to arrest the *Fuhrer* and his executive staff and replace them with our own government." The Admiral shook his head as though that was an unrealistic dream. "We intended to place Hitler and his *Nazis* on trial for treason and offer a conditional surrender to the Allies that would not humiliate the German people."

Oster crossed a polished boot over the razor-crease of his gray jodhpurs. "That does not seem possible now."

"What do you need me for?"

Neither man answered for several moments and I was conscious of the noise of traffic that filtered up from the street below. Through the parted curtains on the open window I could see the standing walls of bombed-out buildings jutting up from piles of rubble, broken trees and leveled homes in the distance.

Finally, Admiral Canaris said, "To prevent the next generation of Nazis from conquering the world during the second half of the twenty-first century."

* * * * * *

They moved Anna and me to a new apartment in a different neighborhood on the same gas line as Fabian, our trusted resistance contact. Berlin had taken a horrible beating from the Allied air raids that had been dropping tons of explosive and incendiary bombs on the city day and night. In some sections, entire blocks of buildings were heaps of rubble, yet the pipes beneath the streets in our district were intact, even though gas might not be running through them. One of my first chores was to reinstate our radio connection to Fabian.

Our rooms were on the top floor of a six-story building in a residential area that Allied airmen had apparently been instructed to avoid. The apartment consisted of a sitting room with traditional gas fireplace, a bay window overlooking a narrow tree-lined street, a tiny bedroom in the rear and a kitchen the size of a closet. It was completely furnished and each floor had its communal bathroom. Despite the six flights of stairs, we would have been happy with the *Admiral*'s generosity except for the knowledge that those rooms had been the home of a Jewish couple who had not been rescued from the camps.

Before our internment in *Belsen*, Anna had been a vibrant girl of constant energy, fully aware of the dangers of her existence as a Jew in the heart of *Nazi* Germany and from our activities as espionage agents securing valuable information the Allies would use against the hated *Nazi* regime. Once she was off the streets and living with me she seemed convinced of her own immortality, like many adolescents, acquiring a dismissive attitude toward discovery and its inevitable consequence.

After *Belsen*, Anna developed a facial tick and became

remote. As usual, I told her none of the details of the messages we sent to London, but I could sense that she had to steel herself to contact Fabian to verify our release and set up the transmission schedule so I could reassure James Barnum that we were back in business.

Canaris and his *Schwarze Kapelle* wanted me to make my Resistance organized and *OSS* assisted exit from Germany with some document Canaris claimed could prevent World War III. The *Admiral's* changed status, however, my internment in *Belsen*, the possibility that I had been broken by the *SS*, whether to include Anna in my escape and several other issues invented by Barnum, precipitated confusion in the *OSS*, resulting in a series of queries and conditions regarding my departure from Berlin and *Nazi* occupied Europe.

On the day after Christmas, I sent a harshly worded demand for a date and details of our flight from enemy territory. A month later, Anna picked up the reply which I shared with Hans Oster. I was on my own.

Anna asked Fabian to set up an escape route through his Resistance group, but so far, they were 'working on it.' We knew running people was more difficult than sending messages, yet I suspected Fabian and his superiors also thought we were too hot to handle.

Ten days later, Hans Oster picked me up after curfew in his gray Mercedes. I noticed an *StG 44* assault rifle on the back seat, its long-curved magazine protruding from the base of the chamber. "Are you expecting trouble?" I asked him.

"A precaution."

I was not reassured. When I pressed for more information about our appointment with the *Admiral*, he changed the subject. We entered Canaris' office to find the *Admiral* slumped behind the big desk, his usually well-barbered hair longer, his eyelids puffed and heavy.

"Working for two years in the midst of enemy intelligence could not have been a pleasant existence," he observed, "even for the most seasoned agent."

I looked from him to Oster. "You made it easier."

"If Naujocks or others had exposed you," Oster said, "we could not have prevented your execution. We nearly failed as it was."

"You have served your country well," Canaris told me. He gestured to a door at the far end of the room without looking at it. "I would like you to wait with General Oster in my secretary's office during a meeting that is scheduled in one hour."

"*Mein Admiral*, I thought we were going to discuss getting Anna and me out of Germany."

We had been cooped up in our apartment for two months, trying to avoid Naujocks and his troopers who'd been looking for us relentlessly. "What about sending us home?"

He waved a listless hand in the air. "We will speak about that," he said, but refused to do so until after his meeting.

I must admit that I was more concerned about escaping from Germany than some meeting about events that wouldn't take place for almost one-hundred years, if at all.

"Who's going to be in it?"

"You will understand later." The assault rifle propped against a table beside him, Oster sat in a padded wooden armchair across the room from the Admiral; I sat on opposite him at end of the leather couch. We waited in the reflective silence that Canaris never seemed compelled to fill. I noticed the three brass monkeys on his desk with their hands covering eyes, ears and mouth, his private symbol of the intelligence service, one of the two possessions he had brought from his *Abwehr* office. The other was a ship's model which I had always wanted to ask him about. He remained silent for a few minutes until I thought he would not answer me. Then he allowed me to glimpse a sliver of his soul, which would help me make some difficult decisions in the months to come.

He told me about his first assignment out of the Imperial Naval Academy at Kiel as an intelligence officer's billet on the cruiser, *Dresden*, during the First World War, which was scuttled during the battle of the Falkland Islands in 1915; his escape by submarine to Spain, where he worked with the notorious spy, Mata Hari collecting intelligence on British shipping from Madrid.

After the war, he married Erika Waag, the daughter of a wealthy industrialist, living comfortably in their *Schlachtensee* home where they kept horses and dogs, and *Frau* Canaris invited Reinhard Heydrich to join her string quartet. During the 1920's Canaris was a confirmed anti-socialist, patriot and monarchist, who became involved in the *Kapp Putsch* against the *Weimar* Republic and issued false passports to the murderers of two socialist leaders. He seemed to avoid dismissal from the navy for these and other confrontations throughout his life by dodging issues with an ambiguous grin and clever rebuttal designed to offend no one. In 1935, he was posted to Admiral and placed in charge of *Spionage Abwehr.* When he learned of Hitler's plans of world domination and the ruthless methods he would use to achieve them, he organized the *Schwarze Kapelle* and began his tenacious conspiracy to save his country from destruction by a madman.

During that melancholy reverie I recognized the outwardly benevolent little man as a driven, intelligent human being with an insatiable curiosity and astute sense of morality. If he had a fatal flaw, it was his inability to resist personal involvement in the constant intrigue which his responsibilities and very nature demanded.

At a quarter to midnight, Oster and I moved into the adjoining office where he locked the connecting door, motioned me into the swivel chair behind the desk and took a seat in a straight back chair beside it with the rifle leaning against his knee. A red light appeared on the intercom and I started to speak, but he put a finger to his lips and shook his head. We waited.

The distant, metallic voice of the Admiral came over the speaker as he greeted *Reichsleiter* Martin Bormann, Head of the *Nazi* Party and prime force in the execution of the *Fuhrer's* Final Solution; and *Arztin* Joseph Goebbels, Hitler's Minister of Propaganda, who had issued the orders for

Kristallnacht in 1938, the worst pogrom in the Third Reich to that date. Alfred Naujocks needed no introduction and seemed largely ignored by his superiors.

I looked at Oster with raised eyebrows as he picked up a magazine from a small table and pretended to read it. I listened to Bormann introduce Canaris to Ernst Weber, President of the National Bank of Switzerland; Alberto Caflisch, Secretary of the Swiss Bankers Association; Walter Stucki from the Swiss Foreign Minister's Office; and Swiss attorney Walter Keller-Staub. My interest in the clandestine conference sharpened considerably.

Canaris had brought me into the culmination of secret negotiations between the *Nazi* hierarchy and Swiss bankers which had been initiated by the *Devisenstellen [Foreign Trade Board]* established in 1938 to camouflage German investments abroad and had been personally supervised by his predecessor for years. Prior to and throughout WW II, purportedly neutral Switzerland had supplied Germany with arms, munitions and massive loans totaling billions of Swiss francs. Since the mid-1800's this tiny, insular democracy had allowed its bankers to make their own rules based on self-aggrandizement, which included a 1922 statute permitting anonymous numbered accounts protected by law against inquiry or disclosure, that had been stimulated by a threatened tax on capital and a device to attract more customers.

This guaranteed confidentiality encouraged thousands of persecuted Jewish families to deposit their savings in Switzerland since the 1930's. That same law enabled the *Devisenstellen]* to convert confiscated Jewish loot, property, priceless stolen art and gold into Swiss francs via numbered accounts. I felt sick at the thought of the dental work Anna had been forced to plunder from the mouths of murder victims at *Bergen-Belsen.* Most *SS* officers in charge of camps, who were responsible for rounding up and transporting prisoners or the loot itself, had also opened numbered accounts with the Swiss.

Half paralyzed by shock, I heard the Swiss Bankers review

298

the status of *Nazi* and Jewish deposits totaling billions of francs and the final documents whose comprehensive details slammed a ball of revulsion in the pit of my stomach. I must have started to get up, because Oster gripped my arm with strong fingers until I settled back in the chair.

My movement must have been heard through the intercom in the next room because suddenly the voice of Naujocks became louder through our listening device, as though he was moving closer to the speaker of the two-way communications system on the Admiral's desk. Canaris called his name and Naujocks must have seen the speaker light, because he shouted some expletive and the next thing we heard was the rattling of the doorknob and pounding of a pistol butt on other side of the heavy wooden door.

Oster grabbed his rifle, motioned me under the desk and unlocked the door. Naujocks burst through it, pistol raised, pushing both hands against Oster's chest. Amid the brief scuffle, Naujocks smashed his nose against the gun-sight of Oster's weapon. Canaris followed quickly behind him scanning the room while pretending concern for Naujocks' bleeding nostrils, explaining to all that Oster was his personal security assistant, as thoroughly cleared for top secrets as any of them. Knowing the Admiral's quirky penchant for schemes and deception, the *Nazi* generals calmed the Swiss civilians down and they resumed their seats at the table. Canaris found a compress for Naujocks' broken nose, and the *SS* Major grabbed Oster's rifle with a belligerent sneer before marching back into the meeting.

Despite the under-heated office, I was perspiring profusely when I crawled out from under the desk, gingerly regained my seat and stared at the still functioning listening device, about which the meeting participants had either tacitly deferred to the Admiral's wishes, forgotten amid Naujocks blustering confrontation or were united against the unpopular *SS* bully known to have the ear of the *Fuhrer*.

Concentrating again on those *Nazi* leaders gathered around the Admiral's conference table, I began to absorb their concession to one another of their imminent defeat by the Allied forces. The agreement ready for signatures would link all German and Jewish deposits to several anonymous accounts whose numbers would reside in a safe deposit box in the *Schweiz* National Bank.

"We ran out of money, we ran out of men and we ran out of time," Bormann said to the Swiss. "This will likely be the last war of its kind on earth. The contest will no longer be for land, but for power."

"Money is power," a *Schweizer* voice said.

"History proves that entire nations can be conquered," the *Reichsleiter* continued, "by small bands of men who engage not huge armies, but strike fear in the lives of unsuspecting citizens. Genghis Kahn, Attila the Hun---the same way the Boers effectively won their independence from the British."

"We will find the malcontents of the third world, fund them," Goebbles added, "train them if necessary and point them at international events, political leaders, passenger ships and commercial airliners."

It sounded as though those military representatives of Nazi Germany had already surrendered, realized that many of them would not survive the postwar tribunals and were consolidating the means for world domination within the financial institutions of the trusted representatives of the *Schweizer* Bankers Association. All of its members were not mentioned during that meeting, but Credit Suisse was, Union Bank, *Basler Handelsbank*, and of course *Schweizer* National. In the future, Bormann, Goebbles, or their surrogates and followers would use this financial cache to fund any country, political or religious group who would terrorize the United States, Great Britain, our allies and the entire planet.

If they had their way, toward the end of the twenty-first century, our civilian population would be gripped by fear, close to anarchy in opposition to governments who could not retaliate effectively against the terrorists and certainly not the invisible, behind-the–scenes perpetrators. Our resources would be spent on security, our liberties restricted, and the financial cartels of Hitler's heirs would dominate the free nations of the western hemisphere, if not the entire world with all its resources.

"This document," Canaris said, "contains the detailed plan, the numbers of the various deposit accounts, plus a bearer authorization to access them. Your master key, *Herr* Webber, plus either one of theirs will open the box in your Swiss National Bank, which will contain this document with the access codes to the multiple accounts containing the funds."

Naujocks began to object but was silenced by Bormann.

"There are several issues directed by you patriotic Generals, that I received too late to include in the completed document. I will personally guarantee that the document with corrected additions will be given to *Herr* Weber to hand-carry under seal, accompanied by military escort tomorrow, and disburse them on the following day."

Naujocks asked, "Who will receive the other two keys?

"For security purposes," Canaris answered, "both recipients of a key will be anonymous to one another. If the persons with the second and third keys make inquiries regarding the other key holder, that will alert *Shwarze Kapelle* members to the planned theft and deal with it as you will.

"So, the keys are the key to billions of *deutschmarks,* Naujocks said, unable to keep a sly grin off his face.

They all laughed at the weak pun.

* * * * * *

I had barely stopped shaking a half hour later.

"Do you think they can they do that?" I asked.

"This is not the work of idiots." He extracted a *Zigaretten* from a silver case and paused to light it. "They have murdered hundreds of thousands of people, stolen their wealth and placed it in legitimate institutions that will divulge its existence to no one, much less allow its facile withdrawal. The security precautions have been designed to make the Swiss believe the money is secure from further theft by any one individual, to give the appearance of participation by our Ministry of Economy under the natural control of *Devisenstellen* and create the illusion that their monstrous booty is in the safekeeping of someone they cannot force to relinquish."

Oster stared at his boots.

Canaris was the fiercest national I had met. "What's your problem, Admiral? Isn't this a perfect way for Germany to dominate the world without all the bloodshed you detest?"

"No bloodshed?" The bushy brows rose above those pale blue eyes. "These are *Nazis, Herr* Andeweg. Butchers, who kill their old and sick, frail children like your friend Anna. You were there." His glance returned to the document on his desk. "Last June the *SS* massacred 600 French civilians in the village of *Oradour-sur-Glane.* Every living person they could find in retaliation for the killing of one *SS* officer by the resistance." He shook his head in an expression of infinite sadness. "Inhuman torture, medical experiments, starvation." He looked at me with moisture in his eyes. "What a world they would make, *wurden sie nicht?*"

"We'll defeat those people again, the savages who do that."

"Yes," Canaris replied. "But do individuals commit such crimes or do these *Nazis* possess an inherent genetic aberration which allow the elders to order cruel behavior and their young men to carry it out?" The Admiral sucked on his *Zigaretten* and squinted at me through its pungent smoke. "Given the chance, will they continue to repeat these cruelties again and again, throughout history?"

I was recovering from my initial astonishment at the idea that the losers in the war seemed confident of their ultimate victory.

"And you think they could do that?"

Canaris held my gaze for a moment. "What was your impression?"

I thought for a second. "The Swiss didn't seem sincere."

"You are quite observant." Canaris nodded his large head. "I suspect they have their own plan, which eventually excludes their co-conspirators." He folded his arms and glanced again at the keys lying on a copy of the document. "They will accommodate the *Nazis* to an extent but ignore the agreement if no one claims the money—which they might have a plan to arrange."

"They just signed a legal instrument," I said. "One of them boasted that a small country must live by their laws to survive."

"The Swiss speak of honor, morality, but change the rules to fit their greed. At least the *Nazis* make no pretense at integrity."

"Then why trust them with all that money?"

"Expediency. The *Nazis* are desperate." Canaris smiled at his sudden insight. "The Swiss are an arrogant race without conscience--perhaps we deserve each other."

I was distressed that both the *Nazis* and Swiss would profit from the ultimate evil of genocide but found it difficult to keep my mind on their long-range plan with the thought of Naujocks getting a brainstorm, following me and popping up here with a troop of *SS* goons any minute. But I was curious. I pointed to the pair of small silver keys lying on top of a three-ring binder at the corner of his desk.

"I thought you were going to give the master key to Webber?"

"I invited *Herr* Webber to be a weekend guest in my home, ostensibly to review the document and security procedures, where I was able to substitute the safe deposit keys in his briefcase for two identical ones--almost."

"Why, *Mein* Admiral?"

"Knowledge of these deposits, this agreement with the Swiss, could help the world to prevent it."

"You promised to get me out of here," I said with a wave of my good arm at the keys. "What's all this got to do with me anyway?"

He picked up the three-ring binder that contained the Swiss agreement and handed them to me with the master key. "Guard these well," he warned me. "Do not give them up easily."

From recent developments and the tone of their comments, Canaris and Oster did not expect to outlive the war and were obsessed with a financial pact, as heinous as it was, that probably wouldn't bear fruit for a couple of generations.

I said, "We can discuss this when the fighting is over."

"It is over," he said, and I knew he didn't mean the army.

We stood, all moving together in front of Canaris' desk and I shook Oster's hand in the abrupt European manner. The general turned and walked to the door, paused with his hand on the knob, looking back at me. "I will explain your escape route from Berlin on the drive back to the City."

Admiral Canaris looked up at me as though he had just awoken from an idle daydream. He grasped my hand in both of his. "*Aufwiedersehn*, my young American friend. Listen to your heart. Never settle for less."

CHAPTER TWENTY-NINE
Potsdam, Germany
January 1945

Our tires jumped the frozen ruts on the unplowed street where ice crystals permeated the slush and mud. It was well after midnight and the streets on the outskirts of Potsdam were deserted. Total darkness enveloped the faint images of bombed-out buildings. Oster did his best to avoid the larger chunks of rubble in the road as I used a map and penlight trying to direct him around the center city onto the Autobahn back to Berlin.

I found the access road that led to the highway and told Hans to turn left. When he did, an *SS*-Staff car was parked across our path, its motor running, dim headlights illuminating the pile of debris blocking the single lane ahead, forcing us to stop. Before he could back up, a beam of light burst through the side window on Oster's right.

"Do not move, General," Alfred Naujocks' voice said, through the window glass or your days of high treason will end tonight."

Oster's hand started for his Lugar, but I grabbed his arm. "No, Hans," I whispered, "he's right."

A look of pain and sadness crossed Oster's features. Then he rolled down the window to reveal Naujocks pointing a pistol at us, a bloody bandage on his nose contrasting with his shadowy features. The light shifted to my face. "Ha, ha!" he shouted. "I knew something was cooking, but this! Get out of the car, *Herr* Kramers. Slowly. No tricks tonight, please."

When I was standing outside the car, Naujocks instructed me to close the door, Oster to squeeze the Mercedes around his staff car and get on the Autobahn back to Berlin. There was nothing either one of us could do. We watched the fading red pinpricks of two taillights as the big car receded up the access ramp and disappeared into the darkness.

Naujocks swung the beam of his flashlight behind me into the doorway of a brick building still half standing. "Over there, *Herr* Kramers, where we can speak in private."

The brainy hoodlum had a sense of humor and was going to enjoy this. "Now, *Herr* American spy, where is your Jewess traitor?"

His flashlight was aimed at my face but threw an eerie glow around the beams, bricks and mortar fragments protruding from under the snow that had fallen through the roofless structure. The dank smell of wet ashes and charred wood tickled my nostrils.

I laughed. "You're going to kill me anyway, Alfred, why should I give up Anna?"

"Because if you do I will end it quickly. If you do not, you will tell me eventually and beg to die. Do you understand that?"

"I know what you *SS* cretins are capable of."

Now he laughed. A passerby would think we were a couple of pals having fun.

Suddenly he took a half step at me and smashed the heavy flashlight against my right elbow. The pain shot all the way up to my shoulder and I grabbed the throbbing joint with my left hand, bending at the waist, my entire right arm on fire, useless.

"Bastard!" I hissed through clenched teeth.

"Once again, *Herr* Spy. Where is the Jew traitor?"

I realized he was going to beat me up until I was a clump of broken bones he'd shove under a pile of bricks. If he kept hitting me like that for another couple of minutes I wouldn't have a chance. I straightened up clutching my elbow. It might be a bad risk, but it was all I could think of. "How about a trade, Alfred?"

He laughed longer this time. "You have nothing to offer, *Herr* Kramers. I will take from you the information I wish and then your life. What can you have that I would exchange for those?"

"You're supposed to be a smart guy, Alfred. You know

why the Admiral was meeting with Bormann, Goebbels and Swiss bankers tonight. I was in the room with Oster under the desk."

He stood frozen for a moment, then spoke softly. "That old traitor." His face brightened like the morning sun as comprehension flooded his mind. With a little prodding on his part, I told him the truth. When he had my key to the Swiss safe deposit box he could pilfer the bank accounts at will. His next demand sounded almost giddy.

"Give me the key."

"It's in the car," I said. "I slipped it to Oster."

"No!" he shouted, lunging at me, holding the gun to my temple as he stuffed the light in the pocket of his greatcoat and twirled me around by my injured arm. I screamed with pain, almost fainting.

"Move and I will shoot," he warned me, groping into the side pockets of my overcoat, then the pockets of my tunic from behind. He turned me again from my left this time, but I screamed anyway. Naujocks was breathing hard, consumed with finding the key on me, hoping desperately that I was lying, that his chance at unbelievable wealth was not traveling in the Mercedes to Berlin. As he jammed his hand inside my pants pocket, I pulled my head back, apparently to allow him better access to it, stiffened my neck and slammed my forehead into Naujocks broken nose with the full weight of my upper body. He gave up a violent squeal of pure agony, stumbled back a few steps, dropped the pistol and went down flat on his back, both hands covering his gushing proboscis. I picked up his gun and pressed the muzzle against his forehead. I knew then that I should have done it but could not lower myself to his level. If I escaped and tried to live a normal existence after the war, I did not want that debasing moment haunting the rest of my life. I tied his hands and feet with his Sam Browne belt and dragged him as far I could to the rear of the building with my good arm. Then I ran to his staff car and drove toward Berlin.

* * * * * *

I could not go charging back to my apartment. But if I could reach him, Fabian could contact Anna through our radio hookup and send her to one of their regular drop locations. I left the car in an alley and snuck through the half-plowed streets of Berlin, dodging snowdrifts, hiding behind ruined buildings to avoid the occasional beam of a *Polizist* flashlight until I found a shelter jammed with hundreds of people whose homes the Allied bombers had destroyed, then spent the rest of the night huddled in the common fear that our luck would run out before dawn.

By noon the following day, I had spoken to Fabian on a pay phone and told him to alert London that I was coming out with or without their help. The message we sent hinted at top secret information in the hope that they would finally treat my situation with some immediacy. Fabian played von Wagner's *Gotterdammerung* on the gas pipe from a safe house requesting the all clear signal from Anna in my apartment. She didn't respond, and I was afraid the worst had happened.

The next afternoon Fabian met me at the *Zum Goldenen Hahn* across town from my district.

"Someone played Deutschland *Uber Alles*," he said. Our all clear signal. He did not mention the awkward way I held my broken elbow or the wooden slats that bound it under my coat.

"Someone?"

He was a thin man in his late forties with a haggard face. Neither one of us had used a razor recently, but that was not unusual in war-torn Berlin.

"Where has she been the past two days and nights?" Fabian asked.

I hadn't wanted to think about that. "They must have let her go."

"Not before she told them about the welcome song."

"I can't go off and leave her," I said, "without knowing. What if she's there, waiting?"

We were the only customers drinking beer at a sidewalk

table under a weak winter sun. We were both cold but would not be overheard.

"Do as you wish." Fabian ground out his foul-smelling *Zigaretten* in the ashtray and prepared to get up. "The *Gestapo* arrested Canaris, Oster and other *Schwarze Kapelle* this morning. They are combing the entire countryside to the southwest for you."

"Thinking I'd avoid Berlin."

"Naujocks told them you escaped." A phlegmy cough wracked the resistance fighter's body. "They found the car this afternoon."

We both knew what that meant.

"OK, someone in the *Abwehr* told them where my apartment was and they took Anna in for interrogation," I argued. "She doesn't know where I am, so they let her go."

"A *Juedin*? Naujocks? After she explained the crystal set and microphone?"

"We hid that in the basement."

Fabian leaned across the table. "*Du spinnst!*" [You're crazy!] he whispered. "Walking off with some key that leads to billions of Swiss francs," he thrust his unshaved jaw at my inside pocket, "they will hunt you down as long as you live."

He was right, and I knew it. If Naujocks told Bormann and Goebbels I escaped with the second key and a signed copy of the Swiss agreement, the *Nazis* would never let me leave Germany. Even if I slipped through, they would hunt me down to eliminate the only outside witness to the signature meeting. What the hell had the Admiral been thinking?

Fabian stood up. "I will observe the Krupp factory until dark." He extended his hand and I shook it with my left. "If you do not come...."

I watched the gaunt figure trudge down the street and realized I wasn't thinking clearly. But I knew I'd never have a dreamless night if I abandoned Anna without knowing if she was alive or beyond hope of rescue. My second regret was that some perverse sense of responsibility would not allow me to let Fabian hold on to the Admiral's bequest. I tried to convince my rattled brain that it would be just as safe with me but couldn't do that either.

Around six o'clock, when the streets became filled with homebound workers and shoppers, I began walking toward my neighborhood. That residential section of the city had been spared the heaviest bombing and most families had permitted their less fortunate relatives to move in with them. There was no petrol for cars, but the narrow street carried enough pedestrian traffic and makeshift sleds to give me anonymity. Women clutching shawls over winter coats gossiped on the stoops of semi-intact buildings before their evening meal as their children played on the dingy snow banks piled up beside the sidewalks.

Allied air-raids could come at any time and suddenly the rooftop sirens began their terrifying wail as people bolted for the shelters or the nearest basement. I was a block and a half from my building and welcomed the steady rumbling of B-26 engines merging with the sound of the sirens and agitated voices of scurrying people. Anna and I would have a better chance of getting out of the city by blending into the confusion after the raid.

I glanced up at our apartment as I ran down the street with women and old men hurrying toward the shelters, holding the hands of children, clutching food and blankets to their chests. The setting sun was behind me, reflecting off our bay window. I saw a movement behind the glare and waved at Anna above the crowd, motioning her to come downstairs and meet me on the street. The activity in the window stopped, and for a second, I thought she understood.

Suddenly, a dark object crashed through the panes of the bay window as though an explosion had been detonated in our rooms, blasting broken glass and splintered wood into the air amid the free fall of Anna's flailing arms and legs, her frail body plummeting six stories down to the icy sidewalk. Two men in black *SS* uniforms poked their heads out of the window and shouted at a man who stopped to stand beside the twisted figure at his feet then hurried off. One of the *SS* pointed in my direction, then withdrew from the window.

Poor Anna was dead or beyond my help. I turned and ran in the opposite direction against the tide of people moving toward the shelters, leaving a trail of indignant shouts as I pushed and jostled anyone in my way. I heard cars revving, shrill whistles and motorcycles kicked to life behind me over the strident sounds of babbling Germans and keening sirens that filled the air. Cutting through an alley I bumped into an old man riding a delivery tricycle with a basket between the two rear wheels and knocked him to the ground. The pain in my elbow felt like a hot knife, but the old man was dazed and slow getting up. I was halfway down the alley on his adult tricycle before he regained his feet and limped after me shouting obscenities.

The raid continued as the bombers circled for a second pass. The main streets were almost deserted as I sloshed through the wet snow on the maze of rubble-strewn footpaths between crumpled buildings that bore little resemblance to the prewar topography. Sirens continued to pierce the gathering dusk as the sounds of bombs punctuated the steady drone of aircraft overhead.

My twofold hope was that the determination of motorized *Gestapo* in pursuit would goad them into accelerating their powerful engines and spin out of control on the ice. I hoped the bikes and staff cars would have trouble following me in the rutted snow through a neighborhood with which I had become familiar.

Fabian would be waiting for me at a partially destroyed Krupp plant on the edge of an industrial area that was always the target of Allied pilots. I pedaled as fast as I could toward the remnants of an orange sunset with clouds of black smoke rising up before it, silhouettes of bombs falling from the open bays of Lancasters and Flying Fortresses lumbering stubbornly through the flack of German anti-aircraft.

Dense gray smoke and flames rose above the battered factories ahead, but I would have a better chance against the falling bombs than with the fanatical *SS* intent on capturing me. Fabian would not wait inside our partially destroyed rendezvous because I might lead the Nazis right to him. He would keep it under observation from some vantage point nearby and join me as soon as he saw I was clear.

I threw the bike behind a pile of crumbled cement walls two streets away and ran into the factory through a side entrance, its door askew on twisted hinges. The brick outer walls of the building were still standing, but half the roof was missing and the machinery on the cavernous floor was blackened by fire and covered with soot-flecked snow and debris. The damage had been inflicted by previous raids and the cleanup crews had not begun to restore it. Our fliers might not hit this broken shell again.

Bombs were exploding all over the area. The concrete floor trembled beneath my feet and flames erupted beyond the shattered windows in the near distance. The stench of cordite and burning rubber made my eye water and the air difficult to breath. The noise was so terrifying that I almost ran outside to roll the dice with the *Gestapo*. But Fabian knew the escape route, safe houses and how to avoid detection better than I did. If the building did not take a direct hit, we could wait for dark. With a little luck and Fabian's skill at evasion, we might get past the search net the *Gestapo* would throw over the area.

A massive brick forge reinforced with wide bands of metal strapping stood undamaged off to the side of the room. Its tempered steel door was ajar, revealing a dark interior. If the bombs got any closer, the inside of that furnace looked like the safest place to be. I hunkered down on a pile of damp ashes in the darkest corner of the forge, pressing my forehead into my knees, shins clutched with my trembling left arm, thighs pressed against my chest. The image of Anna crashing through that bay window into the air burned my eyelids as they squeezed tears for that frail, brave, innocent girl and toxic smoke.

The *Gestapo* had been looking for me and had taken her. When they finally extracted the all-clear music from her, they brought her back to our apartment and made her play the *Nazi* national anthem to Fabian over the gas pipe. When the *SS* saw me coming down the street, little Anna gave me the only warning she could.

I don't know how long I sat there like that, but I lifted my head when the far end of the building took a direct hit. The furnace shook violently with the shock of the blast and the chimney rained soot and ashes on me. Through the half-open door, I saw a hunched figure dash through the entrance I had come in through and crouch in the shadows. Seconds later a burst of light shone through the doorway and I could make out the angular helmets and rifles of two *SS* troopers beyond it.

Bombs were exploding all around the building. The troopers seemed undecided whether to chase their quarry or take cover until the raid was over. A brilliant flash filled the yard outside, the concussion lifting the troopers off their feet, tossing them ten meters into the building. They lay sprawled on the floor, apparently unconscious. I jumped up, waving my arms, shouting from the doorway of the forge.

"Fabian! This way. Over here!" Fabian started running toward me across the slippery floor, dodging the ruined machinery and litter. He was twenty meters away when another blinding light and compressed air slammed the heavy steel door against my shoulder, throwing me back into the furnace.

I don't know how long I was unconscious, but the fires in and outside the building. were still raging. I forced the door of the forge ajar and squeezed through the narrow opening. The remaining roof had fallen in and both walls at the front corner of the building were gone. The night was bright with flames, and the smoke made it difficult to see or breathe. I moved to the spot where I last saw Fabian and looked around for several minutes before I found him under a charred timber that was still on fire. His clothes had burned away, and his skin was charred black. Fabian's tenuous existence undermining *Nazi* gangsters was over.

Without his knowledge of the escape network, my chances of making it out of Germany were slim. As he said, they would not give up on me until I was captured or dead. I pulled the collar of my coat up and started toward the rear of the building.

The *SS* probably saw Fabian run in here and thought it was me. They might not know any different when they examined the charred body. I stopped.... then went back to the blackened corpse. If the *Gestapo* were convinced I was dead, they wouldn't try to follow me. There'd be no alert out. I might be able to make it. I knelt down and said a simple prayer for both of us. Then removed my prosthesis and the gelatinous mass that had been Fabian's left eye. I placed Pieter Kramers' glass eye in the empty socket. If they believed this, they'd assume the stolen Swiss agreement was part of the ashes, the key melted or lost.

Now we were all dead. Anna, Fabian, Kramers--and it would probably take years for the *Nazis* and Naujocks to learn the deceased one-eyed corpse was John Andeweg.

CHAPTER THIRTY
Vlissingen,
The Netherlands
April 1945

"I don't read German," Frank DePrete said. He looked naked without his blue serge FBI uniform, even though he was dressed as a deckhand from the Belgian fishing trawler that had taken him into the Dutch port with apparent engine trouble.

"I told you what it says." We were dangling hand lines off a stone quay in the harbor on the *Westerschelde* River which opened into the North Sea.

I'd traveled west from Berlin across snow-clogged northern Germany, seven-hundred kilometers, mostly on foot, through knee-high drifts on farmlands and forests, avoiding cities and battlefields, hitching rides on horse drawn-carts and rattletrap trucks when I could. The few details of Fabian's escape route I could remember took me around Magdeburg where I bought an eye patch and change of clothes, *Gutersloh*, *Wesel*, across the Rhine and into occupied Holland. I had avoided the main highways during the day, then burrowed down to bare ground to sleep in sodden blankets in the woods or snuck into the barns of certain farmers who brought me home-made sausage and bread at night.

Frank DePrete was the last person I expected to meet me. But the agreement I had hinted at in Fabian's last transmission probably sounded too sensitive to entrust to someone outside our closely guarded *Spionage* unit. DePrete spoke fluent French and knew me on sight, even with a month's growth of beard. The red-haired agent thumbed through the document as I dangled my line, listening to the noise of commerce mingled with the raised voices of boat crews and merchants hawking their meager stock from open carts along the retaining wall. DePrete tied the piece of twine holding the key to the safe deposit box around the folded agreement, stuffed them both back in my oilskin packet and set it down on the quay between us.

"I need to take this back for verification," he said.

"I'm the verification, Frank. I heard them signing it. It's the real McCoy."

"I'm sure it is." He was wearing a navy beret and an old wool sea coat, the collar pulled up around his ears against the chill wind. His baggy twill trousers were stuffed into heavy knit stockings and rubber boots swinging back and forth over the edge of the retaining wall in the northern sunlight.

"We have to check it. You could have been set up."

"By who?"

"Canaris.

"Who's been plotting against Hitler since 1935?"

DePrete made a plosive sound with his lips.

"You think he launched a monumental fabrication--complete with hot and cold running Swiss bankers--days after he was fired from the *Abwehr*? The same guy they arrested for trying to assassinate Hitler concocted this," I slapped the packet between us, "for you, me and posterity?"

I jiggled my line in the cold water and watched the movement disturb the reflections on the rippling surface. Another reason DePrete had come to identify me in person was that they had heard I was dead. When they received my last message through the Dutch underground, they wanted to be sure.

The *OSS* had also learned the details of Hitler's swift retribution on members of the *Schwarze Kapelle*: immediately after their conviction for high treason in a summary court martial, *Oberst* Klaus Count von Stauffenberg and the men directly involved in attempting to assassinate Hitler on 20 July were taken from the dock to a courtyard below and shot by the *Schutzstaffeln*. Hitler had been so incensed at Stauffenberg that he ordered his body exhumed so he could personally verify his death.

Some of the Black Choir committed suicide before they could be apprehended. Among them were General Henning von Tresckow, the perpetrator of a failed attempt on Hitler's life in 1943, and *Feldmarshall* Erwin Rommel. Others were executed during that autumn and winter, right through the spring of 1945 and the end of the war: General Karl Heinrich Stuelpnagle, one of Canaris' closest friends, *Doktor* Hans von Dohnanyi, a brilliant young attorney with the Ministry of Justice, and General Hans Oster, the same day as his mentor. It wasn't until the British debriefed me that summer that I learned Admiral Canaris had been given a cursory trial on

April 9, exactly one month before the Germans surrendered. Later that same day he was dragged naked from his underground jail cell in *Flossenburg* Concentration Camp and hanged by the neck from an iron collar at the end of a chain.

"The Admiral did not set me up," I said.

"Then what's your problem?"

'Do not give this up easily,' Canaris had warned me.

"I'm going to deliver the agreement and the key to Barnum myself," I said.

Months after the surgery, I discovered my peripheral vision had improved and I could watch people without turning my head much if I kept them on my right. DePrete seemed mesmerized by the cork bobbing on his line on the glistening water.

"You're still in the Navy, Andeweg. Under wartime orders."

"Not from the FBI."

"I represent James Barnum. He reports to Colonel Donovan who takes his orders directly from FDR." DePrete turned to look at me. "So, you might say your orders come right from the President."

"Who wants me to hand the agreement over to you and stay in place with a blown cover."

"Your cover's not blown, John! It's perfect. Everyone but Barnum and I are convinced you're dead."

"I just go back into Germany, sneak around behind enemy

lines with this new Dutch identity and keep you posted?"

"Something big's coming. The war will be over in less than a year. Months.... Eisenhower wants daily reports on *Nazi* troops in northern Europe."

"He can put anyone in to do that."

"Not with the knowledge you gained in the *Abwehr.*"

I lowered my hand to the packet between us. "No one else can validate this."

"It's probably bullshit anyway."

"Fuck you, Frank."

A cold wind cut through the sweater under my ragged tweed jacket carrying the pungent odor of fish and brackish water across the harbor. The Germans had transferred most of their occupation troops to the front, but *Wehrmacht* soldiers still scrutinized the fishing craft coming and going from the tiny port, ignoring the men and boys mending nets on the quay, smiling at the blond women in home-sewn coats and knee stockings terminating in wooden shoes who haggled with fishmongers at their quay-side stalls.

The maroon sails of a *Botter* luffed in the breeze as she tacked between the stone jetties into the river. She was one of those traditional Dutch boats with a rounded canoe hull and lee-boards that Mr. Van Oudgaarden used to reminisce about when we sailed on Narragansett Bay.

DePrete wound his fishing line around its piece of wood and tucked the hook into the spool. "You win." He sighed as he stood up and slipped into a pair of knit mittens. "Eisenhower needs the information you can provide from behind their lines more than we need those bogus papers."

J. Edgar would not have been proud of one of his agents caving in like that.

"Great," I said. "You have my new ID?"

DePrete spread his hands, palms up. "Come on, John. You know I can't carry two IDs."

"How do I get it?"

"Tonight," he said. "The Krauts cleared my trawler to leave at 0200 for Ostend. Meet me at the end of the quay a couple of minutes before that." He started to walk away, then came back and pointed at the packet with the toe of his boot. "Oh, bring that, will you? Might as well photograph a couple of pages for Barnum."

* * * * * *

Maybe it's the way their tiny country is practically squeezed off the top of Europe into the North Sea and the constant battle they wage to keep it out with dikes and latticed windmills that struggle to drain the lowlands. Maybe the ambivalent pride and isolation they feel at the difficulty of their language contributes to it.

Wencky told me about a resistance cell that validated spies and questionable strangers in an unusual manner. The man was made to pronounce the name of a Dutch town impossible for non-Dutch people to pronounce correctly. Those who failed the test were shot summarily.

The Netherlands is little club that will risk anything to help one of their own against external forces. I had established contact with Bono Wenckebach of the Dutch underground when I arrived. After I explained my predicament, it didn't take much to enlist his services. His first concern was my elbow, which had to be re-broken and set properly in a neighbor's basement by a doctor on a legitimate maternity call. He apologized profusely for having no anesthesia, but he was quick, and a half bottle of *Geneva Junge* took the edge off his ministrations.

An hour before meeting DePrete, we stitched my copy of the Swiss agreement and the key into a rubber inner tube from an old tractor tire. We sealed it from the elements by immersing it in a hot pan of wax. After midnight, we buried the packet a meter down in a fresh grave in the town cemetery.

The *Nazis* had imposed a curfew throughout Holland, but at that stage of the war they didn't have enough troops to enforce it. Wencky and I slipped through alleys and backyards in the freezing night air until we reached the harbor. The moon gave a murky luster to a thin mist rolling in from the sea, creating imagined movement in the deepest corners of the blacked-out town. Two armed men emerged from the shadows. Wencky conferred with them briefly, and all three figures disappeared into the darkness. I tucked my oilskin packet into my coat and moved down the slippery cobbled path above the quay.

Standing beneath the eaves of a stone warehouse, I listened to the tide lapping against the seawall and wondered if I had spent too much time under the influence of Germany's master spy. There I was questioning the wisdom and explicit orders of my government on the advice of a high-ranking enemy officer. An unfathomable personality obscured in life by layers of intrigue and duplicity and would remain so in death by contradiction and innuendo. Was I on the verge of becoming a traitor to my country as he was to his? Or was he really a patriot, governed by moral judgment and integrity?

The diesel engine of a trawler thrummed to life at quayside one hundred meters away as the outlines of two German soldiers appeared in silhouette before the yellow glow of a lantern amidships. A woman's laughter mingled with deeper male voices and someone extinguished the oil lamp. The short scruffy figure of Frank DePrete materialized at my elbow.

"Our cook," he said. "Her boyfriends came down to see her off."

"You think of everything, Frank."

"Did you bring the agreement?"

I patted the bulge under my jacket. "Where's my ID?"

DePrete led me around the corner of the building and shone a pencil flashlight on the dog-eared identity papers of a Dutch magazine correspondent that carried signature authorization of a German army commander.

"Anything I should know about these?" I asked.

"The man was killed in a car accident while home on leave. The units he was attached to are stamped inside. Don't go near them."

I put the ID in my pocket and could hear the grin in DePrete's voice.

"Now show me yours."

"Maybe you should take them back after all," I said, reaching into my coat. I withdrew the packet and handed it to him. "See you stateside, Frank."

"Hold up a minute." DePrete opened the oilskin and snapped on his flashlight. I sensed the presence of someone behind me and turned my head to see two crewmen from the trawler blocking my retreat.

"You bastard! DePrete whispered, pawing through the bundle of newspapers I had put in the packet. "Where are they?"

"I'll bring them with me when I come out."

"What if you don't make it?"

"Somehow, I think I'm more likely to come out with them, than if I give them to you."

"That's ridiculous." He didn't sound convincing. "Suppose something happens?"

"I've made arrangements to get it to Barnum."

DePrete spoke French to the men behind me and one strong arm snaked around my neck as another pressed a sharp blade against my throat.

"Where is it?" DePrete hissed.

A low voice gave a harsh command in Dutch from the darkness.

The arm released me and the knife dropped away as DePrete swore in English. Wencky held a Pistol under DePrete's chin and his two compatriots jabbed the muzzles of their rifles into the ribs of the crewmen.

I said, "Compromise, Frank. I'll stay behind the lines and bring the key and agreement out when I come."

I could hear the threat in DePrete's voice. "You're making a big mistake, John."

"I don't think so." Someone in our government had decided that the *Nazi/Swiss* Banker's agreement should be suppressed. Maybe me along with it.

"How can we reach you?" DePrete asked.

"I'll be in touch."

* * * * * *

Nine months earlier, on the 6th of June 1944, the largest invasion force in the history of warfare had been launched by Allied forces on the beaches of Normandy. For the first time since it began, the end of the war seemed near.

In August, General Charles De Gaulle marched into Paris leading a tumultuous parade of French tanks to the exultant strains of the *Marseillaise* and hundreds of waving tricolor flags in the hands of damp-eyed citizens lining the streets.

In October, General Omar Bradley burst through the heavily defended Siegfried line and the Allies took Aachen, their first plot of German soil. General George Patton's tank division rolled into the Saar Basin, Germany's critical mining and factory region.

Bottled up with a handful of American paratroopers in Bastogne during the Battle of the Bulge, Brigadier General Anthony McAuliffe issued his one-word reply to the surrender demands of five *Nazi* divisions: "Nuts!"

In the Pacific, General Douglas MacArthur waded ashore on Leyte Island to fulfill his 1941 promise that, "I will return," to the Philippines. And B-29 Super-fortresses dropped tons of bombs on Tokyo.

During the spring and summer of 1945, I operated behind enemy lines in northern Europe, feeding German troop strength and movement through Wencky to the Allied commanders in London. From the Ardennes, I was able to warn them of booby traps left behind by the Germans under the bridge at *Remagen*, and American soldiers crossed the Rhine for the first time.

During that month of April 1945, President Roosevelt died of a cerebral hemorrhage; Benito Mussolini was tried, executed and hung on display by the heels in Milan with his mistress Clara Petacci; and Adolph Hitler committed suicide with his mistress Eva Braun in his command bunker under the Chancellery in Berlin--their bodies soaked with petrol by *Arztin* Josef Goebbels and Martin Bormann, then set on fire in the courtyard.

* * * * * *

That spring, the civilized world was sickened by the horrors of *Nazi* concentration camps liberated by the Allies: medical experiments conducted at *Auschwitz*, crematoria in *Dachau*, gas chambers at *Treblinka*, naked corpses stacked ten meters high like broken tree limbs in *Buchenwald*, lamp shades made from human skin at *Mauthausen*, hollow-eyed survivors emaciated by starvation at *Flossenburg, Belzec, Chelmno*--a network of over nine hundred satellite camps connected to fifteen large extermination and holding centers throughout Germany and occupied Europe.

Photographs in *Life Magazine* showed battle-hardened GIs weeping at their discovery of these atrocities as they liberated the sick and dying inhabitants of those earthly hells. Not war by any past or present definition, but an inconceivable genocide orchestrated by a madman, executed by sociopathic troglodytes with the silent complicity of almost an entire nation. War correspondents did not report the rumors of angry retribution, however, such as the platoon of American soldiers who machine-gunned 360 *SS* camp guards without trial or remorse.

Bergen-Belsen was liberated on 15 April 1945 by the British 8th Corps that found rampant typhus, starvation and evidence of mass executions right up to the previous day. The English officer in charge reported that if they had arrived a fortnight later, none of the prisoners would have been alive.

When I learned the magnitude of these repulsive crimes against humanity that were documented at the close of the war, I could understand why men like Canaris, Oster, and von-Stauffenberg became 'traitors' to their country. This Holocaust, I was certain, would be the daily topic of newspapers, magazines, radio, universities, synagogues, churches, public discussion and government forums throughout the world for centuries.

On May 8th, *Feldmarshall* Wilhelm Keitel, *General* Hans-Jurgen Stumpff, and *Gross Admiral* Hans Georg von Friedeburg surrendered unconditionally to the Allied commanders in Berlin.

The war in Europe had been won.

* * * * * *

As far as the outside world was concerned, John Andeweg had been dead for six months. If I walked up to a U.S. Army Colonel and told my story, I'd be detained pending verification by James Barnum. I remained in Paris through the end of June, sleeping, drinking more wine than I should have, trying to purge the foul depression I felt from Anna's death and the millions of innocent people-turned-numbers I had not known. Barnum's sudden mistrust didn't help.

I could not expel the vision of Anna kneeling among that travesty of gassed corpses, which became bound in my mind to the last words of Kurtz in Conrad's *Heart of Darkness*, when "*He spoke in a whisper at some image, some vision--he cried out twice, a cry that was no more than a breath--'The horror! The horror!'*"

Finally, I made my way north, waiting in Holland while Wencky arranged to get me to London. By mid-July I was anxious to go home regardless of what awaited me. But Colonel Dick White, Chief of British Intelligence was determined to debrief me regarding the data I'd provided the Allies during my years at the *Abwehr* and the last several months; then took his time doing it.

After they had extracted all the information they needed, the two MI6 operatives who would drive me to the airport turned their Austin sedan southeast into Kent County, the opposite direction from Heathrow. No amount of questioning could prompt them to divulge our destination and the only reassurance I received was that the BOC flight on which I held a reservation would not depart without me.

We traveled through bombed-out London suburbs under an overcast sky and persistent drizzle, along broken country roads, between broad meadows spotted with decimated clusters of sheep and cattle, farmland pocked with bomb craters, three-wall barns, farm houses and unkempt estates with shuttered manors. The German army had not invaded England, but Hitler had brought a devastating war here, killing almost one-half million citizens of the Commonwealth, including over 60,000 civilians. Waging their six-year conflict with the Axis powers across the globe, and the resultant destruction of property at home and abroad had sapped one-fourth of their national wealth and virtually bankrupt this once-great empire.

The rain stopped, the sky brightened, and we left the worst of the ruin behind us, inhaling the damp earth-smell of country air through lowered windows as though we had encountered proof of the promise of peace. Soon after we passed through the little town of Westerham, we turned off the water-filled potholes of the macadam highway onto a gravel road that led through a copse of trees to a wide roundabout in front of a sprawling brick home with the words, "Chartwell Manor" chiseled in a stone plaque beside the huge double oak doors.

"What's this?" I asked the agents.

The man in the left-hand passenger seat turned and grinned at me. "Command p'formance, y'might say. Don't spoil it f'y'self makin' us tell ya. G'won git in 'ere."

Their expressions were vacant as they assured me that I was expected and remained in the car. A uniformed Bobby sans helmet opened the door, checked the Voorhees passport stamped by MI6, and handed me off to a male functionary in a double-breasted suit who led me down a broad hallway to the rear of the house, through a pair of French doors onto a large patio with a flooring of pink flagstones.

A heavyset man with sloping shoulders under a wide-brimmed hat sat with his back to us, gazing at an expanse of gray lake set in the midst of acres of unmowed grass, brush and distant trees, daubing at a canvas perched on the wooden easel before him.

"Excuse me sir," the secretary said. "Mr. Carl Voorhees is here for his appointment."

The man made a stroke on his painting, wiped the brush on a cloth and set them down on a low table beside him. He placed his cigar in a pewter ashtray and used a silver-handled ebony cane to help himself to his feet.

Winston Churchill looked up over his round tortoiseshell

reading glasses as he turned and faced me, nodding to the secretary, who left the patio, closing the doors behind him.

The genius statesman who had led his island-based commonwealth through her "finest hours" had been turned out of office less than two months after the war's end by a weary British electorate. The brilliant crisis rhetoric seemed to have abandoned the equally exhausted seventy-year-old politician who failed to judge their mood and had no peacetime message.

Standing before me, the real man resembled a caricature of the photographs and political cartoons that had appeared daily in newspapers and magazines throughout the world: the round bulldog face, balding head, piercing eyes, short, stooped stature. He wore a white shirt with bow tie, dark linen jacket with paint stains over protruding vest, a gold watch chain hanging from a lapel buttonhole terminating in his breast pocket.

He came to where I stood in the center of the brick-walled patio covered with dark green leaves of ivy and floor to ceiling windows.

"I won't address you by name or ask you to sit," he said, extending his hand for me to shake. "But I did want to proffer my gratitude--and that of Great Britain, for all you have done."

I was only twenty-five years old and almost as nervous as the day I was marched into that first meeting with the Admiral at the *Abwehr*. "No more than a lot of others, sir."

"True, true," he said, appraising me for several moments. Then he picked up a black velvet box from the table. "By the power invested in me by His Royal Majesty George the Sixth, King of England," he said, lifting from the box a gold medallion embossed with the seal of Great Britain, "for personal service to The Commonwealth in her time of need, I hereby confer upon you the Royal Order of Knights Victoria Cross."

He reached up and I lowered my head, so he could place the wide red ribbon around my neck.

"You'll not be able to wear that again, I suspect." Mr.

Churchill handed a leather folder to me. It was the official documentation of the awarded medal, signed by the King, witnessed by Churchill, Prime Minister Clement Attlee and dated. Only the name of the recipient was blank.

"When your new identity is established, a competent calligrapher can fill in the appropriate name."

Maybe I was in line for some kind of recognition from my own government, but not England's highest honor. "Mr. Prime Minister, I don't deserve...."

"The least we could do," he placed his hand on my arm and walked me to the French doors. "Call it our heartfelt appreciation for retaining your sanity under what must have been considerable stress--the sacrificial eye and broken elbow."

Before I figured out what had happened, I was back in the Austin, the boxed medal and leather encased parchment on my lap driving west to the airport with the two MI6 agents. Churchill couldn't have known all the details, but he must have learned about my run-in with DePrete and was telling me it was serious. He had also given me a blank birth certificate. I could have John Andeweg inscribed on it or any identity I chose. Then my existence after the war would be verified by the political powers of Great Britain and the King of England.

If anyone wanted me dead they'd have a lot of explaining to do.

CHAPTER THIRTY-ONE
Washington, DC
August 1945

My British Overseas Airways plane landed at LaGuardia at seven in the morning and I was checked through customs on Carl Voorhees' Dutch passport. It was August 17th, 1945, forty-eight hours after V-J Day--the first time I had set foot on American soil in three years. My eye got sort of blurry on the bus ride into Manhattan, and when we arrived in the city people were still celebrating the surrender of Japan.

Confetti and strips of newspaper littered the main thoroughfares. Soldiers, sailors, marines and airmen sauntered along the sidewalks in the morning sunshine, arms linked together or around the waists of laughing girls. I stood on the corner of 56th and Park on my way to Penn Station watching mounted police shepherd a parade of Veterans of Foreign Wars followed by a half-dozen high school bands marching up the Avenue. The music of John Phillip Sousa rose above the good-natured blare of automobile horns as men in uniform stepped into the wide urban road to join the parade. People leaned out the open windows of skyscrapers waving and shouting, filling the air with colored balloons, streamers and scraps of paper.

The full impact of victory suddenly dawned on me. A tiny old woman in a black dress and veiled hat stood beside me waving a little blue flag with the Gold Star attached to a wooden stick, tears of pride and anguish streaming down her face. She looked from the canvas bag in my hand, the European clothes, to the black patch over my left eye.

"You were in it then," she said.

"Yes."

"The Germans killed my Paulie. In Africa."

It occurred to me that this was the first American casualty

of the war whose name I knew. "I'm very sorry."

"Where did they take your eye?" she asked.

"Germany."

The woman reached out and put her arms around my waist, sobbing into my chest. When she released me, she pulled a handkerchief out of the sleeve of her cardigan sweater and wiped her eyes. I rubbed my fist across my cheek and smiled at her. It was probably the only homecoming I was likely to get.

"I pray to God it was worth it," she said.

"Yes." I touched her arm and started walking in the direction of Penn Station. "So do I."

* * * * * *

The Office of Strategic Services was housed in a square ten-story building of gray sandstone on Louisiana Avenue in downtown Washington. I told the uniformed guard I was there to see James Barnum and presented the same passport Frank DePrete had given me in Holland in April.

The guard picked up the phone and announced me, then instructed me to go to an address in Alexandria where Mr. Barnum would meet me that afternoon. I asked the guard to tell Barnum that I wanted to see him immediately or I was going to visit a classmate who worked at the *Washington Post.*

Ten minutes later I was sitting in a windowless room with bare walls. After a strained greeting from Mr. Barnum, a nod from DePrete and an introduction to a man named Allan Dulles, I faced the three men across a narrow table.

"You may understand a certain degree of ambivalence we have toward you, John," Barnum said through a forced smile.

I smiled back. "And I toward you."

"The nation is deeply in your debt for your sacrifice and invaluable work." James Barnum had not aged a week in the past three years. The same haughty carriage, tailored suit and placid expression on his craggy features. "On the other hand," he turned his palms up on the surface before him, "your refusal to cooperate on the so-called Swiss agreement is rather disconcerting."

329

"Disobedience of a direct order during engagement with the enemy while serving in the United States Navy," DePrete said, "withholding intelligence data, impeding the war effort." He was still angry about our confrontation on the quay in Vlissingen. "Court martial offenses," he added, "maybe treason. You could be shot."

Mr. Barnum continued staring at me and said, "Be quiet, Frank."

"Where is the document and key?" Dulles asked. He looked like an academic with his steel-rimmed glasses, tweed suit and brush mustache.

"It's safe."

"Why won't you hand it over," Mr. Barnum wanted to know, "as you did with all the other intelligence information?"

"That was raw data. I was just a conduit."

"And the key to this purported multi-billion-dollar conspiracy?" Dulles asked.

"The key was entrusted to me," I said. "Before I give it to anyone, I want to know what's going to happen to the money."

Dulles frowned. "Entrusted by whom?"

"Admiral Canaris."

DePrete made a derisive noise in his throat but didn't speak. "Alfred Naujocks claims you had a suspicious relationship with Canaris," Dulles said. "He claims you were doubled."

"Naujocks!"

"He deserted last fall," Mr. Barnum said, "and gave us some interesting testimony."

I couldn't help laughing. "If you gentlemen believe a man like that, I'll tell you about the Easter Bunny."

"He was there," DePrete said.

"Where the hell do you think I was, Antarctica?"

Mr. Barnum's voice adopted a conciliatory tone. "We don't doubt your loyalty, John, but you are behaving strangely on this."

"I'll set you straight on Naujocks in five minutes. Where is that little bastard?"

Dulles shifted in his seat. "He escaped from Nuremberg Prison."

I tossed my head back and laughed again.

"If you're so positive this conspiracy constitutes a serious threat to the country," Dulles argued, "why are you reluctant to allow the government to handle It?"

"Because I don't think you will."

Barnum and Dulles exchanged looks.

"And you wish to deliver a message to the American people from the deceased head of German military intelligence," Barnum said, "that the worst elements of a country we just defeated has the financial means to terrorize the civilized world."

"The Swiss bankers and terms of this... arrangement are spelled out in that document with the numbers of the secret accounts?" Dulles asked.

"Not the account numbers. That's what the two keys are for. The numbers are in a safe deposit-box named in the agreement. I have one key, the last I knew Naujocks had the other. Unless Goebbles or Bormann took it."

"Goebbles is dead," Dulles said. "A confirmed suicide."

"How about Bormann?"

"Killed when a tank blew up during his escape as an enlisted *Wehrmacht* soldier," Barnum answered.

Dulles frowned. "We think."

"Oh, great! Now we have two vicious *Nazis* sworn to terrorize the west running around loose with the potential of billions of dollars at their disposal to do so."

"John," Barnum said, "don't you think they'll just steal it and burrow down for a life of luxury in some remote country?"

"Not without my key, I don't."

Dulles removed his glasses and wiped them with his handkerchief. "But we cannot act without it, either."

"What action would you take?"

"With the agreement and key in hand we could address the matter with the Swiss. The money is obviously stolen, the booty of war."

"Neutrals caught dead to rights in the world press," Dulles added, "would place tremendous pressure on them to relinquish those deposits."

"Neutrals! The damned Swiss did more to support Germany and prolong the war than any other country on the planet."

"We have to move on, John," Barnum said. "We have enough on our plate with Nuremberg, the occupation, making sure the civilian populations of our defeated enemies do not starve to death next winter or fester for another twenty-years until the next Hitler decides to start world war three."

"Not to mention the Russians," Dulles said.

"How about the two or three million people the *Nazis* executed?" I asked. "Isn't that the latest count?"

"Jews," Barnum said. "Six million, by the way."

"People! Human beings! Most of those Swiss deposits were pried out of their corpses or confiscated from abandoned accounts."

The two senior men exchanged looks again, as though they had anticipated my sentiments. "They're dead, John."

"Some of their children aren't, their relatives."

"Are you proposing that we try to identify the heirs to those billions, then disburse them to hundreds of thousands of Jews scattered all over the world now?"

I sat there and looked at them. I had expected reluctance, but not this. Will every man cross the line when the stakes are high enough?

"Men like us are the government."

"You're going to steal the money yourselves."

Dulles stiffened in his straight-backed chair. "It would be virtually impossible to apportion it to the legitimate descendants of the deceased Jews," Barnum contended, "and take decades to do it. The bulk of the money was probably deposited legitimately by *Nazis* after they. . . appropriated it. What can be done about that?"

"Split it up among the descendants and people who

escaped the death camps. God knows they suffered enough while you and the rest of the world stood around with your thumbs up where the sun don't shine."

"I resent that," Dulles said.

"Resent all you want, mister. You can't roust millions of people out of their homes, take their businesses, transport them through cities and towns in broad daylight, employ hundreds of civilian train crews, thousands of *SS* guards, tmurder Jews in several hundred locations--some on the outskirts of major cities, the smoke and stench of burning flesh carried on the wind--and hope to keep it a secret!"

I was out of control and I knew it. I did not see James Barnum, Allan Dulles and Frank DePrete before me in that sterile room. I was back in *Bergen-Belsen* standing naked with a thousand condemned souls in the freezing snow watching that *SS-Hauptsturmfuhrer* smash an old man's cock with a swagger stick.

"Rumors, they claim! Practically every single adult in Germany knew. *Knew!* In Poland and other occupied countries where they had concentration camps. Churchill denounced a million camp murders in a 1941 speech on the BBC. The White House knew. Didn't Roosevelt freeze Swiss bank accounts here in 1941?"

"We were fighting as hard as we could to get in there as it was," Mr. Barnum reminded me. "How could we stop it?"

I shook my head, trying to push those horrible images out of my mind. "By parachuting Airborne and Marine battalions into every godamned slaughter house in Europe, for one."

"How would you like to work for me?" Dulles offered.

"I don't even know who you are."

Mr. Barnum was getting impatient. "Mr. Dulles is *OSS* Chief of Station in Berlin, responsible for gathering information to be used at the Nuremberg Trials." Flown back home to take control of the Swiss deposits.

"What kind of work would I do?"

"Head up the group that will ascertain how to access this money and what to do with it."

"I know what to do with it."

"That issue is moot," Barnum said, "until we can circumvent the Swiss banking laws or acquire the *Nazi* key."

I had heard British MI6 agents speculate the *OSS* was doomed under President Truman, so there didn't seem to be much future in that job offer even if I had been naive enough to take it.

"Work for the government," I said, "under some sworn secrets act."

Dulles was getting annoyed. "Of course."

"What if I promoted a disbursement plan you didn't agree with?"

Mr. Barnum spoke up and his exasperation was clear. "Look here, John, Frank is right. You are in the military and subject to orders. Produce the key and agreement or face the consequences."

"You'd let all this come out in a court martial?"

DePrete couldn't help himself. "Maybe it wouldn't get that far. Everybody thinks you're already dead."

I pulled the velvet box out of my pocket and slid it across the table. "Not everyone."

Barnum opened the lid and frowned at the gold medal, then handed it to Dulles who stared at it for several moments before asking me, "And the certificate of award?"

I smiled at him. "Safe."

"Check," Barnum said, reminding me of the endless games of chess we had played aboard *Dutch Master*. Then the two spies resorted to their last line of defense--the truth.

When they had learned of the *Nazi/Swiss* agreement that would fund a plan to terrorize civilians during the last half of the twenty-first century, Colonel Donovan and his top *OSS* advisers had decided to suppress it: some of them didn't believe it; others didn't think it could be carried off; allied administrators hired Nazis to critical posts to ensure a continuum of running the defeated country; and the rest simply did not want to deal with it. Regardless of their rationale, the spies were unanimous--the American people should not have their hard-won victory undermined by this ephemeral financial specter of the future.

The war was over. They wanted peace. The Allies had agreed not to make the same mistake following this world war that they had after the first one. The victors were determined to help the vanquished rebuild their countries, not allow them to founder waiting for another Adolph Hitler or sneak attack on Pearl Harbor. The United States was the strongest military power on Earth: we had the atom bomb and the greatest industrial capacity the world had ever known. Whatever the *Nazis* had planned, the powers that be had determined that America would prevail.

"You will not bring this to public attention," I said.

"Never," Dulles answered, getting to his feet. "It would do irreparable damage to the morale and purpose of the nation."

Mr. Barnum summed up the prevailing consensus. "It would make them question what all their sons and husbands had died for."

"I do not want the American people...." Dulles began, until I interrupted him.

"Isn't this something for President Truman to decide?"

"The world is changing." His answer sounded like he was quoting some position paper he'd prepared for a congressional committee. "Compartmentalization of responsibilities, the constancy of certain agencies compared to the short tenure and often shortsightedness of transient elected officials. Knee-jerk political reaction vis-à-vis the appreciation of longer range subtleties within the international intelligence community...."

I couldn't believe what I was hearing. "But a decision like this has to come from the people American voters have elected—-the President, Senators, Representatives, right?"

Dulles reminded Barnum: "No paper on this, right?"

"Mr. Hoover will keep a file," DePrete said.

Mr. Barnum chuckled. "Might as well be on the moon."

Dulles left the room and closed the door before Mr. Barnum answered my question. "The need to know goes up as well as down, John."

"Geezes!"

"We're doing what we think best for the country."

My old navigator and chess opponent stared me down for a few seconds. I wasn't sure, but a look of chagrin may have crossed his face as he lowered his eyes to the file folder he had placed on the table before him but never opened. They were probably good men, decent husbands, fathers and neighbors, just as patriotic as the German bureaucrats who believed they were serving their fatherland by improvising on government policies which they often interpreted to their own advantage or agenda. It dawned on me that that devoted concept of loyalty was one of the subtle implements Hitler used to get ordinary Germans to execute his insane strategies: by using everyman's inherent thirst for unchecked power to accomplish his personal goals as he saw them, justified by his selective rationale.

But that was no excuse. Barnum and Dulles had not heard the *Nazis* tell the Swiss bankers how they planned to use the money to inflict terror on our civilian population.

"So where's the key?" DePrete asked again.

"Where it's going to stay," I answered,

Mr. Barnum's expression registered disapproval. "That is unwise, John."

"As long as I remain healthy, it stays where it is," I assured them. "If I don't, the agreement goes to the press and the Brits will make things pretty embarrassing for you. They think they owe me."

"Mate," Mr. Barnum acknowledged. Your game has improved immeasurably, John."

"I had good teachers."

"What do you require?" he asked.

"A new identity. After interrogating Admiral Canaris, the *Nazis* must know that Pieter Kramers, alias John Andeweg was in the next room and has the second key and a copy of the document spelling out their agreement. Naujocks does, anyway. But they think I'm dead."

Barnum nodded. "If they realized you were alive...."

"It's in your best interest to see they don't." Mr. Barnum chuckled, shaking his head. "You have mastered the craft, my worthy young adversary."

Then he turned to DePrete. "It appears that you have a new assignment, Frank."

DePrete had slumped in his chair with a sullen expression. "I wish you'd get somebody else."

"The best way to keep a secret," Barnum said, "is to limit access to it. No one outside this room must know his new identity."

DePrete's response was dispirited. "Sounds like my career advancement just stopped dead."

"He is in your charge, Frank." Mr. Barnum inclined his head at me. "Your fortunes will rise and fall with this man."

I said, "The new ID should take me from birth to today and account for my whereabouts during the past three years."

James Barnum was not pleased. "You seem to have us at a disadvantage--temporarily."

"Not so, James. It will be permanent," I assured them, "not temporary at all."

Mr. Barnum seemed anxious to end the meeting and turned to DePrete. "Fortunately, we did anticipate this. What is his name, Frank?"

The FBI agent sat up straight in his chair and withdrew an envelope from his inside coat pocket. He extracted several sheets of paper and smoothed them out on the table in front of him.

"This is a pretty good fit. Same age, general appearance, no close relatives, just like our friend here. Came from Lusten, a little town in northern Minnesota, killed in action on Okinawa a month ago."

"You can drill him on all that later," Barnum said. "What is his name, Frank?"

"Robinson," DePrete answered. "Charles Norris Robinson."

1976

CHAPTER THIRTY-TWO
Vineyard Sound, MA
August 1976

Senator Robinson finished speaking as night dissolved into a leaden day. A light breeze picked up out of the southwest, moving the ghostly mist across the heaving ocean, creating a false impression of visibility.

Jared placed the Uzi on the cockpit seat and checked the chart. He hauled sheets to point the bow of the cutter toward Tarpaulin Cove on the west coast of Naushon, leaned out over the leeward combing to check the trim of the jib then stood facing Robinson

"How can you prove all that?"

"Talk to Frank DePrete," Senator Robinson answered.

"Hah!"

The Senator pushed the left sleeve of his jacket up on his forearm to reveal the tattoo of an American eagle that almost obliterated the hairless patch of yellowish skin. "If you put that under a microscope or some sort of Infrared scanner, you might make out the numbers."

Stephanie removed the blanket she had thrown over her shoulders to ward off the chill of the damp sea air. "That must have been horrible."

The Senator stared into the fog with a look of anguish. "Not just six million Jews, which was bad enough; eight, twelve million people all told--gypsies, homosexuals, mentally ill, recalcitrant functionaries, anti-Nazis, resistance fighters, prisoners of war—all murdered by one deranged man. Compared to 20 million combatants killed in action." Robinson shook his head in profound lamentation. "My God, my God."

They were silent for several moments until Stephanie addressed Jared. "Maybe you owe Senator Robinson an

339

apology."

"He couldn't have known," the Senator said.

"Where's the key now?" Jared asked. "And the document?"

Senator Robinson smiled. "In the safe-deposit box of a bank in this country. I retrieved them from Holland years ago."

"Will you show them to me?"

Robinson hesitated. "I suppose I could do that."

"How did the Germans know you had it?"

"When I announced for the presidency and came under the international spotlight, Naujocks, Bormann or some other old *Nazi* intent on funding *Baader-Meinhof* must have recognized me or conducted a background check that indicated I was the spy, Kramers who they believed had been killed in the war."

"They must have strong connections in their government and ours," Stephanie said, "to sneak three terrorists into their embassy."

The Senator shook his head in disagreement. "Powerful old *Nazis* blackmailing present day politicians with Brown Shirt pasts? The Federal Republic of Germany wouldn't touch this. It's an East German group working with old guard *Nazis,* both scheming to stay alive."

"Then why didn't you expose them?" Jared asked. "Let the *Bundespolizei* handle it back there."

"Even after I realized what was happening, I couldn't divulge the conspiracy before the election--the ensuing controversy could put this country through a political hurricane. If it was leaked before the truth came out It could make adversaries of two friendly nations and exacerbate our problems with Russia."

"Not to mention," Jared injected, "that your false identity would scuttle your candidacy."

"Jared!" Stephanie admonished.

"That's true," the Senator admitted. "But if I get elected, I can reveal the agreement with impunity, then take executive action to pressure the Swiss into disbursing the funds to living Holocaust victims and descendants of the deceased."

"Nothing has been done so far?" Stephanie asked.

"Sure, it has," Robinson answered. "But the world's ignorance of that travesty is part of the problem I can fix—as president."

"How?"

"Acknowledge and support individuals like Elie Wiesel and Sam Klaus, several other people and organizations such as the 'American Joint Distribution Committee' and 'World Jewish Congress,' who have been stonewalled by the Swiss bankers for thirty years. They've probably stolen some of the money already."

"They'll try to kill you again."

"The president of the United States?" Senator Robinson asked. "They must realize that if the American people become fully cognizant of the secret or stolen billions, we would hunt down those old *Nazis*, the remnants of *Baader-Meinhof*, and any other terrorist groups they support and scoop them out of their hideaways like the vermin they are. Then bring the Swiss bankers before the World Court and launch a financial assault that will drive them back to the Dark Ages."

Jared was still preoccupied with the events of the previous months. "When I caught on to the Germans and kept digging into your phony past, they tried to prevent me from learning your real identity and stumbling onto the document that would lead me to the Swiss accounts."

"It didn't help matters," Stephanie added, "when Jared talked to my mother and Edmund Gilmore."

Senator Robinson shook his head. "When they tried to kill you in the Florida Keys, I thought it would be safer to put Jared on permanent assignment to my protective detail where he'd be out of harm's way."

"And incidentally," Stephanie said, "too busy to run down your background."

"That, too," the Senator admitted with an acknowledging grin.

Jared came back to a personal issue that had settled like bile in his throat. "So, you used my mother and grandfather as much as my father did--to insinuate yourself into their confidence, to trap and murder my father under the legitimacy of war."

"That's not the way it was supposed to happen. I was trying to do the right thing for our country."

"Sounds familiar," Jared muttered.

The Senator's smile was faint beneath his matted beard. "I still don't have your vote, do I?"

All three were silent for several moments.

"OK, maybe I do owe you an apology," Jared offered, without looking at either one of them.

"Maybe!"

Stephanie began folding the blanket with abrupt movements.

"I apologize to both of you," Jared said, looking across the cockpit into the eyes of the man and woman sitting opposite him. "I guess I got more than I bargained for." Then he stood up, handed the tiller to the Senator and went below.

He turned on the VHF radio and listened to Channel 16 as the Coast Guard continued coordinating their search for *Dutchman* with the Secret Service. He'd have a good deal of explaining to do unless Senator Robinson agreed to say they just went for a harmless night sail. Then there wouldn't be a lot Burnett or anyone else could do about it. He didn't plan on being associated with the Secret Service much longer, anyway.

"Coast Guard, Coast Guard, this is the sailing vessel *Dutchman*, Whiskey Charley Echo three-four-two-zero, do you read me, over?"

There was a flurry of response from several Coast Guard search craft and shore stations until the controlled fury of Ken Burnett came over the speaker. "Is CANDY secure?"

"Affirmative." They knew Jared had sailed his boat up the coast from Annapolis and figured that was the most logical way he and the Senator could have left the island.

"What is your present position?"

"We're three miles south of Cuttyhunk."

"Come up Vineyard Sound to Tarpaulin Cove," Burnett

said. "Got that Coughlin?"

"Affirmative."

"Drop anchor off the southwest end of the beach under the abandoned lighthouse and wait for us," Burnett said. "Do you read me?"

"Copy."

"You damned well better, mister! What's your ETA?""

Jared consulted his watch and made a quick calculation in the log. "ETA Tarpaulin is one hour and forty-five minutes. Repeat, one hour and forty-five minutes."

Wherever Burnett was, he seemed to be holding a conference at his end of the emergency transmission frequency. Jared listened to static as he waited for the voice of his superior to come back on Channel 16.

Jared came up through the companionway, climbed out of the cockpit without speaking and went forward along the windward catwalk to the foredeck.

Stephanie hugged the folded blanket to her chest and watched him standing at the headstay, peering out into the dissipating fog. She turned to look at Senator Robinson. "That's not all of it, is it?"

Droplets of moisture from the night mist adhered to the Senator's beard and he ran a hand across his face to wipe them off. "Please.... This has been painful enough for both of us."

"You've just told him he's the son of a traitor, a *Nazi* spy who married his mother as a matter of convenience." She rose to her feet still pressing the blanket to her body. "If there's anything else in your heroic tale of deceit that can soften his anguish, you should tell him."

"No," he said. "There's nothing."

"You're so alike," she said. "Can you always justify whatever means you use to achieve your goals?"

"Only if both are honorable," he answered. "We do not live in a perfect world, Stephanie. Saints and martyrs set good examples but have rarely improved the lives of men on Earth."

She held his gaze without speaking, then went below to

343

make coffee as Senator Robinson steered a compass course toward the abandoned lighthouse on the southern tip of the shallow cove. Jared hadn't moved from the stem head, standing motionless, looking out into the wispy fog with one hand gripping the forestay.

A shiver ran through his body as he emerged from his confusing reverie. He turned, released the main halyard and lowered it in preparation to anchor. His hands furled it automatically as his mind grappled with the events of the past six months and the Senator's confession. True? Contrived? Still obscuring some devastating secret that would generate revulsion and enmity among voters?

When Jared persisted probing into the fiasco in the Senator's condo, the Germans had tried to eliminate him in the Florida Keys. DePrete had surely kept the Senator apprised of these events, so when Jared confronted him in his hotel room in Nashville, the candidate tried to take him out of play by getting him fired. Everyone must have breathed a sigh of relief when he and *Dutchman* had disappeared from her slip in Annapolis. Then he prevented Gunter Knopf from assassinating Robinson at the Convention, and the only recourse Burnett had was to accede to the Senator's request to put him back on duty. Which once again placed him inside the impenetrable cordon of defense and gave him an advantage that no outsider would ever achieve--an opportunity to abduct an elected federal official of the United States under Secret Service protection.

Jared lashed the main around the boom. He untied the marlin on the anchor and made sure the rode would run free from the chain locker in the forepeak. The sun was burning the fog off and the dark outline of the headland was visible through the wafting mist ahead. Burnett would insist that Jared accompany the Senator back to the Forbes compound for debriefing and his inevitable reprimand or termination that even Senator Robinson might not be able to prevent. Or want to.

Standing on the foredeck by the mast, he signaled the

Senator to turn the cutter head to wind. As the jib luffed and the boat lost way, Jared dropped anchor and began to play out rode, waiting for the hi-tensile Danforth to dig its flukes into the ocean bottom. No wonder his mother drank and remained so reticent about his father. Was that why her relationship with Pieter Kramers' son had been so strained? Had she known John Andeweg killed her husband? Misguided in his wartime loyalty or not, Pieter Kramers was his father! Had she known his murderer was still alive, masquerading as a United States Senator?

Jared was uncleating the jib halyard when he heard the sound of a single-engine plane coming in from the east. He stood by the boom listening to the aircraft circle to the north as the pilot adjusted the pitch of his motor for a slower approach. The lifting fog lingered in the distance, melding the morning sky with the surface of the water where there should have been a distinct horizon. Overhead, the ceiling was only a couple of hundred feet and the plane was not visible.

Moments later, an unmarked four-passenger seaplane broke through the mist directly overhead, then banked sharply, its engine roaring to gain altitude as it headed back toward the direction it came from.

"Stephanie!" Jared called below. "Raise the Coast Guard and ask if they have a seaplane in the area."

He stood on the cabin housing squinting off into the bright glare of the rising sun, listening. The plane throttled its engine back and dropped out of the mist like a gigantic white bird, tail straight, wings steady, pontoons skimming the gray water, carving a shallow wake on the rippled surface.

"Senator, get below!"

The pilot decreased his speed, steering a course that would take them upwind, thirty yards off *Dutchman*'s bow. Senator Robinson stood in the cockpit as the near window of the plane rolled down to reveal FBI Agent Roger Talbot waving at them. The Senator stayed where he was. Talbot's voice rose through a megaphone above the diminishing revs of the engine, the little aircraft trying to maintain it's position off their starboard bow.

"I was already in the air, so Burnett told me to take the Senator off your boat immediately."

The plane's passenger door opened, and a gray bundle dropped out into the gently undulating surface, inflating into an emergency life raft when it hit the water. Talbot began playing its pendant out and the current drifted the rubber raft down toward *Dutchman* on the nylon line.

"Just get in the raft, Senator," Talbot shouted, "and we'll pull you back up on a winch."

"Stephanie, any word from Burnett?" Jared asked.

"All I'm getting is static, no matter how I squelch." Like somebody is keeping their mike open to jam the frequency, Jared thought.

"No can do, Talbot," Jared yelled at the plane through a hailer. "The candidate is a Service responsibility, not the Bureau's. Stand by if you want, but I'm waiting for Burnett."

For a few minutes, nothing happened, then the fat snout of a Ruger Mini-14 machine automatic carbine was thrust out the window and Talbot shouted, "Get in the raft, Senator or you both die."

Jared started moving even before he saw the gun, pushing off the cabin top in a running leap that ended in a body block catching the Senator mid-chest, the plane's revving engine drowning out the prolonged burst from the automatic rifle, lead slugs ripping a row of jagged holes along the teak-planked catwalk as Jared knocked Senator Robinson down on the cockpit sole, the Secret Service agent sprawled on top of him.

The raft drifted loose, the door of the plane closed, and the plane turned to run a parallel course back down their starboard side. Stephanie shouted into the mike for medical assistance as the seaplane picked up speed. Senator Robinson shoved Jared off him, his hand smeared with blood from the dark stain seeping through the agent's sweater.

The Senator grabbed the Uzi from the seat cushion,

checked the magazine and flipped the safety off as he knelt at the after end of the cockpit. The seaplane gunned its engine, rounding up under the cutter's stern, aiming its nose back up their port side toward the bow of the sailboat to close the range, the gunner positioned at the window behind the pilot. Senator Robinson held his fire until the plane was less than fifty-yards away, then raked the passenger compartment with a single burst and emptied the rest of the magazine into the fuel tank. The explosion sent red and yellow flames soaring into the air, blowing fiery debris in all directions, falling on *Dutchman*, setting her sails on fire and smoldering black bullet-holes on the teak deck.

The Senator laid the machine pistol aside and used Jared's rigging knife to cut away the agent's blood-soaked sweater. Stephanie came through the companionway and knelt beside them, placing a white tin box with a red cross on the cockpit seat.

"I'll do that," she said, feeling Jared's neck to confirm his pulse. She finished cutting the wet sweater and polo shirt away to expose four puckered holes in his back, oozing blood into the cockpit drain.

"Oh, my God!"

"How bad is it?" Robinson asked.

"Not good. He's losing blood."

Stephanie slipped on a pair of surgical gloves and set stainless steel clamps on the red-rimmed holes in Jared's back as the Senator covered the rest of his body with blankets.

"They might have nicked an artery, but the flow seems to have been reduced. I hope there isn't much internal bleeding."

She fought to maintain a professional tone as she took sterile compresses from the first aid kit and she showed the Senator how to press them on the wounds to slow the bleeding. Then they turned Jared over carefully to examine the rest of his body.

"That's it," she said, "but he could go into shock. Get those blankets from the forward berth."

smeared antibacterial salve on the wounds and applied clean bandages. "I can't tell where the bullets are, but I couldn't do anything about them anyway." She snapped off the Latex gloves and brushed a strand of auburn hair behind her ear. "If they hit a vital organ...."

Jared's eyes opened and focused on the bearded face above him. "You bastard!" he whispered.

Stephanie stroked his arm beneath the blanket. "Don't talk." She wiped the perspiration from his forehead with a piece of damp gauze. "They'll be here any second."

Jared's words were almost inaudible. "He killed my father."

"No!" Senator Robinson's voice was hoarse with emotion.

"You admitted it!"

The Senator stared at the wounded agent. Then he reached inside his jacket, withdrew his leather wallet and took a creased sheet of yellow stationary from it.

"I have hoped and feared that I would never have to do this."

He unfolded the paper and stared at the handwriting on it. "Your mother wrote to me five years ago," he told Jared. "She recognized me from the news photographs."

Jared winced and began to shiver.

Stephanie dug around in the kit until she found a morphine syringe. "I'm going to give you a shot."

Jared opened his eyes and tried to move his head. "No.!" His voice was weak but determined. "I have to hear this."

Stephanie frowned, found his hand beneath the blanket and squeezed it.

"'*Dear Dutch,*'" the Senator read. "'*I'm not positive this is you after thirty-five years, but I've been watching your committee hearings, so I'm sure enough to write this. I've been sick lately and want to get something off my chest that has colored my life more than anything else I've ever done--or haven't done.*

"*The only one who seemed to know what happened the night Pieter was lost overboard was Jim Barnum. Because the FBI whisked him off Dutch Master and away from the rest of us before we could ask him questions or sail back to Newport. I still have dreams about it. If this is really you, Dutch, I don't want to know the truth...not anymore.'"*

The Senator looked up and Stephanie leaned over and spoke to Jared. "I told them you were wounded; they'll be lifting you off to a hospital in a few minutes."

His voice was barely a whisper. "Not 'til I hear the rest."

The Senator took a deep breath. "'*You know I had a son,"* he continued reading, *"he's always been a solitary boy, but I suspect there's a lot going on under the surface that I've never been able to get at. Like, you, my old friend...hard to reach. I suppose I haven't been a good mother to him, but God knows I've loved him. I guess I don't know how to show it."*

Senator Robinson had evidently committed that part of the letter to memory and continued speaking as his blue eye probed the younger man's face.

"So, I guess I've let you down again, Dutch. "*Because Jared was conceived during that awful homecoming weekend at Brown in the fall of 1941. He is not Pieter Kramers' son--he is yours."*

Jared squeezed his eyes shut and groaned as much from the significance of his mother's words as the pain from his wounds. Stephanie broke the cover on the hypodermic and slipped the needle into a vein on the back of his hand.

The Senator seemed compelled to finish now. "'You will probably never be able to acknowledge him, but someday you might be in the same room together. I thought at least one of you should know.'"

The helicopter hovered overhead, kicking up spray on the water around them, the noise of the twin turbo engines competing with the Senator's voice raised to speak the last line of the letter.

"'I did love you once, Dutch--I am sorry. Marijke.'"

A coast guardsman lowered a padded metal basket from the open doorway high above them as Senator Robinson lashed the main boom to the portside lifelines to allow clear access for the basket into the cockpit. They lifted Jared into it, strapped him in and watched him ascend. Stephanie waved the basket down again and rode up in it as the pilot began to pull away toward the mainland.

Senator Robinson stood in *Dutchman's* cockpit, replacing the dog-eared letter in his wallet as he watched the helicopter diminish into thin fog in the distance.

CHAPTER THIRTY-THREE
Wickford, RI
October 1976

"Thanks for speeding up the process getting my boat repaired. And released."

"If you waited through the usual procedures for the government to pay your claim," Senator Robinson said, "you'd be leaving during the next eclipse."

Jared smiled. "Maybe you can change all that bureaucratic horseshit."

The Senator chuckled. "I doubt it."

They were standing on the end of the town dock gazing out through the jetties at the sun-struck waters of Narragansett Bay beyond the Wickford harbor entrance. His wounds had healed, *Dutchman* was repaired and provisioned. He was anxious to set sail.

"Good luck next week," Jared said.

"It's in the hands of the voters, now."

Thirty or forty supporters holding blue-and-white ROBINSON placards stood behind a half-dozen Secret Service agents wearing aviator sunglasses, standing beside three black sedans parked twenty yards away.

"I'm sorry I put you through all this," Senator Robinson said. "Getting shot twice on my account, nearly killed." His eye was fixed on some point beyond the distant horizon. "My own son."

"Hindsight...."

"It's so easy to get caught up in the convolutions of solving seemingly momentous problems," the Senator said, "that have the capacity to nudge us into that gray area between right and wrong."

"Good men making bad decisions?"

"Even the best of us make mistakes. Circumstances we

have no control over confront us and we're forced to act. Some of us behave well according to our conscience. Others do not."

"Regardless of the consequences?"

"An honest man must act on his beliefs, his best judgment at the time."

"And a dishonest man?"

"I doubt he believes in anything."

The minute Frank DePrete had learned the Senator was missing from the island he clamped a lid on the story, flew up and coordinated the search with Ken Burnett. When they located CANDY, on Jared's boat, they smuggled him ashore and pretended he had been asleep all night in his room. The remnants of the seaplane with its renegade FBI agent were loaded on a Coast Guard barge and sunk in the Atlantic Ocean three hundred miles off the coast of Nova Scotia. Jared's wounds were attributed to an accident. He was awarded a disability pension and discharged from the Secret Service.

It hadn't taken the FBI long to discover that their own Roger Talbot had been selling information to the last stragglers of the *Baader-Meinhof* gang masquerading as staff personnel in the West German embassy.

They watched a powerboat back out of a slip in the marina across the way and turn toward the jetties. Her twin diesels rumbled under the five-knot limit, anxious to rev up to cruising speed out on the open water. She was rigged for tuna, with a long bow pulpit and tall rods raked aft high in the air. Jared felt the urge to cast off and follow the fishing boat, but wanted to prolong the moment, too.

"How can you force the Swiss bankers to ante up the money if they stole it?"

"That depends on how the election goes." Senator Robinson paused and swept his eye across the sleepy harbor. "If I lose, I intend to dedicate my life to getting retribution to the survivors and descendants of the Holocaust. If I win, I'll make it the top priority of United States foreign policy. Either way, I intend to ensure that neither the Swiss nor anyone else will walk off with the billions stolen from millions of murdered people."

"We've grown pretty complacent," Jared said. "D'you think the public will back you up?"

"Every American was behind World War II. We were fighting for something we believed in--the hope of our American Dream. Our country. Freedom from miscreants like Hitler. Terrorists like *Baader-Meinhof.* They'll back me."

"Seems like you've done your share already."

"The only ones who've done that are the boys who didn't come home. Innocent civilians. My war. Yours." Senator Robinson watched the stern of the power boat settle into the water as she picked up speed beyond the jetties. "We owe them."

"How do you repay a debt like that?"

"Throw the self-serving thieves out of government; run greedy brigands out of business and industry; give the public reasons to stop whimpering and start rebuilding our country before it's too late."

"That's a tall order," Jared said. "Eliminate the moral vacuum of the late twentieth century?"

"Someone needs to set a good example. Educate. Encourage. Punish."

"Change human nature?"

"That depends on whether you believe man is inherently good or evil." The Senator paused and squinted into the far horizon. "All we can do is follow our hearts. Never settle for less."

Jared did not respond for several moments. "Chucking everything over with no concrete plans for the future must seem pretty irresponsible to you."

"No plans at all?"

"Just a vague idea about hiring out to corporations as a security consultant."

"In Washington?"

"I don't know." They both looked down at the finger piers where Stephanie and Cindy Farrell were perched on the floating dock next to his boat, shoes off, swishing their feet through the water. "I'll have to figure that out when I get back home."

"What's that cliché?" the Senator asked. "Home is where the...."

".... heart is. Yeah, yeah, I know. But the other heart isn't convinced this one is fully committed."

"To her?"

"The kid."

"Are you?"

"I don't know!"

"Sailing back here after your 'round the world cruise would be as good an answer as any."

"I decided to change that. Cruising the Windward Islands."

Senator Robinson laughed. "You're a scheming Dutchman just like your ancestors."

"What?"

"Get back here before some four-f dandy scoops her up."

"Am I that transparent?" Jared asked.

"I'm sure Stephanie will see through your subterfuge."

Jared scuffed the toe of a boat shoe against a smear of tar on the timbered dock, then looked up grinning at him.

"You're starting to sound like my father."

The Senator laughed. "Nobody's perfect."

"I wish I had known you when I was growing up."

"So do I."

"I never did understand my mother."

"She was a lovely woman, Jared. Her life was not the one she wanted."

"I wish...."

The Senator cut him off. "Don't do that to yourself. Or her."

"Keep it up," Jared said.

They laughed together until Jared turned serious again.

"Why didn't you try to find her?"

The Senator did not answer right away. "When I came back from the war she was married to your stepfather, Maxwell Coughlin. What good would it have done to reveal myself? I killed her first husband, the man she rejected to marry

Kramers." He compressed his lips beneath the white beard. "I learned she was drinking heavily. If she knew my secret, it could have endangered my life. Maybe hers."

"And when she wrote you that letter?"

"She did not enclose a return address," he said. "She did not want me to find her."

Both men stood silent in the warmth of the autumn sun. The Senator in a white dress shirt and tie, sharply creased trousers and polished wing tips; Jared in scuffed leather Topsiders, khaki pants and a Georgetown sweatshirt splattered with green paint.

"I'd better get a move on if I'm going to catch the tide."

"I have a speech to give in Providence," the Senator said.

"Your alma mater?"

"John Andeweg's."

They began walking along the concrete path above the retaining bulkhead toward the ramp that led down to *Dutchman* where Stephanie was standing now, watching Cindy leaning over the float trying to scoop minnows into a paper cup.

The Senator placed a hand on Jared's arm and walked alone down the ramp to the pier where Stephanie and Cindy were waiting. They spoke for several minutes until Senator Robinson extended his hand. Stephanie ignored it, put her arms around his neck and gave him a warm hug which seemed to surprise him.

When he returned to the head of the dock Jared said, "I'll be listening to the returns next Tuesday."

They shook hands, the Senator clasping Jared's in both of his. "Call me once in a while."

Jared's left hand grasped his father's and held it. "*Auf wiedersehen.*" [Good-bye]

"*Nein,*" Senator Robinson said. "*Bis dann, stimmt's.* [So long.]"

Jared nodded, and the two men held one another's gaze for several moments. Then the tall, bearded candidate walked toward his constituents, paused before them to say a few words and got into his limo. An agent closed the rear door behind him as the remaining humps got into their vehicles and the caravan pulled out of the parking lot.

Jared walked down the ramp to his slip and stopped a few feet from Stephanie. They just looked at each other. He was sullen and reserved: on the one hand, anxious to leave a painful situation on the other, compelled to make a final effort to resolve it. They both realized this might be their last opportunity to do so.

A bullet from the Ruger carbine had damaged a nerve in his lower back and paralyzed his left leg which had required physical therapy after surgery. During Stephanie's initial visits at Mass General they were able to dissipate her anger at his duplicity in enlisting her help to kidnap the Senator, and his threat of murder if Robinson had not made his astounding confession. They had also tried to plan their future, which invariably led to a discussion of how, or if Cindy Farrell could be part of it.

The contrary teen had been living with Stephanie and Mrs. Graham in their Wickford home supervised by her mother's nurse while Stephanie worked, attended special summer classes and was enrolled at Wheeler, a private girls school in Providence. Stephanie was phasing out her Boston practice and increasing her Providence clientele in order to spend more time with Cindy.

Jared was convinced that Stephanie felt responsible for Cindy because of her failure to counsel her mother successfully. That she was the only positive link to the girl's life before her mother's incarceration. Unless Stephanie intervened, she believed, the girl would be cast adrift for years by some state institution or the round of foster homes in which disturbed children were often placed.

Although Jared agreed that Stephanie had achieved remarkable progress with the girl during the past three months, Cindy's occasional lapse into sulky retreat, unfocused anger and marijuana, persuaded Jared that if adopted, they would be forced to deal with a mercurial, unpredictable personality for the next ten years and possibly beyond. Another objection Jared had to adopting Cindy was the girl's aversion to sailing, the main joy in his own and Stephanie's lives. What would they do with her when they sailed every summer weekend or cruised Maine for a couple of weeks--leave her at home? Would her surrogate mother do that?

Stephanie had listened patiently to his concerns, acknowledging that many were well-founded, trying not to sound accusative when she voiced her contention that Cindy posed no more threat to their happiness than the scores of difficulties loving couples brought to thousands of relationships and survived: different religions, geography, work schedules, finance, addiction, poor health, abuse, squeezing the wrong end of the toothpaste tube or lousy cooking. If Jared loved Stephanie enough to accept Cindy as her daughter and he agreed to adopt her legally and intellectually as his own," Stephanie contended, "all of his fears would vanish, including his jealousy of her attention to Cindy. They would have as much opportunity for a good marriage as any couple. As a psychologist and woman, Stephanie knew she was fighting not only for the two people she loved most, but in all likelihood the man who was the best chance she would ever have at happiness. She tried to show Jared that he had not made any real effort to get to know Cindy. That he had treated the teenage girl with a supercilious attitude since her childish attempt at revenge on his boat, and consciously or otherwise had reinforced his assumption of the girl's temporary status ever since.

"How the hell do you think I'm going to feel," Jared had asked her, "if I try to enforce the normal discipline of a father, afraid she's going to turn me in for child abuse?"

"That's over, Jared. The rape accusation was the desperate lashing out of a defenseless little girl with the only weapon she ever had. Sex."

They had been sitting in plastic arm chairs beside the window in his private room in the hospital two months ago. He got up, hobbling around the bed on crutches in obvious frustration.

"So I can relax, never worry about a relapse. Geeze, Steph,

women have started accusing their .fathers of abuse twenty years after the fact."

"And it's been mostly true."

"Mostly!"

"Jared, the poor kid had been sold by her mother for drugs, tried to commit suicide, was headed for five years in the hands of the state--and you can't forgive her one mistake?"

"I told her I did, but she doesn't buy it.

"'Pigs lie.' She thinks I'm waiting to get back at her."

"Then why don't you try affection? She needs that more than the discipline you're always harping on."

Jared stopped pacing and stood before her. "Steph, this is your business and you're damn good at it. So I'm sure you've considered this streetwise kid could be playing on your affection, using you to get out from under State supervision."

"Maybe she is, a little."

"Maybe a lot?"

"No. Not a lot. And that will change with time, as she begins to appreciate the advantages of a private school. She has a fine mind, Jared."

"That's what scares me." He began pacing again. "And you're trying to be her mother and shrink at the same time. Surgeons don't operate on their immediate family, do they?"

Stephanie turned to look at him. "So you think she's outsmarting me? Gee, thanks for the vote of confidence."

"Steph, you're easy on her, she puts it all over you."

"Now you're giving me the benefit of your vast experience as a parent and telling me how to treat a patient."

After his wounds had healed, his doctors moved him three blocks north to Spaulding Rehabilitation Center to begin PT for his leg that had immobilized him for three weeks following surgery. They agreed to a hiatus on discussing Cindy. Jared persuaded Stephanie to use her medical prerogatives with the nurses to overstay the official visitor's hours and invoke privacy during which she could ply her own special therapy in his darkened hospital room.

During those extended sessions after Stephanie had undressed and joined him between the starched sheets of the narrow hospital bed in that strange, motel-like room devoid of ambient warmth or romance, they seemed to achieve temporary relief from their polarized, apparently irreconcilable attitudes regarding the thirteen-year-old-girl. Their physical and inner need for one another, their exultant immersion in the act itself, the almost violent hunger to meld bodies and souls, their urgent proclamations of unrestrained love had the power to banish the paucity of acceptable solutions to their problem and their growing despair regarding its outcome. Later, Jared believed those late-night hours in that gloomy room had simply postponed the inevitable.

But lying in that hospital bed at Mass General, then stuck in a wheelchair between workouts at Spaulding, contemplating his predominately singular existence to that point and the repeated failure of previous 'serious' relationships, Jared had come to the conclusion that life without Stephanie Graham would leave a large piece missing from his remaining time on Earth, that would cause him distress for years to come.

It also became clear that she was adamant about Cindy; less and less willing to explore any compromise that did not include Cindy Farrell. He could not dissuade her from her absolute refusal to give her up or mitigate their psychologist/mother relationship. Despite their differences, regardless of the consequences, but with the obvious reluctance of a man in defeat, he decided to put his misgivings about Cindy Farrell aside. He wanted this woman at all costs and would do anything, endure anything, to get her.

On a warm sunny afternoon in late September, Stephanie checked him out of Spaulding for a walk along the Charles River. They crossed the Monsignor O'Brien Highway at the lights near the Museum of Science, Stephanie slowing to Jared's pace as he limped down the Esplanade on his cane, past the Hatch Shell until they found an empty bench at the edge of the Lagoon.

"I've got a bad leg," he said, "so I'm not going to be able to give this the full treatment."

"What are you talking about?"

"I love you, Steph. More than anything." He held her hand between his. "Will you marry me? Please?"

He felt the little tug of her arm, possibly involuntary, but a pulling away nevertheless. She looked out at a one-man shell stroking evenly up the near side of the river, avoiding the beginner sailors in dinghies launched from the Community Boat Club.

"No, Jared, I will not marry you," she spoke decisively with a shake of her head at the city of Cambridge on the opposite shore. Her hand had remained in his and she squeezed it.

"Steph! I mean Cindy too, she's part of the package."

She turned and looked in his eyes and he could read her sadness. "You're not convinced," she said, "committed to her as our daughter, an inseparable member of our family." She removed her hand from his and placed it in her lap, staring again across the river, unseeing. "Part of the package isn't good enough, Jared."

"Jesus H. Christ!" he exploded, "how much more committed can I get than legal adoption, giving the kid my name, feeding, clothing her, sending her to college, probably?"

"The kid? Did I hear 'loving her?'"

"I'm willing to give it a damned good try, Steph, bet the rest of my life on it. What more can you ask?"

"More than you're able to give, I think." She turned to search his eyes again. There were tears in hers.

"I don't get it."

She picked up his hand again, with the little grin that drove him crazy. "That's the problem, lover. I don't want to spend the next fifty years watching you trying to like my daughter, consciously avoiding giving offense or taking it, treating her like some conditional baggage, eventually maybe a bad bargain you'll want to get out of."

It was Jared's turn to scrutinize the narrow band of

brackish water, standing in the lagoon below them, pretending to squint at the sun dancing on the surface. "You think I'd make a mess of it."

"With your present attitude."

He shook his head. "I guess I never figured out how you could change your attitude at the snap of a finger. I thought that was something you had to work at."

"When you want to."

"But I'm telling you I do."

"After spending the last few months trying to talk me into getting rid of her?"

"Geezes, Steph, give me a break."

She gave his hand a final squeeze and stood up. "You can make it back on your own, right?"

He stood, too. "That's it?"

"Jared, I can see that you're resigned to Cindy and I love you even more for that, dammit." He took a step toward her, lifting his arms to embrace her, but she raised her hands between them and backed away.

"No, let me say this. I'm caught up in Cindy Farrell, obsessed, you may think, and you may be right. I admit it. Because of the tragic circumstances she was born into, the degradation and fear created by her own mother. Compelled emotionally, irrationally, irrevocably—to try to salvage this unfortunate girl from a future of devastating mental problems, poor prospects...a lousy, degrading, dangerous life.

"You obviously don't empathize with any of that, how I feel, as a woman, a mother." She emitted a deprecating laugh that did not diminish the intensity of her feelings. "You cannot envision making anywhere near that kind of commitment to her or us or me, can you, Jared?" Her expression told him that this last accusation came as a revelation to her as she said it. "Even to me?"

* * * * * *

She was wearing denim jeans with a red chamois shirt to see him off, standing apart on the dock in silence, both of them aware that this could be their final encounter, speechless for several moments.

He spoke at last. "Nothing I can say, huh?"

"I think we said it all during the past couple of months, don't you?"

He took a step, reached around her waist and clasped his hands behind her. "I don't want to leave you. Lose you."

Their arms encircled one another in a lingering embrace, bodies pressed together in a desperate attempt to banish their differences.

"We should stay in touch. Friends?"

He raised his eyebrows, a pleading query: "Cruise Maine next year."

"We'll see."

He turned to *Dutchman* reluctantly, uncleated the spring lines, tossed them on deck, gazed up at the masthead fly to gauge the wind and climbed aboard to start the engine.

Cindy stopped swishing her feet in the water and stood beside Stephanie holding her hand. She seemed taller since living in Wickford and had filled out, an expression of whimsical curiosity replacing the sullen look, a creamy tan in lieu of the urban pallor. A new hairdo made her seem older, white shorts and blue jersey.

A pair of gulls swooped out of the vibrant azure sky and began tearing at a dead menhaden floating in the water. The smell of salt and kelp and sea life filled the Indian Summer air, but Jared could think only of not parting on an unpleasant note. He stepped off the boat and tried again, standing there, hands jammed in pockets, angry, impotent, feeling his life slipping away.

"All the bricks are stacked and cemented in place. I don't think life works that way, Steph."

"This will be best for all of us."

He looked out beyond the harbor entrance at a sloop sailing down the bay.

"Nobody's life is exactly what they want."

Cindy looked up at Stephanie. "Is this gonna take much longer?"

She hugged the girl to her side. "No, it's not. It's over."

Jared acknowledged Cindy for the first time. "Hi, Brat."

"G'bye, pig."

He had to laugh, then spoke to Cindy. "May I have one last word with you?"

Jared looked at Stephanie, who shrugged, turned and walked away toward the end of the pier.

"Congratulations."

"No sweat," Cindy said. The old look of disdain had returned.

"It doesn't bother you screwing up two lives, maybe three?"

"Hey! I got a good deal here. You're a hard-ass ball-buster sees my game, right?"

"So, you're going to use Stephanie to your own advantage and the hell with her feelings."

That infuriating grin was back, too. "Hey, Man, what are friends for? Fuck 'em!"

"No aspirations for a normal life, college, career, marriage, kids?

"That's all bull."

"Who do you want to grow up as, a happy woman, contributing member of society or the screwed-up bitch who pulled that stunt on my boat?"

"An' you wanna change me, be my daddy. Maybe take my panties down, give me a spankin'."

All of the frustration of arguing with Stephanie and losing her because of this duplicitous little tramp hit him at once.

"You know you're right, Cindy? Except for one thing." Jared grabbed the girl by the arm, propped his foot against a guard rail and threw her over his knee.

"You can keep your pants on."

He slapped her bottom repeatedly with enough force to produce screams of pain and indignation from the outraged teen. Stephanie came running up the dock shouting at him to stop but had to hold his arm in both hands to make him do it.

"Is that the way you want to administer discipline?" she asked him, gathering a sobbing Cindy to her, for some reason more confused than angry.

"That's what fathers used to do when the ineffectual pleas of permissive mothers failed, before the application of child psychology that sustains little manipulators like this!"

Stephanie held Cindy at arm's length. "You OK, Honey?"

Cindy had stopped crying, her wide eyes fixed on Jared.

"Sorry, kid," Jared said. "I had no right to do that."

She nodded, her confused gaze never leaving his face.

Jared stepped aboard again and Stephanie uncleated the bow line, holding *Dutchman* to the dock. Jared doubled up on the stern line and brought the bitter end aboard. When he glanced back, Cindy was standing alone on the pier wiping her eyes with her fist. Jared took a turn around the stern cleat and stepped back on the dock. "Good-bye, Cindy," he said.

"Yeah. Don't sink."

Jared reached his hand out and she took it. "I didn't do that because I hate you. I do care about you."

She nodded again, her lips compressed. Jared climbed aboard. Stephanie tossed the bow line on deck, Jared engaged the engine, backed her down, turned *Dutchman* into the harbor and raised his arm.

They waved back. Then watched *Dutchman* motor out through the jetties until the little cutter turned the corner and only her masthead was visible above the riprap.

Stephanie brushed the tips of her fingers across her cheeks and they started walking back up the dock.

That, she thought, was the end of Jared Coughlin.

* * * * * *

The wind was almost nonexistent. If he hoist sail now he'd be bobbing around like a cork. Better continue under power until he passed Point Judith into open water. Jared stood at the tiller feeling unusually low instead of the exuberance that usually accompanied the prospect of a long cruise into distant islands, coves, harbors and adventures.

Was this going to be a fun trip? he wondered.

Jared found himself depressed at the thought of going forward and reluctant to turn back.

After his last conversation/argument with Burnett, if he stayed in the Service, he'd endure the humility of losing the prestige and responsibility of a field agent, sent down to the degrading job of an inside administrator working in a small cubicle with bare walls and no window. What else could he do? Probably wouldn't get a decent letter of recommendation.

He had always marveled at corporations that were so focused on their primary business that they paid little attention to security and were victims of the theft of highly confidential product formulas, embezzlement or computer hacking. With his background he could establish a security consulting business for corporations. Eventually bring on specialists such as Alex Shertinsky and Paul Hunsacker.

Jared shifted the engine into neutral and the sloop coasted with the last of the ebb tide until they were sitting in place, practically dead in the water as the current changed to slack.

With almost twenty-years of romantic and/or sexual relationships, Jared realized, he had struck out every time at bat. Now that he had found the one woman in the universe with whom he believed he could share happiness, Stephanie conjures up some altruistic challenge that only she can resolve. If this is her modus operandi, what next? A houseful of disadvantaged kids? What about their own children? That hadn't even been discussed or considered, with practically every conversation focused on Cindy.

Bottom line: would he rather continue on to the Islands, have a somber, wistful cruise and return to---what? The loss of Stephanie Graham forever or did he want her badly enough to try to help her with Cindy instead of his constant opposition and criticism?

Anything could happen during the six or eight months he planned to be away. Worst case, she could find someone else. The way they left it seemed pretty final. At least on her part. Could he support Stephanie in her efforts to turn Cindy away from her absence of values to a responsible young woman? Could he do that without letting the kid ruin their marriage or drive him crazy?

What the hell was he doing? Screwing his life up again? Was he going to let Stephanie slip through his fingers just because some little brat annoyed him? He'd handled worse. Much worse.

Jared forced himself to shake off his pensive lethargy, turned Dutchman one-hundred-eighty-degrees and pushed the throttle forward.

* * * * * *

"So, what was that about with Jared?" Stephanie asked.

"Nothin'."

"Noth*ing*," Stephanie corrected.

Cindy stopped and shouted, "Nothin', nothin', nothin', goddammit!"

"Cindy, what's wrong?"

"Wrong? Everything! You're on me all the time, raggin' me about the way I talk, the way I dress, my friends...."

"Speaking and dressing properly is important because that's how people get their first impression of you."

"Yeah, well, friends aren't supposed to care about that."

"No. Those kids you brought home last weekend wouldn't. They didn't seem like the pick of the Wheeler crop. Aren't they older than you?"

"So what? I don't have any friends at Wheeler. They're townies from the high school."

"Oh, Cindy, how could you lie to me like that?"

"A hell of a lot easier," she jabbed a thumb out at the bay, "than him." Cindy squinted out over the riprap, taking a step forward, then stopped.

"Look." she pointed at *Dutchman*'s masthead approaching the channel between the jetties that led back into Wickford Harbor.

Stephanie turned to follow her gesture, both watching Jared crossing the harbor, returning to his slip.

"Hey! He's coming back," Cindy said with barely repressed excitement.

"What?" Stephanie was still immersed in the disappointment of Jared's departure and Cindy's deceit.

"Jared," Cindy said, pointing toward the harbor channel.

366

"He's back."

Dutchman turned in between her pilings and gently nudged the side of the slip with her fenders. Jared killed the engine, jumped off the boat and tied bow and stern lines to dock cleats.

They were standing at the top of the ramp. Stephanie couldn't suppress the little smile tugging at the corners of her mouth. "*Well, isn't that strange,*" she murmured.

"He musta forgot somethin'," Cindy said, jogging down the ramp toward *Dutchman*, stopping at mid-point between the ramp and the boat.

Stephanie walked slowly down the ramp to the dock, standing silent with no tell-tale expression. "*Yeah. I wonder what it is?' Or maybe he's just the big loveable dope I thought he was.*"

Cindy was standing between the ramp and *Dutchman* watching Jared secure his boat in the slip. Jared looked at Stephanie just standing there, arms folded across her breasts, her hand feeling, the beat of her heart beneath her ribs, her expression unreadable. He flipped a fender off *Dutchman's* deck. to hang between the dock and his boat, then started jogging toward the ramp and Stephanie, but suddenly changed direction to grab Cindy playfully around the neck in the crook of his arm. Cindy let out a high-pitched squeal, but her arm snaked around Jared's waist automatically as she let herself be pulled into him, not sure whether to resist or giggle.

"Hey, Jared," Cindy asked, her words muffled by her lips pressed into the wool strands of his sweater, "what'd ya forget?"

"Forgot you!"

THE END

Check out Jack Quinn's next
suspense novel:
"The Testimony of Two Witnesses."
In bookstores & Online this Fall

The Testimony of Two Witnesses
by Jack Quinn

CHAPTER ONE

The old man was different: his placid expression, his austere bearing, the pace he set between the two bailiffs that made them appear subservient. Unlike the prisoners arraigned earlier, he did not pull his coat over his head to hide his face from the cameras, but stood in the dock with shoulders back, chin high.

The clerk moved beside the bench, consulted documents in a manila file folder and leaned up on tiptoes so he could speak to Judge Pagano without being overheard. After a brief exchange, the judge looked across the courtroom in my direction and frowned, as the clerk turned and beckoned, calling my name.

"Attorney Jake Cotnoir approach the bench."

Pagano's scowl from under heavy black eyebrows reeled me in until I stood at the corner of the wide mahogany platform next to the witness chair. The gel on his pepper-salt hair glistened under the fluorescent lighting, his midwinter tan setting him apart from the rest of us paleface drones. He shot his cuffs inside the loose fabric of the black robe, folding his hands on the polished surface before him.

"Are you ready to practice law again, Mr. Cotnoir?"

Six months suspension for attempted jury tampering had given me a lot to think about. Studying three years for my profession, working ten years at it, then being deprived of the only way I know to earn a living injected a bit of humility in my knees.

"Yes, Your Honor."

Paul Thompson, Clerk of Boston's Second District Criminal Court treats information like money. "You speak French, right, Cotnoir?"

"Canadian. My parents came down from Montreal during the depression."

"French is French isn't it?"

"Ever try understanding the machine-gun accent of a Mississippi delta chicken farmer?"

Pagano said, "Cut the bullshit, Cotnoir," flapping a hand at Paul urging him to proceed.

"The old man doesn't speak English," the clerk explained. "Asks for things in French, according to the police."

"Get an interpreter," I suggested.

"We have one," Pagano growled. "He won't cooperate. The French and Canadian consuls came in over the weekend. He wouldn't talk to them, so they disowned him."

"Been in custody since Friday night," Paul said. "We need to establish probable cause or release him."

"I intend to do that this morning." The judge glanced at his watch. "And I want a defense attorney who speaks his language to prevent getting reversed for any communications problems later on."

I'd been camping in the courthouse for two weeks hoping to get assigned as public defender to some drug dealer, a real loser I could squeeze a couple of extra grand out of, who might refer his *compadres* to me. The old man sounded like a dead-end case at 45 bucks an hour.

"What's the charge?"

"Murder," Pagano answered.

I turned to glance at the old guy in the prisoner's dock. He looked sixty-five, seventy, average height, pretty good shape for his age. His large head was almost bald, the crescent of lon,g, damp, white hair swept behind his ears by the furrows of a wide-tooth comb, the double-breasted suit that might have been tailor-made.

"Who'd he kill?"

Thompson consulted the folder in his hand. "Some other

old geezer name of Leo Benays in the Madison Hotel."

"Circumstances?"

"It's a gay hangout."

"Oh, great!"

The judge was getting annoyed. "If you don't want it, Cotnoir, I can have your name removed from the public defender list."

"Thank you, Your Honor. I appreciate the opportunity."

Pagano smirked,. I tried not to, holding my hand out for the arrest report held by Paul Thompson and started flipping through pages "I'll need some time with my client."

Judge Pagano leaned forward, his neck stretching out of his robe like a turtle, palms flat on the bench and glared at me. "They've had French speakers, detectives, another PD and an ADA quizzing the old bastard for two days." Then continued in an angry whisper. "Will you stop wasting my fucking time and plead him?"

Knowing when to back off had never been one of my strong points, but I got the message. As I walked over to the defense side, Pagano began informing the accused of his right to due process, including his privilege against self-incrimination and right to counsel, pausing regularly for the court interpreter's translation of his words into French. When he was satisfied the old man should have understood the purpose of the hearing and the procedures involved Pagano nodded to the assistant district attorney and leaned back in his tall, throne-like, black leather chair.

Leah Goldman stood up behind the prosecutor's table and began reading the charges, pausing frequently as the female interpreter standing beside the prisoner converted her indictment into French.

I whirled back toward the bench when I heard the accused referred to as 'John Doe.'

"'John Doe,' Your Honor? Surely the Commonwealth can read the Roman alphabet well enough to identify a person they see fit to accuse of a capital crime."

The assistant district attorney removed her glasses and lowered the document she'd been scanning. She was an attractive woman, bereft of makeup and must have been wearing an old bra. Bright, pleasant, a little heavy in the fashionable dresses she preferred to the severe suits worn by most female attorneys.

"The accused requests bail of $25,000," I said before the ADA could say a word.

"Not when the accused has no identification to read, Your Honor," she interrupted, smiling at me. "And refuses to divulge his name to the police."

Leah Goldman was a no-nonsense prosecutor five or six years out of law school. Our paths had crossed before and we seemed to share a guarded respect one another's talents. Prior to my suspension, anyway.

When I turned to my client, his black brows were raised, the corner of his mouth lifted in expectation.

"*Qu'appelez-vous*?" I asked him.

"*Je refuse.*"

I was going to earn my fee on this one, but I didn't want to start off by arguing with my client the first time we appeared in court together.

"Stipulate 'John Doe' for the time being," I said.

A preliminary hearing is usually a simple procedure to determine probable cause for continued detention, which must take place within 72 hours of a suspect's arrest: A person is formally charged with a crime by the authorities, informed of his rights, legal counsel appointed if he is indigent, and with the exception of capital crimes, bail is considered. This standard preliminary or Gerstein Hearing is non-adversarial, and the accused has no right to cross-examine witnesses. The role of a defense lawyer is to plead his client not guilty and try for low bail. Then both sides go home to prepare for trial. Which is where the action starts.

Murder is different. This murder was different. As I said in the beginning--my client was different.

Leah Goldman finished reciting her prepared statement and the interpreter translated her final phrases.

Paul Thompson stood behind the wide desk below the bench and addressed the accused: 'How do you plead, John

Doe, to the charge of premeditated murder in the first degree: guilty' or 'not guilty?'"

"If it please the court," I said, "defense requests 'Review of Prosecutor's Decision to Charge'."

Without lifting his head Pagano glared down at me from under those bushy eyebrows, then back at his clerk, whose idea to appoint me as defense counsel must have seemed considerably less astute to the magistrate than it had a few minutes earlier.

The ADA was on her feet before Pagano could respond. "On what grounds, Your Honor? The arrest was straightforward, virtually at the scene of the crime, an eyewitness can place the accused in the proximity of the murder minutes after commission, the defendant refuses to identify himself, and to this point, has not even protested his innocence. A Gerstein is not required."

"Unless otherwise requested by the defendant," I said, "as my learned colleague is aware."

"Requested in advance, in writing, challenging the competency of evidence of each element of the charges," the judge intoned. Pagano was a pain in the ass, but unlike some of his peers he knew the law. "Under ordinary circumstances I'd agree with the prosecution. Since Mr. Cotnoir has been dropped in the middle of this case rather precipitously at the court's instigation, however, I'm inclined to allow some latitude." He looked at me. "Grounds, Counselor?"

"The entire charge," I answered, "is apparently based on the assertion of one witness, Your Honor, who was at the scene when the victim expired."

I could feel the old man's eyes on me, shucking my physical characteristics, groping at the core of my being as the interpreter caught up with my response to Pagano's ruling. I moved away from the dock toward the bench, using the information I had scanned in the reports. "How can we be certain this critical eyewitness didn't kill Benays himself? How do we know the deceased didn't die of natural causes or slip and fall? Maybe the poor old fellow wasn't murdered at all...."

Pagano continued to glare at me but the look had become less hostile. Not only did he know the law, he was a stickler on its interpretation, priding himself on never having been reversed on appeal for technical errors during his seventeen years on the bench.

"Can we do it now?" Pagano asked the ADA.

She looked around the courtroom. "One of the arresting officers is present but no witnesses. However, Sergeant Butler personally interrogated all of them."

"You're on thin ice, Counselor, and you know it," Pagano told me. "I'll permit Review of Decision now, if you agree to admission of hearsay allowed by Gerstein."

I didn't have much hope of getting the charges dismissed, but I'd be flailing around in the dark if I didn't probe them under Pagano's scrutiny before the district attorney's office had a chance to get its act together and put up a smoke screen during discovery later on. Butler probably had ninety percent of the testimony from the key witness, anyway.

"Agreed, Your Honor. Thank you."

Sergeant Phil Butler was sworn in at the witness stand. A big, rumpled, Black man with a pockmarked face, the veteran homicide detective was cautiously referred to as the 'Unmade Bed', although never within his hearing.

"We took the call Friday night," Butler glanced at his notebook. "Ten-forty-seven P.M., February 27th."

"Who placed the call, Sergeant?"

"James Keneally, security officer at the Madison Hotel."

"What was the substance of that phone call, Sergeant Butler?"

"A witness," the detective consulted his notes again, "Randall Collins seen the accused John Doe leaving the victim's room a couple minutes before he finds Leo Benays dead, buck naked, face down in the bathtub full of water."

"What did Collins do?"

"The victim's mouth and nose were under water, but Collins rolled him over anyway. Then called the desk, told him what he found and described the accused."

The courtroom-savvy homicide detective would not give

anything away.

"What happened next," I prompted.

"Security Officer Keneally apprehended John Doe as he tried to leave the hotel."

Leah Goldman stood to request that Butler point out the man detained by Keneally for the record, subsequently identified by Collins and arrested. The policeman extended a beefy arm toward my client.

"That's him, right there in the prisoner's dock."

"What time did you arrive on the scene, Sergeant?"

"Eleven-fourteen, right after the beat cops."

"What did you find?"

"Same as the witness--Benays floating in the tub, except Collins had rolled him face up and drained the water to give CPR."

"What else?"

Goldman stood again. "Your Honor is this a fishing expedition or Review of Charges?"

"She's got a point, Cotnoir," Pagano said.

"My basic challenge is the credibility of the eyewitness, Your Honor. I intend to show that his accusation could be self-serving and fabricated."

"Then get on with it."

I turned back to Butler: "Do you have the preliminary findings of the medical examiner's autopsy?"

Butler flipped a couple of pages of his notebook. "Leo Benays drowned, all right, but the coroner found a couple of bumps on the head, bruises, welts around his shins."

"Have you determined the cause if those abrasions?"

"One way to drown somebody is hold 'em up by the ankles with his head in the water." The detective lifted his massive shoulders. "Victim thrashes around, inhales water, loses consciousness."

"Sergeant Butler, who was the deceased, Leo Benays?"

"We're checking that out."

"Would you care to elaborate, Sergeant?"

The detective shifted his weight in the witness chair. "His New York driver's license and credit cards give a name and address we haven't been able to confirm yet."

"You mean the Leo Benays identity is false...."

"We don't know that for sure at this time."

"Well, Sergeant, what do you know for sure about the deceased at this time?"

Butler looked at his notes. "Male, Caucasian, about seventy, eighty years old, six foot three, 168 pounds, white hair, mustache, couple of ragged old scars on his chest and arm."

I glanced at Judge Pagano scowling down at me, but he seemed interested. "So you don't know who the deceased is, who the accused is or if there is any prior relationship between these two men, is that correct, Detective Butler?"

"We're working on it."

"And you really don't know if a crime was committed, and if it was, how it was committed or why--do you?"

"We have a witness," Butler said, casting a glance at Leah Goldman that pled for her intervention. "Strong circumstantial evidence and a lot of unanswered questions by the defendant."

"Accused, Sergeant. He is not a defendant until he's been charged--which on the basis of what I've heard so far, he does not even belong in this courtroom, never mind accused of an extremely questionable homicide."

"Are you finished, Mr. Cotnoir? Pagano growled. "I have other matters I'd like to hear before the Governor's Easter Egg hunt." An appreciative chuckle rippled through the political cognoscenti in sparsely filled gallery.

"No, Your Honor."

"Then do so with dispatch, please."

I nodded toward the bench and took a step to Butler's right, so he'd have to crane his neck to get signals from Goldman. "Where was the witness Randall Collins when he first observed the accused?"

"Gettin' off the elevator on the 17th floor."

"How far is that from the room of the deceased?

The big detective consulted his notes. "Eighty-three feet. Direct line of sight."

"How could Collins be sure that the accused had been

inside Leo Benay's room?"

"He saw him leave it."

I took a couple of steps toward the dock to include my elderly client in the proceedings. "Describe exactly what Mr. Collins saw, please."

Butler flipped several pages again and read the verbatim statement of the witness from his notes. "I got off the elevator, started walking down the hall and this old guy comes out of Leo's room walking toward me. I was kind of surprised and interested, you know? So, I took a good look as he passed me It was him all right "The policeman smiled at me expectantly.

"Collins actually saw Mr. Doe come out of the room, step across the threshold and close the door behind him?"

Butler glanced at his note pad again. "I'm not sure he said that specifically."

"So, Mr. Doe could have had other business in the hotel and Collins just happened to observe him passing Mr. Benays door, isn't that correct, Detective Butler?"

The seasoned policeman knew where I was going. He adjusted the nonexistent crease in his trousers and crossed his legs, looking at Leah Goldman amid the movement.

She stood up. "Objection. That response calls for speculation on the part of the witness."

"Sustained," Pagano said.

"Did you find the fingerprints of the accused on the doorknob or inside the room?"

"No, but he could have...."

"You answered my question Sergeant. What took place after Collins passed the accused in the hotel corridor?"

"Collins entered the room and found Benays floating face down in the tub of water."

My expression registered surprise. "The door wasn't locked, chained on the inside?"

"Locked, not chained."

"And Benays was already dead."

"Yes sir."

"How did Collins get in the room?"

"He picked up a key at the desk."

"On Benays authorization."

"Yes sir."

"Ah, ha!" I turned automatically to play to a jury that wasn't there, then switched my appeal to the judge. "Your Honor, who is this Randall Collins? He had a key to Benay's room, an assignation with him," I raised the volume of my voice again, this time feigning indignation, "and probably more motive to kill him than an old Frenchman strolling down the corridor--conceivably suffering from Alzheimer's disease!"

Pagano looked annoyed and turned his tanned face to the prosecution. "Ms. Goldman?"

Leah smiled. "It's 'Miss', Your Honor."

The Judge shook his head in mock bewilderment. "We never know anymore, do we?"

The ADA smiled, slid a piece of paper from a file folder on the table before her and stood. "Randall Collins is a Boston resident, an acquaintance of the deceased."

"What kind of acquaintance?" I asked her.

"Homosexual," Leah admitted, "which has no bearing on his powers of observation."

"Unless he had a reason to kill his lover, Leo Benays."

"Then why report it?"

"To deflect suspicion."

"Mr. Collins is a registered voter, a local businessman and member of the community with no prior record."

"Does that preclude a violent act of passion?" I moved closer to my client, who stood at ease in the dock following the words of the interpreter and put my hand next to his on the wood railing. "But an old man who is not linked to the deceased in any way, who happened to be in the hotel when a guest drowned in his bathwater is a suspect--because, quite obviously," I lifted my hand toward the Frenchman, "he does not fully comprehend what's going on."

"The witness Randall Collins has been thoroughly interrogated by the police," Leah said, "and is not a suspect at this time."

"Not *thoroughly* interrogated, Ms. Goldman. But an old man who cannot speak our language," my voice was getting louder again, and it was no act this time, "who may not understand his predicament, was probably not fully interrogated or apprised of his rights, I'll wager--is accused of premeditated homicide based solely on the unsubstantiated word of a man who should be a suspect himself!" I turned to face Butler in the witness chair.

"Isn't it true, Detective, that an interrogation of a secondary suspect is often casual and incomplete when the police have a primary suspect with motive, circumstances and opportunity to commit the crime?"

"I remind you, Mr. Cotnoir, this is only a preliminary hearing," Pagano said.

"Was that your summation?"

Another smattering of laughter from the regulars.

I took a deep breath. "A few more questions for Officer Butler, Your Honor."

I addressed the homicide detective, who had remained immobile during the previous exchange except for his eyes that followed every object and nuance of our comments. "You say Mr. Collins claimed he found Benays face down in his bathwater?"

"Dead in the tub, yes sir."

"How could he be sure Benays was dead?"

Butler looked at me like I was an idiot. "Cause his head was under water and he wasn't blowing bubbles."

More chuckles from the gallery. I smiled dutifully waiting for them to finish.

"But Collins claims he applied CPR anyway."

"Yes sir."

"While Benays was in the tub or did he lift him out of it?"

"In the tub after he drained the water out."

"Then Collins claims he called the desk and described the old man he saw in the corridor."

"That's correct.

"Did the accused try to run, resist the security guard?" I asked.

"He's an old man," the detective answered. "Keneally's in his thirties, lifts weights."

"Did Mr. Doe protest verbally?"

Butler grinned like I should know better. "Maybe so, but nobody understood him."

"Then what happened?"

"Keneally brought Mr. Doe up to the room to confirm Collins' story and called it in.The beat cops showed up a few minutes later."

"Could you summarize their initial report on the scene?"

"Benays still wasn't breathing."

More laughter.

"Any sign of a fight, blood," I asked, "wounds, or deep lacerations?"

"There was water on the floor like there might have been a struggle; bruises, scrapes like I said on the deceased shins and ankles."

"Isn't it possible he could have felt sick, nauseous from something he ate, had the flu, splashed water trying to get out of the tub and fell back in unconscious, getting bruised and scraped in the process?"

"I can't...."

"Or Collins splashed water turning him over, giving CPR?" I waited for his answer this time.

"Possible," Butler admitted.

"What shape was Mr. Collins in when you first saw him?"

"Pretty flustered. His clothes were soaked from leaning into the tub."

I started back to the defense table frowning and shaking my head, pretending I didn't understand. Then as though an afterthought stopped, turned towards Butler asking, "Isn't it true that some people--hetro and homosexuals who engage in passionate sex practice what's known as bondage?"

"So I understand."

"And couldn't the welts on Mr. Benay's ankles have come from being tied to bedposts, for example, with some kind of rope or abrasive material?"

"We didn't find anything in the room to suggest that, so we

have no way of knowing," Butler answered.

"Just as you have absolutely no way of knowing that the accused or any other senior citizen could hold 168 pounds of thrashing Leo Benays up in the air by his ankles for the length of time it would take to drown him."

"There is no evidence Benays had sex recently."

"Correction, Detective Butler. You mean there is no evidence that the sex act was consummated, don't you?" I walked back toward the witness box and raised my voice in controlled outrage. "Which doesn't rule out foreplay, the inability of an old man to ejaculate or a number of other circumstances neither one of us is privy to, is that not a fact, Detective?"

"You're flying pretty close to the trees, Cotnoir," Pagano said. "Let's wrap this up, save something for the trial."

I shook my head and gave a little laugh. "Your Honor, please! There shouldn't be a trial."

I took a couple of steps toward the bench ticking my arguments off on my fingers. "We know that Leo Benays or whoever he is drowned. One man purportedly outside the victim's room had no means of access to it, no prints inside it, no known connection to the deceased or motive to kill him. The other man, who was found visibly distraught and soaking wet, did have access to the room, did have a sexual relationship with the victim, a possible motive to kill him and therefore good reason to accuse an innocent bystander of his act of murder."

"It would help if the defendant would identify himself," Leah said. "Tell us what he was doing in the hotel."

I waited for the interpreter's translation, then used my rusty French to urge my client to answer the questions posed by me, the police earlier, and the prosecution now.

"*Je refuse,*" he said.

"This arraignment is premature, Your Honor. My client is obviously not competent to appreciate the gravity of the charge or participate in his defense against it. We need a psychiatric workup first.

"Agreed in principle, Your Honor," Leah said, "but the

Commonwealth has sufficient grounds to arraign and detain this man under law as an accused murderer, not hold him in a hospital as a harmless bystander."

Unless I had lost my touch, my tone was incredulous. "For being in a hotel where an old man probably slipped in the tub and drowned?"

"The accused was seen leaving Mr. Benays room," she said, "he refuses to cooperate with the investigation. This is not the portrait of an innocent man."

"Not *seen* leaving the room," I corrected. "And your so-called witness may in fact be the real killer--if a homicide was actually perpetrated. I move for dismissal."

Judge Pagano struck his gavel on its wooden base. "Enough, Mr. Cotnoir. We're not trying the case this morning. There are adequate grounds to arraign. Motion for dismissal denied."

He nodded to the clerk and Paul Jackson rose from his chair at the circular desk before the bench. to ask, "John Doe, how do you plead to the charge of first-degree murder: guilty, or not guilty?"

After the translation I prompted my client, "*Pas guilte*," and prepared to repeat his plea in English.

"*Nolo contendere*," the Frenchman said, his strong voice slashed the expectant silence of the courtroom, now crowded since the word of the unusual hearing had scampered through the building, stimulating a murmur of disbelief.

"Your Honor, we seem to have a different language problem. A moment with my client, please."

I explained that in an American court, the Latin phrase '*Nolo contendere*' meant, 'I do not contest the charge'.

"You can't plead that to murder," I told him. "A jury would slaughter you."

The old bugger understood my rusty Canadian, but he wouldn't change his plea. I convinced Pagano to allow me to enter 'not guilty' on the man's behalf, and even though he had no right to bail in a capital offense, I mustered all the brass I had to ask for his release on a $50,000 bond.

Leah nearly knocked her chair over objecting to that one

and I couldn't blame her. The old man had no ID, no English, offered no defense, and apparently had no idea of the severity of the crime he was charged with. I didn't want him running around loose, either.

* * * * * *

"You should get your consul back here," I told him in French. "Get them to assign one of their staff lawyers for you, hire some high-priced criminal attorney."

"You will serve admirably," he replied in his formal Parisian dialect.

According to the cops, this was the first real conversation he 'd had with anyone since his arrest. We were sitting at a chipped metal table bolted to the floor in one of the little conference rooms off the basement holding cells of Suffolk County Courthouse in downtown Boston. After his arraignment, I secured a complete copy of the police investigation to date, the allegations of the prosecution, questioned one of the beat cops who had picked him up and conferred with Leah Goldman. My initial exchange with John Doe made the opposition seem more cooperative than my own client.

"*Monsieur!* You will not tell me who you are, where you are from, what you were doing in the hotel, if you knew the victim--how the hell do you expect me to defend you?"

He lifted his shoulders beneath the pin-striped fabric of his suit coat in the classic Gallic mannerism of my father which used to drive my mother crazy. "You will do the best you can."

I pointed my finger in his face and stood up. "Get yourself a new lawyer, *mon vieux.* I don't need this.*"

"The judge will allow you abandon me?"

Not without cause. Not with my track record. Not Pagano.

I gestured at his suit. "You don't look like you need a public   defender.   Call   a   high-profile   criminal hotshot. Someone you trust."

"I have my trust in you."

Some French-speaking jailbird must have bent his ear in the

382

holding cell while I was questioning the opposition. "I did not suborn a juror. They did not find me guilty of that. I would never do it for you."

"You did well for me this morning."

"I like to win."

"And perhaps you have something to prove also, *nest pas?*"

He was right about that. I had to show I could try a case again without the Bar Association and the whole damned Massachusetts judicial system sniffing around for illegal conduct. If I was going to regain the lucrative practice I had two years ago, I would have to be brilliant, not just win. On the other hand, defendants have enough problems without an albatross for a lawyer. Why me?

I sat down again and pulled a yellow pad out of my brief-case. Maybe this would be a good opportunity to start a comeback after all. No pressure from a front-page spotlight, but enough human interest to get me back in the game. I didn't need my hands tied to make me look like a moron, though.

"Trust works both ways, *Monsieur.* Ill never prove anything for either one of us if you don't help me."

"What I could tell you would not improve our chances of success."

"Terrific!"

An ironic smile accompanied the shrug this time.

"I'm your attorney. I'm bound by law not to reveal anything you tell me against your wishes."

"I know the law."

Before I could respond, a guard knocked, stuck his head in the door and told me Judge Pagano wanted to see me in chambers.

I stood up. "Do you need anything?"

"Your American cigarettes are for children."

"Maybe that's why so many kids smoke."

****

When I walked into his book-lined office, the judge was seated behind his desk in shirtsleeves with Leah Goldman on a sofa to his right, Frank Borkowski, the inimical district attorney of Suffolk County occupied one of the leather partner chairs opposite His Honor.

Pagano gestured me into the other and asked, "Did you learn anything more from your client?"

"Privileged," I replied.

His tanned features became darkened by a maroon flush. "I'm removing you from this case, Cotnoir."

"On what grounds?"

"My review of your re-admission testimony before the Bar Association indicates you are unsuited to it."

"In what way?"

Pagano's fingers groped on the desk as though searching for his wooden mallet. "I'll cite you for contempt, if necessary, you snotty bastard!"

I made the wise choice of remaining silent.

"It seems we have a slight complication in your John Doe matter," Borkowski said. Frank was not the sharpest tack in the box, but his innate political instincts had kept him firmly in the DA's seat for almost fifteen years. "You don't need the hassle, 'Cotnor.'"

"It's 'Cot-nwah,' Frank. What are you, coming down with polish Alzheimer's?" I had worked under Frank for three years in the DA's office as lead prosecutor and ever since I told him to stuff it when I quit, he tried to piss me off by mispronouncing my name.

His condescending smile followed by, "*Mea culpa.*"

"Hassle for whom?" I asked.

"We now know the victim did register at the Madison under an alias. Had a fake driver's license, used a valid credit card based on the false name."

"Concealing his identity during a homosexual encounter," I said. Not everybody was out of the closet, after all. But I sensed the shocker would be the noble reputation the deceased Leo Benays had been trying to protect.

Pagano's intercom buzzed at his elbow and he pressed a button on his speaker phone. A sexy female voice I knew belonged to a sixtyish grandmother said, "Mrs. Delacroix is back, Your Honor."

"Send her in."

The door opened and the tall, thin, blond woman who had translated the proceedings of the preliminary hearing entered the room. Judge Pagano introduced Mrs. Delacroix from Social Services.

"Did you explain the situation to the John Doe prisoner?" he demanded.

"Repeatedly, Your Honor."

"Will he agree to choose a more qualified attorney?"

"He will not, Your Honor. He says he is perfectly satisfied with *Monsieur,* with Mr. Cotnoir."

Pagano scowled at me as he asked the interpreter, "Did you learn anything else?   His name, for god sakes?"

I said, "Your honor, I object to my client being questioned in my absence."

The judge raised his voice to the interpreter as though he was angry with her instead of me. "Did you learn anything at all about the man?"

"No, Your Honor, he refused to answer... to say anything," Mrs. Delacroix replied.

"That's all then," Pagano said in a lower tone of voice.   Thank you."

The woman closed the door behind her, obviously happy to remove herself from the line of fire we all knew was coming.

The magistrate turned to Borkowski. "You're going to handle this personally."

"Yes, judge, along with my able chief assistant," the DA smiled at the young lady on the couch, "Miss Goldman."

Pagano took a deep breath, leaned forward, folding his hands on the desk. "Look, Cotnoir, this thing has become rather delicate. It's not just another random killing, now."

"Because the victim was gay?"

"Channel 3 has already implied a homosexual lover's angle," Borkowski said. "*Queer Nation* called suggesting the murder constituted gay bashing."

"The victim is a French national," Pagano argued, "your client too, probably. The international press will castrate us for putting a sleaze shyster on a case like this."

I glanced at Leah whose wide eyes were crossed in feigned horror at the judge's graphic verb.

Suddenly, I needed this case as much as the blood in my veins. "On what grounds will you remove me, Your Honor?"

Pagano was almost unable to speak. "Step down!" he shouted.

"Not unless my client requests it." Chances were the old man knew more about this case than anyone else. And for some reason he wanted me to represent him.

"You don't need the hassle," the DA said.

"Who's the victim?" I asked.

Pagano slammed his fist on the desk and swiveled around to glare out the window behind him. "Tell him."

"The murdered man was actually Georges Vachon." Borkowski paused for effect. "The French Deputy Ambassador to the United Nations."

I couldn't help myself. "*Le gai Parisien.*"

(To be continued)

www.ingramcontent.com/pod-product-compliance
Lightning Source LLC
Chambersburg PA
CBHW051551250626
47157CB00001B/262